Alison Lurie was born in Chicago, Illinois in 1926, but grew up in New York. A graduate of Radcliffe College, she has received both Guggenheim and Rockefeller grants for her work, and currently teaches studies in children's literature at Cornell University. Her first novel, *Love and Friendship*, was published in 1962, followed by *The Nowhere City* (1965), *Imaginary Friends* (1967), *Real People* (1970), *The War Between the Tates* (1974), *Only Children* (1979), and a non-fiction work, *The Language of Clothes* (1982).

Alison Lurie is based in New York, but divides her time between New York, London and Florida.

Also by Alison Lurie in Abacus:

LOVE AND FRIENDSHIP
THE NOWHERE CITY
THE WAR BETWEEN THE TATES

Alison Lurie

FOREIGN AFFAIRS

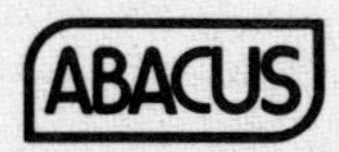

First published in Great Britain by
Michael Joseph Ltd 1985
Published in Abacus by Sphere Books Ltd 1986
27 Wrights Lane, London W8 5TZ

Reprinted 1986 (three times), 1987

Set in Times

Printed and bound in Great Britain by
Collins, Glasgow

For Diane Johnson

1

As I walked by myself
And talked to myself,
  Myself said unto me,
Look to thyself,
Take care of thyself,
  For nobody cares for thee.

Old song

On a cold blowy February day a woman is boarding the ten a.m. flight to London, followed by an invisible dog. The woman's name is Virginia Miner: she is fifty-four years old, small, plain, and unmarried – the sort of person that no one ever notices, though she is an Ivy League college professor who has published several books and has a well-established reputation in the expanding field of children's literature.

The dog that is trailing Vinnie, visible only to her imagination, is her familiar demon or demon familiar, known to her privately as Fido and representing self-pity. She visualizes him as a medium-sized dirty-white long-haired mutt, mainly Welsh terrier: sometimes trailing her silently, at other times whining and panting and nipping at her heels; when bolder, dashing round in circles trying to trip her up, or at least get her to stoop down so that he may rush at her, knock her to the ground, and cover her with sloppy kisses. Vinnie knows very well that Fido wants to get onto the plane with her, but she hopes to leave him behind, as she has successfully done on other trips abroad. Recent events, however, and the projected length of her stay, make this unlikely.

Vinnie is leaving today for six months in England on a foundation grant. There, under her professional name of V. A. Miner, she will continue her study of the folk-rhymes of schoolchildren. She has made this journey a number of times, and through a process of trial and error reduced its expense and discomfort to a minimum. She always chooses a daytime charter flight, preferring those on which no films are shown. If she could afford it, she would pay the regular fare so as to avoid boarding delays (she has already stood in various lines for nearly an hour); but that would be foolishly extravagant. Her grant is small, and she will have to watch expenses carefully as it is.

Though patience is held to be a virtue most appropriate to women, especially aging women, Vinnie has always particularly disliked waiting for anything, and never does so if it can be avoided. Now, for instance, she elbows her way deftly past less experienced passengers who are searching for their seat numbers or are encumbered with excess luggage or with children, excusing herself in a thin pleasant voice. By crossing through the galley to the far aisle and back again between two rows of seats, she outflanks a massed confusion of obvious rubes with carry-on bags labelled SUN TOURS. In less time than it takes to read this paragraph she has made her way to a window seat near an exit in the non-smoking section, pausing only to extract the London *Times* and British *Vogue* from a magazine rack. (Once the plane is airborne, the stewardess will distribute periodicals to all the passengers, but those Vinnie prefers may vanish before they reach her.)

Following her usual procedure, Vinnie slides into her place and unzips her boots. In stocking feet she climbs onto the seat and opens the overhead locker; since she is barely over five feet tall, this is the only way she can reach it. She removes two pillows and a loose-woven blue blanket, which she drops onto the center seat beside her handbag and her British periodicals, thus tacitly claiming this space if – as is likely in midweek and mid-February – it hasn't been assigned to anyone. Then she arranges her worn wool-lined raincoat, her floppy beige felt hat, and her amber-and-beige Liberty-print wool shawl in the locker, in such a way that only the rudest of fellow passengers will attempt to encroach upon them. She slams the locker shut with some difficulty, and sits down. She stows her boots under her own seat along with a carton of duty-free Bristol Cream sherry, and puts on a pair of folding slippers. She arranges one pillow beside her head and wedges the other between her hip and the arm of the chair. Finally she smooths her crisply cut graying hair, leans back, and with a sigh fastens the seatbelt across her tan wool sweater and skirt.

A disinterested observer, Vinnie is quite aware, might well consider these maneuvers and condemn her as self-concerned and grasping. In this culture, where energy and egotism are rewarded in the young and good-looking, plain aging women are supposed to be self-effacing, uncomplaining – to take up as little space and breathe as little air as possible. All very well, she thinks, if you travel with someone dear to you or at least familiar: someone who will help you stow away your coat, tuck a pillow behind your head, find you a newspaper – or if you choose, converse with you.

But what of those who travel alone? Why should Vinnie Miner, whose comfort has been disregarded by others for most of her adult life, disregard her own comfort? Why should she allow her coat, hat, and belongings to be crushed by the coats and hats and belongings of younger, larger, handsomer persons? Why should she sit alone for seven or eight hours, pillowless and chilled, reading an outdated copy of *Punch*, with her feet swollen and her pale amber eyes watering from the smoke of the cigarette fiends in the adjoining seats? As she often says to herself – though never aloud, for she knows how unpleasant it would sound – why shouldn't she look out for herself? Nobody else will.

But such internal arguments, frequent as they are with Vinnie, occupy little of her mind now. The uneven, uncharacteristically loud sigh she gave as she sank back against the scratchy blue plush was not a sigh of contentment, or even one of relief: it was an exhalation of wretchedness. Her travel routine has been performed by rote; if she were alone, she would break into wails of misery and vexation, and stain the London *Times* with her tears.

Twenty minutes ago, while waiting in the departure lounge in a cheerful mood, Vinnie read in a magazine of national circulation a scornful and disparaging reference to her life's work. Projects such as hers, the article stated, are a prime example of the waste of public funds, the proliferation of petty and useless scholarship, and the general weakness and folly of the humanities in America today. Do we really need a scholarly study of playground doggerel? inquired the writer, one L. D. Zimmern, a professor of English at Columbia. No doubt Mr or

Ms Miner would answer this query by assuring us of the social, historical, or literary value of "Ring-around-a-rosy,' he continued, sawing through the supports of any possible answer; but he, for one, was not convinced.

What makes this unprovoked attack especially hideous is that for over thirty years the *Atlantic* has been Vinnie's favorite magazine. Though she was raised in the suburbs of New York and teaches at an upstate university, her imaginative loyalties are to New England. She has often thought that American culture took a long downward step when its hegemony passed from Boston to New York in the late nineteenth century; and it has been a comfort to her that the *Atlantic* continues to be edited from Back Bay. When she pictures her work receiving general public recognition, it is to this magazine that she awards the honor of discovery. She has fantasized the process often: the initial letter of inquiry, the respectfully eager manner of the interviewer, the title of the finished essay; the moment when her colleagues at Corinth University and elsewhere will open the magazine and see her name printed on its glossy pages in its characteristic and elegant typeface. (Vinnie's ambition, though steady and ardent, is comparatively modest: it hasn't occurred to her that her name might be printed upon the cover of the *Atlantic*.) She has imagined all that will follow: the sudden delighted smiles of her friends; the graceless grins of those who are not her friends and have undervalued both her and her subject. The latter group, alas, will be much more numerous.

For the truth is that children's literature is a poor relation in her department – indeed, in most English departments; a stepdaughter grudgingly tolerated because, as in the old tales, her words are glittering jewels of a sort that attract large if not equally brilliant masses of undergraduates. Within the departmental family she sits in the chimney-corner, while her idle, ugly siblings dine at the chairman's table – though, to judge by enrollment figures, many of them must spout toads and lizards.

Well, Vinnie thinks bitterly, now she has got her wish; her work has been mentioned in the *Atlantic*. Just her luck – because surely there were others whose project titles might have attracted the spiteful attention of L. D. Zimmern. But of course it was her he chose, what else could she expect? Vinnie realizes that Fido has followed her onto the plane and is snuffling at her legs, but she lacks the energy to push him away.

Above her seat the warning light has been turned on; the engines begin to vibrate as if with her own internal tremor. Vinnie stares through the streaked, distorting oblong of glass at gray tarmac, pitted heaps of dirty congealed snow, other planes taxiing toward takeoff; but what she sees is a crowd of *Atlantic* magazines queuing for departure or already en route, singly or in squadrons, flying over the United States in the hands and briefcases of travelers, hitching their way in automobiles, loaded onto trucks and trains, bundled and tied for sale on newsstands. She visualizes what must come or has already come of this mass migration: she sees, all over the country – in homes and offices, in libraries and dentists' waiting rooms – her colleagues, ex-colleagues, students, ex-students, neighbors, ex-neighbors, friends, and ex-friends (not to mention the members of the Foundation Grants Committee). All of them, at this moment or some other moment, are opening the *Atlantic*, turning its glossy white pages, coming upon that awful paragraph. She imagines which ones will laugh aloud; which will read the sentences out with a sneering smile; which will gasp with sympathy; and which will groan, thinking or saying how bad it looks for the Department or for the Foundation. 'Hard on Vinnie,' one will remark. 'But you have to admit there's something a little comic about the title of her proposal: "A comparative investigation of the play-rhymes of British and American Children" – well now, really.'

About its title, perhaps; not about its content, as she has spent years proving. Trivial as it may seem, her material is rich in meaning. For example – Vinnie, almost involuntarily, begins composing in her head a letter to the editor of the *Atlantic* – consider the verse to which Professor Zimmern took such particular exception:

Ring around a rosy
Pocketful of posies.
Ashes, ashes,
We all fall down.

– This rhyme appears from internal as well as external evidence to date very possibly from the Great Plague of 1665. If so, the 'posies' may be the nosegays of flowers and herbs carried by citizens of London to ward off infection, while 'Ashes, ashes,' perhaps refers to the burning of dead bodies that littered the streets.

– If Professor Zimmern had troubled to do his research . . . if he had merely taken the time to inquire of any authority in the field – Vinnie continues her imaginary letter – he . . . he would be alive today. Unbidden, these words appear in her mind to complete the sentence. She sees L. D. Zimmern, whom she has never met but imagines (inaccurately) to be fat and bald, as a plague-swollen, discolored corpse. He is lying on the cobblestones of a seventeenth-century London alley, his clothes foully stained with vomit, his face blackened and contorted, his limbs hideously askew in the death agony, his faded posy of herbs wilting beside him.

– Many more of these apparently 'meaningless' verses, she resumes, a little shocked by her own imagination, have similar hidden historical and social referents, and preserve in oral form . . .

While the stewardess, in a strained BBC accent, begins her rote exhortation, Vinnie continues her letter to the editor. Phrases she has used many times in lectures and articles repeat themselves within her head, interspersed with those coming over the loudspeakers. 'Children's game-rhymes/Place the life vest over your head/oldest universal literature/Bring the straps to the front and fasten them securely/representing for millions of people their earliest and often their only exposure to/Pulling on the cord will cause the vest to become inflated with air.' Inflated with air, indeed. As she knows from bitter experiences, nothing is ever gained by sending such letters. Either they are blandly refused ('We regret that our limited space prevents . . .') or, worse, they are accepted and printed weeks or months later, reminding everyone of your discomfiture long after they had forgotten about it, and making you seem a sore loser.

Not only mustn't she write to the *Atlantic*: she must take care never to mention its attack on her to anyone, friend or foe. In academic life it is considered weak and undignified to complain of your reviews. Indeed, in Vinnie's experience, the only afflictions it is really safe to mention are those shared by all your colleagues: the weather, inflation, delinquent students, and so forth. Bad publicity must be dealt with as Vinnie was once taught by her mother to deal with flaws in her adolescent appearance: in total silence. 'If you have a spot on your face or your dress, Vinnie, for goodness' sake don't mention it. At best you'll be reminding people of something unpleasant about yourself; at worst you'll call it to the attention of those who might never have noticed.' Yes; no doubt a very sensible policy. Its only disadvantage is that Vinnie will never know who has noticed this new ugly spot and who hasn't. Never, never know. Fido, who has been standing with his forepaws on her knees, whining hopefully, now scrambles into her lap.

The rackety roar of the engines increases; the plane begins to trundle down the runway, gathering speed. At what seems the last possible moment it lurches unevenly upward, causing the usual shudder in Vinnie's bowels and the sensation of having been struck on the back of the neck with the seat-cushion. She swallows with difficulty and glances towards the window, where a frozen gray section of Long Island suburb is wheeling by at an unnatural angle. She feels queasy, disoriented, damaged. And no wonder, whines Fido: this public sneer will be in her life forever, part of her shabby history of losses and failures.

Vinnie knows, of course, that she ought not to take it so hard. But she knows too that those who have no significant identity outside their careers – no spouse, no lover, no parents, no children – do take such things hard. In the brief distant time when she was married, professional reverses did not damage the core of her life; they could not disrupt the comfort (or, later, the discomfort) of what went on at home. They were, so to speak, outside the plane, muffled by social insulation and the hum of the marital engines. Now these blows fall on her directly, as if the heavy oblong of glass had been removed so that Vinnie could be slapped full in the face with the Atlantic – not the magazine, but a cold half-congealed sopping-wet arm of the ocean after which it is named, over which they are passing; slapped again and again and –

'Excuse me.' It is a real voice that Vinnie now hears, the voice of the passenger in the aisle seat: a bulky, balding man in a tan Western-cut suit and rawhide tie.

'Yes?'

'I just said, mind if I take a look at your newspaper?'

Though Vinnie does mind, she is constrained by convention from saying so. 'Not at all.'

'Thanks.'

She acknowledges the man's grin with the faintest possible nod; then, to protect herself from his conversation and her own thoughts, picks up *Vogue*. Listlessly she turns its shiny pages, stopping at an article on winter soups and again at one on indoor gardening. The references to marrowbones, parsnips, and partridges, to Christmas roses and ivy, the erudite yet cosily confiding style – so different from the hysterical exhortation of American fashion magazines – make her smile as if recognizing an old friend. The pieces on clothes and beauty, on the other hand, she passes over rapidly. She has now no use for, and has never derived any benefit from, their advice.

For nearly forty years Vinnie has suffered from the peculiar disadvantages of the woman born without physical charms. Even as a child she had a nondescript sort of face, which gave the impression of a small wild rodent: the nose sharp and narrow, the eyes round and rather too close-set, the mouth a nibbling slit. For the first eleven years of her life, however, her looks gave no one any concern. But as she approached puberty, first her suddenly anxious mother and then Vinnie herself attempted to improve upon her naturally meager endowments. Faithfully, they followed the changing recommendations of acquaintances and of the media, but never with any success. The ringlets and ruffles popular in Vinnie's late childhood did not become her; the austerely cut, square-shouldered clothes of World War II emphasized her adolescent scrawniness; the New Look drowned her in excess yardage, and so on through every subsequent change of fashion. Indeed, it would be kinder to draw a veil over some of Vinnie's later attempts at stylishness: her bony forty-year-old legs in an orange leather miniskirt; her narrow mouse's face peering from behind teased hair and an oversized pair of mirrored aviator sunglasses.

When she reached fifty, however, Vinnie began to abandon these strenuous efforts. She ceased tinting her hair a juvenile and unnatural shade of auburn and let it grow out its natural piebald gray-beige; she gave away half her clothes and threw out most of her makeup. She might as well face facts, she told herself: she was a disadvantaged woman, doubly disadvantaged now by age; someone men would not charge at with bullish enthusiasm no matter how many brightly colored objects she waved to attract their attention. Well, at least she could avoid being a figure of fun. If she couldn't look like an attractive woman, she could at least look like a lady.

But just as she was resigning herself to total defeat, the odds began to alter in Vinnie's favor. Within the last couple of years she has in a sense caught up with, even passed, some of her better-equipped contemporaries. The comparison of her appearance to that of other women of her age is no longer a constant source of mortification. She is no better looking than she ever was, but they have lost more ground. Her slim, modestly proportioned figure has not been made bulgy and flabby by childbearing or by overeating and overdieting; her small but rather nice breasts (creamy, pink-tipped) have not fallen. Her features have not taken on the injured, strained expression of the former beauty, nor does she paint and decorate or simper and coo in a desperate attempt to arouse the male interest she feels to be her due. She is not consumed with rage and grief at the cessation of attentions that were in any case moderate, undependable, and intermittent.

As a result men – even men she had been intimate with – do not now gaze upon her with dismay, as upon a beloved landscape devastated by fire, flood, or urban development. They do not mind that Vinnie Miner, who was never much to look at, now looks old. After all, they hadn't slept with her out of romantic passion, but out of comradeship and temporary mutual need – often almost absent-mindedly, to relieve the pressure of their desire for some more glamorous female. It wasn't uncommon for a man who had just made love to Vinnie to sit up naked in bed, light a cigarette, and relate to her the vicissitudes of his current romance with some temperamental beauty – breaking off occasionally to say how great it was to have a pal like her.

Some may be surprised to learn that there is this side to Professor Miner's life. But it is a mistake to believe that plain women are more or less celibate. The error is common, since in the popular mind – and especially in the media – the idea of sex is linked with the idea of beauty. Partly as a result, men are not eager to boast of their liaisons with unattractive women, or to display such liaisons in public. As for the women, painful experience and a natural sense of self-preservation often keep them from publicizing these relationships, in which they seldom have the status of a declared lover, though often that of a good friend.

As has sometimes been remarked, almost any woman can find a man to sleep with if she sets her standards low enough. But what must be lowered are not necessarily standards of character, intelligence, sexual energy, good looks, and worldly achievement. Rather, far more often, she must relax her requirements for commitment, constancy, and romantic passion; she must cease to hope for declarations of love, admiring stares, witty telegrams, eloquent letters, birthday cards, valentines, candy, and flowers. No; plain women often have a sex life. What they lack, rather, is a love life.

Vinnie has now reached an article in *Vogue* devoted to new ideas for children's birthday parties, which arouses her professional dismay because of its emphasis on adult-directed commercial entertainment: the hiring of professional magicians and clowns, the organization of sightseeing trips, etc. – just the sort of thing that is tending more and more to replace the traditional rituals and games. Partly as a result of such articles, the ancient and precious folk culture of childhood is rapidly being destroyed. Meanwhile, those who hope to record and preserve this vanishing heritage are sneered at, denigrated, slandered in popular magazines. Woof, woof.

'Here's your paper.' Vinnie's seatmate holds out the London *Times*, clumsily refolded.

'Oh. Thank you.' To avoid further requests for it from other passengers, she places the newspaper in her lap beneath *Vogue*.

'Thank *you*. Not much in it.'

Since this is not phrased as a question, Vinnie is not obliged to respond and does not. Not much of what? she wonders. Perhaps of American news, sports events, middlebrow comment, or even advertisements, in comparison to whatever paper he habitually reads. Or perhaps, being used to screaming headlines and exclamatory one-sentence paragraphs, he has been misled by the typographical and stylistic restraint of the *Times* into thinking that nothing of importance occurred in the world yesterday. And perhaps nothing has, though to her, to

V. A. Miner, arf, arf, awooo! Stop that, Fido.

Setting aside *Vogue*, she unfolds the newspaper. Gradually, the leisurely *Times* style, with its air of measured consideration and its undertone of educated irony, begins to calm her, as the voice of an English nanny might quiet a hurt, overwrought child.

'You on your way to London?'

'What? Yes.' Caught as it were in the act, she admits her destination and returns her glance to the story Nanny is telling her about Prince Charles.

'Glad to get out of that New York weather, I bet.'

Again Vinnie agrees, but in such a way as to make it clear that she does not choose to converse. She shifts her body and the tissuey sheets of the paper toward the window, though nothing can be seen there. The plane seems to stand still, shuddering with a monotonous regularity, while ragged gray billows of cloud churn past.

However long the flight, Vinnie always tries to avoid striking up acquaintance with anyone, especially on transatlantic journeys. According to her calculations, there is far more chance of having to listen to some bore for seven-and-a-half hours than of meeting someone interesting – and after all, whom even among her friends would she want to converse with for so long?

Besides, this man looks like someone Vinnie would hardly want to converse with for seven-and-a-half minutes. His dress and speech proclaim him to be, probably, a Southern Plains States businessman of no particular education or distinction; the sort of person who goes on package tours to Europe. And indeed the carry-on bag that rests between his oversize Western-style leather boots is pasted with the same SUN TOURS logo she had noticed earlier: fat comic-book letters enclosing a grinning Disney sun. Physically too he is of a type she has never cared for: big, ruddy, blunt-featured, with cropped coarse graying red hair. Some women would consider him attractive in a weather-beaten Western way; but Vinnie has always preferred in men an elegant slimness, fair fine hair and skin, small well-cut features – the sort of looks that are an idealized male version of her own.

Half an hour later, as she refolds the *Times* and gets out a novel, she glances again at her companion. He is wedged heavily in his seat, neither dozing nor reading, although the airline magazine lies limp on his broad knees. For a moment she speculates as to what sort of man would embark on a transatlantic flight without reading materials, categorizing him as philistine and as improvident. It was foolish of him to count on passing the time in conversation: even if he didn't happen to be seated beside someone like Vinnie, he might well have been placed next to foreigners or children. What will he do now, just sit there?

As the plane drones on, Vinnie's question is answered. At intervals her seatmate gets up and walks toward the rear, returning each time smelling unpleasantly of burnt tobacco. Vinnie, who detests cigarettes, wonders irritably why he didn't request a seat in the smoking section. He rents headphones from the stewardess, fits the plastic pieces into his large red ears, and listens to the low-grade recorded noise – evidently without satisfaction, since he keeps switching channels. Finally he rises again and, standing in the aisle, converses with a member of his tour group in the seat ahead, and then for even longer with two others in the seats behind. Vinnie realizes that she is surrounded by Sun Tourists, the representatives of all she deplores and despises in her native land and is going to London to get away from.

Though she has no wish to eavesdrop, she cannot avoid hearing them complain in loud drawling guffawing Western voices about their delayed departure, the lack of movies on this flight, and the real bum steer given to them in this matter by their travel agent. As this phrase is repeated, Vinnie visualizes the Real Bum Steer as a passenger on the plane. Scrawny, sway-backed, probably lamed, it stands on three legs in the aisle with a SUN TOURS label glued on its scruffy brown haunch.

Unable to concentrate on her novel while the conversation continues, Vinnie gets up and walks toward the rear. She finds a washroom that looks reasonably clean and wipes the seat, first with a wet, then with a dry paper towel. Before leaving, she removes the plastic containers of Blue Grass cologne, skin freshener, and moisturizer from their rack and places them in her handbag, as is her custom. As is her custom, she tells herself that British Airways and Elizabeth Arden expect, perhaps even hope, that some passenger will appropriate these products; that they are offered to the public as a form of advertising.

This kind of confiscation – borrowing, some might call it,

though nothing of course is ever returned – is habitual with Professor Miner. Stores are out of bounds – she is no common shoplifter, after all – and the possessions of her acquaintances are usually safe, though you must be careful when lending her your pen, particularly if it has an extra-fine point; she is apt to return it absent-mindedly to her own purse. But planes, restaurants, hotels, and offices are fair game. As a result, Vinnie has a rather nice collection of guest towels, and a very large revolving supply of coasters, matches, paper napkins, coat hangers, pencils, pens, chalk, and expensive magazines of the sort found in expensive doctors' and dentists' waiting rooms. She owns quantities of Corinth and University College (London) stationery and a quaint little pewter cream pitcher from a lobster house in Maine, about which her only regret is that she hadn't taken the matching sugar bowl too. Well, perhaps one day . . .

It should not be imagined that these confiscations are of common occurrence. Weeks or months may pass without Vinnie feeling any need to add to her hoard of unpurchased objects. But when things are not going well she begins to look round, and annexations take place. Each one causes a tiny ascent in her spirits, as if she sat on one of a pair of scales so delicately hung that even the weight of a free box of paper clips on the opposite pan would make hers rise in the air.

Now and then, instead of appropriating something she likes that doesn't belong to her, Vinnie improves her world by getting rid of something she dislikes. During her short marriage, she caused several of her husband's ties and a camp souvenir ashtray in the shape of a bathtub to vanish completely. Twice she has removed from the women's faculty washroom in her building at Corinth an offensive sign reading WASH HANDS BEFORE LEAVING: YOUR HEALTH DEPENDS ON IT.

None of Vinnie's acquaintances are aware of these habits of hers, which might best be explained as the consequence of a vague but recurrent belief that life owes her a little something. It is not miserliness: she pays her bills promptly, is generous with her possessions (both bought and borrowed), and scrupulous about splitting the check at lunch. As she sometimes says on these occasions, her salary is perfectly adequate for one person with no dependents.

Her superego does sometimes complain to Vinnie about this

do-it-yourself justice, most often when her morale is so low that nothing can raise it. Now, for instance, as she stands in the narrow toilet cubicle surrounded by multilingual scolding and warning signs, a shrill and penetrating interior voice sounds above the roar of the plane. 'Petty thief,' it whines. 'Neurotic kleptomaniac. Author of a research proposal nobody needs.'

With effort Vinnie pulls her clothes together and returns to her seat. The red-faced man rises to let her in, looking uncomfortable and rumpled. An inexperienced traveler, he has worn a too-tight suit of some synthetically woolly material that crumples under pressure.

'Pain in the neck,' he mutters. 'They oughta build these seats farther apart.'

'Yes, that would be nice,' she agrees politely.

'What it is, they're trying to save dough.' He sits down again heavily. 'Packing the customers in like cattle in a damn boxcar.'

'Mm,' Vinnie utters vaguely, picking up her novel.

'I guess they're all pretty much the same, though, the airlines. I don't travel all that much myself.'

Vinnie sighs. It is clear to her that unless she takes definite action this Western businessman or rancher or whatever he is will prevent her reading *The Singapore Grip* and make the rest of the flight very boring.

'No, it's never awfully comfortable,' she says. 'Really I think the best thing to do is bring along something interesting to read, so one doesn't notice.'

'Yeh. I shoulda thought of that, I guess.' He gives Vinnie a sad, baffled look, arousing the irritation she feels at her more helpless students – students on athletic scholarships, often, who should never have come to Corinth in the first place.

'I have some other books with me, if you'd like to look at them.' Vinnie reaches down and pulls from her tote bag *The Oxford Book of Light Verse*; a pocket guide to British flowers; and *Little Lord Fauntleroy*, which she has to reread for a scholarly article. She places the volumes on the middle seat, aware as she does so of their individual and collective inappropriateness.

'Hey. Thanks,' her seatmate exclaims as each one appears. 'Wal, if you're sure you don't need them now.'

Vinnie assures him that she does not. She is already reading a book, she points out, suppressing a sigh of impatience. Then, with a sigh of relief, she returns to *The Singapore Grip*. For a few moments she is aware of the flipping of pages on her right, but soon she is absorbed.

While the shadows of war darken over Singapore in Jim Farrell's last completed novel, the atmosphere outside the cabin windows brightens. The damp grayness becomes suffused with gold; the plane, breaking through the cloudbank, levels off in sunlight over an expanse of whipped cream. Vinnie looks at her watch; they are halfway to London. Not only has the light altered, she senses a change in the sound of the engines: a shift to a lower, steadier hum as the plane passes midpoint on its homeward journey. Within too she feels a more harmonic vibration, a brightening of anticipation.

England, for Vinnie, is and has always been the imagined and desired country. For a quarter of a century she visited it in her mind, where it had been slowly and lovingly shaped and furnished out of her favorite books, from Beatrix Potter to Anthony Powell. When at last she saw it she felt like the children in John Masefield's *The Box of Delights* who discover that they can climb into the picture on their sitting-room wall. The landscape of her interior vision had become life-size and three-dimensional; she could literally walk into the country of her mind. From the first hour England seemed dear and familiar to her: London, especially, was almost an experience of déjà vu. She also felt that she was a nicer person there and that her life was more interesting. These sensations increased rather than diminished with time, and have been repeated as often as Vinnie could afford. Over the past decade she has visited England nearly every year – though usually, alas, for only a few weeks. Tonight she will begin her longest stay yet: an entire six months. Her fantasy is that one day she will be able to live in London permanently, even perhaps become an Englishwoman. A host of difficulties – legal, financial, practical – are involved in this fantasy, and Vinnie has no idea how she could ever solve them all; but she wants it so much that perhaps one day it can be managed.

Many teachers of English, like Vinnie, fall in love with England as well as with her literature. With familiarity, however, their infatuation often declines into indifference or even contempt. If they long for her now, it is as she was in the past – most often, in the period of their own specialization: for the colorful, vital England of Shakespeare's time, or the lavish elegance and charm of the Edwardian period. With the bitterness of disillusioned lovers, they complain that contemporary Britain is cold, wet, and overpriced; its natives unfriendly; its landscape and even its climate ruined. England is past her prime, they say; she is worn-out and old; and, like most of the old, boring.

Vinnie not only disagrees, she secretly pities those of her friends and colleagues who claim to have rejected England, since it is clear to her that in truth England has rejected them. The chill they complain of is a matter of style. Englishmen and Englishwoman do not open their arms and hearts to every casual passerby, just as English lawns do not flow into the lawns next door. Rather they conceal themselves behind high brick walls and dense prickly hedges, turning their coolest and most formal side to strangers. Only those who have been inside know how warm and cozy it can be there.

Her colleagues' complaints about the weather and the scenery Vinnie puts down to mere blind pique, issuing as they do from people whose native landscape is devastated by billboards, used-car lots, ice storms, and tornadoes. As for the claim that nothing much ever happens here, this is one of England's greatest charms for Vinnie, who has just escaped from a nation plagued by sensational and horrible news events, and from a university periodically disrupted by political demonstrations and drunken student brawls. She sinks into the English life as into a large warm bath agitated only by the gentle ripples she herself makes and by the popping of bubbles of foam as some small scandal swells up and breaks, spraying the air with the delightful soapy spume of gossip. In Vinnie's private England a great deal happens; quite enough for her, at least.

England is also a country in which folklore is an old and honorable study. The three collections of fairytales for children that Vinnie has edited, and her book on children's literature, have been much better received there than in America, and she is in greater demand as a reviewer. Besides, it now occurs to her, the *Atlantic* is not widely distributed in Britain; and even if by some remote chance her friends there should see Zimmern's essay, they won't be much impressed. English intellectuals, she has noticed, have little respect for American critical opinion.

As Vinnie smiles to herself, recalling remarks made by her London friends about the American Press, the cabin crew begins to serve lunch – or perhaps, since it is now seven o'clock in London, it should be considered dinner. Vinnie purchases a miniature bottle of sherry, and accepts a cup of tea. As usual, she refuses the plastic tray upon which have been arranged mounds of some tasteless neutral substance (wet sawdust? farina?) that has been colored and shaped to resemble beef stew, Brussels sprouts, mashed potatoes, and lemon pudding. It does not deceive her any longer, though once she assumed that the altitude, or a mild anxiety condition when airborne, was responsible for the taste of airplane food. But the homemade lunches that she now brings with her are just as nice as they would be at sea level.

'Hey, that looks good,' her seatmate exclaims, regarding Vinnie's chicken sandwich with a longing she has seen before in the eyes of other travelers. 'This stuff tastes like silage.'

'Yes, I know.' She gives him a perfunctory smile.

'They must do something funny to it. Radiate it or something.'

'Mm.' Vinnie finishes her sandwich, folds the wax paper up tidily, unwraps a large shiny McIntosh apple and an extra-bittersweet Tobler chocolate bar, and reopens her novel. Her companion returns to his silage, chewing in a slow, discouraged manner. Finally he shoves the tray aside and picks up *Little Lord Fauntleroy*.

'Guess you're glad to be getting back to England,' he says presently, as Vinnie accepts a second cup of tea from the steward.

'Mm, yes,' she agrees, without looking up. She finishes the sentence she is reading, stops, and frowns. Has she been talking to herself out loud, as she sometimes does? No; rather, misled by her New England accent and her academic intonation – plus, no doubt, her preference for tea – this western American believes that she is British.

Vinnie smiles. Ignorant as the man is, in a sense he is onto something, like those of her British friends who sometimes remark that she isn't really much like an American. Vinnie knows that their idea of 'an American' is a media convention. Nevertheless, she has often thought that, having been born and raised in what they call 'the States,' she is an anomaly; that both psychologically and intellectually she is essentially English. That her seatmate should assume the same thing is pleasing; it will make a nice story for her friends.

But Vinnie also feels uneasy about the misunderstanding. As a teacher and a scholar she finds errors of fact displeasing; her instinct is to correct them as soon as possible. Besides, if she doesn't correct this particular error, the heavy red-faced man in the aisle seat will realize his mistake when he sees her in the queue labeled 'NON-COMMONWEALTH PASSPORTS.' Or possibly he will think Vinnie is making a mistake, and will loudly try to help her out. No; she must explain to him before they land that she isn't British.

A bare announcement, however, seems graceless; and having discouraged her seatmate's attempt to interrupt her reading so often, Vinnie hesitates to interrupt his– particularly since he is now deep into *Little Lord Fauntleroy*, one of whose minor characters, the outspoken democratic grocer Mr Hobbs, he somewhat resembles. She sighs and looks out the window, where the air is now darkening above the scarlet horizon line, planning a casual reference to her American citizenship. When I first read that book, when I was a little girl in Connecticut . . . Then she looks at Mr Hobbs, willing him to turn and speak; but he does not do so. He reads steadily on, increasing Vinnie's respect both for him and for Frances Hodgson Burnett, the book's author.

It is not until they are over Ireland, some hours later, that Mr Hobbs finishes *Little Lord Fauntleroy* and returns it with thanks, and Vinnie is able to clear up the misunderstanding.

'You mean you're an American?' He blinks slowly. 'You sure fooled me. Where you from?'

Since they have almost reached their destination, and her eyes are tired from reading, Vinnie relaxes her unsociability and replies graciously. In the next twenty minutes she learns that her seatmate is called Charles (Chuck) Mumpson; that he is an engineer from Tulsa specializing in waste-disposal systems; educated at the University of Oklahoma; married with two grown children, one of each sex, and three grandchildren (the names, ages, and occupations of all these relatives are supplied);

and on a two-week Sun Tour of England. His wife, who is 'in real estate,' hasn't been able to accompany him ('There's a big property explosion on now in Tulsa; she's up to her ass in deals'). His older sister and her husband, however, are on the tour, which consists mainly of employees of the electric company for which his brother-in-law works, and their relatives. At this point Hobbs/Mumpson heaves himself up in his seat and insists on introducing Vinnie to Sis and her husband, of whom it is only necessary to report that they are a very nice sixtyish couple from Forth Worth, Texas, now visiting Europe for the first time.

As Vinnie listens to these facts, and under friendly interrogation supplies a few of her own, she wonders why citizens of the United States who have nothing in common and will never see one another again feel it necessary to exchange such information. It can only clog up their brain cells with useless data, and is moreover often invidious, tending to estrange casual acquaintances. (Mumpson's brother-in-law, like many before him, has just remarked to her, 'You're an English teacher? Gosh, I better watch my language, I was always a dumbhead in English.') In the British Isles, on the other hand, the anonymity of travelers is preserved. If strangers who find themselves sharing a railway compartment converse, it will be on topics of general interest, and usually without revealing their origin, destination, occupation, or name.

By the time the plane is over Heathrow, Vinnie is already tired of Chuck Mumpson and his relatives. Unfairly, it is then announced over the loudspeaker that due to air-traffic congestion they will be placed in a holding pattern. As the plane drones in a tilting circle through wet blackness, no doubt narrowly missing other planes. Vinnie learns more about the climate and population growth of Tulsa and Fort Worth, public utilities and their energy sources, crocheting (Sis is making a baby afghan for an expected fifth grandchild), and the proposed itinerary of Sun Tours than she has ever wished to know. When at last the tail of the plane thumps onto the runway at Heathrow she not only congratulates herself, as usual, on having survived the journey, but on being able to part with her new acquaintances.

Because of her percipient choice of seat Vinnie is among the first to leave the plane and go through immigration and passport control. Celerity is important now, since the flight is over half an hour late and the buses to London will soon stop running.

In the baggage-claim area, however, her expertise is of only limited use. She knows where to find a handcart, and the best place to stand by the conveyor in order to see and snare her suitcases as soon as they appear. The first one arrives almost immediately; but her other and larger bag fails to materialize.

The long low-ceilinged chilly hall fills with disoriented travelers; the minute hand of Vinnie's watch jerks on; unfamiliar suitcases, garment bags, backpacks, and cardboard cartons trundle past her. She begins to review the contents of her (lost? stolen?) suitcase, which include not only most of her warm clothes but also and more fatefully the notes for her research project, vital reference books and reprints, and all the rhymes she has collected in America and intends to compare with British rhymes – nearly a hundred pages of essential material. While pieces of unclaimed luggage dumbly circle past her, she imagines what she will have to go through to replace all that was in that suitcase: the trips to department stores, drugstores, and bookshops; the Xeroxing at 15p a page (at Corinth it is free); the letter to the visiting professor who is now using her office, begging someone she has never met to open the sealed cartons in which the contents of her filing cabinet are stored and search for a folder marked – what the hell is it marked? And is it actually in one of those cartons, or is it at home in the locked spare room to which her tenants do not have the key? Should she mail a copy of this key to her tenants, thus giving two graduate students in architecture access to all her private letters and journals, her original editions of books illustrated by Arthur Rackham and Edmund Dulac, and her store of wine and spirits? Alien luggage continues to revolve in front of her, along with an invisible dirty-white dog, who whines pathetically at Vinnie each time he comes round. Poor Vinnie, what did you expect? he whines; just your luck.

Twenty minutes later, when the baggage claim area is nearly empty, Vinnie's suitcase stumbles into view, with one corner bashed in and the lock on that side sprung. She is now too exhausted and low in spirits to be much relieved or to face making a claim for damages. Dully she hauls the bag off the conveyor and wrestles it onto her cart. The customs inspector, yawning, waves her past him into the lobby. There, in spite of the lateness of the hour, people of many nationalities are still waiting. Some hold infants, others cardboard signs bearing the names of those they hope to meet. As Vinnie appears, all of them glance at her for a moment, then past her. They stare, wave, exclaim, lunge, embrace, shoving her aside to reach their friends and relations.

Vinnie, unwanted and unmet, checks her watch and with an indrawn breath of anxiety begins pushing the cart toward the far end of the building as swiftly as possible, with Fido trotting at her heels. Soon she is panting, her heart pounding; she has to slow down. No doubt about it, she is getting older, weaker in body and in spirit. Her luggage feels heavier; one year, sooner than she imagines, she will be too old and weak and sickly to travel alone, the only way she ever travels – Fido rubs against her leg with a mournful snuffling. Stop it! Her luggage is heavier because she's staying longer and there's more of it, that's all. And surely, since all the flights are delayed tonight, the bus will wait. There's no need to rush, to pant, to panic.

As it turns out, this is a mistake. When Vinnie, at a carefully moderate pace, shoves her cart out into the rainy, lamp-streaked night, she sees a red double-decker pulling away from the curb in the middle distance. Her cries of 'Wait! Stop!' are not heard, or perhaps not heeded. Still worse, there are no cabs at the taxi rank, only a queue of exhausted-looking people. As she stands, chilled and weary, in the queue, jet-lag depression rises within her like cold brackish water. What is she doing at midnight in this wet, bare, ugly place? Why has she come so far, at such great expense? Nobody invited her; nobody wants her here or anywhere. Nobody needs her silly study of children's rhymes. Fido, who is now sitting atop the broken suitcase, lets out a foghorn howl.

And if she doesn't do something sensible instantly, Vinnie realizes with dismay, she is going to start howling too. She can feel the rising sob in her throat, the sting and ache of tears behind her eyes.

Something. What? Well, she could go back into the terminal and try to telephone for a minicab, though they are notorious for not turning up when promised. And for overcharging. And if they do overcharge, does she have enough English money?

No use worrying about that, not yet. Taking a couple of deep breaths to calm herself, Vinnie shoves her luggage back toward the terminal, hoping for the miraculous apparition of a taxi. There is none, of course; only a mob of Sun Tourists and their luggage waiting to board a chartered bus. She is about to retreat when Mr Hobbs/Mumpson hails her. He is now wearing a tan cowboy hat trimmed with feathers and a fleece-lined sheepskin coat, and is hung about with cameras, making him look even more than ever like the caricature of an American tourist, Western division.

'Hi there! What's the trouble?'

'Nothing,' says Vinnie repressively, realizing that her state of mind must be engraved upon her countenance. 'I was just looking for a taxi.'

Mr Mumpson stares out across the empty, rain-sloshed, light-streaked pavement. 'Don't seem to be any here.'

'No.' She manages a brief defensive smile. 'Apparently they all turn into pumpkins at midnight.'

'Huh? Oh, ha-ha. Listen, I know what. You can come on the bus with us. It's going right into town: centrally located hotel, said so in the brochure. Bet you can get a cab there.'

Over her weak, weary protests, he plunges into the crowd and returns a minute later to report that it is all fixed up. Luckily, since Vinnie and Mr Mumpson are the last to board, they have to sit separately, and she is spared any more of his conversation.

The journey to London passes in a silent blur of weariness. Though Vinnie has often been abroad, this is her first (and she hopes last) ride on a tour bus. She has of course often seen them from the street, and observed with a mixture of scorn and pity the tourists packed inside, gazing out with weak fishy stares through the thick green distorting glass of their rolling aquariums at the strange, soundless world outside.

The bus stops at a large anonymous hotel near the Air Terminal, where several taxis are actually waiting. Mr Mumpson helps her stow her luggage into one of them, and she parts from him with sincere thanks and insincere agreement with his hope that they will 'run into each other' again.

It is now nearly one in the morning. As her cab splashes north through the rain, Vinnie, exhausted, wonders what new disasters await her at the flat on Regent's Park Road she has rented for the third time from an Oxford don. Probably there won't be anyone at home downstairs to give her the keys, Fido whines; or the place will be filthy; or the lights won't work. If anything can go wrong for her it will.

But the young woman in the garden flat is in and still awake; the keys turn smoothly in their locks; the light switch is where Vinnie remembers it, just inside the door. There is the white telephone with its familiar number, and the stack of phone books in their elegant pastel colors: A–D cream, E–K geranium pink, L–R fern green, S–Z forget-me-not blue, holding between their closed petals the names of all her London friends. The sofa and chairs are in their proper places; the gold-framed engravings of Oxford colleges glow quietly on either side of the mantel. The clean grate is decorated as always with a white paper fan that echoes the white enameled pots of English ivy on their stand in the tall bay window. For the second time that evening tears ache behind Vinnie's eyes; but these are tears of relief, even of joy.

Since she is unobserved, she allows them to fall. Weeping quietly, she hauls her bags into the flat, bolts the door behind them, and is safe at last, home in London.

2

Every man hath a right to enjoy life.

John Gay, *The Beggar's Opera*

In the Underground station at Notting Hill Gate a tall dark handsome American is waiting for the eastbound train. Restlessly, he stamps from one foot to the other, staring across the dark dirty tracks at bright colored advertisements of products he will never purchase: Black Magic chocolates and Craven cigarettes. Trained in the close reading of texts (he is an assistant professor of English), he wonders how the British public can be persuaded to buy candy that suggests an evil spell and tobacco designated as cowardly. Maybe there is a darker meaning to the glossy social and sexual occasions illustrated in these posters. Is the scarlet-mouthed blonde offering the box of chocolates about to poison or bewitch her guests? Are the smiling, smoke-breathing young man and woman secretly terrified of each other? In Fred Turner's present mood both scenes seem empty and false like the city above him, almost sinister.

Though he has been in London for three weeks, this is the first time Fred has used the Underground. Usually he walks everywhere, regardless of the distance or the weather, in imitation of the eighteenth-century author John Gay, about whom he is supposed to be writing a book. In Gay's long poem, *Trivia, or the Art of Walking the Streets of London*, mechanical transport is scorned:

> What walker shall his mean ambition fix
> On the false lustre of a coach and six?
> O rather give me sweet content on foot,
> Wrapped in my virtue, and a good surtout!

In a vain search for sweet content, Fred has tramped half over London. Unless it rains hard, he also runs two miles every morning in Kensington Gardens, pounding along past dripping empty benches and gnarled bare trees, under a dark or dappled sky. While his lungs fill with damp chill air and the thin smoke of his breath steams away, he asks himself what the hell he is doing here, alone in this cold, unpleasant city. This evening, however, an icy sleet is falling, and Fred is expected for dinner in Hampstead; even Gay, he decided, wouldn't have walked so far in weather like this.

Most of the other people on the Underground platform are not gazing at the advertisements, but – more or less covertly – at Fred Turner. They are wondering if they haven't seen him somewhere before, maybe in some film or on the telly. A miniskirted billing clerk thinks he looks exactly like the hero on the cover of *The Secret of Rosewyn*, one of her favorite Gothics. a grammar-school teacher, collapsed on a bench with a bulging string bag, believes she saw him in *Love's Labour's Lost* at Stratford last summer, in one of the main supporting roles. The manager of a small menswear shop, professionally noting the transatlantic cut of Fred's duffel coat, wonders if he was in that American detective series his kids always watch. None of Fred's fellow passengers connect him with a comedy or a game show: something in the tense set of his broad shoulders, the angle of his jaw, and the way the dark arches of his eyebrows are drawn together precludes these associations.

Fred is not embarrassed by this attention. He is used to it, regards it as normal, doesn't in fact realize that few other humans are gazed at so often or so intensely. Since babyhood his appearance has attracted admiration, and often comment. It was soon clear that he had inherited his mother's brunette, lushly romantic good looks: her thick wavy dark hair, her wide-set cilia-fringed brown eyes ('wasted on a boy,' many remarked). If anything, Fred is less conscious of being oberved now than he was at home, for the polite British are taught as children that it is rude to stare, and have learnt to disguise their public curiosity. They are also taught not to speak to strangers; and as yet no citizen has broken this rule in Fred's case – though two Canadians stopped him on the street last week to ask if he wasn't the guy that fought the giant man-eating extraterrestrial cabbage in *The Thing from Beyond*.

Fred Turner knows, of course, that he is a handsome, athletic-looking young man, the type that directors employ to battle carnivorous vegetables. It would be going too far to say that he has never derived any satisfaction from this fact, but he has often wished that his appearance was less striking. He has the features, and the physique, of an Edwardian hero: classically sculptured, over-finished, like the men in Charles Dana Gibson's drawings. If he had lived before World War II, he might have been more grateful for his looks; but since then it has not been fashionable for Anglo-Saxon men to be handsome in this style unless they are homosexual. For modern straight tastes his chin is too firmly rounded and cleft, his carriage too erect, his hair too wavy, and his eyelashes much too long.

Were Fred in fact an actor his appearance might be an asset. But he has no histrionic ability or ambition; and in his profession beauty is a considerable handicap, as he has been made to realize over the last five years. While he was in school there was no problem. Boys are allowed to be handsome, as long as that is not their only asset, and Fred was an all-round achiever: energetic, outgoing, good at both lessons and games; the sort of child teachers naturally favor. Later he became the kind of prep-school boy who is elected class president and the kind of undergraduate and graduate student who is described in letters of recommendation as 'incidentally, also a most attractive young man.'

The real disadvantages of Fred's appearance did not surface until he began to teach. As anyone who has been to college knows, most professors are not especially strong or beautiful; and though they may appreciate or at least forgive these qualities in their students they do not much care for them in their peers. If Fred had been in Theater Arts or Painting and Design, he might not have stood out so from his colleagues or had so much trouble with them. In English, his appearance was held against him: he was suspected, quite unfairly, of being vain, self-centered, unintellectual, and unserious.

Fred's looks also interfered with his teaching. In his first term as a TA at least a third of his female students, and one or two of the males as well, developed crushes on him. When he called on these students they went all woozy and breathless and became quite incapable of concentrating on the topic of discussion. They hung round him after class, followed him to his office, leant over his desk in tight sweaters or shirts open nearly to the waist, clutched his arm in mute appeal, and in some cases openly declared their passion either in notes or in person ('I just think about you all the time, it's really screwing up my head'). But Fred had no wish to sleep with ten screwed-up freshmen, or even with one carefully selected well-balanced freshman. He wasn't attracted to puppy fat and unformed minds; and though in a couple of cases he was tempted, he had a strong sense of professional ethics. He also suspected correctly that if he fell and was found out he might be in serious professional trouble.

During that first year of teaching, Fred learnt to put more social distance between himself and his students; for one thing, though with irritation and regret, he stopped asking them to call him Fred. As time passed, the emotional and sexual pressure moderated – especially after he had met a woman whose appearance and temperament kept him fully occupied. But he still feels uncomfortable in the classroom. It bothers him to be 'Professor Turner', to have to maintain at all times a cool distance from his students, a dry manner, to give up hope of achieving the warm, relaxed, but in no way steamy and loose pedagogic climate enjoyed by his less-attractive colleagues. Time will solve his problem, but not for perhaps a quarter of a century, which from the perspective of twenty-eight might as well be forever. Meanwhile he has to put up with the belief of students that he is cold and formal – a belief promulgated every fall in the student-published *Confidential Guide to Courses*.

At the moment these academic difficulties are far from Fred's mind, which is fixed, as it has been intermittently for the past two months, on the collapse of his marriage. Before that, he had assumed that his wife Ruth, known to him as Roo, would be coming abroad with him. They had prepared for the trip together, read books, studied maps, consulted all their friends – Roo even more excited by their plans than he was.

But a domestic storm had blown up: thunder, lightning, and a torrential downpour of tears. Just before Christmas Fred and Roo parted in a cloudy, electrically charged atmosphere for what was announced to their friends and relatives as a 'trial separation'. Privately Fred suspects that the trial is already over, the verdict Guilty, and the sentence on their marriage Death.

No good thinking about it, going over the bad memories of a

bad time. Roo is not here and she won't ever be here. She hasn't answered either of his brief but carefully composed, neutrally friendly letters, and she probably isn't going to. Fred is alone for five months in a London empty of joy and meaning, where a cold drizzly rain seems to fall perpetually both within and without. He is more steadily miserable than he has ever been in his life.

He had come here prepared, even without Roo, to have an intense, vivid experience of the city of John Gay – and of Johnson, Fielding, Hogarth, and many more. Dutifully and mechanically, he has gone along on foot to the places he and she had planned to visit together: St Paul's, London Bridge, Dr Johnson's house, and the rest. But everything he saw looked false and empty: façades of cardboard brick and stone, hollow, without meaning. Physically he is in London, but emotionally he remains in Corinth, in a part of his life that's ceased to exist. He is living in the historic past, as he had planned and hoped to do – but not in eighteenth-century London. Instead he inhabits a more recent, private, and dismal era of his own history.

But Fred doesn't believe that there is no real and desirable London. That city exists: he dwelt there for six months as a child of ten, and last week he revisited it. Though some of its landmarks have vanished, those that remain shimmer with meaning and presence as if benignly radioactive. The house his family once lived in is gone; the jungly, catacombed, sunken bomb-site where he and his grammar-school friends played Nazis and Allies or Cops and Villains has been built over with council flats. But there is the sweetshop on the corner, thick with the odor of anise, cinnamon drops, and slabs of milk chocolate; there are the wide, shallow, unevenly worn stone steps in the passageway beside the church where Freddy (as he was then known) often stopped on his way home to eat shiny twisted black ropes of licorice from a paper bag and read *Beano* comics, unable to postpone either pleasure.

Across the road is the surgery to which Freddy was carried by his father when he fell off his bike, where an old-lady doctor with chopped-off white hair put three prickly black stitches in his chin and called him a 'brave handsome Yankee lad' – giving him, he realizes now, not only an encomium but an identity. The name on the brass plate is unfamiliar, but the heavy door with its stained-glass panel of haloed tomatoes is intact, and still seems to be a sign that this house is a kind of church – though now he knows the glass to be Art Nouveau and the holy tomatoes pomegranates. For a few hundred feet along one road in Kensington, Fred's senses and his sensibility function supernormally; everywhere else London remains cold, dim, flat, and flavorless.

He doesn't blame his inability to have an authentic experience of the city entirely on the loss of Roo. Partly he attributes it to tourist disorientation; he has noticed the same reaction in other Americans who have recently arrived, and back home he has seen it in friends and relatives returned from abroad. The main problem is, he thinks, that visitors to a foreign country are allowed the full use of only two of their five senses. Sight is permitted – hence the term 'sightseeing'. The sense of taste is also encouraged, and even takes on a weird, almost sexual importance: consumption of the native food and drink becomes a highly charged event, a proof that you were 'really there'.

But hearing in the full sense is blocked. Intelligible foreign sounds are limited to the voices of waiters, shopkeepeers, professional guides, and hotel clerks – plus snatches of dubiously 'native' music. Even in Britain, accent, intonation, and vocabulary are often unfamiliar; tourists do not recognize many of the noises they hear, and they speak mostly to functionaries. The sense of smell still operates; but it is likely to be baffled or disgusted by many foreign odors. Above all, the sense of touch is frustrated; visible or invisible Keep Off signs appear on almost everything and everyone.

Two senses aren't enough for contact with the world, and as a result places visited as a tourist tend to be experienced as blurry silent areas spotted with flashes of light. A window box bursting with purple-veined white crocuses; the shouting, anger-gorged red face of a taxi driver; a handful of hot fish-and-chips wrapped in the *News of the World* – these rare moments of sensation stand out in Fred's memory of the past month like colored snapshots against the gray blotting-paper of an old photograph album. Appropriately – for what tourists take home are, typically, snapshots.

Tourists also bring back special meretricious objects called 'souvenirs' – which as the word suggests are not so much actual things as embodied memories; and like all memories somewhat exaggerated and distorted. Souvenirs have little in common with anything actually made for and used by the natives – who's ever seen a real Greek woman in a headscarf bordered by fake tinny gold coins, or a French fisherman wearing the kind of Authentic Fisherman's Smock sold in tourist shops? But these false symbolic objects are meant to indemnify the tourist for having been, for weeks or months, cut off from an authentic experience of the world, from physical contact with other human beings –

Yeh, that's where it's at. If Roo were here, he wouldn't be having these theories, probably. His state of mind is unnatural, the grayness of London projection. What he probably ought to do is find someone who would not replace Roo or make him forget her – that's impossible – but distract him and warm him.

Preceded by a rush of chilly air, a hollow roar, the inbound Underground train arrives. It is more than half empty, for it's after six in the evening and most travelers are on their way home to the suburbs. Several of the people in the car glance with interest at Fred as he sits down. Directly across from him a pretty young woman in a dark-green wool cape gives him a half smile as their eyes meet, and then looks down at her book. Here, and not for the first time, is a good example of what Fred probably needs in London, but he doesn't feel able to do anything about it.

Two things stand in the way of his taking any useful action. One is inexperience. Unlike most moderately attractive or positively unattractive men, Fred as never learnt to pick up women. He has never had to learn, because since he was very young there have always been plenty of females among his acquaintance who were ready, even eager, to know him better. It wasn't his looks alone that interested them, but his high spirits, his good manners, his casual and modest skill in sports, his excellent but never arrogant intelligence. All he has ever had to do, really, is indicate a choice.

Even now, when his spirits are so low, there is no doubt that Fred could pick up women if he tried – that any initial awkwardness would be overlooked by most of those he might approach. But there is another and worse problem. Every woman or girl Fred sees in London has something wrong with her: she is not Roo. He knows it's stupid and counterproductive to go on feeling this way about somebody who has cut you out of her life, to go on remembering and fantasizing. As his childhood friend Roberto Frank said once, all you get from carrying a torch is sore fingers.

If Roberto were here now, instead of teaching French in Wisconsin, he would advise Fred to move in on the girl in the green cape and try to score tonight. As far back as junior high Roberto had begun recommending casual sex as a panacea. 'What you need is a good fast fuck,' he would declare when any chum complained of being bummed out because of a cold, a sprained ankle, too much homework, unsympathetic parents, a bike or a car on the fritz – or any sort of jealousy, infidelity, or sexual reluctance on the part of a current steady. Since then, Roberto has collected women as he once collected baseball cards, always preferring quantity to quality: in grade school he once traded Mickey Mantle to Fred for three obscure and inept Red Sox. It is his contention that the world is full of good-looking horny women who are interested in a no-strings relationship. 'I'm not saying you have to sweet-talk them or pull a fast one. When I meet a mama who turns me on, I lay it on the line. If she doesn't want to play by those rules, okay; so long, no hard feelings.' Fred doesn't agree. In his experience, no matter what is said in the preliminary negotiations, there are always strings. After even one or two dates he often felt like a tomcat entangled in an emotional ball of red yarn.

Yeh, Fred thinks, but maybe Roberto is right in a way, maybe if he could meet somebody –

The train stops at Tottenham Court Road. Fred gets off to change to the Northern Line, and so does the young woman in the green cape; he notices that she has been reading Joseph Conrad's *Chance*. He quickens his pace, for he is a Conrad fan; then, uncertain of what he's going to say to her, slows down. The young woman gives him a regretful backward glance as she turns toward the stairs to the southbound platform.

An opening remark has formed in Fred's mind, and he starts to follow her in order to deliver it; but then he remembers that he is supposed to be on his way to supper in Hampstead with Joe and Debby Vogeler, who will take it badly if he doesn't turn up. The Vogelers, who were in graduate school with him, are the only people of his own age he knows in London, and their continued good will is therefore important. Fred's other acquaintances here consist of several middle-aged friends of his parents, and a member of his own department: an aging spinster named Virginia Miner who is also on leave and working in the British Museum. Toward the former he feels a polite obligation, but no social enthusiasm; in the case of Professor Miner his instinct is toward avoidance. Although she has never had a serious conversation with him on any topic, Professor Miner will presently vote on whether Fred is allowed to stay on at the University or cast into outer joblessness. She is know to be eccentric and touchy, and is also a devout Anglophile. In any encounter Fred probably has more of a chance of alienating her than of pleasing her; and if he admits his depression and his dislike of London and of the British Museum, her opinion of him, whatever it may be now, will sink. On top of all this, he doesn't know whether he should address her as Professor Miner, Miss Miner, Ms Miner, Virginia, or Vinnie. In order to avoid offense, he accepted her invitation to a 'drinks party' later this week, but he plans to call up and say he is sick – no, he corrects himself, *ill* – to say you are sick in this country means you are about to vomit.

Another reason for not disappointing Joe and Debby is that they will give him a free dinner – and since Debby is a competent if unimaginative cook, a good one. For the first time in his life, Fred is broke. He hadn't known how expensive London would be, or how long it would take his salary checks to clear. The flat he and Roo had rented by mail costs too much for one person, and he has never learnt to cook. At first he ate out, in cheaper and cheaper restaurants and pubs, to the detriment of his budget and digestion; now he exists mainly on bread and cheese, canned beans, soup, boiled eggs, and paper cartons of orange juice. If his financial situation gets desperate, he can cable or write his parents for money, but this will suggest a childish improvidence. After all, for Christ's sake, he is nearly twenty-nine and has a Ph.D.

'Have some more chocolate pie,' Debby says.

'No thanks.'

'It doesn't taste right, does it?' A vertical dent appears in Debby's round face, between her nearly invisible eyebrows.

'No, it was great, it's just that –'

'The crust is different, I think,' says Joe, delivering this opinion with his usual philosphical detachment.

'Yeh, it's kind of soggy,' Debby agrees. 'And the filling's much too sweet. Those were the wrong kind of cookies, and I couldn't get real baking chocolate in any of the stores. But that's how it is with everything here, you know?'

Fred does not answer. He should know by now, since Debby and Joe have spent most of the evening telling him, describing with warm indignation (Debby) or ironic resignation (Joe) their disillusion with England in general and London in particular. After making a big effort for over a month they have given up on the whole scene. They are also really pissed off at themselves for having been dumb enough to come here on leave from the adjacent Southern Californian colleges at which they teach, with a year-old baby on top of everything. They were warned, but they had been brainwashed by their admiration for British literature (Debby) and British philosophy (Joe). Why hadn't they listened to their friends? they keep asking each other. Why hadn't they gone to Italy or to Greece, or even stayed home in Claremont, for God's sake? Britain might have been great in the past, all right, but in their opinion modern London sucks.

'For instance, the way they are in the stores. That man at the grocery was really disagreeable, as if I'd insulted him or something by saying he ought to carry unsweetened baking chocolate, and he was glad he'd never heard of it.'

'They're in collusion. That's what we decided,' Joe says. 'They meet once a week in some local pub. "Okay, let's get those dumb young American professors," they say, "the ones who were so bloody pleased with themselves for being in London."' He laughs, then blows his nose.

'That's why the plumber didn't come when our kitchen sink clogged up. He refused to say when he could get here, or if he would ever even come at all.'

'Or like today, that woman at the dry cleaners. She looked at my pants as if they had a smell. "No, sir, we couldn't do anything with those oily spots, one pound ten please."' Joe's imitation of a phony-refined British accent is marred by a natural tin ear and a bad cold.

'It's so ugly, that's what I think I mind the most,' Debby says. 'Everything's so gray and damp, and of course all the modern buildings are absolutely hideous. And they put up public housing and hamburger restaurants and billboards right in the middle of the most beautiful old streets. What's happened to their aesthetic sense?'

'Frozen out of them,' her husband says. Joe, a native of California, is thin, narrow-chested, and easily chilled; he has been ill ever since he arrived in London and sometimes sick as well. At first he tried to ignore the whole thing, he tells Fred while Debby is below in the dark, damp kitchen making coffee. Then he went to bed and waited for four days to feel better; finally, despairing of recovery, he got up again. At present he has a fever, a headache, a sore throat, a cough, and blocked sinuses. What he wants most is to go upstairs, lie down, and pass out; but he is a student and professor of philosophy and a natural stoic. Debby and their baby Jakie also have colds.

'The real downer is the climate,' says Joe, hauling on the ropes of the dumbwaiter in response to his wife's shout. 'They probably fix that too.'

'When I think what the weather's like right now in Claremont!' Debby exlaims a moment later, pouring coffee. 'It makes me feel really stupid and cheated. Well, hell, we *were* cheated. You know, maybe I told you before' – she has – 'we rented this house by mail; the agent sent us a photograph and description. The morning we got here, off the plane, Flask Walk was so pretty: the sun was shining for once, and when the taxi stopped it looked just like the picture, only better because it was in color, a perfect Georgian cottage. And I thought well, damn it, it's really worth all that rent and plane fare and those eight hellish hours with Jakie on the plane. And then we went inside, and the back of the house wasn't there, like it had been sliced off. Of course the real estate agent hadn't said anything about that.' The Vogeler's house is on a sharp-angled corner; it consists of a basement kitchen, a sitting room, and two bedrooms, one above the other. Each room is narrowly triangular, the shape of a piece of pie cut far less generously than those Debby has just served.

'"Drawing room eighteen by twelve feet *at best*," the description said,' she goes on. 'I thought that meant not counting the baseboards or the closets or something. And this awful plastic furniture, squeezed into the corners. And of course there wasn't any garden. It made me feel kind of dizzy and kind of crazy, all at the same time. I just burst out crying, and then of course Jakie started bawling too, the way babies do when you're upset.'

'We were totally disoriented, no kidding,' Joe admits. 'Partly jet lag, I guess. Only it's been nearly six weeks, and we're not recovered.'

'I know what you mean.' Fred holds out his cup for more coffee. 'I get the weird idea sometimes that I'm not really in London; that this place isn't London, it's some kind of imitation.'

'That's just how we felt when we first got here.' Debby leans forward, her square-cut brown hair swinging. 'Especially every time we went to look at something, say Westminster Abbey or the Houses of Parliament or whatever. They were always smaller than we expected, and overrun with busloads of American and French and German and Japanese tourists. So we decided the hell with it.'

'Of course that's inevitable anywhere,' her husband explains. 'Tourism is a self-degrading process, kind of like oxidation of iron.' Joe has a fondness for scientific metaphor, the precipitate of undergraduate years as a biochemistry major. 'Some place is designated a sight because it's typical or symbolic – it stands for the ideal Britain. So hundreds of tourists go there, and then of course all they see is other tourists.'

'And when you get to a sight it probably doesn't look right anyhow,' Debby adds, 'because you've already seen a prettied-up picture of it, taken on some bright summer day with all the tour buses and candy-wrappers and cigarette butts swept away. So the real place seems kind of dirty and shabby in comparison. We've just about given up sightseeing. Well, at least it prevents distractions.'

'Right,' Joe says. 'And if you don't go looking at things, in a climate like this, you're bound to write a lot. Nothing else to do but play with the baby or watch TV – Hey, what time is it?'

'Nearly eight,' Debby says. Joe unfolds his long legs and goes to turn on the rented television set that has been installed in the pointed end of the pie-shaped sitting room.

As they move their chairs round and wait with the sound off for this week's episode of a BBC serial based on a James novel, Fred considers putting forth his own ideas about tourism, but decides against it, realizing that his most important point doesn't apply to the Vogelers, neither of whom – as their juxtaposition on the ugly sofa demonstrates – is deprived of the sense of touch.

Joe turns up the sound, and a minor-key theme announces the start of the program. Fred, who has missed the earlier episodes, watches with less than his whole attention. Gloomily, he compares the Vogelers' situation with his own. They have each other and their baby, and apparently they are getting some writing done, whereas his work on John Gay in the British Museum (now referred to by Roo as the BM or Bowel Movement) is going very badly.

Fred is active, energetic, impatient of confinement. When he's in a library he likes to range through the stacks finding the books he wants, and coming across others he hadn't known about. In the BM he is forbidden to enter the stacks; he can't always get what he wants, and he can never get what he doesn't know he needs. Often he has to wait up to four hours for the constipated digestive system of the ancient library to disgorge a pathetic few of the volumes whose numbers he has copied from the complex, unwieldy catalogue. And even when they arrive all is far from well. Fred is used to working in a study of his own, away from noise and distraction. Now he is surrounded by other readers, many of them eccentric or even possibly insane, to judge by their appearance and mannerisms – filling dusty volumes with multicolored paper slips, tapping with their fingers or feet, mumbling to themselves, conversing in nervous whispers, coughing and blowing their noses in a contagious way.

He also likes to spread out at work, and to move around; at home his notes covered two tables and a bed in the spare room, and books lay open on the carpet. In the BM his tall, muscular frame is cramped into a chair at a narrow section of desk between two other scholars or lunatics and their encroaching heaps of volumes, in an ill-ventilated hall full of identical radiating seats constructed on the same plan as the model prisons designed by Victorian moral philosophers.

Fred is convinced that the BM is having a baleful effect on his work. In order to write decently about John Gay he must (to quote his subject) 'take the road'. He must be able to 'rove like the bee', to bring together not only literary criticism and dramatic history but folklore, musicology, and the annals of eighteenth-century crime. Crouched over whatever books he has managed to get that day, in this huge stuffy scholarly prison, it is no wonder the sentences he strains to produce are cramped and heavy. Again and again he rises to consult the catalogue unnecessarily, or to pace about the room. Glimpses of those habitual readers he now knows by sight, or in a few cases is acquainted with, depress him further. Often either Joe or Debby Vogeler is there, steadily grinding away; they went through graduate school together and have a scrupulously egalitarian partnership, sharing the care of little Jakie. The Vogelers are untroubled by working conditions in the Bowel Movement. As he passes, whichever one of them is present is apt to glance up and smile rather patronizingly. Too bad Fred never learnt to concentrate, he can sense them thinking.

The closing theme of the program comes on; the faces of its hero and heroine are frozen between a background of lush Edwardian architecture and a foreground of television credits.

'Well,' Fred says, rising. 'I guess I'd better – '

'Hey, don't go yet,' Joe snuffles.

'Stay and tell us some news. Uh, how is Ruth?' Debby or her husband ask this question at weekly intervals, alternating as if by prearrangement.

'I don't know. I haven't heard from her,' he replies for the fourth time.

'Still haven't heard, huh.' Behind this seemingly neutral comment and Debby's neutral question Fred senses hostility. His friends do not know Roo very well or like her very much. On both occasions when they met they had made evident efforts to know and like her, but – as with London – these efforts had not succeeded.

'She was never really right for you,' Debby says, breaking a three-year silence. 'We always saw that.'

'Yes,' Joe agrees. 'I mean, she was obviously a decent person. But she was always in overdrive.'

'Those photogaphs of hers. They were so kind of frantic and weird. And she seemed awful immature compared to you.' Roo, admittedly, is four years younger than Debby and three years younger than Joe and Fred.

'She just wasn't on the same wavelength.'

'Evidently not.' Fred picks up that morning's *Guardian* from the plastic imitation-oak coffee table.

'Listen. Don't let it get you down,' Joe instructs him.

'Yeh, that's easy to say,' he replies, turning the pages of the newspaper without seeing them.

'You made a mistake, that's all,' Debby says. 'Anybody can do that; even you.'

'Right,' Joe agrees.

'You know, I'm still really sorry it didn't work out for you and Carissa,' his wife murmurs. 'I've always liked her so much. And you know she's really brilliant.'

'She has a fine mind,' Joe says.

'Mmf,' Fred utters, noticing that Carissa is described in the present tense, whereas Roo by implication not only has a mediocre or coarse mind but has ceased to exist.

'She's a unique person,' Debby goes on.

A unique person is exactly what Carissa is not, Fred thinks. She is a conventional, frightened academic: intelligent, granted; but forever anxious to seem even more intelligent. Whereas Roo –

'Let's not talk about it, all right?' he says abruptly.

'Oh, God. I'm sorry –'

'Hey, we didn't mean –'

It takes Fred nearly ten minutes to convince his friends that he is not really offended, understands their concern, enjoyed dinner, and is looking forward to seeing them again.

As he strides up Flask Walk toward the Underground station through the cold, misty night, Fred's mood is one of angry discomfort. When things have gone wrong it is no consolation to hear that your friends expected it all along and could have told you so if they hadn't been so polite.

He doesn't condemn the Vogelers for their opinion, since when he himself met Roo he also would have said they weren't on the same wavelength, though in fact the signals she broadcast made him hum like a stereo amplifier. Everything about her seemed to send out an electrical pulse: not only the full round breasts under the orange SOLAR ENERGY T-shirt, but the wide liquid eyes, the flushed tanned skin, and the long braided cable of copper-brown hair from which wiry filaments escaped in every direction.

Their meeting took place during Fred's second month at Corinth University, at a reception for a visiting lecturer. Roo attended because she had been assigned to take a photograph for the local paper, and Fred because of his admiration for the views of the speaker – which she emphatically did not share, and said so. Their initial impressions of each other were unfavorable, even scornful. Complete polarization was avoided by the discovery of a mutual interest: Roo had been out horseback riding earlier that afternoon, and hadn't bothered to change; and when Fred learnt that her jodhpurs and high waxed boots were functional rather than – or as well as – theatrical, his hostility relaxed. When Roo, with what he would soon come to recognize as her characteristic impulsiveness masked by a deadpan manner, said that if he wanted to go riding with her that weekened he could, he accepted enthusiastically. Roo, as she told him later, was slower to come around. 'I was like blown away, I wanted to make it with you so much; but all the time my superego was saying Hey, whoa, wait a minute, this is an uptight woolly liberal professor type, probably a real pig in disguise; all you'll get from him is grief, baby.'

Turning off the High Street, Fred plunges into Hampstead Tube Station, buys a ticket to Notting Hill Gate, and enters an ancient iron lift decorated with advertising posters of half-naked young women. As it descends into the cold, damp shaft, so he descends, against his will, into naked memories.

October, over three years ago. He and Roo, whom he had known for three days, were lying in an abandoned apple orchard above her mother's and stepfather's farm, while their two horses tore at the long tough autumn grass in a nearby meadow.

'You know something?' Roo said, turning on her side so that sunlight and shadow flowed over her warm tanned skin as they do over ripe hayfields on a partly cloudy day. 'It's a lie that when your childhood fantasies come true it's always a let down.'

'Did you use to imagine a scene like this?' Fred did not move, but lay on his back looking past the interlaced limbs of the trees into a sky the burning blue of a gas flame.

'Oh yeh. Some day my prince will come, all that sappy stuff. From about age seven.'

'That young?'

'Sure. I never heard of the latency period till I got to college. I was always trying to get the little boys I knew to play doctor, but mostly they weren't all that interested. Of course my ideas about what would happen after the prince came were pretty out of focus. I could visualize the scenery all right, and the way the guy would look riding out of the woods, just about exactly like you, only of course at first he was seven years old.'

'Was that when you learnt to ride, when you were seven?'

'No. Not seriously anyhow.' Roo sat up. Her thick dark-russet braid (the same hue, he had realized earlier, as her horse Shara's coat) had come undone during their recent struggles. Now it spread down her back, uncoiling as if with an inner volition. 'I was wild to, but I didn't get much chance, except for a couple weeks in the summer at day camp. I didn't really learn till I was thirteen, after Ma met Bernie. What about you?'

'I don't know exactly. One of the first things I remember is being put up on a pony at my grandfather's: it seemed miles high, and broad as a sofa. I was two or three, I guess.'

'Lucky bastard.' Roo made a fist and hit him playfully, but not lightly. 'I would've given anything – I was crazy for horses when I was a kid, and so were most of my friends. We were a little nuts about it really.'

'Yeh, I knew girls like that. Funny social phenomenon. I always thought it must be a reaction against this mechanized world – women maybe mind that more than men do, even as kids.'

'Some women.' Roo shrugged. 'Then there's also the Freudian explanation, but personally I think that's all crap. I never imagined I was making it with a horse; I thought I *was* a horse. It was the same for the rest of us, I'm positive. Y'know there were two kinds of little girls in my elementary school: the goody-two-shoes types who liked pretty clothes and baking cookies and playing with dolls; and then me and my friends who wanted to run around outside in old jeans and sneakers and get dirty and were crazy about horses. The way I figure it, it was sort of identification with energy and strength and freedom. Wanting to be a different kind of female than everybody wanted us to be.'

'I remember those good little girls,' Fred said. 'They were no use for anything.' He pulled Roo down towards him. 'Ahh.'

'Hey,' he said a little later. 'You really mean you never went out riding with anyone before and ended up like this?'

'Oh, well.' Roo's breath was warm against his face. 'Sure, a couple of times.' She rolled back so that she could look at him. 'But it wasn't the same. A lot of guys I've known can't ride, not worth a damn anyhow – it's worse when they pretend they can. And the ones who could, they were mostly nice sexless dopes like my stepbrothers . . . I never brought anyone up here before; not to this place.' Her voice thickened, and their glances locked.

'Thank you.'

'Don't think you're so fucking special,' Roo said presently. 'I mean, you can't keep waiting forever for some goddamn prince. I was getting old, you know, and I just figured it was about time.'

'Yeh. Twenty-two.' Fred stroked her face; but Roo turned away from him, propping her chin on one hand and gazing downhill through the trees toward the horses.

'Besides, there was Shara. You know, like I told you, I wanted to get the fuck out of the Boston area last spring because my boss on the paper was such a chauvinist shit, and the relationship I was in turned into a real bummer. I didn't have to come home, though. I could've gone to New York or the West Coast – I had some decent leads on jobs. But I wanted to be with Shara. I figure this might be her last good year – she's nearly as old as I am, and after twenty you never know with a horse. She can still work up a fair speed, but she gets winded. Of course, I could ride one of the other horses, but it wouldn't be the same. In my fantasies I was always on Shara, and that's how I wanted it to be you know? And it's October already. In a couple of weeks, maybe sooner, it'll be too cold to fuck outdoors. So in a way it was now or never.' Roo gave an uneven laugh. 'So don't think you're so special,' she repeated.

But Fred did think so, and rejoiced in it.

In other quarters the rejoicing was less. As he paces the bare, freezing, nearly empty London Underground platform Fred hears again in his mind the recent remarks of Joe and Debby, and of other friends and relatives, some of whom hadn't hesitated to congratulate him on the breakup of his marriage. Most of these people had never been very enthusiastic about Roo from the start. She was not the sort of girl/woman they had expected Fred to become serious about, and their congratulations had been manifested in the conventional form of faint and damning praise.

By Fred's father, for instance: 'Well, she's certainly good-looking. And she seems like a very warm-hearted kind of girl. Those photographs she took in the Mexican slums show a lot of feeling for her subject; you know what she thinks, all right.' The photographs were of Mexicans in an upstate New York farmworker's camp, but Fred had given up trying to correct this error, typical of his father, who prefers to locate all social disagreeableness at the greatest possible mental distance.

Or as Joe and Debby had put it: 'Pretty far out, those disco pictures of Ruth's. You can see she really knows her stuff technically.' 'She's obviously a high-energy kind of person.' 'That was a really unusual dress she was wearing, with the red embroidery and all those mirrors, Albanian or whatever it was.' 'She reminds me of some of my students from New York. We were surprised she grew up in a place like Corinth.'

Translation: Roo is too emotional, too political, too arty, too noisy, and too Jewish. As it happens, Joe himself is Jewish, but from a very different tradition: Princeton-trained, scholarly, retiring.

Many of Fred's graduate school friends, and most of his relatives, are obviously relieved that Roo is, as one of them put it, 'out of the picture'. They assume or at least hope that she won't re-enter it, but will remain in the more far-out and slummy world of her own photographs. Fred's mother, on the other hand, very much wants them to get back together. Maybe for sentimental and conventional reasons: he can remember her saying in another context, with a placid pride, 'You know, darling, there's never been a divorce in my family.' But it is not only that she wishes to preserve this record; his mother had taken to Roo from the start, though they could hardly be less alike: Roo so arty, noisy, etc., and Emily Turner such a lady, her tastes so elegant, her voice so well modulated.

Roo, though more grudgingly, also took to his mother. 'I don't care if it's raining, I want to go for a walk,' she said as soon as they were alone on the first afternoon of her first visit to his family. 'It really gets to me after a while, this whole uptight place. . . . Well, your mother's okay. She had to put us in separate rooms, so it'd look respectable, but I notice she gave us ones with a connecting bath. And she sure is great-looking; almost as great-looking as you.' Roo leant warmly against Fred. 'I bet she's had a lot of adventures.'

'How do you mean, adventures?' Fred stopped caressing Roo's left breast.

'Like, you know: love affairs and stuff. Well, maybe not a *lot*,' Roo qualified, registering his expression. 'But enough to make her life interesting. I mean, hell, you'd have to do something to stay awake in a place like this.'

'You've got her all wrong,' Fred said. For the first time he considered his mother as a possible adulteress, and recognized that her qualifications for this role were excellent. His memory, without any prompting, even suggested possible partners. There was a visiting professor in History she used to dance with at parties; his father always made sour cracks about him. And of course the old guy that ran the riding stable – it was a family joke how he had a crush on her. And once when he was little (four? five?) he suddenly remembers, there was a man sitting in their dining-room fixing a toaster, and Freddy hates him, and his mother, in a red sweater, is standing too near the man, and Freddy hates her too – what was all that about? No, certainly not; his parents are very happy together. 'Not that I don't think she could have, if she's ever wanted to, but –'

'Okay, okay. Forget I said it. She's your mother, so you want her to be like one of those Virgin Mary statues in your church. Maybe she is, how should I know?'

'And you've got the wrong set of stereotypes,' he said, hugging her. 'There are no Virgin Mary statues in our church; it's all very abstract, very Reformation. Come on, get your coat, I'll show you.'

Though he had known Roo for nearly three months at this point, Fred was still intoxicated with her – and not only sexually. As if she had been some mind-expanding drug, he was in a constant state of heightened awareness: what he saw seemed both strange and amazingly familiar. The transformation had begun with her photographs, but did not depend on them. In Roo's presence at first, and then even when he was alone, Fred saw that farm workers had the expressions and gestures of Gothic carvings – elongated, creased, hollowed; and disco dancers, those of a Francis Bacon painting – all pale, screaming, metamorphosing mouths and limbs. He saw that the gate of the college was a frozen iron flower, and that the university officials resembled a convocation of barnyard fowl. Moreover, he knew that these visions were real – that he now saw the world as it was and always had been: like Roo herself, naked, beautiful, full of meaning.

Soon he no longer cared if Roo's pictures and Roo's conversation shocked his kith or kin. Indeed he privately enjoyed it, as she pointed out later: 'You know something: you use me to say things you're too polite to say yourself. It's like that ventriloquist I used to watch on TV when I was a little kid. He wore this big crazy puppet on his arm, sort of a woolly yellow bear with goggle eyes and a big pumpkin mouth, that was always making smartass cracks and insulting everybody else on the show. And the guy always pretended to be surprised, like he had nothing to do with it: 'Ow, that's awful! I can't control him, he's so naughty!' . . . Hell no, I don't mind. It's a good act.'

'Besides, it's reciprocal,' Fred told her. 'You use me to say all the conventional things you don't want to say. For instance, last week you got me to tell your mother we were getting married and take the blame for being a square.' The reaction of Roo's mother was: 'Really? How come? I thought nobody your age got married anymore unless – Oh, hey! Are you two having a baby? . . . Well then, I don't get it, but it's fine by me if you want to.' (Needless to say, on the one occasion when Roo and Fred had stayed overnight with her mother and stepfather, due to blizzard conditions following a party, they were put in the same room.)

It had in fact been Fred's suggestion that they might get married, ostensibly to simplify his relations with his students and hers with his colleagues ('This is Fred's er – friend.'). But it was also a way of proving to everyone that he took Roo seriously – that she wasn't just, as one of his cousins had suggested, the kind of girl you can have a lot of fun with for a while. And Roo, he thought, had wanted to marry him because in spite of appearances (her radical views and getups, her tough manner) she was deeply romantic.

As their plans progressed it became clear that he had been cast in another of her youthful fantasies: the Perfect Wedding. Sunlight on the lawn, massed bouquets of flowers, Mozart and Bartók, strawberries, homemade wedding cake and elderflower champagne. Romantic, but still a radical feminist. Roo had, for instance, refused to take his name; nor would she remain Ruth Zimmern. Her relations with her father, L. D. Zimmern, an English professor and critic of some reputation in New York, were friendly; but still, why should any feminist go through life with a patronymic, particularly that of a *pater* who had walked out on his *familias* when Roo was a small child? Instead, she used the occasion of her marriage to become legally Ruth March. The new surname was chosen because it was the month of her birth; and also in tribute to the favorite book of her childhood, *Little Women*, with whose heroine Jo March she had deeply identified. (She was determined that if they had children, the boys would take his ancestral surname and the girls her new one, establishing a matrilineal line of descent.)

Just as Fred is beginning to wonder if the Northern – or as the London papers call it, the Misery – Line has stopped running, a train arrives. He gets into it, is carried by slow stages to Tottenham Court Road station, and makes his way through a series of cold tiled sewerlike tunnels plastered with posters advertising cultural attractions available in London in February. He pays them no heed. Because of the desperate condition of his finances he cannot afford to go to any of these concerts, plays, films, exhibitions, or sporting events; nor can he afford to travel anywhere outside of London. Last fall when he and Roo were planning their trip together, counting on his study leave, both their savings, and the sublet of their apartment, it seemed as if time were the only barrier to their plans for exploring London, and beyond: Oxford, Cambridge; Cornwall, Wales, Scotland; Ireland; the Continent. He wanted to see everything then, to travel forever; he felt that forever was hardly long enough for him and Roo. Now, even if he had the funds, he lacks the spirit to explore Notting Hill Gate.

Roo, for instance, wanted to go to Lapland in June to photograph the midnight sun, the glaciers, the Northern Lights, the reindeer – the whole landscape, she explained, of Andersen's 'Snow Queen'. But there is no point in thinking about Roo, Fred tells himself as he waits on the platform for a westbound train. She cares nothing for him and never did; she has insulted him and probably betrayed him and said she never wants to see him again. And he doesn't want to see her again; how could he, after what has happened?

But in spite of this he can see her now: her dark eyes wide, her hair electrically springy, talking about the green ice of the glaciers, the mountain flowers – and then, even then, Roo was destroying him, photographing and possibly, probably, fucking – you couldn't use a more polite word – both of those – And what made it worse, at the exact same time she was photographing and fucking him. She was even more full of energy those last, unseasonably warm November weeks, even more beautiful, alight with joy because she was about to have her first one-woman exhibition in Corinth and because (she thought) she was going with him to London.

Her show, Roo had decided, would be called 'Natural Forms' and would include mostly pictures taken in Hopkins County, some of them for her newspaper. She claimed afterward that she had offered to let him see the prints before they were framed, and that he hadn't taken her up on it. As Fred recalled it, Roo had suggested it would be better if he saw the show as a whole.

Roo also claimed she had warned him to expect surprises, and had said she was worried about whether he would like them; but Fred has no recollection of this. He did remember her saying at one point: 'I'm going to use some of the shots I took of you last summer, okay? Your face won't show much.' To which he must, unfortunately – probably he was working at the time – have replied 'Okay.' Certainly she had said more than once that her exhibition was going to bother some people; but there are ways of telling the truth that are worse than an outright lie. Fred knew that Roo's photographs had always bothered some people, people who didn't like sharp-focus views of poverty or of the hysterical underside of the American dream.

On a cold bright afternoon in November, then, an hour before Roo's show was to open, Fred walked into the gallery. As he stood with her in the first and larger of the two rooms beside a bowl of blood-red punch and symmetrical plates of cheese cubes, each pierced by a toothpick, they exchanged their last warm, untroubled embrace. Around them, Roo's photographs were hung in groups of two. What she had done was to pair views of natural and manmade objects in such a way as to emphasize their similarity. A few of the combinations he had already seen. Others were new to him: insects waving antennae and TV roof aerials; Shara's rump and a peach. Some of the juxtapositions were personal and humorous, some strongly political: two overweight politicians and a pair of beef cattle. But the overall tone, in contrast to that of earlier exhibitions, was sympathetic and even lyrical. Three years of happiness, he had thought stupidly as he stood with his arms round his gifted wife, have made her see the comedy and beauty of the world as well as its ugliness and tragedy.

'Roo, it's so damn good,' he said. 'Really fine.' Then he released her and entered the other room of the gallery.

What he saw first were photographs of himself, or rather of bits of himself: his left eye, its long lashes magnified, placed next to a magnified spider; his mouth with its light pout, its infolded curve, likened to a spray of bougainvillea; his reddened knees compared to a basket of reddening apples. He admired the wit, but was somewhat embarrassed. As Roo had promised, his face didn't really show; nobody could be sure that it was him, though many might guess. He glanced at Roo, whose own face expressed – there was no doubt about it – anxiety and suspense; then at the next two photographs. These, paired with a beautiful color shot of woodland mushrooms, dew-dappled, springing strongly from moss and mold, was an unmistakable portrait of his own erect cock, also holding aloft a drop of dew. Fred recognized the picture – or rather, the photograph from which this detail had been grossly enlarged – but had never thought to see it on public view.

'Roo. For God's sake.'

'I told you.' Her large soft mouth quivered. 'I had to put it in, it's just so beautiful. And anyhow' – her voice modulated, as it did sometimes, into a strained toughness – 'who's going to know it's yours?'

'Well, for Christ's sake, who else's would it be?'

Roo didn't answer. But the question, he soon saw, was not a rhetorical one. One the walls beyond his own partial portraits were others not his own. Including other penises – two others, to be exact. Neither was as fully enlarged (in either sense) as his, but both displayed some interest. One tended to length at the expense of breadth and rose from sparse blond tendrils; it was compared by juxtaposition to a stalk of asparagus. The other, stubbier and mottled a darker red, was displayed next to a high-focus photograph of the heavy, rusted bolt of an ancient barn door.

The battles that followed this private view were fierce, painful, and prolonged. Roo refused to take down a single one of her photographs before the show opened or at any time thereafter – a decision in which she was upheld by the owners of the gallery, two small, deceptively quiet and pretty radical feminists whom Fred had once liked very much. She also refused to identify her other models, whose feelings she was evidently more considerate of than her own husband's. ('Honestly, I can't, I like *swore* I wouldn't say.')

When he protested, using phrases like 'good taste', Roo started screaming at him. 'Yeh, well you know what that is, baby, that's a pile of chauvinist shit. What about all the male painters and sculptors that've been exploiting women's bodies for thousands of years – and photographers too, posing women to look like fruit or sand-dunes or teacups? A room full of breasts and asses, oh yes, that's really nice, that's Art. But don't let the cunts think they can try the same thing on us. Well, too bad. Goose sauce, sauce for the gander!'

Okay, all right, Fred conceded for the sake of argument. If she wanted to take photographs of good-looking men, their physiques, he guessed he could see the point of that, their chests and shoulders and arms and legs. Or even their asses – 'great buns', he had heard that was the term – But Roo, still fuming, interrupted him. 'That's not where it's at, pal. Women aren't interested in men's behinds, that's a fag thing.' What they are interested in, she didn't say, didn't have to say, was cocks.

At the same time, Roo insisted and kept on insisting that neither of her unknown models had been physically intimate with her. 'I don't *know* how they got aroused like that. Being photographed turns a lot of people on. You really think if I'd fucked some other guy I'd put a picture of his cock in my show, you think I'm that kind of bitch?'

'I don't know,' Fred said, angry and weary. 'Hell, I don't know what you might do any more. I mean, what's the difference?'

Roo looked at him with rage. 'Kate and Harriet were right,' she said. 'You really are a pig.'

Far below Tottenham Court Road a train pulls up beside the cold dirty platform on which Fred is standing. He gets in, feeling gloomy and tense – as always when, against his better judgment, he allows himself to think of Roo. She is something he has to put behind himself, to forget, to recover from. The marriage is an emotional disaster, a failed adventure which has, inevitably, shrunk his view of himself and of the world; he is wiser, maybe, but at the expense of being that much sourer and sadder.

Fred's choice of Roo had felt to him like a bold and expansive act, a defiance of conventions – and also of his own conventional self. For years he had been aware that in spite of all his abilities and advantages his life was a litle unexciting. From babyhood on he had been what he once heard his father describe as 'a very satisfactory child' – bright, good-looking, successful in everything, above all well behaved. His adolescent rebellion was of the most ordinary variety, and gave his parents no serious anxiety. Fred would have liked to worry them a little more – but not at the cost of failing school, scrambling his brains permanently with acid, or wrecking the battered tail-finned Buick he had delivered papers in zero weather and mowed lawns for five years to earn.

Roo was his red flag, his declaration of independence – and in the beginning, the less comfortable his family and more conventional friends were with her, the better pleased he was. Now he feels shamed and enraged to realize that they had judged her more accurately than he. His father, for instance, held the unspoken but clearly evident opinion that Roo was not a lady. Once Fred would have indignantly denied this, or rather condemned the concept as outmoded and meaningless. Now he has to recognize its validity. Even if you suppose, just for the sake of argument, that Roo never slept with either of the two guys whose semi-erect cocks were featured in her show, those photos were pretty vulgar. And worse, she didn't even know it. As Joe had put it, she wasn't on the same wavelength; they weren't, as Debby had said, 'coming from the same place' – though in fact they had both grown up in university towns with fathers who were professors.

Possibly it was this similarity of background that had helped mislead him into assuming that Roo and he were, whatever her language and manners, essentially in cahoots. It wasn't his fault; Debby had said so: 'Anyone can make a mistake – even you.'

As Fred hears her remark again in his head, however, it begins to deconstruct, becoming condescending, chilly, and spiteful. It occurs to him for the first time that Debby does not like him, possibly has never liked him, that she is glad to see him depressed and discomfited. Why this should be so, however, he has no idea. He has known Debby even longer than he has known Joe, since their first year in graduate school, and had always thought of her as a friend, though not an intimate one.

As a matter of fact, though he doesn't know it, Debby had originally liked Fred very much – too much for her peace of mind. When they met – almost daily, in class or at some lecture or party – or when they had lunch together, usually in a group but now and then alone, Fred remained unaware of her feelings. With the good-natured vanity of the extremely good-looking, it didn't occur to him that dumpy, dish-faced Debby might hope he was developing a romantic interest in her, or that as time passed she regarded herself as a woman scorned. At present Debby would tell anyone who asked that she 'likes' Fred, but privately she thinks of him as rather immature and thoroughly spoilt. She resents him professionally too, both on her own account and on her husband's. Why should Fred, who did no better in graduate school than they, and has published no more, have a job in an Ivy League university, while they are at California colleges nobody ever heard of? It is only because he dresses well and has a smooth manner at interviews, and because of his connections: because his father is a dean at another Ivy League school. Fred, according to an article Debby once read, is an example of Entitlement Psychology: he has been brought up to get, and think he deserves, all the good things of this world. So why should she mind seeing him stumble, even fall? It will do him good to get a few bruises and a little mud in his eye. The fact that Joe doesn't resent Fred the way she does, though he is in her opinion basically much more brilliant and has a more original mind, is for Debby just another proof of her husband's inner superiority.

Fred, however, has never been agile at discovering unpleasant motives for his friends' behaviour. What he thinks now is that he must somehow have offended Debby, maybe by coming to dinner too often. Maybe she thinks he is sponging on them; maybe he *is* sponging on them. (Actually, this idea has never occurred to either Joe or Debby.) He has to ease up, Fred thinks as the train jolts toward Notting Hill Gate; he has got to meet some other people in London.

He decides that he will go to Professor Miner's party after all. Probably there will be nobody there but other elderly, touchy academics; but you never know. And at least there will be drinks, and more important, maybe food – enough hors d'oeuvres so that for once he won't have to buy supper.

3

Raspberry, strawberry, blackberry jam,
Tell me the name of your young man.

Old rhyme

In Monsieur Thompson's, a small but chic restaurant in Kensington Park Road, Vinnie Miner is waiting for her oldest London friend, a children's book editor, writer, and critic called Edwin Francis. She is not anxious, for Edwin has thoughtfully called the restaurant to say he may be late; nor is she impatient. She is content to sit enjoying the book she's just bought, the yellow and white chiffon of the fresh jonquils on the table, the matching alternation of sun and shade on the whitewashed houses outside, and the sensation of being in London in early spring.

Unless you knew Vinnie well, you would hardly recognize her as the miserable professor who got onto the plane in Chapter One. Perched on an oak settle with her legs tucked under her she looks girlish. Her small size and the illustrated cover of her book (on Australian playground games) add to the illusion. Her costume is also juvenile by academic standards: a ruffled white blouse and a deep-flounced tan wool jumper. Round her narrow shoulders is her Liberty wool shawl, which gives her the look of a junior high school student, playing the part of a kindly grandmother. Her spectacles might well be a prop, the lines in her face drawn with eyebrow pencil, and her hair incompletely powdered gray.

'Vinnie darling. Forgive me.' Edwin Francis leans over the table to brush her cheek with his. 'How are you? . . . Oh, thank you, dear.' He removes his coat and presents it to the waiter. 'You won't believe what I've just heard.'

'I might. Try me,' Vinnie says.

'Well.' Edwin leans forward. Though he is some years younger than Vinnie, his appearance – when he is in good form, as now

– also suggests an artificially aged child. In his case, too, smallness of stature plays a part in the illusion; his short limbs, round face and torso, high color, and curly fair hair – now becoming rather sparse – also contribute to the effect. (When he is not in good form – depressed, drinking too much, unhappily in love – he resembles an afflicted Hobbit.) In spite of his innocuous appearance, and a manner that matches it – amused, offhand, self-deprecating – Edwin is a figure of power in the children's book world and a formidable critic of both juvenile and adult literature: learned, sharp-witted, and, when he chooses, sharp-tongued.

'Well,' he continues. 'You know Posy Billings.'

'Yes, of course.' Contrary to Fred Turner's assumption, Vinnie's London circle isn't composed exclusively or mainly of academics. Through Edwin and other friends she is acquainted with publishers, writers, artists, journalists, people in the theater, and even one or two society hostesses like Lady Billings.

'I was talking to Posy this morning, and you were quite wrong. Rosemary *has* taken up with your colleague Mr Turner. She's even proposed bringing him to Posy's place in Oxfordshire for a weekend.'

'Really,' Vinnie says, frowning a little. Rosemary Radley, an old friend of Edwin's, is a television and film actress. She is extremely pretty and charming; she also has a history of brief, impetuous, usually disastrous affairs. When Edwin first announced that she had 'taken up with' Fred Turner, Vinnie frankly didn't believe it. They had been seen together at a play, at a party? Very possibly they had; that didn't mean they had come together, or were romantically involved. Perhaps Rosemary *had* invited Fred to the event, because after all he is a nice-looking young man, and one whose transatlantic origin might lend a piquant variety to her usual crowd of admirers. Or perhaps she hadn't: people always gossiped about Rosemary, often inaccurately: she'd been the heroine of so many BBC and real-life romantic serials.

Edwin particularly enjoys fantasizing about his friends and acquaintances. He likes to hover over their adventures or presumed adventures as he does over whatever Vinnie is cooking when he comes to dinner, occasionally giving the pot a stir or adding a pinch of spices himself. 'Really,' Vinnie had once said to him, 'you should have been a novelist.' 'Oh no,' he had replied. 'Much more fun this way.'

Even if things have gone as far as Edwin is claiming now, it can't be very serious. Rosemary, after all, has frequent impulsive sexual lapses – referred to later with laughter in phrases like 'I just don't know what came over me' or 'It must have been the champagne' – and Fred might be a relatively harmless instance of this habit. But she can hardly be serious about him. It isn't just that she's older, but that her world is so much more complex and resonant. If talking to Fred for any length of time rather bores Vinnie, who after all is in the same profession and department, what on earth can he have to say that would interest Rosemary Radley? On the other hand, perhaps you don't have to interest her, as long as you are sufficiently interested *in* her. Perhaps what she wants is fans, not rival entertainers.

'Of course it's all your doing,' Edwin remarks, breaking off his loving contemplation of the menu. 'If you hadn't given that party –'

'I never meant for Rosemary to take up with Fred.' Vinnie laughs, for surely Edwin is teasing. 'I never even considered –'

'The intentional fallacy.'

'I never even considered it. I thought Fred ought to meet some young people, so I invited Mariana's eldest daughter. How was I to know she'd turned into a punk rocker? She was perfectly presentable when I saw her at her mother's last month.'

'Well, you might have asked me,' Edwin says, breaking his current diet and liberally buttering one of the whole-wheat rolls for which Thompson's is celebrated. Vinnie does not pick this up; if Edwin had his way, she is quite aware, he would dictate the guest lists of all her parties. His social circle is wider and considerably more glamorous than hers, and though she is perfectly happy to have him bring one or two of his well-known friends to her house – as he had brought Rosemary – she doesn't want it to go any further. One or two celebrities are a social asset; but if you have too many, she has noticed, all they ever do is talk to one another.

'Besides, if Mariana's daughter's so punk,' she asks, 'why did she bother to come to a party like mine, with that awful spotty young man in black zip-up leather?'

'To annoy her mother, of course.'

'Oh dear. Was her mother annoyed?'

'I think so, very,' Edwin says. 'Of course she wouldn't ever let it show, *noblesse oblige*.'

'No,' Vinnie agrees, and sighs. 'It's not safe any more, is it, giving parties? One never knows what fateful events are going to be precipitated.'

'The hostess as demiurge.' He giggles, and Vinnie, reassured, joins in.

'Fred's being at that party wasn't my fault,' says Vinnie, returning to the subject somewhat later. 'It was yours, really. I only asked him because you said I didn't know any Americans,' she lies.

'I never said any such thing,' Edwin lies, though both of them know that he had recently made this remark, which flattered Vinnie and also aroused in her a guilty patriotism.

'Anyhow, I don't see why you're complaining. I would have thought Fred was about the safest sort of person Rosemary could become involved with. Compared to Lord George, or to Ronnie, you have to admit –'

'Oh, I do. I have nothing against Fred *per se* . . . Thank you, that looks delicious.' Edwin gives his sole véronique a concupiscent glance, then delicately attacks it. 'Mmm. Perfect . . . And I admit he's beautiful.'

'Too theatrical for my taste.' Vinnie, less passionately, begins on her grilled chop.

'Well of course, for Rosemary that could hardly be an objection.'

'No.' Vinnie laughs. 'But the point is, he seems to be almost ideal for a fling.'

'Very likely.' Edwin, against his doctor's advice, plunges into the creamed potatoes. 'But Rosemary isn't looking for a fling. She's looking for an undying passion, the way most of us are.' Edwin, like Rosemary Radley, is known for his disastrous romantic affairs, though his are somewhat less frequent and naturally less well publicized. They tend to involve unstable young men, usually recent émigrés from southern European or Near Eastern countries, with menial jobs (waiter, grocer's clerk, dry cleaner's assistant) and grandiose ambitions (theatrical, financial, artistic). From time to time one of them leaves Edwin's flat unexpectedly, taking with him Edwin's liquor, stereo, fur-collared overcoat, etc. Others have had mental breakdowns in the flat and refused to leave it at all.

Vinnie refrains from remarking that she at least is not looking for an undying passion; Edwin surely knows that by now.

'Maybe it's Fred we should be worrying about,' Edwin continues. 'Her friend Erin thinks she's going to eat him alive.'

'Oh, I doubt that,' Vinnie exclaims. After twenty years she feels a certain amount of loyalty to and identification with the Corinth English Department; and the idea that one of its members (no matter how junior) could be totally consumed by an English actress is displeasing. 'He doesn't look all that digestible to me.'

'Perhaps you're right . . . Ahh. Have you tried the courgettes?'

'Yes, very nice.'

'Tarragon, obviously. And is there perhaps a little dill?' Edwin gives a gourmet's frown.

'Hard to say.' Vinnie's interest in food is comparatively moderate.

'No. Not dill. I must ask the waiter.' Edwin sighs. 'So how do you see the future of the affair, then?'

'I don't know.' Vinnie puts down her fork, considering. 'But whatever happens, it can't last very long. Fred's going back to America in June.'

'Oh? Who says so?'

'Why, Fred does. He told me himself.'

'Yes; but when did he tell you?'

'What? I don't know – in December, before he left, it must have been.'

'Exactly.' Edwin gives the wide smile that increases his resemblance, noted before by Vinnie, to the Cheshire Cat.

'But that won't make any difference. Fred has to be back in Corinth by the middle of June: he's teaching two courses in summer school.'

'Unless he decides not to.'

'Oh no; that's impossible,' Vinnie explains. 'That'd be most inconvenient for the Department. They wouldn't like that at all.'

'Really.' Edwin raises his eyebrows, somehow expressing doubt not of the English Department's annoyance but of its very existence, and even of the existence of Hopkins County, New

York. ('Tell us again the wonderful name of that place where you live in the States,' he occasionally says. 'What is it? Simpkins County?')

'Besides, he couldn't afford it,' Vinnie continues. 'Between us, he's quite hard up.'

'Rosemary has plenty of money,' Edwin says.

This time Vinnie represses her immediate reaction, though the idea that one of her colleagues might allow himself to be kept by an English actress is not only displeasing but disgusting. 'I'm sure that Fred's not serious about her anyhow,' she says. 'For one thing, she must be at least ten years older than he, don't you think?'

'Who knows?' Edwin, who probably does know, shrugs. Officially, and in press releases, Rosemary is thirty-seven; her actual age is a matter of constant speculation among her acquaintances. 'Oh yes, now let's see,' he adds, his eyes lighting as the dessert menu is presented. 'A lemon ice, perhaps? Or a teeny little bit of the apricot tart, would that be too fattening? What do you think, Vinnie?'

'If you're really on a diet, you should have the cantaloupe,' she suggests, refusing for once to be an accessory before the fact; she is annoyed at Edwin both for his discretion about Rosemary's age and his insinuations about Fred's motives.

'No; not the cantaloupe.' Edwin continues to study the menu; his expression is both firm and a little injured.

'Just coffee for me, thanks,' Vinnie tells the waiter, offering a good example.

'Two coffees. And I'll have the apricot tart, please.'

Vinnie does not comment, but it occurs to her for the first time that for such an intelligent man Edwin is disgracefully plump and self-indulgent; that his pretense of dieting is ridiculous; and that his demand that his friends join in the charade is becoming tiresome.

'But we mustn't enjoy ourselves,' he says a few minutes later, wiping a bit of whipped cream from the side of his muzzle. 'We must consider the problem of Rosemary, before there's another disaster like the Ronnie one. If she keeps breaking her professional commitments to go off with some fellow . . . Well, naturally the word gets round: better not cast Rosemary Radley, she's not dependable.' Edwin moves his plump forefinger in a horizontal circle, indicating world-wide distribution of this warning. 'Jonathan, for instance, I know he wouldn't consider it after the Greenwich debacle . . . But she's been working fearfully hard on that TV special, and in July she's got to go on location for her series, she mustn't be upset. I really think it's your job to do something.'

'To do what? Warn Rosemary against Fred Turner?' Vinnie speaks rather impatiently; while watching Edwin's loving consumption of his apricot tart it has struck her that in order to shame him into sticking to his diet – what a silly idea! – she has denied herself any dessert. And to no practical purpose, for she isn't at all overweight; rather the reverse.

'Heaven's, no,' Edwin replies soothingly, with the complacent tolerance of the well fed. 'We all of us know how little use warnings are with Rosemary; they only incite her. When she rushed off to Tuscany with that painter, Daniel what's-it, everyone warned her, but it simply made her more determined.'

'Well then. What could I possibly do?' She laughs.

'I think you just might speak to Fred.' Though Edwin continues to smile, it is clear from the way he pushes his coffee aside and leans over the blue-and-white checked tablecloth that he is not entirely jesting. 'I'm sure he'd listen to you. Considering your position at his college. You could try to persuade him to – what would be his phrase? – cool it, before there's too much damage done.'

The idea that she might use her academic seniority to persuade – *blackmail* would be a more accurate word – Fred into breaking off his love affair is disagreeable. Vinnie enjoys wielding her hard-won professional authority, but only in professional matters. Unlike Edwin, she feels a strong dislike, almost a revulsion, from the idea of meddling in anyone's private life.

'I could, I suppose,' she says, sitting back away from him. 'But I certainly am not going to.'

A March afternoon in St James's Square. In what she has determined by experiment to be the most comfortable and best lit of the chairs in the London Library Reading Room, Vinnie Miner sits working. Unless she needs some volume available only in the British Museum, she prefers to study in these quiet, elegantly shabby surroundings, which for her are agreeably haunted by the shades of writers past and the shapes of writers present. It is easy for her to imagine the portly, well-dressed spirit of Henry James climbing the stairs in a dignified manner, or that of Virginia Woolf trailing limp crushed twenties silks between two shadowy bookstacks. And almost any day she might see Kingsley Amis, John Gross, or Margaret Drabble in their still incarnate state. Many of her friends, too, use the library; there is almost always someone around to lunch with.

Vinnie's scholarly research is nearly complete. As soon as it stops raining and warms up a bit she can begin the more exciting part of her project: collecting playground rhymes in city and suburban schools. Already she has spoken to a number of principals and teachers, some of whom have not only given her permission to visit, but volunteered their help in recording rhymes, or even made this part of a classroom project. Here in Britain, she doesn't have to educate the educators; her interest in folklore is seen as natural and respectable. All that remains is to wait for the weather to improve.

By now Vinnie has more or less forgotten her unpleasant flight to Britain and – most of the time – that hateful article in the *Atlantic*. So far, no one she knows here has mentioned it; probably no one has even seen it. To help ensure this, since many of her friends regularly use the London Library, on her first visit she took the precaution of removing the March issue of the *Atlantic* from the top of its pile in the reading room and sliding it under a stack of *Archaeology* nearby. From time to time the magazine reappears; then she hides it again. One sign of the moderation of her distress is that this morning she merely moved the March issue to the bottom of the heap of *Atlantic*'s. As she did so, she imagined L. D. Zimmern as shrunken to about six inches high and crushed flat between the pages of his own article, a kind of unattractive paper doll, staining the paper with a thin sepia smear. It also occurred to her, as it had before, that she might slip the magazine into her canvas shopping bag, sneak it out of the library, and destroy it at her leisure. But all her training is against this final solution. Magazine-burning, in Vinnie's mind, is nearly as bad as book-burning; besides, in the same issue there is a really excellent article on vanishing wildlife, which many people might enjoy.

The only thing that disturbs her at the moment is her

conversation with Edwin Francis at lunch yesterday. Mentally reviewing it, she is not quite comfortable in the most comfortable chair in the reading room. She is annoyed at Fred Turner, and feels – quite illogically, she realizes – that he is somehow responsible for a slight but definite coolness between her and her oldest London friend and for the fact that Edwin and she had parted yesterday without making plans to meet again. Fred had also somehow deprived her of an apricot tart with whipped cream – a treat that seems even more desirable today ater a pub lunch of wafer-thin salmon-paste sandwiches and a rubbery Scotch egg. Why should she be involved in the affairs of some junior colleague whom she hardly knows? If Fred needs to be recommended for a grant, very well; if he wants to have a frolic with a mutual acquaintance, it is no concern of hers. At the same time, Vinnie is uncomfortably aware that if Fred did ask for a recommendation now, it would take some effort to respond with disinterested good will.

Her mistake had been asking him to her party in the first place. In the past, instinct has always warned Vinnie to keep her American colleagues and her English friends apart. She has suspected that if they did meet, they would probably fail to appreciate or would even dislike one another, and that this dislike might rub off on her, staining both existing relationships ('I just don't understand Vinnie. How could she possibly care for someone like that?'). In one or two cases she had almost disregarded her intuition, but after consideration decided not to risk it. As Edwin once said, social life is like alchemy: mixing foreign elements is dangerous. Last month she had broken her rule for a mere junior colleague; and instead of disliking each other Fred and Rosemary Radley apparently liked each other too well. Trouble either way.

Originally Vinnie had never meant to invited Fred to anything. She knew he was in London, of course – she had seen him several times in the British Museum. She knew he was alone here, having somehow misplaced his wife, though she had no idea how he had done this; one seldom does know personal details about the junior members of one's department, though there is, in Vinnie's opinion, more than enough gossip about one's contemporaries. It had never occurred to her to feel sorry for Fred because he had no spouse with him: after years of detached observation, she doesn't think that much of marriage.

The whole thing was an accident. One gusty wet afternoon, on her way home from a luncheon party, Vinnie had stopped in a grocery store in Notting Hill Gate and run into Fred, who lives nearby. He was looking windblown and damp, and buying two sickly greenish oranges and a can of the wrong kind of vegetable soup for his supper. Vinnie felt an irritated, uncharacteristic concern. At home, except for her students and very close friends, she seldom does anything for anyone else if she can help it; she simply hasn't the energy. But here was a junior member of her own department, hungry and lost in a foreign city. In Corinth she would have passed him by with hardly a nod; but in London, where she is a different, nicer person, the unfamiliar conviction came to her that she ought to do something about him. Well, I suppose I could ask him to my party next week, she thought. He's presentable enough.

Too presentable, almost. There is something overfinished about Fred's looks that reminds Vinnie of the Arrow Collar Man in the advertisements of her childhood – though that isn't his fault, heaven knows. He doesn't dress up or act up to his appearance: he wears ordinary, even colorless preppie-professor clothes and has unremarkable good manners. All the same, his appearance sometimes annoys people, especially men: Vinnie remembers the hostile, jocular remarks that were made after his MLA interview. It was lucky for Fred that he had already published two solid articles and was in the eighteenth century, where good candidates are scarce.

Fred's handsomeness hadn't saved his marriage either, Vinnie thinks. That wasn't so hard to understand, perhaps. Such looks arouse false expectations: the noble exterior is assumed to clothe a mind and soul equally great – the Platonic fallacy. Whereas inside Fred, as far as Vinnie can tell, is simply an ordinary, reasonably intelligent young man who knows something about the eighteenth century. Besides, one might get tired of striking, continual beauty after a while, just as one might get tired of being struck continually.

Even as she issued the invitation, Vinnie had regrets. But at the party Fred caused her no anxiety. She noticed that he didn't spend much time talking to Mariana's punk daughter and her angry-looking boyfriend – well, who could blame him for that?

He ate a good deal, which was understandable considering the financial difficulties suggested by the vegetable soup and his rather desperate inquiries about how one could get Corinth paychecks cashed without a four-week delay. (No way, is the answer.)

Later on at her party Vinnie had noticed that Fred was part of the circle around Rosemary Radley; but then there is always a circle around Rosemary. She has the knack of becoming the center of a group without seeming to dominate it that, Vinnie supposes, any successful actor must possess. Her sphere of influence is rather small – only a few feet in diameter – as you might expect of someone who works mainly in television and films. She cannot, like some stage performers Vinnie has met, effortlessly focus all attention in a large room; but within her range she is invincible. And this somehow without holding forth on any topic, retailing gossip, wholesaling personal confessions, or saying anything especially clever or shocking – anything, really, that would have been out of character for the roles she plays on camera.

Professionally, Rosemary's specialty is ladies: highborn women of every historical period from classical Greece to modern Britain. She doesn't portray queens or empresses: she isn't sufficiently regal or monumental for that. She is extraordinarily pretty rather than in any sense beautiful: pink-and-white-and-gold like a refined Boucher; her features are agreeable but small and unemphatic. What she mainly projects is elegance and breeding – comic, pathetic, or tragic according to the demands of the script – and a sweet, airy graciousness. She is frequently in work, since ladies are overrepresented in British television drama, and is often praised in reviews as one of the few actresses who is totally convincing as an aristocrat. It is sometimes mentioned that this is not surprising, since she is really Lady Rosemary Radley, her father having been an earl.

Rosemary's private life is generally believed to be unsatisfactory. She has been married twice, both times briefly and unhappily and without issue; now she lives alone in a large beautiful untidy house in Chelsea. Of course some people say it is her own fault that she's alone: that she is impossibly romantic, asks too much (or too little) of men, is unreasonably jealous, egotistical/a doormat; sexually insatiable/frigid; and so on – the usual things people say of any unmarried woman, as Vinnie well knows. In all this, Rosemary has Vinnie's sympathy. But, somehow, not her trust.

It is Rosemary's charm that Vinnie doesn't trust: the silken flutter and flurry of her social manner; her assumption of a teasing, impulsive intimacy which yet holds its victim at arm's length. For instance, when someone new comes within her range, Rosemary will often compliment that person extravagantly on some quality or attribute nobody else would have fixed on, or perhaps even noticed. She will declare that she adores some acquaintance, or a cousin, or her greengrocer or dentist, because they are so marvelous at arranging roses, or speak so slowly, or have such curly hair. She always makes this announcement with an air of wondering discovery to everyone who is within listening range, and without regard to whether its subject is sitting next to her or is miles away.

At a luncheon of Edwin's once, for instance, she sang out during a pause in the hubbub that she really loved the way Vinnie's friend Jane ate salad. It was no use asking what she meant by that, as Jane discovered. Even if you could get her attention again, which was never easy, Rosemary would only toss back the pale-gold waves of her hair and give her famous laugh – like sunlight sparkling on crystal, a besotted television reviewer had once written – and cry, 'Oh, I can't explain! – It's just so – wonderful.' And if, as occasionally happened, someone else offered an interpretation, Rosemary would either ignore them or protest that it wasn't that at *all*. She couldn't bear to have her butterfly enthusiasms – or, possibly, her antipathies – analyzed, pinned down.

When they heard – or heard of – Rosemary's paean to their unique qualities, most people were pleased, because it's agreeable to be loved and adored, even casually; and because Rosemary was pretty and well known. Even if they didn't have the least idea what she meant, there was something awfully attractive in the manner of its delivery. Indeed, some of those who hadn't ever thus been complimented, like Vinnie, began to feel a little left out.

Others, however, were made uneasy. One can for instance picture Rosemary's dentist alone in his surgery after his famous patient has left. He twists the magnifying mirror attached to his dental unit toward him and frowns into it. Is there really something unusually lovable about the way his hair curls behind his ears? Or is there, on the other hand, something odd about it, something ugly and bizarre? Had Lady Rosemary been laughing at him?

For days after Edwin's party, Jane said, Rosemary's encomium kept sliding into her mind and nagging at her. Finally one day she took a container of leftover salad out of her fridge and went and stood in front of the dining-room mirror, peeled back the plastic wrap, and watched herself eating the spicy oil-soaked lettuce leaves and soggy slices of tomato, trying to discover what was so damned adorable about it, or so different from the way most people ate salad. What on earth had Rosemary meant?

The truth was, Vinnie told her, Rosemary probably hadn't meant anything. It was just nonsense off the top of her head, a way of focusing attention on herself or changing the topic of conversation, perhaps – a musical noise, that was all. Words don't matter to actors as they do to a literary person. For them meaning is mainly in expression and gesture; the text is just the libretto, a line of empty glasses that the performer can fill with the golden or silver or bronze liquid of his or her voice. At drama schools, Vinnie has heard, they teach you to say 'Please close the door' twenty different ways.

In any social network there are always some people who are as it were 'friends' by social compulsion, though if the net fell apart they would seldom or never see each other. It is thus with Vinnie and Rosemary. Because of Edwin they meet fairly often, and always behave on these occasions as if they were perfectly delighted, but they don't like each other very much. At least, Vinnie does not like Rosemary; and she senses that the feeling is mutual. But nothing can be done about it. Vinnie imagines their social network, or perhaps 'web' is more like it – fine-spun, elaborately joined, strung across the rainy city from Fulham to Islington, anchored by isolated threads in Highgate and Wimbledon. She and Rosemary are points of intersection in the web, held there now by many silken twisted strands. If they were to break off cordial relations it would leave gaping sticky holes, distressing to everyone. And they are probably not the only two thus unwillingly joined, Vinnie thinks. Still, the web holds, and spreads its elastic, dew-spangled pattern over London: that is the important thing.

The fading light on the pages of her book tells Vinnie that it is time to leave if she wants to avoid the homebound crowds. Outside the London Library the air is cold, damp, with rain suspended in it rather than falling. Realizing that she is still hungry, and the cupboard in her flat bare of delicacies, she turns up Duke Street and into Fortnum and Mason's. A clerk in formal morning dress, resembling an Edwardian banker, approaches her with discreet whispered offers of assistance, which she politely declines. No; really it would be foolish to buy anything here; the prices are ridiculous. As she stands debating before a Tower of Babel of international jams and jellies, a much louder voice, much less refined – in fact, blaringly mid-American – hails her.

'Wal, hey! Aren't you, uh, Professor Miner?'

Vinnie turns. A very large man is grinning at her; he wears a semi-transparent greenish plastic raincoat of the most repellant American sort, and locks of graying reddish-brown hair are plastered to his broad, damp red forehead.

'Metchoo on the plane last month. Chuck Mumpson.'

'Oh, yes,' she agrees without enthusiasm.

'How's it going?' He blinks at her in the slow way she recalls from the flight.

It? Presumably, her work. Or life in general, perhaps? 'Very well, thank you. How about you?'

'Oh, doing okay.' There is no enthusiasm in his voice. 'Been shopping.' He holds up a damp-stained paper shopping bag. 'Stuff for the folks at home, wouldn't dare go back without it.' He laughs in a way that strikes Vinnie as nervous and unreal. Either it is in fact the case that Mr Mumpson would be afraid to return to his 'folks' without gifts, or, more likely, the remark is just an example of the debased and meaningless jesting common among half-literate middle Americans.

'Hey, glad I ran into you,' Mumpson continues. 'Wanted to ask you something; you know this country lots better than I do. How about a cup of coffee?'

Though she isn't especially glad that Chuck Mumpson has run into her, Vinnie is moved by the appeal to her expertise and the prospect of immediate refreshment. 'Yes; why not.'

'Great. A drink'd be more like it, but I guess everything's shut now, crazy regulations they have here.'

'Until five-thirty,' Vinnie confirms, glad for once of the licensing laws. She doesn't care for city pubs, and would especially not care to be seen drinking in one with someone dressed like Mumpson. 'There's a tearoom here in the store, but it's awfully expensive.'

'No sweat. I'm taking you.'

'Well. All right.' Vinnie leads the way past elaborate ziggurats of biscuits and candied fruits and up the steps to the mezzanine.

'Hey, did you see those guys?' Mumpson says in a loud whisper, jerking his head back at the small table at the head of the stairs where two Fortnum's employees in Regency dress are having tea and playing chess. 'Weird.'

'What? Oh, yes.' She moves on to a more polite distance. They're often here. They represent Mr Fortnum and Mr Mason; the founders of the store, you know.'

'Oh, yeh.' Turning, Mumpson gives the executives the slow rude animal stare characteristic of tourists. 'I get it. A kinda advertising gimmick.'

Vinnie, irritated, does not assent. Of course it is in a sense an 'advertising gimmick'; but she has always thought of it as an agreeable tradition. She regrets having accepted Mumpson's invitation; for one thing, if she isn't careful she will have to listen for at least half and hour to his tourist experiences, to hear about everything he has seen, bought, and eaten, and what is wrong with his hotel.

'I didn't realize you were planning to be in England so long,' she says, settling herself on one of the pale-green butterfly-design metal chairs that give Fortnum's tearoom the look of an Edwardian conservatory.

'Yeh, wal, I wasn't.' Chuck Mumpson peels off his plastic raincoat, revealing a brown Western-cut leather jacket trimmed with leather fringe, a shiny-looking yellow Western-cut shirt with pearlized studs instead of buttons, and a leather string tie. He hangs the raincoat on an empty chair, where it continues to drip onto the crimson carpet, and sits down heavily. 'Yeh, the rest of them all went home last month. But I figured once I was here, there was plenty I hadn't seen; hell, I might as well stay on a while. I was doing the sights with this couple from Indiana I met at the hotel, but they left Monday.'

'I've never seen the point of those fourteen-day tours,' Vinnie says. 'If you're going to visit England, you really should allow a month at least. If you can spare the time from your work, of course,' she adds, reminding herself that most people do not enjoy an academic schedule.

'Yeh. Wal, no.' He blinks. 'Matter of fact, I don't have to worry about that. I'm retired.'

'Oh, yes?' Vinnie doesn't remember his mentioning this on the plane, but no doubt she wasn't listening. 'You retired early,' she adds, since he doesn't look sixty-five.

'Yeh.' Mumpson shifts about on the pale-green iron chair, which is much too small for his bulk. 'That's what they called it: an early retirement. Wasn't my idea. I was chucked out, you could say.' He laughs in the too-loud manner of someone joining in a joke of which he is the butt.

'Really.' Vinnie recalls articles she has read about the growing trend toward forced obsolescence among middle-aged executives, and congratulates herself on her university's tenure system.

'Yeh, chucked on the heap at fifty-seven,' he repeats, in case she hasn't gotten the pun – after all, she didn't laugh, he is probably thinking. 'Okay, uh – Virginia, what'll you have?'

'Vinnie,' she corrects automatically, then realizes she has tacitly given Mumpson – Chuck – permission to use her first name. She would prefer Professor Miner, Ms Miner, or even Miss, but to say so now would be intolerably rude by the informal standards of middle America.

'Chuck' orders coffee; Vinnie tea and apricot tart. Then, wishing to divert him from, if not console him for, his professional misfortunes, she persuades him to try the trifle.

'I'm sure there are advantages in not having to go to work every day,' she remarks brightly after the waitress has left. 'For instance, you'll have time to do many more things now.' What things? she wonders, realizing she has no idea of the probable recreations of someone like Chuck. 'Travel, visit your friends, read' – Read? Is this likely? – 'play golf, go fishing' – Are there any fish in Oklahoma? – 'take up some hobbies –'

'Yeh, that's what my wife tells me. Problem is, you play golf every day, you get damn sick of it. And I don't go in much for sports otherwise. Used to really enjoy baseball; but I'm pretty well past that now.'

A person without inner resources who splits infinitives, Vinnie thinks. 'It's too bad your wife can't be here with you,' she remarks.

'Yeh, wal. Myrna's in real estate, like I told you, and property is pretty hot now in Tulsa. She's working her a – ' Chuck, in deference to Vinnie's – or the room's – air of old-fashioned gentility, displaces the metaphor from below to above – 'head off. Raking it in, too.' He makes a loose raking gesture with his broad freckled hand, then lets it fall heavy onto the table.

'Really.'

'Yeh, she's a real powerhouse. Matter of fact, the way things are going, she's probably just as glad not to have me hanging round home at loose ends for a while. Can't really blame her.'

'Mm,' says Vinnie, connecting Chuck's loose ends in her mind with the dangling rawhide thongs of his tie, which is fastened by a vulgarly large silver-and-turquoise clasp of the sort favored by elderly ranchers and imitation ranchers in the South-west. She too does not blame Myrna for wanting him out of the house. It is also clear to her that after many days alone in what to him is a strange foreign city Chuck is determined to unburden himself to someone; but she is equally determined not to be this someone. Deliberately she steers the conversation toward neutral tourist subjects, the very subjects she had earlier planned to avoid.

In Chuck's opinion, London isn't much of a place. He doesn't mind the weather: 'Nah. I like the variety. Back home it's the same goddamn thing every day. And if you don't water, the earth dries up hard as rock. When I first got here I couldn't get over how damn green England is, like one of those travel posters.'

On the other hand, he complains, the beds in his hotel are lumpy and the supply of hot water limited. English food tastes like boiled hay; if you want a half-decent meal, you have to go to some foreign restaurant. The traffic is nuts, everybody driving on the wrong side of the road; and he has a hell of a time understanding the natives, who talk English real funny. Vinnie is about to correct his linguistic error rather irritably and suggest that it is in fact we Americans who talk funny, when their tea arrives, creating a diversion.

'Hey, what'd you say this thing was called?' Chuck points with his spoon at the tumulus of fruit, custard, jam, rum-soaked sponge cake, and whipped cream that has just appeared on the marble-topped table before him.

'Trifle.'

'Some trifle. It's bigger than a banana split.' He grins and digs in. 'Not bad, though. And they sure give you a spoon to match.'

Vinnie, enjoying her tart, politely refrains from pointing out that in Britain dessert spoons are always of this size.

Unlike Edwin, Chuck eats rapidly and without style, shoveling in the elaborate dessert as if it were so much alfalfa, while he continues his narration. He has seen most of the standard tourist attractions, he tells Vinnie, but none of them impressed him much. Some actually seem to have offended him — for example, the Tower of London.

'Hell, when you get right down to it, it's nothing but an old abandoned prison. From what the guide told us, it sounded like a lot of the historical characters they shut up in there shouldn't have been in jail in the first place. They were good guys mostly. But they jammed them into those little stone cells about the size of a horse stall, without any heat or light to speak of. Most of them never got out again either, from what he said. They died of some sickness, or they were poisoned or choked to death or had their heads chopped off. Women and little kids too. I can't figure out why they're so damn proud of the place. If you've ever been in jail it could really give you the willies.'

'I see what you mean,' Vinnie agrees politely, wondering if Chuck has ever been in jail.

'And those big black ravens out in the yard, prowling around like spooks.' Chuck makes his thick hands into talons and walks them slowly across the green-veined marble. 'Jailbirds, I guess you'd call them.'

'Yes.' Vinnie smiles.

'Where I come from birds like that mean real bad luck. I figured maybe that's what they put them there for, the guys that built the place. So I asked the guide, was I right.'

'And what did he say?' Vinnie is beginning to find Chuck rather entertaining.

'Aw, he had no idea. He didn't know anything, he just had this spiel memorized. He showed us what he claimed was the crown jewels, we had to pay extra for that. Wal, it turned out they were only copies, fakes; the jewels were colored glass. The real stuff is locked up somewhere else. Hell, anybody could see that: the crowns and all look like what guys in the Shriners of Masons would wear to some big do.'

Vinnie laughs. 'I remember the same thing, years ago. Costume jewelry, I thought.'

'Yeh, right. I complained to the guide, said he must think we were suckers, charging extra for something like that. He got real nervous and huffy; he was kind of a dope anyhow. But I have to admit he was the exception. Most of the people I've met here, they wouldn't mind that kind of talk. They don't keep telling you how great they are, how they've got the biggest and best of everything. They kinda make fun of themselves, even; you can see that from the newspapers.'

'Yes, that's true.'

'Y'know, we've got a lot of boosters back in Tulsa. Smile, accentuate the positive, keep your eye on the doughnut, that kind of thing. It can get you down, 'specially if you're down already. Oral Roberts University, you ever hear of that?'

'No,' says Vinnie, who has but can't remember why.

'Wal, it's this college we have in Tulsa, founded by one of those TV preachers. Their idea is, if you're a Jesus-fearing man or woman and go to church regular you'll get ahead in life, win prizes, succeed in business, anything you want. It used to sound pretty harmless to me. You lose your job, you see the flip side of the pitch. If you aren't producing, you're some kind of sad Christ-forsaken weirdo. Hey, that reminds me. What I wanted to ask you in the first place.' Chuck lowers his spoon. 'I got this idea from that book you lent me on the plane, about the American kid who goes back to England, where his grandfather is a duke or something. I forget the name.'

'*Little Lord Fauntleroy.*'

'Yeh. That's right. Wal, it reminded me of my grandfather when I was a kid, when I was working on a ranch with him summers. He used to talk about how we were descended from some English lord, too.'

'Really.'

'I'm not kidding. Most of our ancestors back in England were just plain folks, he said, but there was one called Charles Mumpson, the same name as him and me, back around Revolutionary times, who was some kind of great lord. He lived on a big estate down in the southwestern part of the country and was a famous local character. Kind of a wise man. He didn't sleep in his castle, my grandfather said; he stayed in a cave out in the woods. And he wore a special costume, sort of a long coat made from the fur of about a dozen different animals. He was called The Hermit of Southley, and people came from all over the countryside to see him.'

'Really,' Vinnie says again, but with a different intonation. For the first time she feels a professional interest in Chuck Mumpson.

'So anyway, I got the notion that while I'm here I should try and look up this guy and find out more about him and all our ancestors over here. Except I don't know how to proceed. I went to the public library, but I couldn't locate anything, I didn't even know where to start. The trouble is, these dukes and knights and things have a lot of different names, sometimes three or four to a family. And there isn't any place in that part of the country called Southley.' He grins, shrugs. 'I tried to phone you, to get some help, but I must have taken down the number wrong. I got a laundry instead.'

'Mm.' Vinnie naturally doesn't explain that she had deliberately altered one digit of her number. 'Well, there are some standard places you might look,' she says. 'There's the Society of Genealogists, for instance.'

While Chuck writes down her suggestions, Vinnie thinks that his quest is also standard: the typical middlebrow, middleclass, nominally democratic American search for a connection with the British aristocracy – for 'ancestors', a family history, a coat of arms, a local habitation, and a noble name.

Conventional, tiresome. But the particular details of Chuck's family legend are intriguing to a folklorist: the eccentric lord and local sage clothed in a patchwork of furs in his woodland cave. Mad deistic philosopher? Follower of Rousseau? Herb doctor? Wizard? Or even possibly, in the local folk imagination, the incarnation of some pagan god of the forest, part beast and part man? Half-formed wraiths of a short but rather interesting article stir in her mind. It also amuses her to think of Chuck as, in a debased and transatlantic form, the final incarnation of this classic folk figure – by coincidence, from the southwestern part of his own country and dressed in assorted animal skins.

When the bill arrives, Vinnie, as usual, insists upon paying her share. Some of her friends attribute this to feminist principles; but though Vinnie accepts their interpretation her policy well predates the women's movement. Essentially, it reflects a deep dislike of being under obligation to anyone. Chuck protests that he owes her something anyhow for her advice; but she reminds him that he got her a ride to London on the Sun Tour bus, so they are now quits.

'Wal. All right.' Chuck crumples up Vinnie's pound notes in his large red fist. 'You know, you remind me of a teacher I had once in fourth grade. She was real nice. She . . . '

Vinnie listens to Chuck's recollections without comment. It is her fate to remind almost everyone she meets of a teacher they had once.

'Anyhow. What I wanted to say is, it looks like I'm going to be in London a while longer. Maybe we could get together again sometime, have lunch.'

Vinnie declines tactfully; she's awfully busy this week, she lies. But why doesn't Chuck let her know how he gets on with his research? She gives him her telephone number – correctly this time – and also her address. If he really wants to find out anything, she adds, he'll probably have to go to the town or village his ancestors lived in, once he discovers where it is.

'Sure, I could do that,' Chuck agrees. 'I could rent a car, maybe, and drive down there.'

'Or you might be able to take a train. Hiring an automobile is frightfully expensive here, you know.'

'That's okay. Money's no problem. When Amalgamated threw me out, I got to admit, they threw a lot of stock after me.'

Money is no problem to Chuck Mumpson, Vinnie thinks as she boards the bus to Camden Town, having declined his offer to find her a taxi; and obviously time is no problem either, except in terms of oversupply. The problems are loneliness, boredom, anomie, and loss of self-esteem, somewhat disguised by a hearty manner which was probably at one time more congruous with his actual condition.

For a moment Vinnie considers adding a fifth problem, sexual frustration, to her list. It is suggested to her by the warm, determined way Chuck grasped her arm – or rather, the arm of her raincoat – just above the elbow as he guided her through Piccadilly Circus toward her bus stop. After all, he is a large, healthy, muscular man; and without those silly, rather vulgar cowboy clothes he would probably not look too bad in a bedroom. Possibly this was what he was, in a blurry way, trying to convey.

But on reflection Vinnie decides this is unlikely. Chuck Mumpson is so obviously a typical middle-American businessman, the sort of person who, if he needs what Kinsey et al. have unromantically called an 'outlet' – when she hears the word Vinnie always thinks of an electrical wall socket – will simply purchase one. And Chuck probably already has purchased this wall socket several times, in the hardware and software markets of Soho, no doubt getting stinking drunk beforehand on each occasion as an excuse. ('I was bombed out – didn't know what I was doing.') Men of this type never think of anyone like Vinnie in connection with sex; they think of some 'cute babe' or 'hot little number' – ideally, a number under thirty. What Chuck was pressing for was sympathy, companionship, an understanding listener. It's probably not very satisfying to talk to whores, and apart from them she is the only woman he knows in Britain.

This conclusion, though unflattering and even, in a very familiar way, irritating and depressing, also reassures Vinnie. There will be no need to fend off the advances of Chuck Mumpson; she only imagined there might be because she is used to thinking of friendship and sex linked.

As related earlier, Vinnie has throughout her life slept mainly with men whose interest in her was casual and comradely rather than romantic. They seldom used the word 'love' to her except in moments of passionate confusion; instead they told her that they were 'very fond' of her and that she was great in bed and a real pal. (Possibly as a result, Vinnie detests the word 'fond', which always suggests to her its archaic or folk meaning of 'foolish' or 'silly'.)

In her youth Vinnie made the painful error of allowing herself to care seriously for some of these people. Against her better judgment, she even married one of them who was on the tearful rebound from a particularly aggravating beauty and, like a waterlogged tennis ball, had rolled into the nearest hole. Over the three subsequent years Vinnie had the experience of seeing her husband gradually regain his confidence and elasticity, begin to bounce about at parties, flirting and dancing with the prettier women; hop briefly into the arms of one of his students; and eventually soar entirely beyond the boundaries of marriage, where he was caught and carried off by someone she had once thought of as a good friend.

After her divorce, Vinnie protected herself against emotional attachment to her occasional bed partners by declaring an extramural involvement of her own. She too was in love with someone else, she would hint, someone in another city – though unlike them she never went into details. This strategy was brilliantly successful. The more generous and sensitive of her lovers were relieved of the fear that Vinnie might take them too seriously, and suffer as a consequence; the less generous and sensitive were relieved of the fear that she might 'make trouble'.

Moreover, as was perhaps necessary for the ploy to work, it wasn't quite a lie. As she had done in early adolescence, Vinnie allowed herself to fix her romantic desires on men she hardly knew and seldom saw. These were not, as previously, film stars, but writers and critics whose work she had read, whom she had heard speak or even briefly met at the receptions that generally follow university readings or lectures. She had thus over the years enjoyed imaginary relationships with, among others, Daniel Aaron, M. H. Abrams, John Cheever, Robert Lowell, Arthur Mizener, Walker Percy, Mark Schorer, Wallace Stegner, Peter Taylor, Lionel Trilling, Robert Penn Warren, and Richard Wilbur. As this list shows, she rather preferred older men; and she insisted on intellectuals. When several members of a women's group she belonged to in the early seventies confessed that they had passionate fantasies about their carpenter, their gardener, or the mechanic at the service station, Vinnie was astonished and a little repelled. What would be the point of going to bed with someone like that?

Vinnie's fantasy affairs tended to be of brief duration, though under the influence of a brilliant new book or lecture she sometimes returned to an earlier passion. When, by coincidence, one or two to these distinguished people came to teach for a term at her own university and established cordial relations with Vinnie, she at once broke off her private affair with him. It wasn't difficult at all, seen at close range, this man was nothing extraordinary, not a patch on Daniel Aaron, M. H. Abrams, or whoever was center stage at the moment.

After the disastrous experience of her marriage, Vinnie always ended her real affairs whenever she found her current lover getting into her bedtime home movies, or when one of them began to use the word 'love' casually, or to announce that he could really imagine getting seriously involved with her. No thanks, chum; I was caught that way before, she would think to herself. Not that there was always a current lover. For long periods Vinnie's only companions were the shades of Richard Wilbur, Robert Penn Warren, etc, who faithfully every evening appeared to admire and embrace her, commending her wit, charm, intelligence, scholarly achievement, and sexual inventiveness.

In all the years she has been coming to England, Vinnie has never found a lover there. Nor is there any sign of one appearing now. And perhaps that's for the best, she thinks. Because really, isn't it time? In the popular imagination, and (more importantly) in English literature, to which in early childhood Vinnie had given her deepest trust – and which for a half a century has suggested to her what she might do, think, feel, desire, and become – women of her age seldom have any sexual or romantic life. If they do, it is either embarrassingly pathetic or vulgarly comic or both.

In the last year or so Vinnie had begun to think more and more often that what she does with her pals is inappropriate – unbecoming to her station on the railway line of her life. The fact that at fifty-four she still had erotic impulses and indulged them with such abandon seemed to her almost shameful. It had been something of a relief to her to be away from home, and chaste; to be as it were on sabbatical from sex – one which might well develop into a long leave of absence or even an early retirement. She is therefore embarrassed and irritated at herself for having, even briefly, imagined Chuck Mumpson standing naked by her bed in Regent's Park Road. She tells herself to act and feel her age, for heaven's sake. She certainly doesn't want someone like

Chuck, she tells herself; she doesn't even want her brilliant, handsome, charming imaginary lovers very much.

As the bus carries her north through the darkening city, away from the sensual attractions of Fortnum and Mason's and the erotic throbbing noises and flashing colored lights of Piccadilly Circus, into the quiet dim elegant streets around Regent's Park, Vinnie tells herself again that it's time, and past time, to leave what her mother used to refer to as All That behind. It is time to steer past the Scylla and Charybdis of the elderly sexual farce and sexual tragedy into the wide, calm sunset sea of abstinence, where the tepid waters are never troubled by the burning heat and chill, the foamy backwash and weed-choked turbulence of passion.

4

> Despair is all folly;
> Hence, melancholy,
> Fortune attends you while youth is in flower.
>
> John Gay, *Polly*

In the hard-lit, almost empty lobby of a small theater in Hammersmith Fred Turner is waiting for Rosemary Radley, who is late as usual. Each time the doors fling open and let in some meaningless person and a gust of damp March evening, he sighs, like a gardener who sees his flowers blowing away in a storm; for each minute that passes is one less alone with her.

Maybe Rosemary won't come at all – that has happened more than once before, though not lately, and wouldn't surprise Fred. What still surprises him is that he should be here in this theater waiting for her, and in this mood of high-charged expectation. A month ago all of London for him was like the empty county fairgrounds outside his home town on some cold evening – a sour, dim expanse of cropped stubble and stones. Now, because of Rosemary Radley, it has been transformed into a kind of circus of light; and Fred, as if he were a small child again, stands wide-eyed just within the entrance of the main tent, wondering how he came there and what to do with the sparkling pink spindle of cotton candy he holds in his hand.

Rationally, of course, his being there can be explained as a result of the interest in eighteenth-century drama that brought him to London in the first place, and later gave him something to talk to Rosemary about. (As it turns out, she is remarkably knowledgeable about theatrical history and stage tradition, and has herself appeared in *The Beggar's Opera* in repertory.) More fancifully his presence can be explained as the reward of virtue – specifically of the eighteenth-century virtues of civility and boldness.

It was civility, for instance, that made Fred stay on at Professor

Virginia Miner's party last month after he had eaten and drunk as much as seemed polite, though nobody he had met interested him or seemed interested in him. As a result he was still there when Rosemary Radley arrived, fashionably and characteristically late.

He saw her first standing near the entrance beside a pot of pink hyacinths: like them in full bloom, and delicately pretty with what he recognized as a typical English prettiness. She had the sort of looks celebrated in eighteenth-century painting: the round face, roguish eye, small pouting mouth, dimpled chin, creamy-white skin flushed with pink, and tumbling flaxen curls. As soon as he could, Fred crossed the room to observe this phenomenon at closer range, and by persistently standing alongside it eventually managed to be introduced to 'Lady Rosemary Radley' (though not by Professor Miner, who knows as Fred now does too that it is not done to use the title socially – just as one wouldn't properly introduce someone as Mr or Miss).

'Oh, how do you do.' Fred, who had never met a member of the British aristocracy, gazed at Rosemary with what he now realizes must have appeared a rude intensity – though, as Rosemary said later, she's used to being stared at; after all she's an actress. He felt like some traveler who for years has read of the existence of snow leopards or poltergeists, but never expected to be this near to one.

'An American! I do love Americans,' Rosemary exclaimed, with the light amused laugh that he was presently to know so well.

'I'm glad to hear that,' Fred replied, a little too late, for already she had turned to greet someone else. For the rest of the party he hovered near her, sometimes trying to claim her attention, more often just gazing and listening with the same kind of baffled fascination he felt last month at the RSC production of *Two Gentlemen of Verona*.

It was only after he was back in his cold empty flat that Fred realized he wanted very much to see Rosemary Radley again, whereas he did not at all want to see another performance of *Two Gentlemen of Verona;* and realized simultaneously that he had no means or encouragement to do so. True, Rosemary Radley had been briefly charming to him; but she had been charming to everyone. She had asked him where he was living; that was a good sign, he had thought, not having yet learnt that in England such inquiries don't precede or hint at an invitation, but rather serve to determine social class; they are the equivalent of the American question 'What do you do?'

But where was Rosemary Radley living? Her name wasn't in the phone book, and phoning to ask Vinnie Miner point-blank would be awkward and probably unproductive; if someone has an unlisted number, their friends are probably expected not to give it out. Fred felt balked and depressed. Then he remembered that Rosemary had said she was going tomorrow to the preview of a new play; she had even suggested that he (and, it must be admitted, everyone else who was listening at the time) should see this play.

Because of his financial circumstances Fred had decided not to see any contemporary theater while he was in London. Now he broke this resolution, replacing his supper with a piece of stale bread and a can of chicken noodle soup in order to stay within his budget; his paychecks from Corinth had begun to clear, but when transformed into pounds they were pathetically small. At this point he did not think of himself as romantically interested in Rosemary Radley. The pursuit of her acquaintance appeared to him only as a distraction from gloom, or at the best as a challenge, undertaken in the same spirit that makes other Americans expend energy and ingenuity to view some art collection or local ceremony that is out of bounds to most tourists.

Though Fred got to the theater early and waited by the entrance until the last possible moment before bounding up the stairs to his balcony seat, Rosemary Radley didn't appear. He watched the play – a witty highbrow farce – distractedly, feeling stupid, desolate, and hungry. But as he descended the stairs during the intermission, restless rather than hopeful, he saw Rosemary below him in the lobby. She was dressed more elaborately than she had been the day before: her pale-gold hair piled high, her creamy round breasts half exposed, nestled in pale-green silky ruffles like some exotic fruit in a Mayfair greengrocer's. As Fred looked down at her she suddenly seemed not only aristocratic and authentically English, but radiantly sexual and desirable.

As might have been expected, Rosemary wasn't alone, but surrounded by friends – among whom was the playwright himself, a tall elegant man in a rumpled trenchcoat. For the first but not the last time it occurred to Fred that Lady Rosemary Radley probably had many famous and/or titled admirers, and that his chances were therefore slim. Another man might have despaired and retreated to the balcony. But Fred's romantic history had made him an optimist; loneliness and gloom made him bold. Hell, why not make the effort? What had he to lose?

As it turned out, the courtship of Rosemary Radley demanded not only boldness but stubborn persistence of a sort new to Fred. In the past, girls and women had more or less fallen into his lap, sometimes even literally – bouncing onto his knees with giggles and squeals at parties or in the back of cars. That had been pleasant and convenient, but not very exciting. Now he knew for the first time the joys of the chase; he breathed the heady animal scent of the hotly pursued quarry. Though always charming, Rosemary was completely undependable. Often she would arrive half an hour or more late, or would ring up to explain that she had to meet him at some other, usually inconvenient time; must bring along a friend; or simply couldn't manage to come at all. Her eager, breathless apologies, her murmurs of regret and distress, always seemed genuine – but of course she was an actress. Money was another problem: Fred couldn't afford to take Rosemary to expensive restaurants or to buy her the flowers that she loved. He did both these things, greatly to the detriment of his bank account; but he can't keep doing them much longer if he wants to eat.

Weeks passed in this way without his making any significant progress. Rosemary had to be courted in the old-fashioned manner, and over a length of time that most of Fred's friends back home would have found irrational. Roberto Frank, for instance, would have roared with disbelief if he knew that it had taken Fred nearly two weeks to get to first base with Rosemary and that after over a month he still hasn't scored. Yeh, well, he isn't in Convers playing sandlot baseball now, Fred says to the imaginary grinning figure of Roberto. This is England; this is the real thing.

Though he was often frustrated, Fred didn't become discouraged; instead the very difficulty of the undertaking ensured its value. Since he had gone through so much for

Rosemary Radley, she must be worth the effort; his feelings must be serious. And indeed, the more he saw of her the more entrancing, the more attractive she seemed.

Part of Rosemary's attraction, Fred realizes, is her being in every way the opposite of his wife. She is small, soft, and fair; Roo large, sturdy, and dark. She is sophisticated, witty; Roo – relatively – naive and serious, even a little humorless by London standards. In manner and speech Rosemary is graceful, melodious; Roo by comparison clumsy and loud – in fact, coarse. Just as, compared with England, America is large, naive, noisy, crude, etc.

As he persisted in the chase, and slowly began to gain on his quarry, other national – and possibly class – differences appeared. Fred's courtship to Roo could hardly be called a pursuit, since she was galloping just as fast in his direction. They circled each other, snuffling; then rushed together just as the horses they had ridden that first memorable afternoon might have done. What had happened in the abandoned orchard on the hill wasn't a seduction, it was a collision of two strong, sweaty, eager young bodies, rolling and panting in the long grass and weeds.

The images Rosemary suggests are not animal but floral. Recalling their first meeting, Fred imagines her as a pot of hyacinths, or some other more exotic flowering plant: fragile, fine-leaved, of some species that quivers and folds up tight at any clumsy touch or cold breeze, but if tended gently and patiently, opens at last into full glorious bloom. And in fact, only two days ago, after six weeks of trial and error, Fred's efforts were almost wholly rewarded: the last soft, creamy, many-layered pink-and-white petals unfurled, revealing the delicate calyx. Tonight, if all goes well, he will have his desire.

As he paces impatiently in the theater lobby, thinking of Rosemary and of Roo, Fred understands for the first time the power of what at Yale is referred to as retrospective influence. Just as Wordsworth forever altered our reading of Milton, so Rosemary Radley has altered his reading of Ruth March. In his mind he sees Rosemary standing on a height that is probably the city of London. In one hand she holds a powerful arc lamp of the sort used in the theater, and from it a cone of white light streams back across time and space three years and more to Corinth, New York.

In this light, Fred's memory of Roo under the apple trees, with the imprint of twigs on her sweaty brown back and butt and bits of dried grass in her thick untidy chestnut hair, seems crudely staged, garishly colored, hardly civilized. Roo's rapid and enthusiastic sexual surrender – which he once believed a warranty of passion and sincerity – seems unfeminine, almost uncouth. Compared with Rosemary's delicate lingering butterfly kisses, Roo's embraces had a greedy animal urgency that should, Fred thinks now, have warned him of her lack of control, of the exhibition – to make a sour pun – that was to come.

Before Fred had known Roo a fortnight she had not only made love with him many times but had lost all sense of modesty – if in fact she ever had any. She told him everything she thought or felt – including details of previous love affairs he could have done without. She showed him everything: from the first she slept naked beside him, or when it was very cold in a sexless red-flannel that tended to bunch up under her arms. She walked about her (later their) Collegetown apartment naked at all times of day, not always remembering to lower the blinds. In his presence she blew her nose, picked her teeth, cut her toenails, washed her cunt, and even, if she was in the midst of an interesting conversation (and to Roo most conversations were interesting) used the toilet. Because he was in love with her, Fred had repressed his embarrassment, even denigrated it. He had defined himself as an uptight preppie, and Roo's behavior as natural and free.

For Rosemary, on the other hand, to yield sexually is not to give up her privacy. Instinctively she surrounds herself with the intimate mystery that preserves romance. She prefers dimmed lights: two tall white candles on the dressing table, or a silk-shaded lamp. She bathes and dresses alone; Fred has never yet seen her completely naked. Psychologically too she doesn't overexpose herself: she is silent about her own history and doesn't demand to learn Fred's. It is only from a phrase dropped here and there that he guesses, for instance, that Rosemary's childhood, though luxurious, was unhappy and disrupted as the result of her parents' frequent changes of partners and residence.

Now and then, it's true, Rosemary carries a good thing too far. Though he doesn't want to invade her physical reserve or her reticence about the past, Fred wishes he could see further into her mind. She is whimsical, impulsive, contradictory: when he tries to speak to her about something serious, he often feels – or is made to feel – like some intrusive insect trying to burrow its way into a prize hothouse rose and finally giving up, dizzied by fragrance and baffled by the continual flurry of pale petals.

It is nearly seven o'clock now. The lobby has filled with people and is beginning to empty in the direction of the auditorium. Fred has been waiting for forty minutes, and Rosemary still isn't here. He is also very hungry; but even if she does arrive there won't be time for the sandwiches they had planned to have before the play.

He has almost given up when a taxi door burst open and Rosemary comes running, almost flying, into the theater, her pink wool cape blowing out behind her like some Rococo angel's wings.

'Darling!' Out of breath – or perhaps only affecting to be so? – she puts a soft white hand on his arm and looks up from under feathery lashes. 'You've got to forgive me, the taxi simply wouldn't come.'

'Okay, I forgive you.' Fred smiles down at her, though not as readily as usual.

'Are you absolutely starving?'

'Not quite.'

'Don't be cross. I've arranged for us to eat after the play with Erin. He knowes a very good place near here, and I'll buy you a lovely dinner to make up . . . Oh, Nadia! I didn't know you were back; how was looney Los Angeles?'

You mustn't do that,' Fred says; but his words are lost. The resolution remains, however. He doesn't want to waste his time alone with Rosemary sitting in a restaurant with some actor from the play they are about to see. Besides, she's bought him too many expensive meals lately. When he protests she gives different excuses: the sale of a TV play she's been in to Australia, a favorable interview in some women's magazine, whatever.

'Rosemary, I want to say something,' he begins as soon as they are alone and making their way to their seats.

'Yes, darling . . . ' She stops to wave and smile brilliantly at someone across the theater.

'I don't want you to take me to dinner tonight.'

'Oh, Freddy.' She looks up at him, widening her fringed azure eyes. 'You're cross because I was so late, but I absolutely couldn't help it, that wretched taxi service –'

'No, I'm not, I just – ' An usher interrupts them; Fred buys two programs at tenpence each. Big spender, he thinks sourly, recalling that Rosemary has been given ? – or paid for? – their tickets.

'What it is,' he begins again as soon as they are seated, 'is that I just don't want you to buy me dinner. It's not right.'

'Oh, don't be silly: I already promised.' Rosemary's eyes are focused past him, sweeping the rows for familiar faces. 'Oh look, there's Mimi, but who can that possibly be with her?'

'No. It bothers me.' Fred plows ahead. 'I mean, what will Erin think? He'll think I'm some kind of gigolo.'

'Of course he won't, darling.' Rosemary focuses on Fred again. 'It's not like that in the theater. When you're in work you treat. Everyone knows that.'

'Well, I'm not in the theater. So I'd like to pay for myself from now on.' Fred remembers that he has with him only eight pounds and some change, which according to his budget has to last till the end of this week. Soon he will be sitting, as he has often lately sat, behind a menu whose size is as inflated as its prices, searching for the cheapest item (usually a bowl of coarse raw greens of some kind), declaring falsely that he had a big lunch and isn't all that hungry. 'What I'd really like,' he goes on, leaning toward Rosemary to gain her attention, which is fluttering off again, 'is for us to go somewhere tonight that I can afford, and then I can take you. I bet there must be some inexpensive places around here –'

'Oh yes, there's lots of nasty cheap restaurants in Hammersmith,' Rosemary says. 'And I've been to most of them. When Mum broke her ankle, and Daddy stopped my allowance, trying to starve me into leaving the rep and coming home to run the house, because he was too lazy to bother. I found out all about that. I've eaten all the fish fingers and macaroni cheese I ever want to eat in my life, darling.'

'All the same. I don't think it's fair that you should pay for me.'

'But you think it's fair that I should have to eat in some disgusting caff –'

'I didn't say that I wanted to go to a disgusting caff –'

' – where we'll probably both be poisoned.' Rosemary's exquisite mouth sets in a sweet-pea pout. Then, as the house lights soften, her pout softens into a smile. 'Besides, you know we can't do that to Erin, he'd think we were out of our minds, or that we absolutely detested his performance and wanted to punish him for it.' She gives a whispery giggle.

Fred doesn't argue further, but for the rest of the evening he continues to feel uncomfortable: during the play and during the dinner that follows, where he orders a chef's salad and also consumes four rolls, a third of Nadia's beef bourguignonne, and half of Rosemary's cherry cheesecake ('Don't be silly, love, I simply can't finish it'). What is he doing eating off other people's plates in this expensive restaurant, in this expensive company?

'You're still cross,' Rosemary says plaintively in the taxi afterward. 'I can tell. You haven't forgiven me for being so frightfully late tonight.'

'No I'm not; yes I have,' he protests.

'Really?' She leans toward him, resting her spun-gold curls against his shoulder.

'I always forgive you.' Fred eases his arm around Rosemary; how soft and yielding she is under the folds of wool! 'I'm in love with you,' he says, imagining how he will soon demonstrate this.

'Oh – love,' she murmurs indulgently but rather dismissively, as if reminded of some childhood pastime: skipping rope, say, or hide-and-seek.

'Don't you believe me?'

'Yes.' She raises her head slightly. 'I suppose I do.'

'And? But?'

'And I love you . . . But it's not that simple, you know.' Rosemary sighs. 'When you're my age –'

Fred sighs too, though silently. That he is just twenty-nine and Rosemary thirty-seven – though she hardly looks thirty – is in his opinion unimportant – in the context of their relationship, even meaningless. Of course he knows that women, perhaps especially actresses, worry about their age; but in Rosemary's case it's ridiculous. She is beautiful and he loves her; it's not as if they were planning to get married and raise a family, for Christ's sake. 'What difference does that make?' he asks aloud.

Fred has been raised in an academic environment; he assumes that even difficult questions must be answered. Rosemary, after years in the theater and long experience of prying and hostile interviewers, assumes the reverse. Instead of replying, she yawns, covering the pink flower of her mouth with one fluttering hand. 'Heavens, I'm exhausted! Classical drama does that to me sometimes. Is it dreadfully late?'

'No; half past eleven.' One possible cause of, or excuse for Rosemary's constant tardiness is her refusal to wear a watch ('I can't bear the idea that Time has me by the wrist, like some awful cross old governess').

'Oh horrors, darling. I think I'd better go straight to bed.'

'Don't do that,' Fred says, grasping her more firmly. 'At least, not alone.'

'I'm afraid I must.' She sighs deeply, as if under some heavy invisible compulsion.

'But I was hoping – ' Fred puts a hand on that part of the angel-wing cape that covers Rosemary's breast.

'Now, love, don't be tiresome. I'll ring you tomorrow.'

So quite casually, Rosemary canceled what was to have been the climax of their evening together. For the next eighteen hours Fred was in a bad state of mind. He called – or, in the British phrase, 'rang' – several times, starting at ten a.m., but couldn't get through her answering service. Either she was out, or she was angry with him. He tried to work, but – as often lately – not with any success; he needed a book that was in the BM, but didn't want to leave the phone.

Finally, about six, Rosemary rang back She was as affectionate as ever, 'simply longing' to see him. She denied she'd been cross; wouldn't even discuss it; welcomed him passionately at her front door an hour later.

Shadowy spring twilight in the library of an English country house often featured in magazines and color supplements, famous both for its architectural and decorative beauty and for the architectural and decorative beauty of its mistress, Penelope (Posy) Billings, and the financial acumen of her husband Sir James (Jimbo). The crimson velvet brocaded walls, buttery buttoned leather and mahogany sofas, gilt bindings, glass cases of curios, and antique varnished globes of the earth and heavens create a slightly campy late-Victorian effect. This is relieved by an orderly profusion of fresh spring flowers, and a table on which are arranged the latest papers and magazines, prominence being given to those of conservative views and to last month's *Harper's/ Queen*, which includes a photograph of Lady Billings in her kitchen and her original recipe for cream-of-watercress-and-avocado soup, as part of a series on 'Country-House Cuisine'.

On the walls are Victorian paintings in thickly flounced gold frames: two portraits of Posy's distinguished military ancestors and one of a mournful prize sheep who strongly resembles George Eliot. All three pictures have been in the family for over a century. The Leighton above the marble chimneypiece, on the other hand, was bought for Posy by Jimbo as a wedding present just before prices skyrocketed, on a tip from one of her best friends – the fashionable decorator, Nadia Phillips. It shows a smooth-limbed statuesque Victorian blonde, much resembling Posy Billings and with the same tumbling masses of brassy hair. This figure is somewhat anachronistically half clad in pink and lavender draperies and is making eyes at a caged bird on a sun-drenched, petal-strewn marble terrace.

Now, six years later, Posy is beginning to be tired of the Leighton, the sheep, the curios, and the ancestors. She'd rather like to send them to the attics and put up something more contemporary. Indeed, she has been wondering lately if it wouldn't be rather amusing to have the library redone, with Nadia Phillips' help, in the style of the 1930s, with lots of deep sexy white sofas, stainless steel and lacquer tables, engraved mirrors, and funny art-deco cushions and lamps and vases.

At the moment Posy is not in the library, but having tea in the nursery with her two small daughters and the *au pair*. The only present occupant of the room is Fred Turner, who would be distressed to learn that its Victorian decor is doomed. As he stands between floor-length curtains of deep-fringed crimson plush, looking out over the lawn – where there is still light enough to see a host of airy daffodils crowding the circular flower bed beyond the gravel drive – he feels both euphoric and slightly unreal. What is he doing here in this perfect Victorian country house, in this misty English spring, instead of a century later in upstate New York where early April is still gray frozen winter? It's as if, by some supernatural slippage between life and art, he has got into a Henry James novel like the one he watched on television two months ago with Joe and Debby Vogeler. How far away they and their carping complaint about London seem now! How secondhand and incomplete their view of England has turned out to be – as secondhand and incomplete as some TV adaptation of a classic novel.

In the last few weeks Fred has entered a world he had before only read of: a world of crowded, electric first nights, leisurely highbrow Sunday lunches in Hampstead and Holland Park; elegant international dinner parties in Connaught Square and Chester Row. He has been backstage at the BBC studios in Ealing, and at the offices of the *Sunday Times*, and has met a score of people who were once only names in magazines or on the syllabi of college courses. What is more amazing, some of these people now seem to consider him a friend, or at least a good acquaintance: they remember that he is writing on John Gay and inquire about the progress of his research; they speak to him in a casually intimate manner about their troubles with reviewers or indigestion. (Others, it's true, forget his name from one party to the next – which is maybe to be expected.)

When he first started seeing Rosemary, Fred wondered why she knew so many celebrities. The answer turns out to be that she herself is a sort of celebrity, though he had never heard of her. As one of the stars of *Tallyho Castle*, a popular comedy-drama series about upper-class country life, she is familiar by sight to millions of British viewers, some of whom occasionally approach her in shops and restaurants or at the theater. ('Excuse me, but aren't you Lady Emma Tally? Oh, I really do enjoy that program so much, and you're one of my very favorite characters!') As a result, she is better known by sight than some of her more famous but nontheatrical friends.

To Rosemary, Fred realizes now, her popular fame is both welcome and unsatisfying. He has seen how she begins to sparkle and glow when a fan appears, as if some inner lamp had been turned up to 200 watts. He has also heard her say, more than once, that she is tired to death of Lady Emma and of all the other nice ladies she has portrayed on television. What she really wants, she has confided to him, is to act 'the great classic parts' – Hedda Gabler, Blanche DuBois, Lady Macbeth – in the theater before she is too old. 'I could do them, Freddy, I know I could do them,' she had insisted. 'I know what it is to feel murderous, coarse, full of hate.' (If she does, Fred thinks, it's only by a magnificent leap in intuition.) 'All that's in me, Freddy, it is. You don't believe me,' she added, turning to look directly at him.

Holding her close, he smiled, then shook his head.

'You don't think I could act those parts.' A frown had appeared between her fair arched brows, as if some invisible evil spirit were cruelly pinching the skin.

'No, I do. Of course I do,' Fred assured her. 'I know you're good, everyone says so. I'm sure you could do anything you liked.'

But no director has ever been willing to cast Rosemary in such roles. When she is invited to appear on the stage – less often than she would like – it is always in light comedy: Shaw or Wilde or Sheridan or Ayckbourn.

The problem is, as Rosemary's friend Edwin Francis explained to Fred, that she just doesn't look like a tragedy queen. Her voice is too high and sweet, and she doesn't project that kind of dark energy. 'Can you see Rosemary as Lady Macbeth? Now really: "Infirm of purpoth! Give me the daggerth."' Edwin imitated Rosemary's voice, with the slight charming lisp that she affects as Lady Emma. 'Nobody would believe for a moment that she'd been involved in a murder; they'd think she wanted to cut the cake at a charity fête.'

Though he doesn't like the way Edwin sometimes makes fun of Rosemary, Fred has to admit that he can't imagine her as Lady Macbeth, or as full of coarse murderous hate, even for dramatic purposes. Her wish to play violent and tragic parts is one of the things about her that still puzzles him.

Something else he would like to understand about Rosemary is why her pretty house in Chelsea is always such a goddamn mess. At first glance the long double sitting room looks very elegant, though a little faded. But soon, especially in the daytime, you notice that the bay windows are smeared and fly-specked, the sills grainy with soot, the gilt moldings of the pictures chipped, the striped gray satin upholstery blotched and worn, the mahogany table-tops branded with rings and burns. Everywhere there are rumpled newspapers, sticky glasses, muddied coffee cups, full ashtrays, empty cigarette packages, and discarded clothing. Below in the kitchen and in the bedroom upstairs it is worse: the closets are jammed with rubbish, and the bathrooms not always clean. How Rosemary can emerge from all that disorder looking so fresh and beautiful is a mystery – and how she can stand to live in it another one.

Of course Rosemary probably doesn't know how to do housework, Fred thinks, and he wouldn't want her to have to learn. But she could certainly hire somebody. Her friends agree with him. What she needs, Posy Billings explained earlier this afternoon when she was showing Fred around her own perfectly kept grounds, is a 'daily' – some strong reliable woman who will come in every morning to clean and shop and do the laundry and make lunch, so that Rosemary won't have to go out to a restaurant. If only Fred could persuade her to hire someone like that – Posy knows of a very reliable agency in London – he would be doing a tremendous good deed.

'Okay,' Fred said as they stood in front of a long perennial border covered by a mulch of clean shredded bark, from which neat clumps of crocus and grape hyacinths emerged. 'Okay, I'll try.'

It won't be easy, though, he thinks now, imagining Rosemary as he had left her a quarter of an hour ago, lying upstairs in what Posy calls the Pink Room. Its oversize bed has a carved and gilded headboard padded in flowered satin, and a matching quilted spread is drawn up in loose folds to Rosemary's breasts. She is wearing a nightgown of delicate ivory silk with semitransparent lace insets in the shape of butterflies scattered over it; her white-gold hair falls in fine tendrils across pale-pink scalloped sheets. The pink-silk-shaded bedside lamp casts a blush over her creamy skin, and over the rococo furniture painted in pink and silver, the French fashion plates on the walls, and the silver vase of narcissus on the dressing-table. It also illuminates a confusion of spilt powders and creams on this dressing-table and a shipwreck of discarded clothes on the Aubusson carpet.

No, it won't be easy to change Rosemary's ways. She hates talking about 'boring practical things' and isn't capable of concentrating on any subject for long. She is – and for Fred it's part of her charm – a creature of sudden, random impulse. He sees her as a rare beautiful lacy butterfly like those which decorate her nightgown, fluttering and hovering, dancing near and then away, difficult to catch hold of for more than a moment.

Her present withdrawal, however, is not idiosyncratic. Going to bed when it isn't bedtime – or at least saying that you are going to bed – is, Fred has discovered, a habitual and respectable social stratagem among the British. To declare fatigue without obvious cause isn't, as in America, to confess physical and/or emotional weakness. Instead, 'having a bit of a rest' or 'lying down for a while' provides a polite excuse for social withdrawal – one that is more effective here than it would be at home, since even here married people usually have separate bedrooms. And the English, at least those Fred has met lately, seem to need and want more solitude than Americans do. Now, for instance, at six in the evening, all Lady Billings' other guests are – as far as he knows – shut up alone in their rooms. After he left Rosemary, Fred tried to stay in his, but restlessness and claustrophobia brought him downstairs again. If it weren't drizzling and nearly dark, he would have gone out into the gardens.

There are three weekend guests at Posy's besides Fred and Rosemary. One is Edwin Francis, the editor and critic, who is almost effusively affectionate to Rosemary and Posy, but speaks to Fred as if he were interviewing him on television, with a pretense of respectful attention that often seems designed to provoke humor at his expense. ('So it was generally known that Mr Reagan had appeared in a film in which his co-star was a chimpanzee? Yet you say that many members of your college voted for him. How do you explain this?' 'Your current project then, I assume it is much influenced by the French school of demolition, excuse me, deconstruction.')

Edwin has brought with him a very young man called Nico, who according to Rosemary is his current 'particular friend'. Rosemary and Posy approve of Nico; they regard him as a great improvement on Edwin's previous particular friends, most of whom Posy says she has 'simply refused to have in the house.' Compared with these persons Nico is well educated, fluent in English, and 'really quite presentable'. He is a Greek Cypriot: slight, smooth-skinned, with abundant dark glossy curls and pronounced artistic and political opinions. His ambition is to work in British – or even better, American – television or cinema, eventually as a director. At lunch today he expressed an interest in Fred's views that was evidently more sincere than

Edwin's, though less disinterested. ('You have very original ideas on the cinema, Fred, I think very exciting. I suppose that you know many people in the American film industry, or in the American theater, perhaps, that you have discussed these theories with? . . . No, none at all? That is a pity. I would like so much sometime the chance to talk with American film makers.') Though Nico is still polite to Fred, it is clear that he now regards him as professionally useless.

The final houseguest is William Just, who is a sort of cousin of Posy's and is referred to by her and Rosemary as Just William. In appearance he is middle-aged and nondescript, with rumpled-looking tweedy clothes and an air of vague detachment. Just William does something at the BBC and is unusually well informed on current events; he also seems to be acquainted with everyone Posy, Rosemary, Edwin, and even Nico know in London. His manner is mild and self-effacing; Fred assumes he has been invited partly out of family obligation (he is no longer married, and probably lonely) and partly because he might be able to get Nico a job at the BBC.

Fred finds Edwin and Nico interesting as types, and William for his behind-the-scenes political knowledge. He is sorry, though, that he won't get to meet Posy's husband, Jimbo Billings. According to the newspapers, Billings is a shrewd and aggressive character who deals in high-risk investments, and knows many world leaders; a large, imposing-looking man (his photograph is prominent on the sitting-room mantelpiece). At the moment, however, he is in the Near East on business.

Nico is even more disappointed that he will not meet Jimbo Billings. 'Yes, I wish the chance to tell him many things, what I think of his government, and of his policies,' he said belligerently to Fred when they were all out for a walk after lunch. 'There is much that he could do for my country, for my friends there, if he would.' But Posy's husband has no connection with the British government, Fred protested, he is only a businessman. 'Only, that is a lie,' Nico said, slashing at Posy's newly leafed box hedges with a willow switch he had broken off beside the ornamental lake. 'He has much influence, more than many politicians here, believe me, but in my country he uses it for evil.'

As the landscape outside darkens, Fred turns away from the

window and takes up one of the four daily newspapers that since lunchtime have been refolded by some unseen hand and neatly ranged on the polished mahogany table. Presently he is joined by Edwin and Nico, and then by Posy, Just William, and Rosemary. Drinks are served, followed by a five-course dinner (sorrel soup, spring lamb, watercress salad, lemon fool, fruit and cheese) and coffee in the long drawing-room. Among the topics discussed are the Common Market, growing exotic bulbs indoors, the films and love life of Werner Fassbinder, the novels and love life of Edna O'Brien, various ways of cooking veal, a current mass murder case, the financial and staffing difficulties of the *TLS*, and hotels in Tortola and Crete. Fred tries to keep up his end of the conversation, but without much success; he has never grown bulbs, cooked veal, seen a film by Fassbinder, etc. He feels provincial and out of it, though Posy and William try to help by asking him about American customs of gardening and cooking and filmgoing. He is glad when Posy proposes that they all stop gossiping and play charades.

As it turns out, the British game of charades differs from the one Fred knows – though each, it occurs to him, is characteristic of its culture. In the American version every player has to act for his team-mates some popular proverb, or the title of a book, play, film, or song, provided by the opposite team; victory goes to the side whose members collectively do this the fastest. America, that is, rewards speed and individual achievement, and encourages frantic attempts to communicate with compatriots who literally or metaphorically don't speak your language.

In the British version of charades – or at least in Posy's version – there is no premium on speed and there are no winners. Each team chooses a single word and acts out its syllables in turn with spoken dialogue that must include the relevant syllable. Though some trouble is taken to confuse the issue and make guessing harder, the game mainly seems to be an excuse for dressing up and behaving in ways that would otherwise be considered silly or shocking. It thus combines verbal ingenuity, in-group loyalty and cooperation, love of elaborate public performance, and private childishness – all traits that Fred has begun to associate with the British, or at least with Rosemary and her friends.

Before the charades can begin, nearly an hour is spent choosing the words and rummaging about in closets and trunks to outfit the players. Rosemary, Edwin, and Just William go first. They seem to have chosen their word (which turns out to be HORTICULTURE) partly for the opportunities it gives Edwin to wear Posy's clothes – which, since she is a large woman and he a small man, fit pretty well. In the first scene (WHORE) he and Rosemary appear as streetwalkers, and William, with a cane and bowler, as their drunken client. Edwin is comically horrifying in a red fright wig, an orange-and-yellow flowered sundress stuffed with facial tissues, and high-heeled gold sandals. Fred is nearly as startled by Rosemary. She is not only vulgarly made up and loaded with costume jewelry, but wearing the lace butterfly nightgown in which, just a few hours ago . . . He wants to protest, but makes himself laugh along with the rest; after all, it's only a game.

In the second scene (TIT) Edwin is a milkmaid (sunbonnet, pink checked pinafore) while Rosemary and William – with the help of a brown woolly blanket, two bone drinking horns, and a pink rubber balloon filled with water – represent the front and back halves of an uncooperative cow. For CULTURE Edwin wears one of Posy's tweed suits, a tweed porkpie hat, horn-rimmed spectacles, and a string of pearls. With his neat, rather handsome features and his well-padded small frame he looks, Fred thinks, better and even more natural as a fortyish matron. He obviously enjoys his part, in which he tries to force a series of highbrow books and records on Rosemary and William, who represent two sulky semi-punk schoolchildren.

After much laughter and applause and another round of drinks, Posy, Nico, and Fred retire to the library to get into costume for the first syllable of their word (CATASTROPHE). Nico and Fred, now in shirtsleeves, are fitted with colorful sashes and black rubber boots (Posy calls them 'Wellies') and breadknife daggers. They represent pirates and will soon pretend to lash her (as a cabin boy) with an improvised clothesline CAT o'nine tails.

'What's that noise outside? It sounds like a car.' In the white sailor-boy blouse she has just pulled on over her long pleated red silk dress, Posy runs to the window and pushes aside the heavy velvet curtain. 'Oh, my God. It's Jimbo. Quick, upstairs, everybody – and don't forget your proper clothes.' She flings open the library doors and dashes across the hall to the drawing room.

'William, it's Jimbo, get upstairs as fast as you can, he's just putting the car away. All of you, come on.' Ignoring their questions and exclamations, Posy herds her guests up the crimson-carpeted staircase and along a hall lined with heavy gilt-framed eighteenth-century portraits.

'Now,' she declares, checking to make sure that none of them are visible from below through the banisters. 'William, dearest, you go straight out by the back stairs and down to the boathouse, the key's in the stone urn under the ivy. Look out when you pass the stables, in case Jimbo's still there. Rosemary, and Edwin, oh Christ – ' She takes in Rosemary's naughty schoolgirl outfit and Edwin's dowager tweeds. 'All right, both of you; get dressed as fast as you can and then come down to the drawing room. I'm counting on you to keep Jimbo occupied for at least five minutes while I change the sheets and tidy up. Fred, and Nico, you've got to help too, darlings, this is a crisis. I want you to pack everything in William's room into his bag, all his clothes and books, every single thing you find. If you're not sure it's his, put it in anyhow. Right, everyone? Let's go.'

Fred hears a door opening below and steps in the hall, then a weary, peremptory male voice. 'Hallo? Is anybody still up?'

'Jimbo!' Posy cries. She drags the sailorboy blouse over her head, stuffs it into an antique oak chest, and runs down the stairs. 'Darling, how lovely! I didn't expect you till Monday.'

'I sent a cable this morning from Ankara.'

'It never came. Never mind, darling. Did you drive all the way from Gatwick? You must be simply exhausted. Come into the drawing room and I'll fix you a lovely strong whisky. I've got a few people here for the weekend, but most of them have gone to bed. Rosemary's still up, I think, and Edwin Francis. I'll go tell them you're here in a moment, but first I want to know all about – ' Her words fade.

'Remarkable,' Edwin says sotto voce, shaking his head under the tweed matron's hat. 'Did you ever see such natural authority, such military decision, such a grasp of strategic essentials? Hereditary, of course,' he adds. 'The Army blood . . . Poor Posy, really, all those Empire-building genes wasted on this sad century. She should have lived a hundred years ago – '

'Edwin, do go on, before Jimbo sees you like that,' Rosemary whispers, giggling.

'– and been a man, of course. Very well. But I must say, I hope Jimbo has the sense to take her into partnership as soon as the babies are safely in school.'

'Okay, let's get started,' Fred says to Nico a few moments later, lifting William's worn leather Gladstone bag onto the bed. 'I'll do the closet, and you can empty the drawers.' He opens the wardrobe door and begins sliding clothes off hangers. 'Lucky there isn't much.'

But when he turns around with a load over his arm Nico is still standing in the middle of the Turkey carpet. In his open-necked white shirt and black rubber boots, with Posy's red fringed scarf knotted around his waist, he looks as if he were playing pirates; his expression is theatrically stormy.

'Hey, let's go,' Fred says.

'No,' Nico hisses through his teeth, in character.

'No?'

'I am not a servant.' Nico's voice is barely under control. 'I don't pack the dirty clothes of people.'

'Oh, for Christ's sake.' Fred rolls up some surprisingly elegant maroon silk pajamas and stuffs them into the bag. 'Don't be a wimp.'

Nico does not move. He looks insulted; probably he has never heard of a wimp and thinks it is something unspeakable. 'Sorry,' Fred says. 'Look, maybe you could just pile up those books and papers, all right?'

'All right,' Nico says sullenly.

'What I don't understand,' Fred goes on, trying to ease the atmosphere in the room, 'is why William has to get out of the way so fast. I can understand that maybe Sir James Billings wouldn't want to meet a lot of strangers when he's just got back from Turkey late at night. But he must be used to William; after all he's Posy's cousin.'

Nico snorts. 'You are wrong, and also stupid,' he says, slinging *Royal Charles* and *Betrayal* onto the bed.

Fred decides not to notice the word *stupid*, which Nico has no doubt used as a riposte for *wimp*. 'But he *is* her cousin; Posy said so when she introduced us before lunch,' he says, starting to pack up William's leather toilet kit.

'Yes, her cousin, I suppose.' Nico's tone is scornful. 'They are all cousins here. And also her lover.'

'Aw, come on.' Fred thinks of Posy, so blond and queenly and tall, in her way as much the real thing as Rosemary. 'I can't believe that.' He imagines Posy naked, a luscious full-bodied late-Victorian nude, in sexual juxtaposition with the lanky, dim, fiftyish William, the relevant part of whom is somehow represented in his mind by the worn beaver shaving brush with dried white soap on it that he has just stowed away.

'No? Why not?'

'Well, I mean, he's too old. And he's not all that attractive either. I mean, hell, Posy's a beautiful woman.'

'Who can calculate these things?' Nico tosses the *Times* untidily beside the books. 'It's a matter of opinions. Myself, I would not want to fuck with Lady Posy; you would not want to fuck with Cousin William.'

'No,' Fred agrees vehemently, reminded that Nico, in spite (or perhaps because) of his macho appearance, presumably fucks regularly with Edwin Francis.

'Also, sex, it is not always a matter of only desire, as you must know.' Nico allows a slight unpleasant pause. 'Cousin William is not wealthy or famous, but he has many connections. With his help Posy is a feature in the magazines, on the television. Soon she introduces for him six programs about English gardens, for a nice payment. He does much for her.'

And if Cousin William would do as much for me, Nico seems to be saying, I might fuck with him. Or even worse: Rosemary is rich and famous, she does much for you. The conviction that Nico is a sly, second-rate, opportunistic person, a blot on the country-house scene, comes over Fred. 'Maybe, but that doesn't prove –'

'Also you see he stays in the room next to Lady Posy's, the customary room of the husband.' With a mocking flourish Nico pulls open a paneled oak door, exposing a vertical slice of Posy's blue-and-white sprigged and ruffled Laura Ashley bedroom.

'So?' Fred says, concealing his fear that Nico is right, but not his dislike.

'So convenient.' Nico smiles.

Fred does not smile. He goes on packing William's clothes, faster than before. Though most of them are clean, they now feel disagreeable: the tightly rolled thin dark lisle socks, the slippery starched shirts with the name of a Belgravia laundry on the paper band. He does not like them; he does not like the paneled room with its deep tapestry-cushioned chairs and window seat, its distorting mullioned panes, its connecting door. An impulse to walk away comes to him, but his training in manners is strong, and he presses on.

'You're saying that William had to get out of the house fast because if Posy's husband saw him here, he'd think they were having an affair,' he says, trying to clarify it in his mind.

'Not think.' Nico's expression is condescending. 'He knows already that they fuck, since a long time.'

'Says who?'

'Edwin says it to me. They have an arrangement, he says.'

'You mean like an open marriage.' Fred begins to pull out the drawers below the wardrobe. They are empty and lined with glazed paper in an overcomplicated and disagreeable red paisley design.

'I don't know what you call it,' says Nico. He has given up all pretense of helping and is lounging on the window seat. 'Edwin says they well understand each other, and if Billings does not have to meet Cousin William he is content, why not? He has still the beautiful aristocratic wife, the pretty children, the rich country house –'

'Yeh, but –'

'He also has his freedom, naturally. His own amusements.'

'Oh, yeh? What amusements?'

'I don't know.' Nico shrugs. 'But Edwin says they are expensive ones, and not very nice.'

Without wanting to, Fred starts trying to imagine the sort of amusements that might be considered not very nice by Edwin Francis, a homosexual who likes to dress up in his hostess's clothes; but he is interrupted.

'Well, how are you getting on?' Posy pauses in the doorway with an armful of scalloped yellow sheets. She is as beautiful and gracious as ever; but she looks different to Fred, somehow fleshy and loose.

'Almost done.' He bundles the *Times* into William's bag and pulls the sides together.

Posy surveys the room, taking in Nico lazily prone on the window seat. 'Very good,' she says to Fred. 'Now, could you be a real sport, and take the bag down to the boathouse?'

'Yeh, sure.'

'I'll show you the way; and then you can come back and have a drink and meet Jimbo. But you mustn't keep him up late, please, he's had such a long trip. I know what; you might say you have to turn in early so you can get up and jog before breakfast. Jimbo will like that, he often runs himself; and it might not be a bad idea if you were to arrange to meet him tomorrow and go jogging together. Then we can make sure he doesn't run in the wrong direction.' Posy smiles at him again, then clicks it off. 'And you. Nico.' She gives him a chilly look. 'I want you to go straight to bed. Don't even think of having a shower tonight, or there won't be enough hot water for Jimbo. You were in there for an hour this afternoon as it is. And please don't come down for breakfast; Jimbo's very grumpy at breakfast. I'll send you up a tray.'

For a long moment Nico does not move. His handsome features have darkened and distorted as Posy spoke and are now set in an angry flush. But her aristocratic stare is too much for him; he rises slowly and moves toward the door.

'Thank you,' she says, gracious again. 'All right now, Freddy darling, it's this way.'

Posy leads him along the hall between two rows of ancestors: plump-jawed self-satisfied countenances in heavy curled wigs. The portraits are hung from near the ceiling in such a way that they tilt outward from the top, creating an oppressive effect.

'He's such a nuisance sometimes, Nico,' she says. 'He's got all sorts of silly ideas about politics, and I'm simply not going to have him bothering poor Jimbo with them, especially not at breakfast. You know how excitable these Mediterranean types can be.' She opens the door to some back stairs, smiling at Fred, inviting him into the company of non-Mediterranean types who are not excitable and have no silly ideas. 'So if you should see him trying to sneak downstairs tomorrow morning, I hope you'll be a dear and head him off.'

'Well. I'll try,' says Fred reluctantly.

'I knew I could count on you.' She stops at the bottom of the stairs and smiles up from under her golden mane, which from this angle looks almost too thick, too perfectly curled – almost like a wig. Maybe it is a wig; maybe underneath all that hair Posy

Billings is bald or stubble-headed, as her eighteenth-century ancestors along the corridor probably were under their powdered headpieces.

'Here you are.' She swings open a door, admitting a gust of cold, dark air. 'Now there's the way down to the lake, where we were this afternoon, you remember?'

'I think so.'

'Very good.' As Edwin has remarked, there is an authoritarian, even a military tone to Posy's manner. 'Here's a torch, but I don't expect you'll need it, it's quite light out. You can almost see the boathouse from here, just past those big pines. And the rain's cleared off nicely. A lovely night, really. Off you go, now.'

Fred starts down the path. It doesn't seem like a lovely night to him. In the circle of light at his feet the gravel is loose and wet; when he points the torch upward he can see the two-hundred-year-old topiary hedges, dark and dripping, on either side. The fanciful shapes of pigeons, peacocks, owls, and urns seem distorted, almost sinister. In the sky above is a lopsided yellowish moon with a pale greasy ring around it, like a badly fried egg. It is bright enough, however, for Fred to circumnavigate the pines and make out the boathouse, a crouching structure of pebblestone with a deep overhanging roof and its feet in inky water.

'Yes?' William opens the door a cautious crack. He is still wearing the baggy knickers and plaid kneesocks in which he portrayed an uncultured schoolboy, and has a rough hairy brown blanket, perhaps the one which earlier was part of the cow, round his shoulders. He looks guilty and disreputable, like some old crazed tramp caught hiding in the outbuildings of an estate. 'What did you want?'

'I brought your things.' Fred decides that if he ever, God forbid, has an affair with a married woman, he won't set foot in her house, not so much on pragmatic or moral grounds as on aesthetic ones.

'Oh, thank you very much.' William opens the door just enough to admit his bag. He doesn't invite Fred to come in, and Fred doesn't want to come in.

'Well, see you,' he says, turning away.

From the lake Posy's house looks unnaturally tall and somehow misshapen; an effect perhaps of its elevation, the shadows and shrubberies that surround it, and the fried-egg moonlight. As Fred walks slowly back up the path past the giant dark vegetable birds and urns, he becomes conscious of a strong impulse not to reenter this house; to hike instead into the nearest village and find a bed for the night somewhere (at the pub, maybe?) and take an early train or bus into London in the morning.

But of course he can't do that, it would be rude and crazy; and besides there's Rosemary. He can't leave her alone with two posturing queers and a bossy adulteress whose hair looks like a wig – though only an hour ago he thought it was all beautiful, the real thing.

James again, Fred thinks: a Jamesian phrase, a Jamesian situation. But in the novels the scandals and secrets of high life are portrayed as more elegant; the people are better mannered. Maybe because it was a century earlier; or maybe only because the mannered elegance of James' prose obfuscates the crude subtext. Maybe, in fact, it as just like now . . .

Because, after all, isn't Rosemary the classic James heroine: beautiful, fine, delicate, fatally impulsive? She thinks of Posy and Edwin as her best friends; she is too generous to see them as they are, too lighthearted and trusting. She needs other, better friends – better in both senses – friends who will shield her from scenes like tonight's –

Well, isn't that what he's here for, the sterling young American champion James himself might have provided? For the second time that day Fred has the giddy sense of having got into a novel, and again it is dizzying, exhilarating. He laughs out loud and plunges into the blackened shrubberies, toward the house.

5

The Devil flew from north to south
With [Miss Miner] in his mouth,
And when he found she was a fool
He dropped her onto [Camden] school.

Old rhyme

Vinnie Miner is sitting on a bench in a primary school playground in Camden Town, watching a group of little girls skipping rope. It is a windy April afternoon; gray and white clouds like jumbled soapy washing slosh across the sky, sending alternate brightness and shadow over her notebook. She already has a thick folder of rhymes recorded in this school and several others; but as a contemporary folklorist she is interested not only in text but in the cultural settings in which they occur, how they are passed on and by whom, the manner of their delivery, and their social function. So far today she has seen and heard nothing strikingly new, but she isn't disappointed. She has spoken to one class and collected material from this and from two others, concentrating her efforts on the ten- and eleven-year-olds who are usually her best informants: younger children know fewer rhymes, and older ones are beginning to forget them under the pernicious influence of mass culture and of puberty.

Overall, Vinnie's working hypothesis about the differences between British and American game rhymes has been supported. The British texts do tend to be older, in some cases suggesting a medieval or even an Anglo-Saxon origin; they are also more literary. The American rhymes are newer, cruder, less lyrical and poetic.

More complex analysis will come later; she can see already, however, that violence is common in the verses of both countries, something that wouldn't surprise any trained observer and doesn't surprise Vinnie, who has never thought of children as particularly sweet or gentle.

Polly on the railway
Picking up stones;
Along came an engine
And broke Polly's bones.
'Oh,' said Polly,
'That's not fair.'
'Oh,' said the engine-driver,
'I don't care.'

How many bones did Polly break?
One, two, three, four . . .

The chant continues, repeats itself; the rope revolves, a vibrating blur in the air, enclosing an ellipsoid of charmed space. Within it a child jumps, her long hair blown out, the gray pleated skirt of her school uniform fanning wide above thin knobbly legs in gray wool stockings. Her expression of unselfconscious concentration, skill, and joy is repeated on the face of the girl next in line, who is already bobbing to the scuffed beat of oxfords on damp tarmac. As Vinnie watches, her strongest sensation – far stronger than professional interest or a shiver whenever the sun skids under a cloud – is envy.

Since she is an authority on children's literature, people assume that Vinnie must love children, and that her own lack of them must be a tragedy. For the sake of public relations, she seldom denies these assumptions outright. But the truth is otherwise. In her private opinion most contemporary children – especially American ones – are competitive, callous, noisy, and shallow, at once jaded and ignorant as a result of overexposure to television, baby-sitters, advertising, and video games. Vinnie wants to be a child, not to have one; she isn't interested in the parental role, but in an extension or recovery of what for her is the best part of life.

Indifference to actual children is fairly common among experts in Vinnie's field, and not unknown among authors of juvenile literature. As she has often noted in her lectures, many of the great classic writers had an idyllic boyhood or girlhood that ended far too soon, often traumatically. Carroll, Macdonald, Kipling, Burnett, Nesbit, Grahame, Tolkien – and the list could be extended. The result of such an early history often seems to be a passionate longing, not for children, but for one's own lost childhood.

As a little girl Vinnie too was unusually happy. Her parents were good-tempered, fond of her, and comfortably circumstanced; her first eleven years were passed in agreeable and varied semirural surroundings. It was no handicap not to be beautiful then, and all children are small. Vinnie was clever, energetic, popular. Though her size prevented her from excelling at most sports, she gained authority through her self-confidence and her good memory for games, rhymes, riddles, stories, and jokes. She loved everything about those years: the chorus in the classroom and on the playground; the thrilling exploration of overgrown vacant lots, alleys, woods, and fields; the visits to stores and museums; the picnics and summer trips to the mountains or seaside with her parents. She loved the books – indeed, she still prefers children's literature to most contemporary adult fiction. She loved the toys, the songs, the games, the Saturday matinees at the neighbourhood movie house, the radio programs (especially 'Little Orphan Annie' and 'The Shadow'). She loved the round of holidays, from January first – when she helped her parents toast the baby New Year in nonalcoholic foamy eggnog – to Christmas with its elaborate family ceremonial and gathering of aunts and uncles and cousins.

Then suddenly, when Vinnie was twelve, her parents moved to the city. In her new school she was skipped a grade, and found that she had lost everything important to her in life and become a disadvantaged adolescent – an undersized, pimply, flat-chested, embarrassingly plain 'grind'. The pain of this transformation is something she has never quite got over.

As it turned out, though, Vinnie didn't have to relinquish childhood forever. No one really has to, she believes, and often declares. The message of all her lectures and books and articles – sometimes explicit, more often implied – is that we must, as she puts it, value and preserve childhood: we must 'cherish the child within us'. This isn't of course an original theme, but one of the basic doctrines of her profession.

The cloudy laundry overhead has thickened; the school building, a castellated structure of sooty Victorian brick, intercepts the declining sun. The skipping rope ceases to define its magical space, falls limp, becomes only a length of old clothesline. As the little girls prepare to leave, Vinnie consults with them to check on some of the textual variations she had heard; she thanks them, and writes down their names and ages. Then she puts away her notebook and follows the children's route across the chilly, darkening playground, wrapping her coat closer, looking forward to her tea.

'Hey! Hey, missis.' The girl who has accosted her is standing against the smoke-stained, graffiti-scrawled brick wall of the narrow passage that runs past the school to the street. She is older than the children who were jumping rope – perhaps twelve or thirteen – skinny, and poorly dressed in a semi-punk style. A soiled once-pink Orlon cardigan is pinned together over her school uniform skirt and a red-and-black T-shirt advertising some rock group. Her complexion is bad; her cropped hair has been dyed a nasty shade of pale magenta, and resembles the synthetic fur of those stuffed toys that are won – or more often not won – at Bank Holiday fairs.

'Yes?' Vinnie says.

'I got somethin' to tell you.' The girl grabs a fold of Vinnie's coat sleeve. 'My sister says you're wantin' rhymes. Rhymes you wouldn't tell the teachers.' She grins unattractively; her teeth are chipped and irregular.

'I'm collecting all sorts of rhymes,' Vinnie says, with a professionally friendly smile. 'What I told your sister's class was that there might be some they wouldn't want to recite in public, because they weren't very polite.'

'Yeh, that's what I mean. I know a lotta those.'

'That's nice,' Vinnie says, repressing her desire for tea. 'I'd like to hear them.' The girl is silent. 'Would you like to say some for me?'

'Maybe.' A precocious shrewdness twists the spotty unformed features. 'How much you paying?'

Vinnie's first impulse is to break off the conversation. No child or adult has ever before proposed to sell material to her; the very idea is unseemly. Folklore by nature is free, uncopyrighted – as a Marxist colleague says, it's not part of the capitalist commodity system – and this for Vinnie is part of its glory. But it's possible that this unpleasant litle girl knows some interesting, even unique rhymes; and Vinnie has learnt in over thirty years never to turn down material, or judge the value of the text by an informant's appearance. Besides, God knows the child looks as if she could use the money.

'I don't know.' She laughs awkwardly. 'How about fifty pence?'

'Okay.' The reply is animated, almost vivid. Vinnie realizes she's offered much more than was expected. She gets out her notebook and pen; then, noticing the child's suspicious stare, she rummages in her purse. When she first came to England, the old silver coinage was still in use; the new octagonal fifty-pence piece, once she finds it, looks more than ever like some sort of cheap medal. Britannia, sitting between her lion and her shield, seems shrunken, defensive.

And where is Vinnie to sit? Reluctantly she lowers herself onto the only available horizontal surface, a ledge of dirty-looking cement alongside the school building.

Clutching the coin, the mauve-haired girl darts down the alley to scan the now-empty playground, then back in the other direction toward the street. Perhaps it was all a begging trick, Vinnie thinks. But after surveying the scene the child sidles back up the passage.

'Okay,' she says.

'Just a moment, please.' Vinnie opens her notebook. 'Could you tell me your name?'

'Wha' for?' The child takes a step back.

'It just for my records,' Vinnie says in a reassuring tone 'I'm not going to tell anyone.' This isn't strictly true: in her published work she always identifies and thanks her informants, and over the years more than one child, coming across Vinnie's books or articles later, has written to thank her in turn.

'Uh. Mary, uh, Maloney.'

The manner of delivery makes Vinnie certain that this is not the child's name; but she writes it down. 'Yes. Go ahead.' 'Mary Maloney' bends toward her and says in a hoarse whisper:

> 'Mother, mother, mother pin a rose on me,
> Two little nigger-boys are after me,
> One is blind and the other can't see,
> So mother, mother, mother pin a rose on me.'

It would be idle to pretend that Vinnie likes this rhyme. But since she has never heard it before she records the lines and then, as is her custom, reads them back for confirmation.

'Yeh. You got it.'

'Thank you. Would you like to say another one?'

Mary Maloney slouches against the sooty bricks above Vinnie, mute. The ripped hem of her skirt hangs down on one side; she wears sagging pink bobby socks and scratched red plastic clogs, and her thin white legs are prickled with gooseflesh. 'You want more, you gotta pay for more,' she whines.

Now it is Vinnie's turn to be silent; the sordidness of the transaction has overcome her.

'I betcha you'll get more brass 'n that when you sell my stuff.'

'I don't sell these rhymes.' Vinnie tries to say this pleasantly, to keep both distaste and rebuke out of her voice.

'Yeh? What d'you do with them, then?'

'I collect them, for, uh' – How can her life's work be explained to a mind like this? – 'for the college where I teach.'

'Oh yeh?' The girl gives her the look one gives a liar whose bluff one has decided not to call. It is clear that she believes Vinnie to be collecting dirty rhymes for some dubious, even perverse purpose. It also seems likely that for enough money she would sell Vinnie, or anyone else, anything they wanted – that she would say and do horrors. 'Okay.' A peeved sigh. 'Tenpence.'

Now that she is in so far Vinnie feels somehow constrained to go on. She reopens her purse and extracts another tinny, debased coin. Mary Maloney leans closer, so close that Vinnie can see the dark, dandruff-clogged roots of her synthetic mauve hair, and smell her sour breath.

> 'I wish I wuz a seagull,
> I wish I wuz a duck,
> So I could fly along the beach
> And watch the people fuck.'

Vinnie's pen pauses in its transcription. She likes this verse even less than the preceding one: not only is it vulgar, it contradicts her thesis. A few more of these and her theory about the difference between British and American playground rhymes will be down the tube, as they say here.

'Thanks, that's enough,' she says, shutting her notebook on the unfinished rhyme and rising to her feet. 'Thank you for your help.' She gives a tight smile. A cold wind has begun to scour the darkening playground and funnel through the passageway, blowing shreds of paper rubbish with it.

'Hey, I ain't finished.' Mary Maloney follows her out into the street.

'That's all right; I have enough now, thank you.' Vinnie begins to walk down Princess Road; but the girl follows closely, clutching at her coat.

'Hey wait! I know lots more rhymes. I know some really dirty ones.' Mary Maloney presses nearer; in her clogs, she is taller than Vinnie, who always wears sensible low heels on field trips.

'Would you let go of me, please,' Vinnie exclaims, her voice tight with revulsion and, it must be admitted, fear. The street is almost empty, the clouds low and unpleasant.

'Mary had a little lamb – '

A dread of hearing what will come next gives Vinnie the strength to pull her coat away. Breathing hard, not looking back, she walks off as fast as she can go without actually running.

Back in the sanctuary of her pleasant warm flat, with a pot of Twining's Queen Mary tea on the table before her next to the bowl of white hyacinths, Vinnie begins to feel better. She is able to pity Mary Maloney for what must surely be a tainted and deprived background, a premature exposure to all that is synthetic and filthy in popular culture.

It might be possible, she decides, buttering the second half of her cinnamon bun, to exclude those last two texts from her study. After all they are not, to paraphrase her projected title, British Rhymes of Childhood, but rather rhymes of a precocious and corrupt adolescence. Besides, she never got Mary Maloney's age; very likely she is older than she looked, undersized like many slum-dwellers, maybe fourteen or even fifteen, not a child at all.

All the same she feels a nagging unease. Mary Maloney remains in her mind: the skinny white gooseflesh legs, the flat dirty face, the chipped teeth, the matted acrylic hair; the pressure of her greed and her need.

It also occurs to Vinnie that in a sense the girl was right: she will get more than tenpence for each rhyme in her notebook when her study is published. And more still if, as she hopes, Janet Elliot in London and Marilyn Krinney in New York agree to print a selection of her rhymes as a children's book; negotiations for this project are already underway. And what would her Marxist friend say to that? Depending on his mood, which is highly unstable, he might say either 'Well, we all have to live' or 'Capitalist bitch'.

Of course if she doesn't use Mary Maloney's contribution she won't be exploiting her. No; she'll only be exploiting the scores, hundreds even, of schoolchildren who for thirty years have told her their rhymes, stories, riddles, and jokes for nothing. But to think this way is ridiculous. It is to condemn every folklorist who ever lived, from the Grimm brothers on.

Yes, Vinnie thinks, she will forget those rhymes, as she prefers to forget much of adult folklore. A scholar, of course, cannot afford to be prudish, and over the years she has recorded a good deal of off-color material with hardly a quiver. Children are given to bathroom humor:

> Milk, milk, lemonade.
> Around the corner fudge is made.

She has even (without the accompanying gestures to parts of the body, of course) used this verse in her lectures as an example of folk metaphor, demonstrating the young child's undifferentiated pre-moral pleasure in both food and bodily products.

But some of the jokes told by grownups and collected by other folklorists really gross Vinnie out, as her students would say. They are not only filthy, they emphasize an aspect of the relations between men and women that she prefers not to look at too closely. However carried away by sex – and at times she has been carried far – Vinnie always returns with a slight sense of embarrassment. Intellectually she considers the physical side of love ridiculous at best, certainly unaesthetic – not one of nature's best inventions. The female organs seem to her damp and cluttered; that of the male positively silly, a pink unnatural toadstool sort of thing. As the only child of modest, even rather squeamish parents, Vinnie was six years old before she saw a naked human male – a friend's baby brother. Because she was a polite child she made no comment on what appeared to her a kind of unfortunate growth on the baby's tummy, a sort of large fleshy wart. Subsequently, through contemplation of public sculptures and her parents' art books, it occurred to her that other males besides little Bobby had this handicap, though in art it was usually concealed, or partly concealed, by a sculptured or painted leaf. Other men, she concluded from a visit to Rockefeller Center and a photograph in *Life* of the Oscar Award, were not so deformed. When she discovered the truth, Vinnie's main feeling was one of pity. A decade later she saw her first erect penis; in spite of all she now knew, her first thought was that it looked infected: sore, red, puffy. Though she has tried to suppress them, these ideas are never far from Vinnie's consciousness. She has never got used to the way sex looks.

But though it looks foolish or even disgusting, Vinnie presently found, sex feels wonderful. She didn't find that odd, since it is the same way with food: an oyster or a plate of spaghetti is far from attractive in itself. The solution to the problem was simple: you either make love in the dark or shut your eyes. Of course, this hasn't always been possible. In graduate school she once broke up with a most attractive man because the wall opposite his bed was one large gold-framed mirror salvaged from a demolished building nearby. Vinnie managed to keep her eyes closed most of the time, but she couldn't help opening them once in a while, and then the sight of her own thin white legs wrapped around her friend Paul Cattleman's brown hairy back filled her with a deep embarrassment that almost wholly quenched her pleasure.

While she was growing up Vinnie often heard the minister of her parents' church say that love (the married sort, of course) was a God-given blessing. Vinnie herself is not religious, though she is somewhat superstitious, and she does not blame the human reproductive process on anyone. But if she were to imagine the sort of God who might have arranged it, he would hardly inspire veneration. She sees one of those fat, undignified, naked bronze deities that are occasionally offered for sale in Oriental shops, whose human avatars are worshiped by the least stable of her students. Some little plump godling, with a limited imagination and the giggly, vulgar sense of humor one sometimes sees in young children.

Before she left America, Vinnie had rather dreaded the prospect of being without physical love for six months, and anticipated with anxiety the frustration and/or unsuitable incidents it might bring into her life – the necessity of calling too desperately on fantasy affairs. But as it turns out, she has been less often painfully troubled by desire than in the past, perhaps because of her age.

Even in her fantasy life, she has noticed, professional recognition has of late tended to replace romance. As she drowses over a book, or lies among her pillows drifting into sleep, public bodies rather than private ones approach her. She accepts their advances as warmly and graciously as before, but now in a vertical rather than a horizontal position, and clad not in her best black nightgown but in the black gown and colored silk hood appropriate to the recipient of various prizes and honorary degrees. It annoys Vinnie that she is enough a woman of her generation to be rather ashamed of these imaginings when fully awake. Among her feminist students they would be thought far less embarrassing than the other sort of fantasy; even admirable. But Vinnie has been brought up to believe that though a man may work for wealth or fame, a woman must labor for love – if not that of a husband or children, at least that of a profession.

No, Vinnie doesn't miss sex as much as she had feared. What she misses is the affectionate and romantic side of love, insofar as she has known it: the leisurely walks in the woods, the exchange of notes, the rapid concealed half-caress at the crowded party, the glance across the lounge at the faculty club, the sense of sharing a complex, secret life. But she is used to missing all this – she has been short of it almost all her life.

And here in London she thinks of it rather less often, for there is so much else to entertain her. Tonight, for instance, she's going to the English National Opera with a friend whom she considers one of the nicest people and best authors of children's fiction in Britain.

At the Coliseum that evening, during the intermission of *Così fan tutte*, Vinnie descends the stairs from the balcony in search of coffee for herself and for her friend Jane, who has a sprained ankle. Her hope is that the lower bar will be less crowded, but it is worse if anything: surrounded by very large, pushing men, none of whom shows the slightest inclination to make way for her. She has noticed before that the British, who unlike Americans queue so politely on all other occasions, become selfish and shoving around any supply of liquor, public or private. It is, she thinks, a sort of national hysteria, probably the result of the licensing laws.

As Vinnie gives up all hope of coffee and heads back toward the stairs, she sees Rosemary Radley and Fred Turner sitting on a bench. That they should be here together doesn't surprise her. Everyone knows about them now: Rosemary has even been mentioned in *Private Eye* as 'discussing Ugandan affairs with a gorgeous young American don'. She has also, presumably because of Fred, cancelled out of a film now being shot in Italy. It wasn't a very large role, admittedly; but a fair amount of money was involved – and, as everyone says, Rosemary has to think of her reputation; she isn't getting any younger.

None of this gossip seems to affect the lovers. They go everywhere together, and Vinnie has to admit that they make a handsome couple. Rosemary of course is famous for her looks, and more than one of her friends has compared Fred's profile to that of Rupert Brooke – which is fine if you like that rather flamboyant sort of appearance, Vinnie thinks. Nor do they seem mismatched as to age: Fred's seriousness of manner, and Rosemary's delicate playfulness, help to cancel the difference. And they are evidently good for each other. Fred has cheered up amazingly, and Rosemary's scatty manner has moderated. She still darts from one topic to the next, but far more smoothly.

What strikes Vinnie about them now isn't so much the way Fred is looking at Rosemary – she's seen plenty of people stare at Rosemary like that, including some who don't much like her – but rather Rosemary's unwavering concentration on Fred.

Like many actors, Rosemary usually broadcasts rather than receives impressions. She also seems unable as a rule to fix her attention on anyone or anything for more than a few moments; perhaps this helps to explain why she hasn't ever had any real success on stage. Television, on the other hand, is shot in tiny segments: it doesn't require an extended and developed performance, only a concentrated brief intensity of expression, something Rosemary is certainly capable of – even famous for – in private life.

Her normal *modus operandi* is to leap charmingly and distractingly from subject to subject, mood to mood, and person to person, often so quickly that the outlines of her conversation and even of her appearance seem to blur; one is left with an impression of sparkle and flutter. Her clothes produce the same effect. Rosemary never follows current fashion, but has developed a style of her own. Everything she wears shimmers and billows and dangles; she seems not so much dressed as loosely draped in flimsy, flowery, lacy stuffs: veils and scarves and floating gauzy blouses and trailing skirts and fringed silk shawls. Her hair too is continually in flux: tinted and streaked in varying shades from pale gold to bisque, it alternately gathers itself up in soft coils, falls in flossy clouds about her shoulders, or extends wayward tendrils and curls in all directions.

Tonight, though, Rosemary seems unusually tranquil. Light but serene blonde waves lie on her brow; her ropes of blue and silver beads and her long chiffon dress printed with shadowy azure flowers fall undisturbed toward the floor; her gaze is steady on Fred. Vinnie has to speak twice before either of them notices her.

'Oh, uh-Vinnie, hello.' Fred rises smoothly, but stumbles over her first name, which she has recently invited him to use. 'I'm glad you're here. I need support; Rosemary's being very stubborn. You'll tell her I'm right.'

'Don't be silly, darling. Vinnie will agree with me. Now, sit down.' With a flutter of sleeve and a tinkle of silver-gilt bangles Rosemary smooths the banquette beside her.

Their dispute turns out to concern – or have as its pretext – the question of whether Rosemary should hire a cleaning lady. Even before Vinnie hears their arguments she's on Fred's side. Rosemary's Chelsea house is famous for its disorder, its elegant slovenliness; every time Vinnie's been there it has been cluttered with things that need mending, scrubbing, dusting, polishing, emptying, and throwing away. But Rosemary claims to be perfectly satisfied with her present method of housekeeping, which is to let everything go until she can't stand it and then ask an agency called Help Yourself to send someone over for a day.

'I can't bear housecleaning,' she tells Vinnie. 'It always

reminds me of my mother's two spinster aunts in Bath, where I was sent to stay as a child during the war – mean, obsessive old things. All their staff had left except this elderly battle-axe Mrs McGowan, but they insisted on keeping that great ugly barn of a house up. Always cleaning, they were, working their fingers to the bone.' Rosemary extends and flexes her soft ringed hands. 'They were fearfully cross with me because I was so careless and untidy. "You're a most inconsiderate child," Aunt Isabel used to tell me' – Rosemary assumes an unfamiliar voice, thin and nasal – '"You can't expect Mrs McGowan to pick up after you, she has other things to do. If you don't change your ways before you're grown, no self-respecting servant will ever want to work for you."'

'Well, I made up my mind right then. I said to them, "I don't want my room picked up. I like it the way it is." Oh, they were shocked. My Aunt Etty said' – another voice, lower and wearier – '"No man'll stay in a house that looks the way your room does now." Little she knew.' Rosemary giggles provocatively.

Besides, she goes on, charladies always get so dreadfully familiar, trying to involve you in their awful pathetic lives. 'You Americans – ' She made a face at Vinnie and Fred. 'You haven't any idea what household help is like nowadays in this country. You think if I phone an agency they'll send me a dear old family retainer out of *Upstairs, Downstairs*.'

'No – ' begins Vinnie, who has never tried to find a cleaning lady in London, because she can't afford one.

'What I'll get instead' – Rosemary rushes on – 'is some miserable immigrant who speaks only Pakistani or Portuguese and is terrified of electricity. Or else some awful slut who can't find a proper job in a shop or a factory because she's too stupid and ill-tempered. And then twice a week I'll have to hear all about her backache and her constipation and her drunken husband and her delinquent children and her squabbles with the Council over her flat.' Rosemary slides into stage Cockney – 'and 'er dawg's worms and 'er cat's fleas and 'er budgie's molt, ooh, the pore dear, 'e's losin' is feathers somethin' awful and won't touch 'is bloody birdseed.'

Fred awards the performance a grin of appreciation, then goes on to criticize the script. 'It doesn't have to be like that,' he tells Vinnie. 'You can still find a good cleaning lady if you go to the right agency; Posy Billings gave me the name of one when we were there last weekend. If the woman talks too much, well, Rosemary can just leave the house. She can't do that with Help Yourself, because they send somebody different every time, right?'

'Mm,' Vinnie assents; but what she is thinking is that Fred Turner has received after only a few weeks' acquaintance what she will probably never receive: an invitation to Posy Billings' house in Oxfordshire.

'Those people from Help Yourself, see, they're out-of-work actors and singers and dancers, most of them,' he explains. 'They don't know anything about how to clean a house. When I come over they're usually just standing holding a dust rag like it was some prop in a play they didn't understand, or they're pushing the vacuum back and forth over the same place in the carpet, talking about the theater and trying to persuade Rosemary to get them a part in *Tallyho Castle*.'

'Not always.' Rosemary protests, with a soft giggle.

'And if she goes out,' he continues, 'if she doesn't watch them every minute, the people from Help Yourself help themselves to her whisky and her pâté and her opera records and sometimes even her clothes. They smear her windows with detergent and ruin her parquet with soap and hot water and tear up her silk scarves for dust rags.'

As Fred relates these disasters, Vinnie is struck not only by his grasp of the details of housekeeping but by his familiarity with Rosemary's domestic circumstances. Evidently he's not actually living with her now; but Vinnie wonders if he might be planning to move in, especially if conditions improve. She thinks of the remark of Rosemary's aunt, that no man would stay in her niece's house because of its disorder. As Rosemary implied, her aunt had been wrong: many men have stayed in her house. On the other hand, none has done so for very long.

Before Vinnie can pronounce any judgment in the dispute, the bell rings for the second act. Just as well, she thinks as she climbs the stairs to the balcony, jostled aside by larger and heavier persons. It's always a mistake for an outsider to venture an opinion in arguments of this sort, which are often largely a sort of amorous play. At least for Rosemary the quarrel seemed no more than a pretext for dramatic monologue and affectionate banter. At times she'd even taken the other side, adding weight to Fred's case by telling how she once came home to find a youth from Help Yourself soaking in pink bubbles in her tub. 'And he wasn't even attractive! He was rather pudgy, and soapy and apologetic, and later I found he'd used up all my Vitabath.'

But Fred, underneath his light manner, is singing the basso part. He has a temperamental commitment to the idea of order, already demonstrated to Vinnie in meetings of the Corinth Library Committee. The dusty chaos of Rosemary's house would surely seem to him a most unsuitable backdrop for their love duet. Also, no doubt, he doesn't much care to have ambitious young actors chatting intimately with Rosemary, or sloshing about (however pudgily) in her bathtub.

Vinnie's guess is that Rosemary will win the argument. She's used to having her own way, and besides it's her house, not to mention her country. But there is something in Fred's manner that suggests he won't give up easily. On the Library Committee this past autumn he was – though always polite – quite stubborn: willing to prolong a meeting well past five o'clock to gain his point. Vinnie had thought that this might be because he didn't want to go home to an empty apartment. On the other hand, perhaps stubbornness was part of Fred's character – and as such possibly a cause rather than a result of his newly single state.

As she lies in bed later that evening, sinking into an agreeable unconsciousness, with Mozart's tunes drifting vaguely through her head, Vinnie hears what is unmistakably the sound of her doorbell. Startled, she lifts her head from the pillow. Her first thought is of the habitués of the local municipal lodging-house – slovenly meat-faced men in soiled clothes who lounge on the benches by the railway underpass in good weather, passing a bottle in a crumpled paper bag, or lurch along the streets near Camden Town tube station mumbling to themselves or to strangers. Her next, crazier notion is that the girl from the playground has somehow found out where she lives and is waiting on the stoop to recite the rest of her filthy nursery rhymes the moment Vinnie opens the front door.

Another longer ring. Cautiously, she crawls out from under the down comforter and pads barefoot along the hall in her flannel nightgown and bathrobe. The light from the entryway spills down through the transom onto the cold black-and-white tiles, and Vinnie feels a shiver up her legs. Her vision of the unknown caller multiplies, and she imagines on the doorstep an aggregation of drunken vagrants, then a gang of mauve-haired teenage punks chanting foul rhymes.

A third ring at the bell, more prolonged, somehow plaintive. It is spiritless of her to cower behind two locked doors like this, Vinnie thinks. London is not, like New York, an anonymously indifferent city. She is acquainted with her neighbours in the house; if she were to scream they would come hastening to see what was the matter, the way everyone (including Vinnie) did when the baby-sitter upstairs scalded herself last month. Holding her bathrobe closely around her, she opens the door of the flat.

'Yes?' she called shrilly. 'Who is it?'

'Professor Miner?' An American male voice, muffled by the heavy slab of oak that is the outer door.

'Yes?' Her tone is less fearful now, more impatient.

'It's Chuck. Chuck Mumpson, from the plane. I hafta tell you something.'

'Just a moment.' Vinnie stands considering. It must be well past eleven, an impossible hour for a social visit, and she hardly knows Chuck Mumpson. She hasn't seen him since they had tea at Fortnum and Mason's, though he phoned once to report on his genealogical search. (Following Vinnie's advice, he had located a village in Wiltshire called South Leigh – 'They spell it different, like you said they might' – and was planning to visit it.) If she tells him to go away, she can return to bed and get enough sleep to be in decent shape for her nine a.m. appointment at a primary school in South London. On the other hand, if he goes away he may never come back, and she will never know what he has found out about his ancestor the local folk figure.

'I'll be with you in a minute,' she calls.

'Okay,' Chuck shouts back.

Vinnie returns to the bedroom and gets back into the dress she wore to the opera. She pulls a brush through her hair and gives a critical, discouraged glance at her face; but neither it nor her guest seem worth the effort of makeup.

Her first impression of Chuck as he steps into the light is unsettling: he looks ill, sagging, disheveled. His leathery tan has faded to a grayed pallor; his piebald hair, what there is of it, is uncombed; his awful plastic raincoat is creased and mildewed. As she shuts the door of the flat he sways and staggers sideways, then recovers and stands gazing down into the hall mirror in a fixed, dull way.

'Are you all right?' she asks.

'No, I guess not.'

Instinctively, Vinnie steps back.

'Don't worry. I'm not drunk or anything. I'd like to sit down, okay?'

'Yes, of course. In here.' She switches on a lamp in the sitting room.

'Been walking a long ways.' Chuck lowers himself heavily onto the sofa, which creaks under his weight; he is still breathing hard. 'I saw your light, figured you were still up.'

'Mm.' Vinnie doesn't explain that she always keeps the desk lamp on in the study, which faces the street, in order to confound burglars. 'Would you like a cup of coffee? Or a drink?'

'Doesn't matter. A drink, if you've got one.'

'I think there's some whisky.' In the kitchen Vinnie pours a rather weak Scotch and water and puts the kettle on so that she can have tea, wondering what disaster it is that has overtaken Chuck Mumpson.

When she returns, he is still sitting there staring out into the room; he looks wrong and too large for her flat and for her sofa. 'Wouldn't you like to take off your raincoat?'

'What?' Chuck blinks toward her. 'Oh yeh.' He grins weakly. 'Forgot.' He heaves himself up, peels off the stained plastic, and drops down again, looking no better. The jacket of his Western suit has been snapped together wrong, so that the left side is higher than the right, and one point of his collar sticks out at an angle. Vinnie makes no comment on this; Chuck Mumpson's appearance is none of her concern.

'Here you are.'

Chuck takes the glass and sits holding it as if stupefied.

'What's happened?' Vinnie asks, both apprehensive and impatient. 'Is it – your family?'

'Nah. They're all right. I guess. Haven't heard lately.' Chuck looks at the glass of whisky, lifts it, swallows, lowers it, all in slow motion.

'Did you find any ancestors in Wiltshire?'

'Yeh.'

'Well, that's nice.' She adds more milk to her tea, to avert heartburn. 'And did you find the wise man, the hermit?'

'Yeh. I found him.'

'That's very good luck,' Vinnie remarks, wishing he would get the hell on with it. 'Lots of Americans come over here to search for their forebears, you know, and most of them don't find anything.'

'Bullshit.' For the first time that evening Chuck speaks with his normal force, or more.

'What?' Vinnie is startled; her china teacup rattles on its saucer.

'The whole thing was bullshit, excuse me. The earl, the castle – My grandfather, he was just shooting me a line. Or somebody shot him one, maybe.'

'Really.' Vinnie affects surprise, though on consideration it doesn't seem strange that Chuck Mumpson isn't descended from the English aristocracy. On the other hand, for her purposes it doesn't matter whether his ancestor the hermit was an earl or not. 'Yes, go on.'

'Okay. Wal, I rented a car from that garage you recommended, and drove down into the country, to this South Leigh. It's not much of a place: old church, a few houses. I checked into a hotel in a town near there. Then I went to the library, asked how I could get to see the parish registers for South Leigh, like you told me, and the tax records. I found a whole mess of Mumpsons, but they weren't anybody special. Farmers, most of them, and none of them was named Charles. It took a hell of a long time. Everything kept being out of commission for different dumb reasons, like for instance it was Thursday afternoon. The whole place just shut down in the middle of the week. All the stores too. Hell, no wonder we've got so far ahead of them, right?'

'Mm.' The last thing Vinnie wants at this time of night is to start an argument about the comparative economic achievements of America and Britain.

'Anyhow, finally this antiquarian society was open. I talked to the secretary, and she found what looked like it might be the right place, a ways out in the country. Her book said a hermit used to live there, back at the end of the eighteenth century. It was on the estate of some people she'd met once, Colonel and Lady Jenkins their name was. So she called them up, and they invited me over. Mind if I smoke?'

'No, go ahead.' Vinnie sighs. Usually she doesn't allow cigarettes in her classroom, office, or home; when she gives a party she asks her nicotine-addicted guests to go outdoors or into another room.

'I keep trying to quit.' Chuck takes out a pack. 'The doctor says I hafta. But I get real crazy without cigarettes. Can't sleep, can't concentrate on anything.' He gives a light false laugh, strikes a match, inhales.

'That's too bad,' says Vinnie, who had often quietly (and on certain occasions noisily) prided herself on never having smoked.

'Ahhh.' A foul, smelly, gray backwash issues from Chuck's mouth. 'Wal, we all gotta go some way.'

With difficulty, Vinnie refrains from remarking that lung cancer and emphysema, according to all reports, are two of the most unpleasant methods of departure.

'Anyhow, I had almost the whole day to kill before I could see Colonel Jenkins. I was hanging round the antiquarian society reading up on the local aristocracy, and I got into a conversation with this archaeologist guy. He's working on a dig outside the town, where there used to be an old village. I mean really old, back in the Middle Ages. For him a couple of hundred years is like yesterday. He was finding some stuff, only the best excavation site they had kept filling up with water. Nobody on his crew could figure out where it was coming from or what to do about it. Wal, that's my line of work; at least it used to be.'

A pained, plaintive note has entered Chuck's voice. Vinnie recognizes it: it is the whistle of self-pity that has so often in the past called Fido to her. Perhaps because she is still a little blurry from sleep, she imagines Fido hearing it too under the sofa where he had been more or less hibernating for the past two months; waking, blinking open his huge mournful brown eyes.

'Wal,' Chuck continues, 'I said I'd go out and look his setup over. Turned out what they'd done was, they'd got one of the pumps hooked up wrong, so most of the water they took out was running right back into that excavation.

'So this guy, Professor Gilson his name is, got his team together, and we moved the pipes, and the water started to go down. I felt real set up with myself. I got my camera and took a load of pictures of them and the site and some of the stuff they'd found. Then we all went and had a beer to celebrate, and then we had lunch in the local pub. Better food than I ever got in my London hotel by a long shot, and a lot cheaper too. I told everybody what I was doing in Wiltshire, and how I was going to locate my ancestor the earl that afternoon. Asshole that I was. I should've known what was coming with my luck.'

'Mm,' Vinnie says. The call is unmistakable now; Fido crawls out from under the sofa to lie at Chuck's feet.

'What I did instead was kinda went back to the hotel and got all spiffed up; I was muddy from the dig, and I wanted to look like I was related to a lord. I was disappointed at first when I saw the Jenkins' place: it wasn't my idea of a castle. No towers or moat or anything. But it was a great big old stone house, over two hundred years old I found out later, with a pediment and columns and sculptures of Roman emperors on the lawn with two-hundred-year-old moss growing on them. And the grass was like Astroturf sprinkled with little flowers. I thought, yeh, this'll do okay. My head was full of blown-up ideas. I knew Colonel and Lady Jenkins had only owned the house for thirty years, so I figured my ancestors must have sold the place sometime. Maybe they were living somewhere else grander, or maybe they'd all died off by now. That'd be too bad in a way, because I wouldn't get to meet them; but then maybe I'd turn out to be the long-lost heir, why not? I mean it could've been like that, right?'

'I suppose so,' says Vinnie, distracted by her vision of Fido, who is now wagging his dirty-white tail and gazing eagerly up at Chuck.

'Only it wasn't. Colonel and Lady Jenkins knew all about it. They took me to see the hermitage down in the woods behind the house. It was what they called a grotto – sort of a natural cave in the rocks next to a stream, built out with cement and pebbles and shells into a kinda little stone room. It had an arched door and one window, and the back walls were dripping wet. It was full of moss and dead leaves and spiderwebs and a couple old pieces of furniture made out of logs with the bark still on, like you see in national parks, y'know.'

'Mm.'

'Of course nobody lives there now, but they said there was a hermit once upon a time. Only he wasn't any lord, he was just some old guy that was hired to stay in the grotto. Rich people used to do that back then, Colonel Jenkins told me, the same way a Tulsa businessman with a ten-acre ranch will buy himself a coupla horses or a few head of cattle: not for profit, just to make the place look good, to decorate it, like. So they bought this guy. The Jenkinses showed me a picture of the grotto, when it was new, in an old book. The hermit was standing in front of it, with scraggy beard and long hair and a droopy straw hat like some old bag lady.'

'Still, there's no proof it was your ancestor,' Vinnie says.

'It was him all right. He was called Old Mumpson, and he got twenty pounds a year and his board, it was all in the book. He couldn't even write, he had to sign his name with an x, he was just a dirty old bum.'

In Vinnie's mind, Fido rises to his legs and places his front paws on Chuck's knee. 'But what about the story your grandfather told you?' she asks. 'About your ancestor being a kind of wise man, and the cloak made out of a dozen kinds of fur?'

'Who knows? It coulda been fur in the picture, you couldn't tell for sure. Colonel and Lady Jenkins'd never heard any of that stuff, though they were interested, said they were going to write it all down. They were real nice to me. They gave me tea and cake and muffins and homemade jam. The jam was kind of a weird green color, but it tasted okay. It was made out of goose berries, whatever they are. And they showed me all over the place and answered all my questions. But I could tell they thought I was a poor dumb jerk, looking for earls in a dirty wet cave in the woods. They're loaded with ancestors themselves, real ones. The house was full of oil paintings of them.'

'That's too bad,' Vinnie says, referring to her own frustration as well as Chuck's.

'It about knocked me out. First thing, I just wanted to get out of there. I drove to London and turned in the car and checked back into that hotel I stayed in before, near the Air Terminal, and all the time I felt worse and worse. I was exhausted, but I couldn't sleep or eat anything or even sit still in the room. Finally

I went out for a walk. Didn't have any idea where I was going, must've walked half over London. Then I thought of you.' He sags back against the sofa and falls silent.

Research has its dangers, Vinnie thinks, looking at him. The study of children's literature, for instance, has revealed to her a number of things she is glad she did not know as a child and is not very glad to know now: for instance, that Christopher Robin Milne's schooldays were made miserable by his association with the Pooh books; or that *The Wind in the Willows* is full of Tory paranoia about the working class. Some adult fantasies, such as Chuck Mumpson's belief in an aristocratic ancestor, might also be better left alone.

'Well, of course it's a disappointment.' Vinnie speaks briskly so as not to encourage Fido. 'But I can't really see why you're so upset. After all, most people don't have ancestors. Some of them don't even have descendants.' Fido turns his head and gives Vinnie a hopeful look. 'I mean, you're no worse off now than you were before.'

'That's what you think.' Chuck gives a suppressed groan that reengages Fido's total attention. 'You don't know what it'll mean for me back in Tulsa. Myrna's relations, they're high-class people: got charts of their family going back to before the Revolution. They've always snooted me. They didn't like what I came from or my language or the kinda jobs I had. Sanitary engineer, Myrna's mother thought that was a dirty word. She told Myrna once it always reminded her of sanitary napkin.'

'Really,' says Vinnie, forming a negative opinion of Myrna's relatives' claims to gentility.

'And her sister, she's a psychologist, got a degree from Stanford University. She said to Myrna the reason I missed my job so bad was my mind was stuck at the age of three, and secretly all I wanted was an excuse to play with my poo-poo.'

'Really.' Vinnie says again, but this time with some indignation.

'After Amalgamated flushed me out it was worse. It was "Wal, Myrna, I always told you so."'

'I suppose everyone has relatives like that,' Vinnie says, though in fact she does not. It was her so-called friends, rather, who had warned her that her husband was still carrying the torch for his former girlfriend and that her marriage wouldn't last – and had later reminded her of how prescient they had been. 'You've simply got to ignore them.'

'Yeh. I try. But Myrna doesn't. When I couldn't find another job she figured her sister was right all along. Thought I wasn't making an effort. Hell, I must've sent out near a hundred enquiries and résumés. But the thing of it is, nobody wants to hire a guy who's fifty - six, fifty - seven. The benefit package is too expensive, and you naturally figure he's past his best effort. Hell, I used to think that way myself.'

'Mm,' Vinnie says, remembering certain meetings of the tenure staff of her department. 'I suppose many people do.'

'After a while I about gave up. I started drinking too much, mostly at night at first, when I couldn't sleep. It was better then. The place was quiet, and I didn't have to talk to Myrna, or watch the maid hustling around, following me all over the house with the damn vacuum cleaner. If I felt real bad, I'd keep at the booze till I passed out. Some days I didn't get out of bed till the middle of the next afternoon. Or I'd get in the car and drive, most of the night sometimes, going nowhere like a goddamn rat out of hell. I mean bat.' Chuck laughs awkwardly. 'So then I was in this smashup.'

'Yes,' Vinnie prompts after a minute, but he does not continue. 'An accident? Were you hurt?'

'Naw; nothing much. I – Never mind. It was bad. I totaled the car, and the cops took me in for DWI. That about finished it for Myrna. She used to like me pretty well once, but after that she didn't even want to look at me. She couldn't wait to get me on that plane. She's ashamed of me now, they all are. Greg and Barbie too.' Fido, triumphant, puts his paws on Chuck's shoulders and enthusiastically licks his broad weatherbeaten face.

'Oh, I don't think – ' Vinnie says, and stops. Maybe Chuck's wife and grown children are ashamed of him; how should she know?

'That's why I didn't go home with the damn package tour. I was sick as hell of London, but I couldn't face Tulsa again. I kept thinking, the best thing for everybody would be if I never came back. Myrna would carry on, but she'd be relieved really. She'd be free, and she'd be respectable. There's this developer, this fat guy she sold a big land parcel to for a shopping plaza, that has a crush on her and a lot of dough and big political ambitions. Myrna would take to that: she always wanted me to run for some office. Her family would've put up the cash, only I couldn't see it; I never liked politicians. But this guy's also got born-again Christian principles, and real conservative fundamentalist backing. He could marry a widow, but not a divorcee.

'Anyhow, I kept thinking, if I was out of the way Myrna could cut her losses. Wal, y'know, I couldn't get the hang of the traffic over here, those tinny little cars they have that you can't hardly see coming at you, and the crazy two-story buses. I tried to remember to look in the wrong direction and do everything backward, but I couldn't concentrate on it. A couple of times it was a damn near thing. I didn't care; I used to think, okay, why not – I've had a pretty fair life.'

A strange impulse comes over Vinnie, and impulse to emulate Fido, to embrace and comfort this large stupid semiliterate man. She's irritated at herself, then at him.

'Oh, come on. Don't overdramatize,' she says to both of them.

'Naw. That's what I thought, honest. Only once I'd talked to you in that restaurant, and 'specially after I located South Leigh, I started to feel better. I thought, okay, maybe I'll show them yet. I'll come home with fancy English relations, a castle, maybe a set of those plates they sell here, with gold rims and a coat of arms painted on them. Hey, look, I'll say to Myrna, I'm not such a worthless bum as you thought. Let's tell your mother and your pissfaced sister about *my* ancestors, honey. And the kids, they'd like it too. It'd be something I could give them, make it up to them, kinda. This afternoon down in South Leigh I mailed Myrna a card; it said, "Hot on the trail of Lord Charles Mumpson the First, looks like Grampa was right." Wait till she finds out. I'll never hear the last of it. Myrna loves a good joke, 'specially if it's on me.'

'Does she,' says Vinnie, forming an even more negative opinion of Chuck's wife.

'Runs in the family. Her Uncle Mervin, he'll work a gag to death. All he needs is a fall guy.'

'Really.' It is a long time since Vinnie has heard this term. She imagines Chuck as a fall guy, a kind of debased stuntman made to perform over and over again for the amusement of his wife's relatives. 'Well, if it's going to be like that, don't tell them.'

'Yeh - uh.' He sits forward. 'Naw. What about the goddamn postcard?'

'Say it was a mistake, a false lead. For heaven's sake, Chuck, show a little initiative!'

'Yeh. That's what Myrna always tells me.' He sags back into the cushions, hugging Fido to him.

'All right then, don't show a little initiative,' Vinnie says, losing her temper. 'Lie down in the street and let a bus run over you if you want to. Only stop being so damn sorry for yourself.'

Chuck's square, heavy jaw falls; he stares at her dumbly.

'I mean for God's sake.' She is breathing hard, suddenly enraged. 'A white Anglo-Saxon American male, with good health, and no obligations, and more money and free time than you know what to do with. Most people in the world would kill to be in your shoes. But you're so stupid you don't even know how to enjoy yourself in London.'

'Yeh? Like for instance?' Chuck sounds angry now as well as hurt, but Vinnie cannot stop herself.

'Staying in that awful tourist hotel, like forinstance, and eating their terrible food, and going to ersatz American musicals; when the town is full of fine restaurants, and you could be at Covent Garden every night.'

Chuck does not respond, only gapes.

'But of course it's none of my business,' she adds in a lower tone, astonished at herself. 'I didn't mean to shout at you, but it's very late, and I have to get up early tomorrow and visit a school in Kennington.'

'Yeh. All right.' Chuck looks at his watch, then stands up slowly; his manner is injured, stuffy, formal. 'Okay, Professor, I'm going. Thanks for the drink.'

'You're welcome.' Vinnie cannot bring herself to apologize further to Chuck Mumpson. She shows him out, washes his glass and her teacup and sets them to dry, gets back into her flannel nightgown, and climbs into bed, noting with disapproval that it is ten minutes past twelve.

But instead of slowing into sleep, her mind continues to revolve with a clogged, grating whir. She is furious at herself for losing her temper and telling Chuck what she thinks of him, as if that could do any good. It is years since she flamed out like that at anyone; her usual expression of anger is a tight-lipped, icy withdrawal.

She is also furious at Chuck: for waking her up and depriving her of necessary sleep, for failing to discover interesting folkloric material in Wiltshire, and for being so large and so unhappy and such a hopeless nincompoop. He and his story remind her of everything she dislikes about America, and also of things she dislikes in England: its tourist hotels, its tourist shops, its cheapened and exaggerated self-exploitation for the tourist trade, the corruption of many of its citizens by American commercial culture into an almost American illiterate coarseness ('I wish I wuz a seagull, I wish I wuz a duck . . .').

Why is she being persecuted by transatlantic vulgarity in this awful manner? It really isn't fair, Vinnie thinks, turning over restlessly. Then, hearing the silent whine in this question, she glances mentally round for Fido. But her imagination, usually so vivid, fails to manifest him. Instead she sees a dirty-white long-haired dog trailing Chuck Mumpson down Regent's Park Road in the fog from streetlamp to streetlamp, panting at his side in the fuzzy yellow glare as Chuck unsuccessfully tries to hail a taxi.

Fido's infidelity astonishes Vinnie. For the nearly twenty years of his life in her imagination he has never shown the slightest interest in or even awareness of anyone except her. What does it mean that she should now so vividly picture him following Chuck Mumpson across London, or making sloppy canine love to him? Does it mean, for instance, that she is really sorry for Chuck, perhaps even sorrier than she is for herself? Or are he and she somehow alike? Is there some awful parallel between Chuck's fantasy of being an English lord and hers of being – in a more subtle and metaphysical sense, of course – an English lady? Might there be someone somewhere as impatiently scornful of her pretensions as she is of his?

Almost as uncomfortable to contemplate is the idea that she is partly responsible for Chuck's illusion – and, as a logical consequence, for his disillusion. As if she'd ever promised that he would turn out to be a scion of some noble family! She began to lose her cool again.

Well, after all, as he said, it might have turned out that way: there are plenty of nincompoops in the British aristocracy. Vinnie's memory provides her at once with examples, including that of Posy Billings, who is not at all what Vinnie means by 'a real English lady'. On the other hand, Rosemary Radley, annoying as she sometimes is, has to be granted the epithet. Rosemary would never have flown into a rage as Vinnie did this evening; she wouldn't have made Chuck Mumpson feel even worse and more stupid that he felt when he arrived. If she had been there to witness the scene, she would have turned her face away as from any unkindness, any unpleasantness.

And what about Chuck himself? Though he probably has only the most conventional idea of what a lady is, he will hardly think of Vinnie as one now. He will think instead that she is uncontrolled and unfeeling – in other words both messy and cold.

Of course in a way it doesn't matter, Vinnie tells herself, turning over in bed, since she will obviously never see Chuck Mumpson again. She has thoroughly depressed and offended him, and presently he will go and do himself in – or, far more likely, lumber on back to Oklahoma – with disagreeable if fading memories both of England and Professor Miner.

It is 12:39 by the poison-green light of the digital alarm clock. Vinnie sighs and turns over in bed again, causing her nightgown to twist itself round her into a tight, wrinkled husk that resembles her thoughts. With an effort she revolves in the opposite direction unwinding herself physically; then she begins to breathe slowly and rhythmically in an attempt to unwind herself mentally. One-out. Two-out. Three-out. Four –

The telephone rings. Vinnie startles, lifts her head, crawls across the bed, and gropes in the dark toward the extension, which rests on the carpet because her landlord has never provided a bedside table. Where the hell is it?

'Hello,' she croaks finally, upside down and half out of the covers.

'Vinnie? This is Chuck. I guess I woke you up.'

'Well yes, you did,' she lies; then, abashed at the sound of this, adds, 'Are you all right?'

'Yeh, sure.'

'I hope you're not still upset about what I said. I don't know why I blew up like that; it was rude of me.'

'No it wasn't,' Chuck says. 'I mean, that's why I called. I figure maybe you were right: maybe I oughta give London another chance before I lie down in front of a bus . . . Wal, so, if you're free sometime this week, I'll take you anywhere you say. You can pick a restaurant. I'll even try the opera, if I can get us some decent seats.'

'Well . . . ' With considerable difficulty Vinnie rights herself and crawls backward into bed, dragging the telephone and the comforter with her. 'I don't know.' If she refuses, she thinks, Chuck will go back to Oklahoma with his low opinion of London and of Vinnie Miner intact; and she will never see him again. Also she will miss a night at Covent Garden, where 'decent seats' cost thirty pounds.

'Yes, why not,' she hears herself say. 'That'd be very nice.'

For heaven's sake, what'd I do that for? Vinnie thinks after she has hung up. I don't even know what's on this week at Covent Garden. I must be half asleep, or out of my mind. But in spite of herself she is smiling.

6

Woman's like the flatt'ring ocean,
Who her pathless ways can find?
Every blast directs her motion,
Now she's angry, now she's kind.

John Gay, *Polly*

May in Kensington Gardens. The broad lawns are as velvet-smooth as the artificial turf of a football field, and ranked tulips sway on their stems like squads of colored birds. Above them brisk sudden breezes pass kites about a sky suffused with light. As Fred Turner crosses the park, one landscape vista after another fans out before him, each complete with appropriate figures: strolling couples, children suspended from red and blue balloons, well-bred dogs on leash, and joggers in shorts and jerseys.

Fred is on his way across town to a drinks party (he has learned not to say 'cocktails') at Rosemary Radley's. Near the Round Pond he checks his watch, then sits down on a bench to wait a few minutes so that he won't arrive too soon. He has offered to come early and help, but Rosemary wouldn't hear of it. 'No, Freddy darling. I want you just to enjoy yourself. You mustn't get here a minute before six. The caterers will do everything – and Mrs Harris, of course.'

For Fred has won their argument, and Rosemary has hired a cleaning lady. He hasn't met her yet, but she sounds great. According to Rosemary she is a hard worker and very thorough: she gets right down on her hands and knees to wax the floors. What's more, she doesn't talk Rosemary's ear off about her husband or her children or her pets: she has no children or pets, and she is long divorced from her drunken husband.

Insisting that she hire Mrs Harris is one good thing Fred has done for Rosemary. She has done much more for him: she has transformed him from a depressed, disoriented visiting scholar to his normal confident self. His earlier anomie, Fred realizes now, was occupational. Psychologically speaking, tourists are disoriented, ghostly beings; they walk London's streets and enter its buildings in a thin ectoplasmal form, like a double-exposed photograph. London isn't real to them, and to Londoners they are equally unreal – pale, featureless, two-dimensional figures who clog up the traffic and block the view.

Before he met Rosemary, Fred didn't really exist for anyone here except a few other academic ghosts. Nor did London really exist for him. He wasn't so much living in Notting Hill Gate as camping out there so that he could walk every day to the British Museum and sit before a heap of damp-stained, crumbling leather-bound books and foxed pamphlets. Now the city is alive for him and he is alive in it. Everything pulses with meaning, with history and possibility, and Rosemary most of all. When he is with her he feels he holds all of England, the best of England, in his arms.

He has wholly recovered from the panic that seized him last month in Oxfordshire, when he was frightened by a few topiary birds and a too-vivid memory of the novels of Henry James into condemning an entire society. His distrust of Edwin and Nico remains – homosexuals have always made Fred uneasy, maybe because so many of them have propositioned him. But he feels fine about Posy Billings and William Just; he looks back on his moral indignation that night as priggish and provincial.

Among Rosemary's long-married friends, he has found, arrangements like that of the Billings are common. More often than not, husbands and wives have agreed to allow each other a discreet sexual freedom, which their friends then take for granted. Everyone knows who Jack or Jill is 'seeing' at the moment, but no one mentions it – except maybe to ask whether Jill would rather have her husband or her lover invited to some party. The couples remain amicable, sharing a house or houses, concerned for each other's welfare and that of their children, giving dinners and celebrating holidays together. As Rosemary says, it's a much more civilized way of coping with passionate impulse than the American system. One avoids open scandal, and also the tantrums of self-righteous possessive jealousy – which, as she points out, usually end in dreadful messy scenes, economically vindictive divorces, and the destruction of homes, children, reputations, and career. Nor is there any of the frantic defensiveness and public display of the so-called open marriages that she's seen among actors in the States (and Fred, now and then, among graduate students) – and which, as Rosemary remarks, never work anyhow. 'It's exactly like leaving all the doors and windows open in a house. You get nasty drafts, and very likely you'll have burglars.'

The strain on Fred's budget has also been eased – at least temporarily – by a loan from the Corinth University Credit Union, arranged by mail with some difficulty. With luck it will just about last until he leaves. He can go to restaurants with Rosemary now without always ordering salad; he can buy her the flowers she loves so much. If he has to skimp and save for the next year or so, hell, it's worth it.

Only two things currently trouble Fred. One is the fact that his work on John Gay isn't getting on too fast. When he was first in London depression slowed him down; now euphoria does so. In comparison to the world outside its walls, the BM seems even more oppressive than before. He is irritated at having to show his pass on entry to the suspicious guard, who ought to know him by now; and he detests having his briefcase searched on departure. He is even more impatient when the volumes he wants turn out to be in the deposit library at Woolwich (two days' wait) or in use by the other readers (one to four days' wait). And the less often he goes to the Bowel Movement the worse it gets, since books placed on temporary reserve by Fred or any other reader fail to rise again on the third day and are, with infinite slowness, returned to their dark tombs.

Though he knows this rule, several days more and more often intervene between Fred's visits to the library, and more and more of the books he has been using have now disappeared somewhere within the system; the slips come back marked NOT ON SHELF, DESTROYED BY BOMBING, or – most infuriatingly of all – OUT TO F. TURNER. Meanwhile there is so much to do in London, so many plays and films and exhibitions to see with Rosemary, so many parties. The hell with it, Fred tells himself almost every day. He'll learn a lot more about British theatrical history and tradition by listening to Rosemary and her friends than sitting in a library – something that, Christ knows, there'll be time enough for back in Corinth.

The other weight on Fred's mind is heavier, though it consists not of a stack of books but of an airletter almost lighter than air. The letter is from his estranged wife Roo, and is her first in four months – though Fred has written her several times: asking her to forward on his mail, returning her health insurance card, and inquiring for the address of a friend who's supposed to be at the University of Sussex. Roo, as he might have expected, hasn't forwarded the mail, acknowledged the card, or provided the address.

But now, like a tardy bluebird of peace returning late to a deserted ark after three times forty days and nights, this blue airletter has flapped across the ocean to him. In its beak it holds, no question about that, a fresh olive branch.

. . . The thing is [Roo writes] I guess I should have told you I was going to put your cock and the rest of those pictures in my show. I'm not sure I would have taken them down even if you raised hell – but I didn't need to make it such a big surprise. If it'd been me, I mean say my pussy, I probably would have freaked out too. Kate says I must have been pissed off at you for something, maybe for being so wound up with school. Or maybe I was scared I wouldn't have the guts to show the photos if you said not to.

Anyhow I wanted to tell you this, okay?

Nothing much happening here, the weather is still foul. I won a second prize in the Gannet contest for those 4-H pictures, Collect $250 but do not pass Go. The emergency room ones were better but not so heartwarming. Everybody misses you. I hope London is fabulous and you're getting your shit together in the BM. Love, Roo.

Here, four months late, is the letter Fred had imagined and desired so often during the dark emptiness of January and February – the letter he had so often fantasized finding on the scratched mahogany table in the front hall of his building, tearing open, laughing and shouting over, cabling or telephoning in response to. He had imagined changing the sheets on his bed, meeting Roo's plane –

Faced with this evidence of Roo's contrition and candor – he has never known her to tell a lie, even when it would have been socially convenient – Fred has to admit that he had accused her falsely. If Roo had had an affair he would have been the first to hear about it, from her. She was telling the truth when she said she never had anything to do with those two other cocks in the exhibit except to photograph them. More than likely they belonged to an old friend of hers from art school who is now working in New York, and his homosexual lover. In fact, she was guilty of nothing worse than bad taste.

But in Rosemary's world bad taste is not nothing: it is the outward and visible sign of an inward and spiritual flaw. Fred remembers her saying only the other day, when discussing a mutual acquaintance with Posy: 'I can understand how anyone might get carried away temporarily by Howie's looks, and his talent, but what I don't see is how Mimi could possibly bring herself to move into that dreadful Kentish Town flat of his, with the plastic ferns and the bullfight posters.' 'And those frightful gold-flocked shiny curtains, like cheap Christmas ribbon,' Posy agreed. 'She must be out of her mind.' Their unspoken assumption was that anyone who would choose such a spuriously natural (the ferns), spuriously virile (the posters), and spuriously elegant enviroment must be false in other ways as well. And probably, Fred thinks now, recalling his own impressions of Howie, an ITV television executive, Rosemary and Posy are right.

Roo's bad taste, of course, is of a different sort, crude rather than phoney – some but not much better. Fred, like Mimi, had been carried away by the looks and talent; that was what Rosemary would have said. Yeh, maybe. But however bad her taste, Roo is a person he used to care for, and his wife. The least she deserves from him now is the truth. But how can he give her that? 'Thanks for your letter, it was great to hear from you, but I'm in love with a beautiful English actress, have a good day.' Not wanting to write these sentences, or some mealy-mouthed equivalent of them, Fred has put off answering Roo's letter for nearly two weeks. He doesn't want to have to think about her now, nor does he want to think ahead to his return to Corinth. When they do meet he will apologize and explain; she will understand. Or maybe she won't understand. It almost didn't matter; nothing matters now except his passion for Rosemary Radley.

Possession hasn't decreased the intensity of Fred's desire. If the excitement of the chase is over, it has been replaced by the knowledge that his triumph must be brief. Joe and Debby Vogeler, typically, take the pessimistic view. Wasn't it really a mistake to get so involved emotionally, Debby wondered, when he knew he had to leave England next month? Since she hadn't exactly framed this remark as a question, Fred didn't have to answer it; but inwardly he swore a strong No. Not for the first time, he thought that the Vogelers' world-view was as limited and narrow as the triangular house that had been allotted to them here, as if by the poetic justice of some supernatural real estate agent.

But then Joe and Debby don't know Rosemary or Rosemary's London. He had told them about Vinnie Miner's party and others that had followed – how amazing Rosemary was, what interesting people she knew, how friendly most of them were. The Vogelers, however, remained sceptical.

'Sure, maybe they were cordial to you for a few minutes,' Debby said, as the three of them sat in the triangular house on a wet dark afternoon, among a clutter of Sunday papers and plastic toys. 'They learn nice manners in their schools. But will you ever see any of them again? That's what it's really all about. When we were first here, Joe and I went to lunch with this elderly writer that his aunt knows, in Kensington, and everybody was very pleasant and said how they hoped to see us again, but nothing ever came of it.'

'It was Jakie.' Joe gestured at his son, who was sitting on the floor in a fuzzy white coverall stained with baby food, tearing up the *Observer Magazine*. 'We shouldn't have brought Jakie.'

'Jakie was perfectly good,' Debbie protested. 'He didn't cry or anything. And he didn't really hurt that old cat, he was just playing. I don't know why they all got so excited.'

'They didn't like him sitting on your lap at lunch, either,' Joe said.

'Well, too bad. What was I supposed to do with him? I bet they wouldn't have liked it any better if Jakie had been crawling round the floor. Besides, he could have hurt himself on that lumpy antique furniture.'

They don't understand, Fred thought then, resolving that he would arrange for Joe and Debby to meet Rosemary soon (and in the absence of Jakie). When they see her, or at least when they get to know her and her friends, he thinks now, sitting on the bench in Kensington Gardens, they'll understand how great most of them are.

After all, even for him it had taken time. Now, though, the doubts he had had earlier – and in a weak moment hinted at to Joe and Debby – seem to him shameful, mean-spirited. It would have been cowardly to hold back from Rosemary because the more he cares for her now, the more he will miss her later. Nothing could be worse than having to say to himself for the rest of his life: 'Rosemary Radley loved me, but I couldn't really get into it because I didn't like some of her friends – because she lived too expensively – because I knew I was leaving London in June and might not see her again for almost a year.'

If Joe and Debby couldn't understand that yet, Rosemary and her world certainly would. Fred remembers an interview in the *Times* last week with a friend of Rosemary's named Lou, in which he announced that he'd told his agent to turn down all television and film offers because he had a chance to play Lear for two weeks in Nottingham. 'Where the theatre is doesn't matter; the length of the run doesn't matter,' he was quoted as declaring. 'When you get a chance like that nothing else counts.'

'What an old dear Lou is,' Rosemary had added, after reading this passage aloud to Fred. 'Of course, I rang up directly to congratulate him. Really, I told him, he should have had the part long ago, he's a marvelous actor, a real genius. And there's no need to go on a diet, I said, why on earth shouldn't Lear be fat? He probably was fat, and his riotous knights too, from eating and drinking so much and using up all Goneril's provisions. You don't hear about them working or exercising, do you? I said to him, "Lou darling, you're quite wrong, you mustn't try to take off a single ounce; you know your voice is always better after a good meal." I only wish I could say the same, but it's just the reverse for me. As soon as I start working again I'll have to starve myself, look at all this flesh.' Rosemary lifted the edge of a kimono embroidered with blue and gray chrysanthemums to reveal a pink, deliciously rounded thigh and hip. 'No, Freddy darling, I didn't mean . . . Oh, dearest . . . Ahhh . . . '

Thinking of this moment again, and the moments that followed it, Fred rises from the bench and, as if drawn by a magnetic force, strides toward Chelsea.

Even before most of the guests have arrived it's clear that Rosemary's party is a success. The weather is fine, the house looks great: the window boxes and the stone urns by the steps have been scoured clean and overflow with white geraniums and satiny ivy; through the open French doors the back garden is a haze of green. Inside, too, everything glows – at least everything that's visible to guests: Fred, looking for a place to put some coats, opens the door to Rosemary's bedroom, then slams it hastily on chaos. Evidently Mrs Harris was so busy downstairs that she didn't have time for anything else.

Descending the stairs again, Fred looks down into a scene that resembles a commercial for some luxury product: the perfectly elegant party. The double drawing room is a dazzle of flowers and light and stylishly dressed people. Many of Rosemary's friends are good-looking, many are well known, and some are both. There are only a few who rather spoil the effect, who would never have been cast if this were in fact a commercial. For instance, little Vinnie Miner, who is wearing one of what Rosemary calls 'her Mrs Tiggy-Winkle costumes' – all starched white cotton and fuzzy pale-brown wool like the fur of some small animal. Fred recalls with amazement how formidable she had seemed to him only a few months ago. Already he has absorbed the view of Rosemary and her friends, that Vinnie, though clever and likeable, is a bit of a comic turn, with her passion for Morris dancing and children's books and everything British that is quaint and out-of-date.

'Vinnie, hello. How are you?'

'Fine, thank you.' Vinnie tilts her head up to look at Fred.

'What a big party, I didn't realize. And how are you? How is your book on Gay coming along?'

'Oh, very well, thanks,' Fred lies.

'That's good. How nice the house looks! It's really amazing. I suppose it's all due to Mrs Harris?'

'Well, more or less.'

'Excuse me, please, ma'am. 'Scuse me.' Behind him Fred hears for the first time in his life an American accent: loud, flat, nasal. Is that how he sounds to everyone here, every damn time he opens his mouth? 'Here you are, Vinnie.' A large balding man in late middle age, got up like an American country-and-western singer in cowboy boots and a suede jacket with a fringe, hands her a glass. 'One dry sherry, honey, like you ordered.'

'Oh, thank you,' Vinnie says. 'Chuck, this is Fred Turner, from my department in Corinth. Chuck Mumpson.'

'Wal, howdy.' Chuck extends a broad, fleshy red hand.

'How do you do,' Fred replies guardedly. His immediate thought is that Chuck's accent and costume, so exaggerated and inappropriate to this party, are assumed – and maybe his name as well. This is not an American, but one of Rosemary's theatrical friends amusing himself by taking on a role – something he has learnt that actors occasionally do when they have been too long between engagements.

'Heard a lot about you.' Chuck grins.

Fred asks himself what this man, whoever he is, has heard. Probably that he is Rosemary's lover. 'I haven't heard anything about you,' he says, consciously listening to his own voice for the first time since adolescence. The pronunciation is similar, he decides, but the tune different. In fact, over the past few months Fred has taken on, not a British accent, but a British intonation and vocabulary. Almost unconsciously, he has begun to imitate the characteristic melody of British speech, with its raised final notes; consciously, so as to be understood, he now uses terms like *lift, lorry,* and *loo* instead of *elevator, truck,* and *bathroom.*

'Chuck's from Oklahoma,' Vinnie says.

'Oh, yeh?' There is still an edge of doubt in Fred's voice – though it seems unlikely that Vinnie would conspire in some actor's impersonation. 'I've never been there, but I saw the movie.'

'Haw-Haw.' Chuck gives a genuine, or very plausible, western guffaw. 'Wal, it isn't much like the movie, not any more.'

'No, I guess not.' This uncomfortable conversation is interrupted by the arrival of more guests, and more behind these. Soon the long high-ceilinged room is thronged. The twin chandeliers, their prisms newly polished, scatter light and echo the tinkle and splash of liquids poured into the crystal, of high-pitched laughter and exclamation.

The miracle wrought by Rosemary's new cleaning lady does not pass unnoticed. All her friends compliment her on it, including some who had speculated earlier that maybe Mrs Harris wasn't as wonderful as Rosemary and Fred made out.

Neither of them might know whether a house had been properly cleaned, some suggested; others said that Mrs Harris sounded too good to be true. Now that the evidence is before them they take another line.

'Perhaps it's a bit too perfectly cared for,' Fred overhears one guest remark. 'One almost feels one's in some National Trust property.'

'Yes, exactly,' agrees her companion. 'I expect Mrs Harris is one of those types who have an absolute obsession with cleanliness. People like that of course they're a little bit crazy,' continues this friend, whose own flat could have used a visit from Mrs Harris. 'Rosemary had better be careful she isn't murdered in her bed one day.'

This sort of spite on the part of Rosemary's friends is a new development. In the past, envy of her prettiness, fame, high spirits, charm, and income – television, even British television, pays well – has always been tempered by compassion for her disorderly living conditions and her history of romantic disaster. Though widely courted, she always seemed to end up with the least stable and attractive of her many suitors. Moreover, the men she chose were usually married, and presently they either returned to their wives or, worse, left both the wife and Rosemary for some other woman. Thus, however pretty and successful she might be, her friends have been able to love and worry about Rosemary, her acquaintances to like and pity her. But now that she has a perfect house in Chelsea and a handsome, apparently unattached young lover, many of them cannot forgive her.

Besides making ominous predictions, some of the guests tonight try to pump Fred about Mrs Harris. As Rosemary had remarked, it isn't easy to find a good English-speaking charlady in London. 'You wait and see,' she told Fred. 'There will be plenty of people who'll want to lure Mrs Harris away, even though they call themselves my friends. You mustn't tell anyone about her, even what her days are; promise me, darling.' Fred, thinking it unnecessary, had nevertheless promised. Now he sees that Rosemary was right. More than one of her guests, when she is out of hearing, makes pointed inquiries: How much does Mrs Harris ask? Does she have a free day? Fred replies truthfully to both questions that he doesn't know. An elderly actress called

Daphne Vane, who had starred with Rosemary in *Tallyho Castle* until her pathetic on-screen death from pneumonia last season, is especially persistent.

'I'd really like so much to meet Mrs Harris,' Daphne murmurs in the wistful, breathy manner that made her a romantic heroine of the stage and screen half-century ago. 'She sounds like the genuine article, and one comes across that so seldom now. I had so much hoped that she would be at the party – helping, you know.' She glances round the room, making great play with her famous feathery eyelashes.

'She's not here,' Fred tells Daphne. 'Rosemary didn't ask her to serve; she says Mrs Harris isn't very presentable.'

'No? Well, one can't have everything, can one? But perhaps she's below in the kitchen?' Fred shakes his head; if he had nodded, he suspects, nothing would have prevented the unworldly, ethereal-looking Daphne from scooting down the back stairs to the basement. 'Do you know what her days are?'

'I'm not sure, no.'

'What a pity.' Daphne gives him the sweet, condescending smile she might give some village idiot; then, without seeming to move, she floats off into another conversation.

In fact Fred knows very well that Mrs Harris comes on Tuesdays and Fridays. Since he can't visit Rosemary then – and, after one attempt, she won't come to his flat. Though he did all he could to make the place attractive, his love hardly spent five minutes there. Drawing her pale fur coat more closely about her, she declared it 'absolutely freezing' and 'frightfully unromantic', and declined even to sit on the sofa bed where Fred had pictured her lying half naked.

Efficient as she is, Mrs Harris has her defects. She can't bear to have anybody 'underfoot' while she cleans. She also refuses to answer the phone and take messages, claiming that it puts her off her work. Occasionally she will snatch up the receiver, shout 'Nobody'ome!' and bang it down again; more often she justs lets it ring. Some of Rosemary's friends view this as another sign of dangerous battiness; Fred's own suspicion is that Mrs Harris is more or less illiterate. That would help to explain why such a hard-working and reliable woman hasn't been able to find a better paying job.

In support of the battiness theory, however, it has to be said that Mrs Harris won't answer the door. Last Tuesday afternoon, when Fred discovered that he was free that evening after all, because the Vogelers' baby had a cold, and he wasn't able to reach Rosemary on her private line or get a message through to her answering service, he decided to go to the house. He knocked, rang, and called out her name; but though he could hear muffled noises within, nobody came. Finally he scribbled a note on the back of an envelope.

As he pushed back the letter-flap, Fred was aware of motion inside the house. He stooped to the newly polished brass slot, and got his first glimpse of Mrs Harris at the other end of the darkened hall, scrubbing the floor on her hands and knees: a shapeless middle-aged woman in a shapeless cotton skirt and cardigan, her hair tied up in a red kerchief. At the sound of the note falling and skidding on the marble tiles, she swiveled her head round, scowling – or maybe her expression had long ago set into a mask of suspicious ill-temper.

'Hello!' Fred called. 'I've left a note for Lady Rosemary – could you give it to her please?' Mrs Harris didn't answer, but turned her back and resumed scrubbing.

Though she won't speak to callers, Mrs Harris does talk freely to her employer, and at length. Her conversation isn't the burden Rosemary feared, but a source of entertainment. Mrs Harris' doings and remarks – maybe somewhat edited or heightened – are now regularly relayed by Rosemary to all her friends. Mrs Harris believes that looking at the full moon through glass makes you loony, unless it's over your left shoulder. She eats Marmite and golden-syrup sandwiches to build up her blood. She goes to the greyhound track and bets on dogs with names that begin with S for Speed or W for Win. 'Them races are fixed, see, everybody knows that,' she has confided to Rosemary. 'But there's clues.'

Mrs Harris' specialty, however, is gnomic, usually sour pronouncements on current events and famous persons. She dislikes all politicians and most members of the royal family, though she remains loyal to 'Princess Margaret Rose' in spite of the scandals about her love life. 'Misguided she was, is all, misguided and betrayed by that midget.' Fred can hear Rosemary repeating this latest *mot* even now, mimicking her charlady's voice – rough and cockney, with a hint of boozy sentiment – and indicating with a broad gesture the supposed height of Lord Snowdon.

Fred has even found himself telling Mrs Harris stories to friends like the Vogelers. In spite of her ill-temper, she has been gradually assimilated to his image of England. Most American visitors – like, say, Vinnie Miner – are attached mainly to the antique, the picturesque, and the noble aspects of Britain. Fred's love is wider-ranging: essentially it comprehends whatever had been hymned in song or told in story. In his present high mood he embraces even what he might deplore in America. Slag heaps remind him of Lawrence, pawnshops of Gissing; the pylons that deface the Sussex hills suggest Auden, the sooty slums of South London, Doris Lessing. In his mouth, canned plum pudding tastes of Dickens; to his ear, every overweight literary man sounds a little like Dr Johnson. Seen through these Rosemary-tinted glasses, Mrs Harris is a character out of eighteenth-century literature: a figure from the subplot of some robust comedy illustrated by Hogarth or Rowlandson. Fred not only appreciates her eccentricities, he takes a proprietary pride in them. After all, if it hadn't been for him she'd never have been hired.

The doorbell sounds again. Fred goes to answer it and sees that Joe and Debby Vogeler have arrived, and that they have brought with them – against his instructions – their baby.

'The sitter never showed up,' Debby says in an aggrieved voice as soon as Fred opens the door, as if this were somehow his fault. 'So we had to bring Jakie.'

'He's been very good all the way here,' Joe says in a more conciliatory tone. 'He's been sleeping mostly.' The baby is suspended against Debby's bosom in a sort of scruffy blue canvas hammock, with his fat legs sticking out on both sides and his bald head lolling against her neck. Debby is got up to match in a washed-out denim jacket, a long ruffled denim skirt, and clogs, as if she were about to appear on *Prairie Home Companion*. Joe wears his usual shabby-academic costume: thick spectacles, worn cord jacket, pilled and sagging gray turtleneck jersey, scuffed loafers. Though Fred is used to seeing the Vogelers in clothes like these, his friends strike him as deliberately and even aggressively ill-dressed for the occasion. In one respect, however, they are improved: the fine weather has restored their health, and for the first time none of them has an obvious cold.

'Come on in; great to see you,' he says, trying to sound enthusiastic. 'You can put the baby upstairs, in one of the spare bedrooms. I'll show you –'

'Certainly not.' Debby wraps her arms protectively around Jakie.

'That wouldn't be right,' Joe explains, looking at Fred as if his suggestion could only issue from an almost criminal ignorance. 'I mean, suppose he was to wake up alone in a strange room? It could be a serious trauma.'

'Well, okay.' For days Fred has been looking forward to the meeting between his old friends and his new love. Now it is with a sense of foreboding that he leads the Vogelers across the drawing room to where Rosemary stands in the bay window beside a flowering orange tree; like it, she is a fragrant spring vision in pale-green many-pleated glistening silk.

'Oh, how nice!' she cries, putting out her soft white ringed hand. 'And you've hiked here all the way from North London, isn't that amazing.' To Fred this appears a pointed reference to their footwear; but Joe and Debby smile, even grin, charmed already.

'Yeh, and we brought our baby,' Debby says, half belligerent, half apologetic.

'Oh yes, I see you did.' Rosemary laughs lightly, managing somehow to convey that it would have been politer not to mention this. 'But Fred, darling, you haven't got your friends anything to drink.'

'Sorry.' Fred goes to order a gin-and-tonic for Debby and – since there's no beer – Scotch-and-water for Joe. Most of the guests, as is usual at warm-weather London parties, are drinking white wine.

On his way back across the room, Edwin Francis stops him. 'If you have a moment, Fred,' he says, gesturing with a cream cracker overloaded with pâté, 'I'd like to speak to you.'

'Sure, just a sec.' Partly because he doesn't much like Edwin, Fred is always careful to be agreeable to him. Having delivered the Vogelers' drinks and introduced them to other guests (Rosemary has drifted away), he follows Edwin into the hall.

'It's about Mrs Harris.' As if casually, Edwin steps onto the bottom tread of the gracefully curving stairs. He is still shorter than Fred, but the difference is now less pronounced.

'Yes?' Fred thinks that Edwin too – whom Rosemary loves and trusts – wants to swipe her cleaning lady.

'I'm becoming a bit concerned about her. She sounds, how shall I put it, such a dominant personality. So suspicious of everyone and everything. And possibly somewhat unbalanced as well. I'm really quite worried about her effect on Rosemary; she seems to be falling more and more under Mrs Harris' influence, if you see what I mean.' Edwin frowns, increasing his resemblance to a plump, solemn child. 'Repeating all her ignorant reactionary opinions, well, you know.'

'Mm.' Fred is familiar with this complaint. Some of Rosemary's friends have put it to him more strongly. 'Rosemary's far too impressed with that woman,' they complain. 'Believes everything she says.'

'You know, for a certain sort of actor it's an advantage to have a rather indefinite sense of self. It makes it much easier to get into various parts. But it can be a problem, too.'

'Oh?' Fred says, expressing doubt. He has no idea what Edwin is waffling on about; Rosemary obviously has a very definite, and wonderful, self. Her ability to mimic Mrs Harris doesn't preclude this.

'I mean, a joke's a joke, right?'

Fred, without enthusiasm, agrees that a joke is a joke.

'But that sort of thing can go too far. What worries me is, I'm off to Japan to lecture next week, I'll be away over a month, and if anything should happen – I mean, with Nadia in Italy and me in Japan and Erin due to go to the States for that film, and poor Posy immured in Oxfordshire with those boring little girls – Well, I won't really feel comfortable unless I know someone's looking out for our Rosemary. So it had better be you.'

'Um,' says Fred, who greatly dislikes the phrase 'our Rosemary' and the idea of sharing his love with Edwin – or for that matter with anyone.

'Promise now. Because she's very delicately balanced, you know. She can get a bit frantic – into rather a difficult state – sometimes.'

Repressing his annoyance, Fred nods. He has never seen Rosemary 'frantic' or in a state; also, he doesn't agree with Edwin that Mrs Harris is imposing her opinions on her employer.

On the contrary, he's begun lately to suspect that Rosemary is imposing her opinions on – or rather, attributing them to – Mrs Harris. It's not just that the lines are too good; they also have a way of echoing Rosemary's less harmonious opinions. For instance, she is rather bored by the ballet; Mrs Harris, according to her, describes it as 'all them faggots jumping and 'opping.' Rosemary despises the current government; Mrs Harris thinks they are a lot of bloody crooks.

Also, more and more often, Mrs Harris gives Rosemary reasons for doing what she wants to do anyhow – or not doing what she doesn't want to do. Recently a late-night variety show was organized in aid of a famous old East London theater. Rosemary declined to participate, not because it would be inconvenient, unprofitable, and exhausting, but because, she claimed, Mrs Harris had told her that 'them people in 'ackney got no use for fancy stage acting, they'd rather watch the telly.' What they really wanted was a kiddies' playground – her niece who lived out that way knew all about it. Anyhow, Mrs Harris – as reported by Rosemary – said, the whole thing was a sell. 'Most of the cash those types take in'll stay in their own pockets, always does with them charity things.' At a lunch party last week Rosemary's friend Erin protested these statements, and tried, with considerable patience and charm, to make her reconsider. She refused to listen. 'Please, darling, don't tell me any more nonsense,' she cried, giving her silvery laugh and spearing a profiterole with the silver tines of her fork (she adores what she calls 'wicked desserts'). 'You don't know the least thing about Hackney, and neither do I. But I know Mrs Harris is right about it; she's always right.'

Feeling annoyed at Edwin, Fred leaves him and returns to the party. He sees at once that the Vogelers are not mixing, but standing by themselves in a corner trying to soothe Jakie, who has begun to make a whimpering squeaking noise, like a stuck drawer.

'Let me take him now, it's my turn,' Joe says, checking his watch. With Fred's help, the surprisingly heavy baby and his canvas sling are transferred to his father's back, where the whimpering and squeaking resume. 'Maybe if he had a cracker or something.'

'Sure.' Fred finds a plate of canapés and scrapes the caviar off one.

'Great. There you are now, ducky.' Jakie reaches for the cracker and stuffs it clumsily into his mouth, shedding crumbs over Joe's jacket.

Asleep and slumped against Debby's chest, Jakie was relatively inconspicuous. Now, because of his father's greater height and his own wakefulness, he is a visible presence in the room – and a rather grotesque one, Fred thinks; from the front Joe seems to have two heads and four arms. Something has got to be done about the Vogelers. He remembers his mother's rule that you mustn't allow anyone at a party to stand alone talking to the people they came with; you must try to separate them.

Taking the easiest first, he leads Debby away and presents her to a woman novelist as 'an American feminist'. (It doesn't much matter what you say when you make introductions, his mother has also advised him, but you've got to say something, to provide a conversational opening.) Then, to avoid parading his two-headed, four-armed, crumb-littered friend across the drawing room, Fred introduces Joe to a drama critic, TV personality, and notorious bore who is leaning against the mantelpiece nearby, under the pretense that Joe is a visiting American anxious to know what shows to see in London. All right, that should do it, he thinks, and goes off in search of Rosemary and a drink.

But the Vogelers remain on Fred's conscience, and he keeps checking to see how they are doing. Twenty minutes later Debby seems to be circulating, but Joe is still trapped in the same spot talking – or rather listening – to the same man. He is clearly not engrossed; in a gesture Fred remembers well from graduate school, he has pushed his spectacles up onto his head. Aloft on his untidy mouse-brown hair, they suggest another pair of eyes fixed upon higher and more philosophical objects of contemplation.

Altogether, in his shabby clothes, with Jakie wiggling on his back, Joe is an incongruous figure at Rosemary's party. He looks especially out of place in front of the white marble fireplace, with its curved mantel crowded with framed photographs, engraved invitations, objets d'art, and tall vases of hothouse flowers doubled into a profusion of bloom by the big gilt-framed rococo mirror. The baby is awake and restless, waving his small fat arms about, grabbing at the air or at his father's hair.

As Fred prepares to go to Joe's rescue there is a movement in the crowd. Joe steps back to let one of the caterer's men pass, and Jakie's clutching baby hand finds a silver vase full of tall white iris and candy-hued freesia. Fred waves, shouts a warning, but this serves only to startle Joe and alert the other guests, many of whom glance up in time to see the vase totter, tip, and fall, sending a torrent of water and foliage over the famous drama critic. As in a thunderstorm, the associated sound effects follow a second or two later: loud curses, shocked exclamations, and infantile howling.

'I'm really sorry about the Vogelers' baby,' Fred says to Rosemary as she closes the door behind her last guests.

'Sorry? Darling, it was wonderful. It made my party.' Rosemary's elaborately piled hairdo has slipped from its moorings, her lipstick has been kissed away by departing friends, and there is a smudge of mascara below her left eye. Fred finds it sentimentally piquant, like the symbolic tear drawn on the cheek of a mime.

'Oh, the expression on Oswald's face!' A ripple of laughter. 'The way his nasty shiny red hair came unstuck from the crown of his head and hung down in strings; of course one always suspected he must be combing it forward into those silly bangs to disguise a bald patch. And there's no damage done at all, really.' Rosemary surveys the drawing-room. The caterers have removed all the glasses and china, and rearranged the furniture; nothing remains of the party but an irregular damp patch on the pale-beige carpet and a few scattered flower petals. 'Perfect.' She sinks onto a low cream-colored sofa heaped with silk tapestry cushions.

'I thought you were furious.' Fred laughs too, recalling Rosemary's startled outcry, her repeated loud apologies and expressions of shock and concern, her demand that he fetch more and more towels to wipe Oswald off – But of course, she's an actress.

'Darling, never for a moment.' She rests her tumbled pale-gold floss of hair against the back of the sofa and holds out her arms. 'Ahh. That's lovely.'

'Lovely,' Fred repeats. A wave of euphoria lifts him. He has never, he thinks, been happier than he is at this moment.

'Really, darling.' Rosemary disengages herself from a second long kiss. 'It was one of the nicest moments of my life. When I think of what Oswald said when I was in *As You Like It* – that was years ago, of course, but I still positively shudder whenever I remember it. And the awful things he's written about poor old Lou over the years. And even Daphne, if you can imagine. He was so beastly clever about her being too old for romantic parts once that she almost left the stage. It was wonderful for all of us to see him looking so ridiculous.' She begins to laugh again. 'And what a silly vulgar fuss he made, far worse than the baby.' Another freshet of giggles. 'And the best thing was, almost everyone saw it.'

'Yeh, they sure did.' The commotion caused by Rosemary's solicitude takes on another meaning. 'You took care of that.' Fred runs his hands down his love's back, feeling the deep lace border of her chemise below the gauzy dress, the rounded convexities below that, marvelling again that anyone so slight, soft, and silky could have so much purpose and will. In a few moments, he decides, he will get up and lower the lights.

'Well, naturally,' Rosemary agrees. She smiles slyly, charmingly. 'But I had help. What a wonderful baby! But you mustn't invite it again, darling, once is enough.'

'I didn't invite the baby. I told Joe and Debby not to bring him. Honestly.'

'I believe you. Honestly.' Rosemary mimics Fred's intonation, then gives him a butterfly kiss. 'One can't trust these hippies, they'll do anything.'

Not wanting to break the mood, Fred refrains from explaining that the Vogelers are not hippies. He kisses Rosemary; she laughs softly and presses him closer. 'Or say anything,' she adds; a little puckered frown appears between the feathery golden arches of her brows. 'Your friend Joe, for instance' – her intonation subtly but definitely conveys that Joe is not and never will be her friend – 'your friend Joe says that you're going back to the States next month. I told him he was quite mistaken, that you'll be here till the autumn at least.'

'I'm afraid he's right,' Fred says reluctantly. 'I've got to start teaching summer school at Corinth June twenty-fourth. I told you about that,' he adds, uncomfortably aware that he hasn't mentioned it lately, or even wanted to think about it.

'Oh, nonsense,' Rosemary purrs. 'You never said a word. Anyhow, you can't leave then, we've got far too many lovely things to do. There's Michael's play opening, and I'm getting tickets for Glyndebourne. And then in July we start shooting the outdoor scenes for next season's *Tallyho Castle* in Ireland – you'll adore that. We always have such a good time: we stay at this perfectly delicious inn run by two of the most amusing old characters. They do marvelous meals: fresh salmon sometimes, and real Irish soda bread and scones. And of course it usually rains half the time, and then we're free all day long.'

'It sounds great,' Fred says. 'I wish I could come. But if I canceled out of summer school they'd be really pissed.'

'Who cares?' Rosemary ruffles his hair. 'Let them rage.'

'I can't. Everyone in the department would think I was irresponsible. It'd count against me in the tenure vote, I know it would.'

'Oh, darling.' Rosemary's voice softens. 'You're worrying about nothing. That's not the way it goes in the world. If you're good, they'll always want you. Look at Daphne: she's absolutely impossible in so many ways, but directors are still falling all over themselves to cast her.'

'It's not like that in academia,' Fred says. 'Not in America, anyway. And anyhow, I'm not a star.'

Rosemary does not contradict him. Instead she sits up away from Fred, with her fair, fine hair tumbling over her face. 'You're not really going back to the States next month,' she says, with a half lazy, half threatening whispery intonation like the sound of his grandfather stropping a razor.

'I have to. But it's not because I want –'

'You're tired of me.'

'No, never –'

'You've been planning to leave me all along.' The blade is almost sharp now.

'No! Well, yeh, but I told you –'

'It was only an act with you, the entire time.' Her voice slashes at him.

'No –'

'Everything you've said to me, all those pretty speeches – ' A half sob.

'No! I love you, oh, Jesus, Rosemary – ' Fred pulls her back to him with force. 'Don't talk like that.' He rocks her against him, feeling again how soft she is, how feathery and fragile.

'Then you mustn't frighten me.'

'No, no,' he says, kissing her face and neck through the light, fallen curls.

'And you're not really going away next month, are you?' she whispers presently. 'Are you?'

'I don't know,' Fred whispers back, wondering what the hell he can possibly tell his department if he doesn't. Rosemary's crinkled pale-green silk dress has been pushed down over her creamy shoulders; his hands are on her naked breasts. 'Oh, darling – '

But she twists sideways, wrenches away. 'You think I'm a little fool, don't you,' she says, her voice shaking in a way Fred has never heard before. 'You think I'm a – what is it you said of your cousin, an easy pushover.'

'No – '

'And when you walk out on me next month and go back to America, you think that will be easy too.'

'Jesus God. I don't want to go back to America. But anyhow, it's not forever. Next summer – ' Fred reaches for Rosemary again, but as he does she stands up abruptly, causing him to lose his balance and flop across the white silky cushions of the sofa.

'Very well,' she says, in a tremulous version of what Edwin Francis calls 'her Lady Emma voice'. Fred has heard this voice before, but not often, and only directed to recalcitrant taxi drivers or waiters. 'In that case I'm afraid I must ask you to leave my house now.' She walks gracefully to the front door, and opens it.

'Rosemary, wait.' Fred hastens after her.

'Out.' Though she speaks through a tangled curtain of pale hair, and with one lovely breast still half exposed, her tone is chilly and formal. 'Out, please.' She points the way at a downward angle, as if speaking to a dog or cat.

Years of training in good manners now work to Fred's disadvantage. Without consciously willing it, he steps across the threshold.

'Listen to me a moment, damn it – ' he begins, but she slams the door on him.

'Wait! This is crazy, Rosemary,' he shouts at the glossy

lavender paint, the brass dolphin knocker. 'I love you, you know that. I've never been so happy in my life . . . Hey, Rosemary. Rosemary!' There is no answer.

7

[Vinnie Miner] is no good,
Chop her up for firewood.
If she is no good for that,
Give her to the old tomcat.

Old rhyme

For the first time this spring Vinnie is ill, with a heavy wet cold that threatens to develop into bronchitis. She lies huddled in bed this mild showery morning under the down-filled comforter, with a flannel-covered hot-water bottle at her feet, and a roll of loo paper by her head because she has used up all the tissues in the flat. The hot-water bottle is lukewarm, and the carpet by the bed is littered with damp wads of paper, offensive to her natural tidiness; but she is too weary and depressed to do anything about either discomfort.

Vinnie's cold is an embarrassment to her as well as an irritation. She has always declared and believed that she never gets ill in England – that the viruses and headaches that afflict her in Corinth cannot follow her across the Atlantic to what she feels is her ecologically correct habitat. What is she to say now?

Even worse, she suspects a psychological source for her affliction, though she doesn't believe in such things. She was perfectly well until last week, when she heard that her grant wasn't going to be extended for another six months. It wasn't this news that made her ill – she hadn't really counted on more support – but a letter in the same mail from an acquaintance in New York: a well-known scholar, one of the judges who had awarded Vinnie her original grant. This woman now wanted to dissociate herself from the recent decision. 'I *really* tried,' she wrote, punctuating her words with a heavy black underline. 'But I simply *couldn't* convince them. I'm afraid it wasn't any help that Lennie Zimmern is on the committee this year – and by the way, I should tell you that *lots* of people consider his remarks about you in the *Atlantic* most unfair.'

In other words, Vinnie thinks, unwinding another length of scratchy paper and blowing her small inflamed nose, if it hadn't been for L. D. Zimmern, I might have had another six months in London. Paranoid ideas, like little invisible bats, unhook themselves from behind the tops of the drawn shutters and flitter about the darkened bedroom, occasionally landing on something with a squashy plop. Why is she being persecuted this way by Professor Zimmern, who doesn't even know her? What has he got against her?

In the view of Chuck Mumpson, there is no use looking for a personal motive. Chuck's views are known to Vinnie because, feeling that she had to talk to somebody, she had selected him as the least likely among her acquaintances to gossip, to judge, or to pity her. Two days ago, over the phone to Wiltshire, she gave him a slightly scaled-down version of Zimmern's continuing persecution, speaking of herself as merely 'very annoyed' and of Zimmern as 'malicious'.

'I d'know, Chuck said. 'It doesn't hafta have been malicious, necessarily. Those things happen sometimes kinda by accident. You know how it is: a guy wants to make a point, so he hasta pick an example. He doesn't always think how there's a person and a career behind what he's attacking. Anybody can do that kinda thing. I've done it myself, when I was younger. There was this superintendent once at a waste treatment plant in East Texas that wasn't testing right; I'll never forget his face. I didn't have it in for him, no way. I didn't even know he existed, so to speak, but I about ruined his life. It could be that way with your professor.'

'You may be right,' Vinnie said into the telephone – her usual response to statements she prefers not to challenge. And of course it's possible that Zimmern has nothing against her personally. His prejudice, rooted no doubt in an unhappy and deprived childhood, may be against childhood itself; or against women in academia, or against folklore, or some combination of all these. But that doesn't exonerate him. Like all offenders, he must be judged by his actions. And condemned. And punished.

If the world were just, Professor Zimmern and not Professor Miner would now have this cold, this headache, this stuffed-up nose, raw throat, honking cough, and general sense of ill-being. Vinnie imagines him afflicted with all her symptoms, only more so if possible, lying in bed at this very moment under a heavy matted mound of blankets (she denies him her down comforter; they are uncommon in the States anyhow). He is in his New York apartment, which she locates in one of those sooty cavernous stone buildings near to and owned by Columbia University. (Actually, L. D. Zimmern lives on the second floor of a brownstone in the West Village.) He has been ill off and on for weeks, Vinnie imagines – for months – ever since he wrote that revolting article. Since he spoke and voted against renewing Vinnie's grant, his symptoms have been unremitting.

Zimmern doesn't know it yet, but he is going to get worse. His cold will turn into bronchitis, his bronchitis into viral pneumonia. Soon he will find himself in one of those huge cold impersonal New York hospitals, at the mercy of impatient anonymous doctors, overworked nurses, and sullen, underpaid, non-English-speaking aides, many of them addicted to drugs. Zimmern will lie in a semi-private room, not getting any better, and his friends, if he has any friends, will grow tired of visiting him. Vinnie can see this room clearly: its dirty window with a view of stained brick walls; its two high stiff white beds, the other one occupied by a coughing, snoring, incontinent, and smelly elderly man; its TV set, always turned to a game show. She can see Zimmern in his washed-out seersucker hospital gown, weakly pushing aside a frayed months-old copy of *Time* magazine, reaching for the plastic cup on the bedtray and sucking up stale lukewarm New York water through a plastic caterpillar straw.

No one has been to see Vinnie in her illness either, mainly because she hasn't encouraged anyone to come. Whenever she's depressed or under the weather her instinct is always to conceal herself until the skies clear. Even a very young and pretty woman is less charming with a bad cold, and Vinnie knows from the bathroom mirror that she looks plainer than ever now; her disposition, too, is at its worst. And though her acquaintance in London is extensive, it is largely composed of what she thinks of as fair-weather friends (with the exception perhaps of Edwin Francis, but Edwin is now in Japan). Fond as she is of them, she has the belief – or delusion – that their reciprocal fondness is the result of their natural sweetness of temper and general good will rather than of profound affection; she fears to test it under adverse conditions. If her friends weren't put off by seeing her as she is this morning, they would probably pity her; and though she sometimes feels sorry for herself, Vinnie hates to be pitied by others, even in her own imagination.

When this danger begins to threaten, her usual resource is to dwell on the misfortunes of others and actively pity them. If she had caught this cold when the weather was consistent with it, early last month, she could have profitably contemplated the tribulations of Chuck Mumpson: his unemployment, his lack of inner resources, his third-rate education, his depression, his loneliness, his dislike of London, and the discovery that his wise and noble English ancestor was really an illiterate pauper. A few weeks later, and she could have added his deprived childhood and his delinquent adolescence.

Chuck's 'folks', he told Vinnie during their first dinner together, were uneducated, 'dirt-poor', and none too law-abiding. 'My dad – he was no good. He spent most of his adult life in jail, if you want to know the truth. And he never gave a hoot in hell for any of us.'

As near as Vinnie can make out, Chuck and his too many brothers and sisters grew up in a kind of rural slum, with an overworked and frequently drunken mother. 'She wasn't a bad woman,' Chuck explained, forking up an overload of Wheeler's sole véronique and parslied potatoes (his table manners leave something to be desired). 'Only she wasn't home much to keep an eye on us. And when things weren't going too good for her she got pissed, and then she slammed us around.'

Unsupervised, half neglected, Chuck and his siblings began to get into trouble as soon as they hit puberty. 'I ran with a rough crowd for a while. By ninth grade we were cutting school pretty regular to hang out in pool rooms and go joy-riding.'

'What's that?' Vinnie asked, marveling at the inappropriateness of Chuck and his history to the old-fashioned British elegance of Wheeler's.

'Aw, you know. You find some car with the keys left in, or you jump start it, and a bunch of you go for a ride. Take the heap out onto the highway and see what it'll do; maybe pick up some girls and drag to the next town. Then when you think the cops might be onto you, or the gas runs out, you shuck it. Or sometimes we'd borrow a couple of horses instead.

'When we got tired of that, we started breaking into empty houses. For the thrill mostly; but if you saw something you wanted, you took it. I used to go for the cameras. Then one time the house wasn't empty; we had to run for it. Afterward nobody wanted to admit he was chicken, so we started talking big, how next time we would bring a gun, and if anybody gave us trouble we would fucking blow him away. One of the guys, he knew where his dad kept a pistol. Wal, we were lucky. Before we could get shot up, or hurt somebody, the law caught up with us. Most of the guys got probation, but they took a look at my family and sent me to a home for bad boys.'

'Hell, no, that didn't reform me.' Chuck continued with his story later, as he and Vinnie sat in the stalls at Covent Garden waiting for *Fidelio* to begin. 'Are you kidding? You ever seen one of those places? . . . Naw, what stopped me was the war. I got drafted, and went to the Pacific with an engineer's unit. If it wasn't for that, I probably would have gone on the way I was going; maybe ended up like my dad. Only after the war, killing a guy didn't look so cute anymore. It was bad enough when it was some Jap that would've got you first if he could. You get home, you hear some old buddy talking, how he went into this all-night gas station maybe, with a gun, and there was this guy. He didn't intend him any harm, but he thought he heard a noise in the back room, he panicked. Pretty soon the guy's laying there dead, and your buddy took the rest of his life away, for what? For maybe a couple hundred dollars. That wasn't for me, y'know?'

'I see what you mean.' Vinnie looked around the great opera house, with its multiplication of shaded lamps and crimson velvet, its festooned golden tiers of balcony – and then, with a sense of the collision of worlds, back at Chuck in his plastic raincoat and leather string tie. 'So you went straight,' she remarked.

'I guess you could say that.' Chuck laughed awkwardly. 'Anyways, after I was discharged I didn't hang around home for too long. I had the GI Bill, and the tests said I was smart enough for engineering college, so I thought, hell, why not.'

'Why not,' Vinnie echoed, marveling at the long fuse of chance that had blasted this unhappy jobless ex-delinquent from rural Oklahoma into the seat next to hers at Covent Garden. She felt a rush of condescending pity, and congratulated herself on her good luck in being born to educated, affectionate, sober, and solvent parents.

In the days that followed that evening at the opera, however, Chuck gradually became less pitiable. Because he was bored and miserable, he was willing to go anywhere, eat anything, and look at anything Vinnie suggested. Sometimes he seemed to enjoy it, or at least find it interesting. After *Fidelio*, for instance, he remarked that it sure wasn't much like real life, but maybe we'd all be better off if when things went wrong we stood around and screamed for a while. His grandad used to do that, he said. 'When he got really riled up he'd stop whatever he was doing and just cuss everybody and everything for maybe ten, fifteen minutes, till he was out of breath.'

Somewhat to Vinnie's embarrassment, Chuck insisted on paying for everything they did together, and thanking her for it as well. From the start he has had a wrong idea of her as helpful and kindly – a misconception born on the flight to London, when all she was really trying to do was protect herself from having to talk to him, and confirmed when she made a few simple suggestions about genealogical research. 'You think I'm a nice person, but I'm not,' she occasionally wants to say, but refrains.

Apart from his misunderstanding of her character and motives, Vinnie decided presently, Chuck wasn't really stupid so much as badly educated – hardly educated at all in her sense of the word. But at least he was willing to learn. Since he'd read practically nothing, she decided to start him at the beginning, with the classics of children's literature: Stevenson, Grahame, Barrie, Tolkien, White. She bought him the books to ensure that he had decent editions, and to make some sort of return for the dinner and theater tickets he kept buying her.

Going with Chuck to the best current plays, films, concerts, and exhibitions, Vinnie of course risked meeting some of her London acquaintances. And indeed, on only their third excursion – to the National Theatre – they ran into Rosemary Radley. Vinnie quailed inwardly as she introduced Chuck, and took him off as soon as was reasonably polite. His subsequent comment was predictable: 'A Lady, is she? Wal, anyhow, I got to meet one real aristocrat over here. Handsome gal, too.'

But Vinnie was astonished when at a lunch party a few days later Rosemary, without any appearance of irony, regretted that she had rushed her 'amusing cowboy friend' away so fast, and declared that she positively must bring him to her house the following week. Vinnie said she would try, at first resolving not to. She might not think all that much of Chuck, but she wasn't going to take him to a Chelsea party to be laughed at. But then, Chuck probably wouldn't notice if someone like Rosemary was laughing at him; and if she was showing him London, shouldn't he see more than just its tourist attractions?

So again Vinnie broke her rule about not mixing English and American acquaintances: she took Chuck to Rosemary's party, hoping that it would be large and various enough to muffle his impact somewhat. To her surprise, his Western costume and Western drawl were an instantaneous hit. Though he explained that he hadn't worked on a ranch since he was a kid, the British clustered round him, inquiring in sentences bristling with invisible quotation marks how exactly one went about roping and branding cattle, and whether there were still many Red Indians on the range. 'I adore your Mr Mumpson,' Daphne Vane, the actress, said to Vinnie. 'He's definitely the real thing, isn't he?' And Posy Billings, pronouncing Chuck 'awfully amusing,' declared that he and Vinnie must come to stay with her soon in Oxfordshire. Vinnie realized that over here Chuck wasn't a banal regional type, but original, even exotic – just as, for instance, a Scots sanitation engineer in a kilt would be in New York.

Chuck's London season was brief, however. Ten days after Rosemary's party he decided to return to Wiltshire, largely because of something Edwin Francis had said. Instead of sympathizing with Chuck's disappointment over Old Mumpson, Edwin had congratulated him. 'Fascinating! A real Hardy character, he sounds. You're so lucky; most of my forebears are dreary beyond words, all lawyers and parsons. You *must* find out more.'

'I've been thinking,' Chuck told Vinnie later. 'I figure Mr Francis has a point. I oughta learn all I can about the old guy.

After all, he was family, whatever else he was.'

So, leaving most of his possessions with Vinnie, Chuck departed. She gave him a book for the train journey and packed him a lunch – well, why not? He'd certainly bought her enough meals in the last few weeks, and British Rail food is famously dreadful. Besides, by now – at least in Chuck's view – they are friends. Many of Vinnie's acquaintances, she is irritatingly aware, suspect that they are also lovers, in spite or even because of her perfectly truthful statements to the contrary.

In all the years she has been coming to England, Vinnie has never made love with an Englishman. Of course her previous visits have been brief, a few weeks at the most. This time, however, she had rather hoped for an adventure; and she had, as always on these trips, recast her fantasies to feature British intellectuals rather than American ones. Not of course that she really expected a romantic interlude with any of these well-known dons, critics, folklorists, or writers. But she certainly hadn't come all the way to London to make it with a sunbelt polyester American left behind by a two-week guided tour, an unemployed sanitary engineer who wears a transparent plastic raincoat and cowboy boots and had never heard of Harold Pinter, Henry Purcell, or William Blake until he was fifty-seven years old and she told him about them. To be suspected unjustly of such a connection causes Vinnie much social discomfort – and also, it must be admitted, a certain amount of irrational pique. Of course she'd turn Chuck down if he made a move, but why hasn't he done so? Either because he forsees her response – unlikely, since he isn't the intuitive type – or because, though he likes her, he finds her unattractive.

The whole situation was beginning to make Vinnie cross and uncomfortable, and she was therefore positively glad to see Chuck leave London. She quite enjoyed imagining him traveling down on the train to Bristol, where he would pick up his rental car: a large red-faced American in a cowboy hat and a fringed leather jacket, eating her excellent ham sandwiches and, to the surprise of the other first-class passengers, reading Jacobs' *English Fairy Tales*. But now that he's gone, though Vinnie doesn't much like to admit it, she misses him. She almost looks forward to the frequent phone calls in which he reports on his research and thanks her for sending on his mail. Most of this seems to be concerned with business: as far as she can tell there has been almost nothing from his wife or his children. Nevertheless, on the phone Chuck sounds in reasonable spirits, sometimes almost cheerful.

Since Chuck is no longer a useful object of pity, Vinnie, lying in bed with her nasty cold, considers pitying Fred Turner. Certainly he seemed miserable enough the last time she saw him.

Lately, Fred hasn't been at any of the parties Vinnie has attended. She met him instead at the British Museum, just before the descent of her cold. It was the first time in weeks that she had gone there, for most of her research is complete and she dislikes the Reading Room – especially in the spring and summer when all the tourists and lunatics come out and it becomes intolerably stuffy, and the staff (perhaps understandably) is harrassed and grumpy.

She was crossing the wet cobbled forecourt after a sudden spatter of rain when she saw Fred sitting under the portico eating a sandwich. Her first thought was that as a single man on a fairly generous study leave he should have no need for such economies. Either he didn't want to wrench himself away from his research for more than a few minutes, or – more likely – the purchase of theater tickets, flowers, and expensive meals for Rosemary Radley had greatly depleted his bank account.

Fred's handsome countenance wore a melancholy, ill-fed expression which brightened only slightly when he saw Vinnie. He invited her to join him on the slatted bench, but agreed only dully with her praise of the day, though the scene before them resembled a British Air travel poster: whipped-cream clouds sailed overhead, the trees were sprinkled with a shiny confetti of new leaves, and the courtyard steamed and glinted with rainbow fragments of light.

'Oh, I'm okay,' he replied to her query, in tones that suggested the reverse. 'Maybe you know, Rosemary and I aren't seeing each other any more.'

'Yes, I heard that.' Vinnie refrained from adding that so had all her London friends, not to mention *Private Eye*. 'I understand she was upset because you have to go back and teach so soon.'

'That's about it. But she thinks – she acts like I've betrayed her or something.' Fred crumpled and uncrumpled his damp paper bag, banging his first into it in an angry way. 'She thinks it'd be easy for me to stay here if I wanted. Damn it, you know that's not true.'

Vinnie assented emphatically. In case he might be thinking of some such move, she pointed out that his sudden and unexcused withdrawal from the Summer School faculty would annoy and inconvenience a great many people at Corinth University; she began to list these people by name and title.

'You don't have to tell me,' Fred interrupted. 'I explained all that to her. Rosemary's a wonderful woman, but she just doesn't listen. When she doesn't like what you're saying she just fucking doesn't listen, excuse me.'

'That's all right.'

'Christ, I'd stay here if I could. I love her, and I love London,' he exclaimed, shedding crumbs of peanut-butter sandwich. 'I don't know what more I can say.'

'No,' Vinnie agreed, sympathizing with one of Fred's passions. 'It's always so hard to leave. I know.'

'But why is she being so goddamned unreasonable? We were going to have such a great time together this month, we had tickets to Glyndebourne . . . I never said I was going to be in England forever, or anything like that. I didn't lie to her. I told her a long time ago I had to go back in June – hell, I know I did.' Fred shook his head while running one hand through his wavy dark hair, a gesture both of puzzlement and of self-reassurance. For the first time, Vinnie saw in him what she had often seen in Rosemary Radley: the assumption of very good-looking persons that as they pass through life they are entitled to take – and to leave – whatever they choose when they choose. In both of them it was the stronger for being largely – in Fred's case perhaps wholly – unconscious.

'Maybe she'll get over it.'

'Yeh. Maybe,' he replied in a dead, unconvinced voice, frowning at the pigeons that had begun to gather. 'Right now she won't see me, or talk to me on the phone, or anything. Oh, okay.' He dropped a crust from the bag onto the pavement; the fat gray birds jostled and pecked. 'She'd better get over it fast; I'll only be around another three weeks.'

'I certainly hope she does,' Vinnie said, though in fact it mattered nothing to her.

'Me, too.' A kind of geological tremor passed over the stormy, handsome landscape of Fred's face. 'Listen, Vinnie,' he added, controlling the threatened volcanic erruption. 'You know Rosemary pretty well.'

'I wouldn't say that.'

'Well, anyhow. You see her all the time. I was wondering . . . Maybe if you were to talk to her.'

'Oh, I don't think – '

'You could explain about summer school; how I can't just walk out on it.' Fred scattered the rest of his half-eaten sandwich, causing a further invasion of pigeons, dozens of them it seemed, flapping and swooping from all directions.

'I really don't think I could do that.' To protect her stockings, Vinnie kicked a particularly intrusive lavender-gray bird away with the side of her shoe.

'She'd listen to you, I bet. All right, get lost! There isn't any more, for Christ's sake.' He stood up, lifting a loaded briefcase. 'Please, Vinnie.'

Vinnie rose too, and retreated several steps from the crowd of pigeons. She looked at Fred Turner standing on the porch of the British Museum, waiting for her answer in a clutter of equally demanding iridescent birds, with his tall athletic figure thrown off-balance by overloaded feelings and an overloaded briefcase. At that moment she realized that he had enrolled himself in the class of persons (usually but not always ex-students) who take it for granted that Vinnie will write them recommendations, give them letters of introduction to colleagues abroad, read their books and articles, and take an interest in their personal and professional happiness. Typically, the fulfillment of any such request does not discharge the obligation, but rather recharges it, just as the use of an automobile recharges its battery. The academic relation of protéger to protégé is a closed electrical circuit not subject to the law of entropy; often it sends out sparks until death.

For Vinnie, one of the advantages of being in England is that she can escape most of these parasites (though a few, of course, have pursued her by mail). Now here is Fred, who has elected himself her protégé simply because they are in the same department, and in the same foreign city, and she is a quarter-century older. And also probably because, quite without having intended it, she is in a sense responsible for his present situation. She was on the department committee that granted him a study leave, and she had invited him to the party at which he met Rosemary Radley.

Sighing, Vinnie told Fred that if the opportunity arose she would try to talk to Rosemary. She had little expectation of succeeding in this assignment, and privately wished that she might have no chance to carry it out. Since she became ill the next day, that wish was granted, though not in a very pleasant manner. But as Vinnie has often noted, both in folklore and in real life, that is the way with most wishes.

Perhaps Fred is somewhat pitiable at the moment, Vinnie thinks as she lies in bed with her lukewarm hot-water bottle, but he is not really the right sort of person for her to contemplate. In the long run, there is no reason to feel sorry for him. He is young, healthy, handsome, smart, well-educated, and – though Vinnie has no intention of ever telling him this – regarded in the English Department as a comer. Right now he feels sore and disoriented because Rosemary has thrown him over, but he will recover. Many other women will love him; his career will steadily advance; and unless he is struck by a car or a deadly disease or some other form of lightning his whole life will be irritatingly fortunate.

Whereas Vinnie is alone, and will probably always be alone. When she is ill, as now, there will never be anyone to listen sympathetically to her symptoms and bring her fresh-squeezed orange juice without being repelled by her appearance or smearing her with condescending pity like glaucous gooseberry jam. She is fifty-four years old; she is going to get older. And as she gets older she will be ill more often and for longer periods of time, and no one will really care very much.

Fido, or Self-Pity, who has been half dozing beside Vinnie for nearly three days, thumps his feathery tail on the comforter, but she shoves him away. Though she has a perfect right to be sorry for herself now, she knows how perilous it is to overindulge it. To go on feeding and petting Fido, even to acknowledge his existence too often, will fatally encourage him. He will begin to grow larger, swelling from the breadth and height of a beagle to that of a retriever – a sheepdog – a Saint Bernard. If she doesn't watch out, one day Vinnie will be followed everywhere by an invisible dirty-white dog the size of a cow. Though other people won't be able to visualize him as she does, they will be subliminally aware of his presence. Next to him she will look shrunken and pathetic, like someone who has accepted for all time the role of Pitiable Person.

'Go away,' Vinnie says to Fido in a half-whisper. 'This is just a bad cold, it'll be gone soon. Get off my bed. Get out of my flat. Go find Mr Mumpson, why don't you?' she adds suddenly aloud, visualizing Chuck alone in the depths of the country, without friends, searching among faded dusty records for his illiterate ancestors.

In her mind, Fido considers the suggestion. He raises his head, then his chest, from the comforter, and sniffs the air. Then he slides off the bed and makes for the door, without even looking back.

Encouraged, Vinnie pushes away the covers and stands up dizzily. She stumbles into the kitchen, pours a glass of orange juice, and drops a black-cherry-flavoured Redoxon tablet into it. Though an agnostic, she has faith in the power of Vitamin C; like most believers, she worships her god more devoutly when things go ill. Now she downs the fizzy, acid-magenta beverage and returns to bed, blows her nose again, pulls her sleep-mask down and the comforter up, and sinks into a snuffly, headachy, slumber.

About an hour later she is roused by the telephone.

'Vinnie? This is Chuck, in Wiltshire. How're you doing?'

'Oh, all right.'

'Sounds like you have a cold.'

'Well, I do, actually.'

'Aw, that's tough. How bad is it? I'm coming up to London this afternoon, I was hoping we could have supper.'

'I don't know. I've been in bed since the day before yesterday. I'm feeling fairly awful, and I look a wreck.' Vinnie feels no hesitation in telling Chuck this. He isn't important in London or in her life, so it doesn't matter what he thinks. 'God knows how I'll be tonight.'

'I'm sorry to hear that. Tell you what. You stay in bed now and keep good and warm, okay?'

'Okay.' It is years since anyone has told Vinnie to stay in bed and keep good and warm.

'I'll phone you when I get in, about seven-thirty. Then, if you're up to it, I can bring something over for us both to eat.'

'That's very kind of you.' Vinnie has a mental picture of her cupboard and refrigerator, now more or less bare except for three quarts of cold soup. 'But you certainly don't have to. This flat is probably teeming with germs.'

'Aw, I'm not scared. I'm tough.' Chuck guffaws.

'Well . . . All right.'

Vinnie hangs up, flops back into bed, and returns to oblivion.

By eight that evening, when Chuck arrives with beer and a complete Indian takeout supper, enough for at least four people, she feels considerably better. It is only the second time that he has been to her flat, and she is struck again by how out of place he looks there, how large and clumsy and Middle American.

Chuck himself, naturally, is not aware of any incongruity. 'Nice place you have here,' he says, looking toward the bow window, which frames a sweep of London back garden, brilliantly and variously gold and green in the declining sun. 'Nice view. Real pretty flowers.' He gestures at a teapot overflowing with overblown yellow roses.

'Thank you.' Vinnie smiles uneasily, aware that her roses were not bought at a shop, but instead removed at dusk two days ago from various nearby front gardens. This petty theft, her first in nearly three months, occurred the day after she heard the story of L. D. Zimmern and her grant renewal, and – like her cold – may be related to it. 'Let me take that shopping bag,' she says, changing the subject.

'Naw. You sit right there and rest. I'll manage.'

In spite of her doubts, Chuck does manage, warming and serving the supper with skill and dispatch. In her present low mood Vinnie finds his clumsy concern soothing, his plodding conversation almost restful. He had a real productive trip to South Leigh this time, Chuck tells her, putting away two-thirds of the Indian dinner and most of the beer as he talks. 'Y'know, this research, it's not like business. Sometimes you do a hell of a sight better if you don't try to zero in on a problem. You start looking for one thing, you come across something else important by accident.'

'Serendipity,' Vinnie says.

'What?'

She explains.

'Yeh, that's what I said. I didn't know there was a word for it.' Clearly, he feels not much is gained by this knowledge. 'Anyways, I was kind of browsing around in the library down there, y'know?'

'Mm.' Vinnie imagines Chuck as a large cow – no, a bull – roaming the stacks of a provincial library, munching on a page here and there.

'Y'know they have these parish records, who lived in a place, who was christened, and married, and buried there. If you go into the churchyard, you can see some of the names on stones. All those names, and every goddamn one of them was a person. They got born, and were babies; and then they were kids, they learned their lessons and played games. Then they grew up and plowed and milked and cut the hay and ate dinner and drank the local beer at the Cock and Hen; and they fell in love and got married and had children and were sick and well and lived and died. And while all that stuff was going on, Tulsa was just a piece of prairie with buffalo ranging over it, and maybe a few Indians. All these people living down there in South Leigh, and everywhere else in this country, for hundreds and hundreds of years, way back to prehistoric times, and now nobody remembers them any more. They're as extinct as the buffalo. It kinda bowls me over.'

'Yes.' In Vinnie's mind, too, shadowy generations rise up; it is what she often feels about England, that every acre of it, every street and building, is thronged with ghosts.

'Wal, so I got to thinking about my ancestor, that I was so ashamed of. I found out some more about him, not much. He was in the parish register for South Leigh, born 1731,died 1801 aged seventy: "Charles Mumpson, known as Old Mumpson". Kind of a honorary title. Seventy doesn't sound real old to us, but back in those days most folks didn't live so long. The doctors didn't really know anything – Wal, they don't know all that much now either, if you ask me.'

'No,' Vinnie agrees.

'Reaching three score and ten, it was a kind of achievement

then, 'specially for a working man.' Chuck takes another swig of beer. 'He must of had a strong constitution.'

'That's true,' Vinnie says, considering the muscular breadth and bulk of Old Mumpson's descendant.

'Anyhow, what I figure, when Old Mumpson was about my age he probably got past farm work, nobody would hire him any more. His wife had died years back, and his two sons had moved away, maybe gone to America – anyways there isn't any record of them marrying or dying in the county. Wal, there probably wasn't much old Mumpson knew how to do besides farming. So he took this hermit job, instead of going on public assistance. The way I figure it, I oughta be proud of him, 'stead of ashamed, y'know?'

'I see what you mean,' Vinnie says, unconvinced, but reluctant to damage Chuck's reconstruction.

'And then this Oxford University professor I told you about, this guy that's in charge of the dig – Mike Gilson his name is. Mike said to me, "Y'know, you don't have to conclude that Old Mumpson was stupid just because he couldn't read and write. It could be that he never had any education; a lot of country folk were illiterate back then." It could be he really was a kind of local wise man, Mike said, and that's why they hired him. Maybe people did come from everywhere round to ask his advice.'

'Yes, of course that's possible,' Vinnie says, wishing she had thought of this comforting argument herself weeks ago.

'There's a hell of a lot of learning that isn't in books.'

'You may be right.' In Vinnie's opinion, the extent of this unpublished learning is less than is generally claimed.

'Anyways, what I wanted to tell you, it's about Mike partly. I've been spending a lot of time out on the dig, like I told you, taking pictures for him. Then Mike has these aerial photos of the area, from the government. You can find out a lot from those things if you know what to look for: ground water and drainage channels, the old foundations and boundary lines and roads – stuff he hadn't noticed, some of it. It helps if you know some geology. Wal, a couple of days ago Mike said, why didn't I stay on for the summer, join his crew. He can't pay me anything, account of I'm not a British citizen, but he's got this big house not too far from the dig rented for the summer, and there's a real nice furnished apartment empty in what used to be one of the tenant cottages. Mike said I could have that for free, and I could eat with them in the main house whenever I wanted.'

'Really?' Vinnie sits forward. 'And are you going to accept?'

'Yeh; I think so.' Chuck grins. 'Hell, I got nothing better to do. And it's nice down there in the country now. Wildflowers everywhere, and so green. Besides, I kinda dig the dig.' He laughs at his own pun. 'And Mike and his crew, I like their attitude. They work damn hard, but they aren't frantic about it. Mike, sometimes he'll just take the afternoon off to think, go for a long walk. And the students too. Course they don't have to worry about production quotas, or showing a profit. In business you can't ever stand still that way. If you're not getting ahead every goddamn minute you feel as if you're sliding back.'

'Like the Red Queen.'

'Yeh?' Chuck blinks at her. 'What queen was that?'

'In *Through the Looking-Glass*.'

'Oh, yeh? I never read that. You think I should?'

'Well.' Vinnie has omitted *Alice in Wonderland* and its sequel from Chuck's reading list, thinking that they would annoy and baffle him as they do many of her students. But if he is to spend the summer with an Oxford don, perhaps he should prepare himself. 'Yes, probably you should.' She sighs, anticipating the explications that will be necessary if Chuck Mumpson is to read *Alice* properly: Victorian education, Victorian social history, Victorian poetry and parody, chess, developmental psychology, Darwinism –

'Okay, if you think so. Hey, Vinnie. How are you feeling?'

'Better, thanks.'

'That's great. Y'know, I could go for a cup of coffee, if you have one around.'

'No, but I could make some,' Vinnie says, thinking that it is typical of men to believe that all women have a cup of coffee concealed about them somewhere.

'Great.' Chuck follows her into the narrow kitchen, getting in her way while she fills the electric kettle and makes coffee for him and rose-hip tea (high in Vitamin C) for herself.

'Thanks, that's swell. You got any milk?'

'I'm not sure – I might.' Vinnie opens her miniature fridge, which rests on the counter and is of a size that in America would be thought fit only for a student dormitory room. At the moment it is almost totally filled by three quarts of avocado-and-watercress soup made by her from Posy Billings' recipe in *Harper's/Queen* and intended for a luncheon party tomorrow that she will have to cancel if she doesn't feel any better.

In order to look for the milk, Vinnie lifts out the bowl of soup and turns to set it on the counter. At the same moment Chuck turns toward Vinnie. There is a collision: the stainless-steel bowl is knocked out of her hands and slides to the floor; she and Chuck are drenched with cold green soup and hot black coffee.

'Aw, fuck! Excuse me.'

'Oh, damn it!'

'I didn't see – Jesus. Sorry. Here, lemme – ' Chuck grabs a dishtowel and begins wiping coffee and soup off the front of Vinnie.

'That's all right,' she says, swallowing with difficulty her irritation and the phrase *You oaf*. 'My fault too.' Seizing a damp sponge, she starts to mop up Chuck. Luckily she is wearing a relatively soup-proofed dress: an olive green, densely flowered Laura Ashley cotton; Chuck's synthetic yellow cowboy shirt and tan Western-cut slacks are much more vulnerable. Because he is so tall, most of the spill is on his pants. As Vinnie moves the sponge over them she suddenly becomes aware that they contain an unmistakable and even impressive bulge – and, simultaneously, that Chuck is to all intents and purposes stroking her breasts with a red checked linen dishtowel.

'Thanks, that's enough,' she says, backing away from him as far a possible in the tiny kitchen.

'Vinnie – '

'Really, I think we'd better just try to soak the stains out, and the sooner the better. Why don't you just go into the bathroom and take your things off. Put them in the tub, and turn on some lukewarm water, not hot.'

'Okay. If you say so.'

Vinnie picks up the broken shards of coffee cup and begins to mop the kitchen floor, then stops, retreats to the bedroom, pulls off her sticky wet dress, and changes into a skirt and shirt. Her mind is full of nervous confusion. Three quarts of soup gone, what can she serve at lunch tomorrow instead? There's no doubt what was going on in Chuck's mind and body – is there? Or was she mistaken? Should she go out tomorrow morning and buy some pâté? Anyhow, she reacted quite fast – fast enough? At least she got him out of the way – Or a pound of shrimps perhaps, from Camden Lock market – Yes, but not very far out of the way. He is in her bathroom now, with almost nothing on and his clothes floating in her tub (she can hear the water running). Maybe the soup stains will come out, if not the coffee, but what the hell is Chuck going to wear instead? She should have sent him back to his hotel, but now it's too late, he can't go anywhere in sopping wet clothes. Her head is muddled by two many aspirin, and she didn't think ahead. If he only had a decent raincoat instead of that awful transparent plastic thing – she gives it a nasty look as it hangs in the hall – then he could wear that while his clothes dried, or even go home in it.

'Hey, Vinnie! Have you got a bathrobe or something?'

Well, now Chuck has thought of this problem too. She'll have to find him something to put on, he can't stay in her bathroom all night; and as soon as he comes out he's going to make a pass at her. Or maybe not. Maybe the whole thing was just a nervous reaction. Maybe she imagined it. Vinnnie begins opening cupboards and drawers, all of which contain only female garments in sizes six and eight.

'Vinnie?'

'Coming.' In desperation she goes into her study and drags the spread off the daybed. 'Here. You can put this round you for now, it's all I've got.' She shoves through the bathroom door a rough bundle of brown homespun with a geometrical border pattern and fringe. Not waiting for any possible objection, she returns to the kitchen floor, which is still splashed and smeared with green soup.

'Aw, what a mess. Lemme help you.'

'No, thanks.' Vinnie, on hands and knees with a bucket of soapy water and the same sponge she used on Chuck, glances up. Scrolled leather boots, thick naked muscled legs furred with pale-red hair, fringed homespun bedspread which, draped round his bulk, looks smaller than before. She stands up.

'You have some kinda green plant stuff in your hair.' Chuck picks it out and presents it to her.

'Watercress.' Vinnie throws it away. 'It was watercress-and-avocado soup. I'd better to put my dress to soak, excuse me.'

'Sure.'

In the bathroom she shakes out her sticky Laura Ashley and lays it in the tub, then checks the mirror to make sure there is no more soup in her hair. How awful I look, how old, gray, unattractive, she thinks. Of course he's not going to make a pass. As she leaves she glances again into the tub, where her dress and Chuck's shirt and slacks lie wetly together in embarrassing proximity. She runs in lukewarm water to give them more room, causing the garments to turn and slosh about in a promiscuous embrace. Come on, get a hold of yourself, she thinks, and returns to the kitchen where, surprisingly, Chuck has just finished mopping the floor.

'I didn't expect – thank you,' she says, noting that the bedspread has managed to transform Chuck from a fake cowboy to a fake Indian. 'Would you like another cup of coffee?'

'No, thanks.' He gives her a brief smile, a longer stare. Vinnie, uneasy, returns neither.

'Well then,' she begins, 'maybe you'd like –'

'Y'know what I'd like?' Before she can answer, the imitation Indian grabs Vinnie by both shoulders and kisses her full on the mouth.

'Mm! No!' she protests, but after the fact.

'Aw, Vinnie. If you knew how long I've been wanting to do that. Ever since that day we had tea. But I didn't have the, I don't know, the nerve. I was too goddamn low.' He hugs her again, warmly rather than hotly – perhaps he only feels especially friendly?

'Please, let's take it easy,' she says. 'And let's get out of the kitchen, before something else spills.'

'Okay.' Chuck stands aside, then follows her into the sitting room. But they are hardly there before he moves closer again, crowding Vinnie against the wall under a watercolor of New College. This time his intention is evidently more than friendly. Vinnie feels the flutter of satisfaction that has always, for her, followed any expression of sexual interest: I may be plain, but I'm not after all hopelessly plain, it says. Then she catches her breath, tries to collect herself. But it is the first time since she left America that anyone has done more than shake her hand or kiss her on the cheek, and Chuck's embrace is close, strong, deeply and alarmingly comforting. A flush of warmth spreads through her, an impulse to relax, to forget who she is, where she is –

'No, no,' she tries to say. 'You're making a mistake, I really don't want this – ' But the words are hardly more than a murmur. Push him away, she commands herself; but her body refuses – though one hand, with great difficulty, manages to keep their lower torsos separated a vital inch or two.

It is Chuck who first pulls back. 'Vinnie. Hold on a minute.' He removes his large warm hand from within her shirt, breathing hard. 'God, this is great. But there's something I've got to tell you.' He drags the bedspread back round his shoulders. 'Let's sit down a minute, okay?'

'Okay,' she echoes shakily.

'What it is, is – ' Chuck, who has lowered himself to the sofa, halts. 'Oh hell.'

'Go on,' she prompts, taking a chair across from him and beginning to regain control. 'I know what you're going to say.'

'You can't. How could you?' He sounds angry, perhaps frightened.

'Because I've heard it before.' Vinnie's voice is almost steady now. She glances at Chuck, thinking how ridiculous he looks: a comic oversized pink-faced Red Indian, incongruous among the English furniture and flowered chintz. 'You're going to tell me that you're awfully fond of me, but you want to be honest, and I should realize that your marriage is very important to you and you really love you wife.'

'The hell I am. I don't love Myrna – I hate her, or pretty near. My marriage is as dead as a skunk.' Chuck looks dark. 'What I hafta say, it's a lot worse than that.' He clutches at the bedspread, clears his throat. 'Uh, you remember I told you I was in an accident back in Tulsa, smashed up my car.'

'Yes,' Vinnie says, wondering if Chuck is about to confess some incapacitating and shameful sexual disability.

'Wal, it wasn't just my car I smashed up. There was this kid in a VW. It was out on the Muskogee Turnpike, about two a.m. I was tearing along, doing near eighty I guess, in my usual midnight funk, and suddenly there was this old VW pulling out from the access road right in front of me, weaving like a drunken chicken. I still keep seeing it. It was this sixteen-year-old kid, half out of his mind on amphetamines. I tried to stop, but my reaction time wasn't fast enough, I was too goddamn pissed.'

'So what happened?' she asks finally.

'So I killed him. That's what happened.' Chuck throws a panicky, searching look towards Vinnie; then, as if afraid of reading her expression, he transfers his gaze to the floor.

'You know those little old foreign cars, they don't have a hope in hell in a crash,' he informs the carpet. 'That beetle crumpled up like a broil-in bag. The Pontiac wasn't in such great shape either, but I got out of it somehow. I had a cracked knee, and my head was bleeding, only I didn't notice it then. But the kid – He was stuck inside the VW with the wheel shaft through him, screaming. I couldn't do anything for him – I couldn't even get the door open.' He looks up at Vinnie again.

'So there we were,' he goes on. 'It was dark all around, black as hell. One of my headlights was still working, and I could see a slice of the road, with ripped-off pieces of metal thrown around, and a lot of smashed glass, looked like crushed ice.

'By the time the cops got there I was kinda incoherent. I had point twelve per cent of alcohol in my blood, and I tried to fight them when they wanted me to get into the patrol car; I had some idea I had to stay with the kid. So naturally they took me in. Resisting arrest, and assaulting an officer, and driving while intoxicated, and exceeding the speed limit, and failure to exercise proper caution . . . And then the kid's parents decided to sue me for manslaughter. I wanted to plead guilty; the way I felt, I didn't care too much what happened to me any more. Myrna thought I was nuts. If I didn't have any self-respect, she said, at least I might have the decency to think of her and the children, of their standing in the community.'

'And did you?'

'Yeh. In the end. I let her get me an expensive lawyer, and he won the case for us. I had the right of way, see, and the kid was on drugs, that's a lot worse than booze in Tulsa. Except if I hadn't been so damn bombed I would have seen him in time, easy.'

'I'm sorry,' Vinnie says. 'What an awful thing to happen.'

'I can't fucking get it out of my mind. At least I couldn't. It's been better lately. For a long time I felt like I oughta die too, to make it up to the kid and his parents. That's what it was mostly. Not so much losing my job like I told you. Whenever I get in a car, even sometimes just crossing the street, I think about it. I keep taking chances, to see if I'll cash in; and if I make it, maybe I'm forgiven. I know that's sort of crazy.'

'Of course it's crazy,' Vinnie says decidedly. 'It wouldn't do that boy or his parents the last bit of good for you to be killed in an accident.'

'"An eye for an eye –"'

'"Makes the whole world blind,"' she finishes.

'Yeh– I see what you mean.' Chuck grins suddenly. 'That's a smart proverb. I never heard it before.'

'Gandhi.'

'What? Oh, yeh, that Indian.' Chuck ceases to smile. 'Anyways.' He shifts uncomfortably on the sofa, causing it to creak in protest. 'I thought you oughta know. I mean, in case you might not want to have anything more to do with me.'

An excuse to draw back has been handed to Vinnie on a platter, but she hesitates. It would be harmful and hurtful to reject Chuck because of what had happened to him on the Muskogee Turnpike. Indeed, now she looks at the platter again, what is on it seems more like a watertight excuse for going ahead.

'Don't be silly,' she says nervously. 'It was a terrible accident, that's all.'

'Aw, Vinnie.' Chuck lunges towards her, so precipitately that he leaves most of the bedspread behind, and folds her in a warm half-naked hug. 'I shoulda known you'd say that. You're a good woman.'

Vinnie does not smile. No one has ever said this to her before, and she knows it to be false: she is not, in Chuck's presumed sense of the word, or any sense of it, a good woman. She is not particularly generous, brave, or affectionate; she steals roses from other people's gardens and enjoys imagining nasty deaths for her enemies. Of course, in her own opinion, she is quite justified in being like this, considering how the world and its inhabitants have treated her; and she has positive qualities as well: intelligence, tact, taste . . .

'You've been so great to me all along,' Chuck continues. 'Hell, you saved my life, just about.' He begins kissing her face, breaking off at intervals to speak. 'Y'know, if I hadn't met you, I probably never woulda thought of looking for my ancestors . . . Or found South Leigh. That time we had tea, I was about ready to give up. If it weren't for you, I wouldn't have found Old

Mumpson, or met Mike or anything. I woulda managed to get myself killed by now, probably. Or else, a damn sight worse, I'd be back in Tulsa.'

'Wait,' Vinnie tries to say between kisses, in which somehow she has begun to join. 'I'm not sure I want . . .' But her voice now entirely refuses to function; and her body – rebellious, greedy – presses itself against Chuck's. Now, now it cries; more, more. Very well, she says to it. Very well, if you insist. Just this once. After all, no one will ever have to know.

8

> The heart when half wounded is changing,
> It here and there leaps like a frog.
>
> John Gay, *Molly Mog*

For the first day or so after Rosemary's party, Fred doesn't take their quarrel very seriously. Her temper is always volatile, and she's been briefly unreasonable before. Once, for instance, she broke a date because she disliked the way her hair had been done: it looked, she said, like some demented mouse's nest and she couldn't bear for him to see it. But she made the disappointment up to him, and more, when they next met. Fred smiled, remembering.

When forty-eight hours have passed and Rosemary still hasn't answered her private telephone or responded to the messages he left with her service, Fred begins to feel uneasy. Then he remembers that she is working: she has a guest role in a historical television series that's filming this week. He makes some phone inquiries, starting with Rosemary's agent, who seems to know nothing of any quarrel (a good sign, Fred thinks), and discovers that they are shooting an outdoor scene early the following morning within walking distance of his flat.

Now full of hope, he rises at eight, gulps some coffee and a piece of half-scorched gritty toast (he has never mastered the British open grill), and hastens toward Holland Park. Early as it is, the square where they are shooting and the streets leading into it are choked with cars and vans and what the British call lorries. Part of the road has been cordoned off; a policeman stands by the barrier in the relaxed posture of one who has drawn an easy assignment; passersby have begun to gather.

Though the sky is heavy with gray, lumpy clouds, a simmering golden light bathes the façade of one tall, elegant brick house and the courtyard and pavement before it. This artificial sunshine emanates from two banks of fluorescent tubes on poles – miniature versions of those he's seen at night baseball games. The building glows not only with light but with fresh paint: glossy white on the pillars and trim, glossy black on the ironwork. The railings and woodwork of the two neighbouring houses have also been freshly painted – but only on the sides visible to the camera: the backs of the pillars, for instance, are dull and cracked. At the other end of the square two men with a ladder are taking down a metal sign reading COOMARASWAMY FOODS and replacing it with a wooden one inscribed CHEMIST in shaded Victorian capitals.

Fred's good looks, his American accent, and his modestly confident manner make it easy for him to talk his way past the barrier. He negotiates a section of pavement jammed with people and equipment and crawling with electrical snakes – yellow, black, poison-green – and accosts an anxious-looking young woman with a clipboard.

'Oh, yes, Rosemary Radley's on location,' she tells him. 'She's inside the house there, but you can't speak to her now' – she snatches at Fred's arm to prevent him ' –we're going to start shooting in a couple of minutes.'

This, as usual in the film business, turns out to be over-optimistic. More than a quarter of an hour passes while Fred leans against the side of a van marked Lee Electrics, watching the scene. A man in a blue smock is wiring white plastic flowers onto the standard rose bushes that flank the front walk of the golden house; two other men are doing something to the lights. A group of actors in Edwardian costume stands by the curb chatting: an old woman in black with a basket, a younger woman twirling a ruffled white parasol, a man in tweeds and a hat, a nanny pushing an empty wicker pram. Many of the crew members also seem to be merely waiting about, though now and then there are outbreaks of activity and shouting. A short plump man resembling an untidy beaver, with an unraveling brown sweater and unraveled gray hair – much the shabbiest and least attractive of the company – seems always to be the focus of these confusions. Fred puts him down as an incompetent technician – some union-protected booby – and blames the continuing delay on him, then realizes he is the director.

At length the tumult focuses to a point and stops. The door

of the golden house opens; a dignified elderly man in Edwardian morning dress steps out, then a beautiful woman in gray and pink, her flaxen hair piled high and floating an immense hat of pink feathers and veiling like a nesting flamingo: Rosemary. The man speaks to her; she replies at length, smiling sweetly up at him. Fred can hear nothing of what they are saying because of traffic noise at the bottom of the square and the shouted instructions of the director. This strikes him as weird; then he notices that there are no microphones in sight. The scene is being photographed, but not recorded – presumably that will be done later, in some studio.

Now Rosemary and her companion descend the marble steps, speaking and laughing animatedly, or appearing to do so. The camera is rolled back; on the sidewalk the nanny begins to push the pram away downhill, the young couple to stroll in the other direction. The beaver raises both hands, shouting 'Cut! Hold it!' Two women and a man in coveralls rush toward Rosemary and the elderly actor and swarm over them, adjusting their clothes, smoothing their hair, powdering their faces. His love and her companion stand there passively, receiving the attention with no more concern than two store-window dummies. The beaver consults with the man operating the camera, then with several others. Finally he gives a signal; Rosemary, who hasn't even glanced in Fred's direction, returns to the house.

Over the next forty minutes this series of events is repeated many times, with only minor variations. Rosemary and the elderly actor exchange sides as they descend the steps; they walk faster, and then slower; the flamingo-pink hat is tilted at a different angle; a dangling branch above the railings is lopped off by a man with a saw and a ladder; the nanny is instructed to walk away more rapidly; the lights are moved again. At other times Fred, unfamiliar with the language of television production, can't figure out what change has been made. Twice the actors get as far as the front gate and are accosted by the shabby woman in black, causing Rosemary to look concerned, smile graciously, and make an inaudible but earnest appeal to her companion.

As he watches, Fred is overwhelmed again by his love's beauty and charm, which seem almost supernatural in the supernatural sunlight, and then by her cheerful endurance. Each time she emerges from the house she smiles with the same soft brilliance, trips down the steps with the same easy grace, laughs at the actor's inaudible joke with the same perfect spontaneity. He understands for the first time that Rosemary is more than a beautiful creation of nature, a lily of the field; he sees that acting for television is hard, boring, skilled work, and admires her even more than before.

At the same time, many details of Rosemary's performance make him uncomfortable. Her way of tilting her head and placing three fingers on the actor's sleeve in half-serious, half-childish appeal, for instance. Until now, he has thought of this gesture as natural, impulsive, private – not a stage mannerism. Is this why Rosemary has never arranged for him to see *Tallyho Castle* on video tape, though the project has so often been discussed?

Finally a halt is called in the shooting. The pram is abandoned in the middle of the street: electricians and carpenters (Rosemary would call them 'sparks' and 'chippies') lean against their equipment and pop open cans of soda; coffee in plastic cups is distributed. At last she emerges from the house again, without her hat. Fred hurries toward her, avoiding the tangle of cables as well as he can, once almost falling.

'Freddy!' Her face lights with pleasure, exactly as it has just done over and over again on camera. 'Where have you been? Why didn't you phone me? No – mustn't touch – I'm plastered with makeup.' She gives him a quick hug, averting her face, which in close-up has an unnaturally flawless pasty surface, like the freshly painted house.

'I did, but all I got was the answering service. And you never called me back.'

'Oh, nonsense, darling. There wasn't any message.'

'I called four or five times at least; and I left my name every time,' Fred insists.

'Really? Those stupid girls; I expect they're jealous. Trying to ruin my love-life.' Rosemary giggles.

'I can't believe – I mean, why the hell should they want to do that?'

'Who knows?' Rosemary shrugs. 'People are so peculiar sometimes.' She reaches up to ruffle his dark curls. 'Not like you. That's what I adore about you, Freddy darling – you're so reasonable. Come into the dressing-room.

I've got to sit down; this corset is murder.'

She leads the way to a bus parked further up the street with its doors open. Within, most of the seats have been removed; the space is filled with mirrors, clothes-racks, and folding metal chairs and tables.

'Oh, darling.' She hugs him again, more closely, then sits, gives a quick, searching look into a glass, and swivels round. 'I'm so happy to see you; I've got wonderful news. Pandora Box has invited us to her tower in Wales for the last week of June, it's the most glorious place, and George owns the fishing rights on the river now – do you like to fish?'

'Yes – but I won't be here at the end of June, you know.'

'Oh, Freddy, please. Don't start that again.' She pivots back to the mirror and begins to smooth stray wisps of silken hair into the white-gold billows above.

'I can't help it, damn it. I have to go back and teach. Besides, I'm broke. I can't afford to stay here any longer even if I could.'

'Oh, Freddy,' Rosemary repeats, but in a very different manner, soft and surprised, leaning over the back of the folding chair toward him and extending round white arms delicately veiled in gray lace. 'You mustn't worry about that, pet. If that's all it is, I can easily help you out. I'm quite flush now from residuals, and this thing we're shooting here – it's a bore, but it does pay rather well.'

'I can't live off you,' Fred says, his voice thickening.

'I'm not offering to keep you, silly. I haven't come to that, I hope.' Rosemary laughs lightly, but there is an edge of impatience in her voice. 'I'm only offering to lend you something.'

'I can't take money from you. It would ruin everything.'

'Oh, for heaven's sake, don't be a ninny. It wouldn't be very much. And you could save something by moving out of that nasty overpriced flat and staying with me for a bit, if you liked. And then once we're in Ireland, everything's practically gratis. Besides, I might ask Al if he couldn't get you into the show as an extra. That'd be rather a lark, don't you think?'

'Well . . .' says Fred, noticing that Rosemary seems to have adopted the slang of the Victorian age along with its fashions.

'You wouldn't have to say anything,' she assures him. 'Well, of course you couldn't anyhow, because of your Yankee accent.'

Fred smiles. Though impossible from a practical point of view, the fantasy of appearing in a British television drama with Rosemary is agreeable.

'But you could be a silent brooding undergardener, or a gypsy tramp, or something like that. And you'd be paid a bit too, of course. I'd insist on that.'

'No,' Fred says with force. He scowls, unconsciously acting the insulting role assigned to him by his love's imagination. 'That'd be as bad as taking money from you. Worse.'

Rosemary's fair, finely penciled eyebrows approach each other in a tiny but somehow threatening frown. She stands up gracefully, smoothing the lacy tiers of her skirt. 'Really, you're being awfully stupid,' she says, gazing down at Fred. 'You think you're in some historical drama; it's you who ought to be in costume. You want to make both of us perfectly miserable, all because of some Victorian moral principle, that a man can't borrow money from a woman.'

'Not from one he loves, no,' says Fred stubbornly.

'I don't understand what's happening.' Her musical voice quavers, and so does her small round chin above the high frilled collar. 'What do you want from me? Oh, damn.' Tearing a tissue from a cardboad box, she blots eyes shiny with moisture. 'You're ruining my makeup.'

Fred rises to embrace her. Avoiding the creamy plastered face and the soot-streaked eyes, he kisses the fine floss of hair behind her ear, the soft neck veiled with lace, the white ringed hand that holds the damp tissue. 'Nothing. Everything. I just want us to go on loving each other. That's all.'

'For four weeks.'

'Yes,' he says, distracted by the contrasting stiffness and softness of Rosemary's body: the heavy, slippery watered silk and frail net and lace; the feel of corseting underneath and soft yielding flesh beneath that; he presses her harder to him.

'You little shit,' says Rosemary in coarse, unfamiliar tones, using a word he has never heard or expected to hear from her. 'Take your bloody hands off me.' Jolted, he steps back.

'I should have listened to Mrs Harris,' she goes on in a voice that is her own, but charged with fury. 'She warned me not to trust you.' She is facing him now, her great fringed eyes narrowed. '"He's a Yankee skip-jack," she told me a long time ago. "He's a low-life deceiver of women."'

'Rosemary, darling –'

'Excuse me, please. I have to get my makeup repaired.' With a swish of her satin fishtail skirt, Rosemary is out the door and tripping down the street.

Fred stands a moment, stunned; then he races after her. 'Rosemary, please –'

Rosemary halts. She looks round coldly at him, then calls to one of the attendant policemen. 'Oh, officer!'

'Yes, Miss?' He approaches, smiling.

'Could you move this man away, please?' She indicates Fred with a toss of her head. 'He's bothering me.'

'Right you are, Miss.'

'Thank you.' She give him a smile made more dazzling by the sooty dampness of the great blue-gray eyes, and trips off.

'All right, you don't have to shove me, I'm going,' Fred says, shaking the policeman's hand from his arm. He picks his way through the electrical snakes, round the barricade, and past a large crowd of spectators. Then he turns and looks back over their heads to the house bathed in brazen unnatural light. In its front courtyard a man with a bucket and brush is methodically painting the plastic roses a brilliant, glamorous crimson.

Even after this scene Fred isn't wholly discouraged. He has never in his life been rejected by any girl or woman he seriously cared for, and he is almost as certain of Rosemary's feelings as he is of his own. Hadn't she been crying at the idea of parting from him?

Not that he takes her tears all that seriously. He has seen his love weep before: at a sad film, or the death of some actor she barely knew; and then, half an hour later, he has seen her dissolved in laughter at some scandal about the same actor relayed by a friend. The theatrical temperament, he suspects, enjoys emotional scenes and tangles of misunderstanding, just as it later enjoys their untangling. The climate of their affair had always been, not stormy, but dramatically various, as changeable as the English spring weather – sunshine succeeding showers with a breezy, careless rapidity.

But as the days and pass he still can't reach Rosemary, Fred becomes more and more tense and desperate..From one hour to the next his mood changes. He is enraged at Rosemary and never wants to see her again; he wants to see her, but only to tell her off, to let her know how angry he is; he wants to plead with her: Hasn't she shut him out long enough? There are so few weeks left; it is perverse and wasteful of her to squander them this way.

Also, for the first time, he seriously asks himself if he should do as Rosemary demands. Should he cable or telephone to the Summer School office in Corinth and say that he won't be able to teach this year – maybe say he is ill? Isn't two months in England with Rosemary worth it – worth angering his senior colleagues and risking his promotion? But if he doesn't teach this summer, what the hell is he going to live on? He's practically broke now, and if he stays on he'll be – there's no getting round it – living on Rosemary, in her house; letting her buy his meals and, when they go to Wales or to Ireland, his train and plane tickets. He will be what is called a kept man – a man who is maintained, enclosed, as one might house and feed and cage an expensive pet. And hadn't Rosemary, when they last met, called him 'pet'? No, no, never.

If he could only find the key to Rosemary's house that she once gave him, he would go there and wait for her to come home. But the damn thing is lost; he must have left it behind the day of the party. Without it, he does what he can: he phones again and again; he even goes to the house in Chelsea, but nobody is ever home, except, once, Mrs Harris, who won't let him in or take a message, only shouts through the locked door something that sounds like 'bugger off!' Is Rosemary staying somewhere else? Has she left town? He tries her agent, but now the man is coolly and smoothly uncommunicative. He is awfully sorry, he says, but he has no idea where Rosemary might be – two evident lies.

Rosemary's friends are most agreeable, but just as unhelpful. And their agreeableness, Fred realizes now, is and always was generic rather than specific. In the past, because he was Rosemary's current boyfriend, they had inquired about his work and solicited his opinions on matters cultural, political, and domestic. Now they have dropped him – though in all cases with the gentlest and most casual motion, as if brushing a crumb to the floor. They all have charming manners; when he telephones they are uniformly pleasant, but rather vague and always 'awfully busy'. Some seem to have difficulty remembering who he is ('Oh yes, Fred Turner. How nice to hear from you'). Though he isn't leaving for several weeks, they wish him a pleasant journey back to 'the States' as if he were about to step onto a plane. His questions about Rosemary are passed over as if unheard, or met with what he is beginning to recongnize as the classic waffling manner of the British upper classes when confronted with the insignificant unpleasant. ('Goodness, I haven't the faintest – wasn't she going to the Auvergne or somewhere like that?') Rosemary's closest friends, who might have been more helpful, and with whom he could have been more direct, are unavailable. Posy lives out of town, and he doesn't have her (unlisted) number; Erin, Nadia, and Edwin are abroad.

His colleague and fellow-citizen Vinnie Miner is also of no use. When he saw her last week at the British Museum she promised to speak to Rosemary for him, promised to explain that Fred didn't want to leave London, that he loves her – Nothing has come of that commission, if she carried it out, which he doubts. And even if she did, Fred thinks, she probably didn't make much of a job of it. If Vinnie ever in her life experienced real romantic love, let alone sexual passion, she has probably forgotten it.

Whereas he, Fred, is – shit, he might as well admit it – emotionally and physically obsessed. All he can think of, day and night both, is Rosemary. He tries to work at home, he goes to the BM, but he can't concentrate, can't read, can't take notes, can't write. And this although he has, for the first time in months, all the time in the world: long empty days and nights.

Again, just as he did last winter, he has taken to wandering about London. But now he knows that the city exists; that a rich, complex, intense life goes on within its walls, behind its shuttered and curtained windows. Everywhere he passes houses, restaurants, office buildings, shops, and blocks of flats where he has been with Rosemary; the streets themselves shimmer with the almost visible ghosts of his love affair. In this keyed-up state he often thinks he sees Rosemary herself at a distance: going into Selfridge's, or in the intermission crowd at a theater; he spots her pale-gold halo of hair and light tripping walk three blocks away down Holland Park Road or getting out of a taxi in Mayfair. His heart pounds; he races, dodging traffic and shoving aside pedestrians, toward what always turns out to be some stranger.

Today Fred is in a part of London where he has little hope of coming upon Rosemary. He is walking along the Regent's Canal above Camden Lock on a glowing June day with Joe and Debby Vogeler. Their progress is slow, since Joe is pushing the baby, and the old towpath is thronged with Sunday strollers. By the time Fred gets back to his flat and his typewriter most of the working day will be gone. On the other hand, if he'd stayed home he probably wouldn't have accomplished damn-all either. His mind cannot focus on the eighteenth century; it is focused too hard on the late twentieth, and specifically on the moment less than twenty-four hours from now when he will be face to face with Rosemary for the first time in a fortnight, and she will have to listen to him.

Joe and Debby are also preoccupied, though in their cases more vocally. What obsesses them is their baby's intellectual development, or rather his lack of it. Jakie is already sixteen months old, for God's sake, and he hasn't started to talk – hasn't said a single damn word, though many kids his age or even younger (examples are cited) are already dauntingly verbal. Their anxiety, it occurs to Fred, is clearly a function of what some modern critics would call an over-valorization of language; it hardly matters to them that Jakie is, as he points out now, a healthy, strong, active child.

'If he'd just start to speak, he'd be so much more like a real person,' Debby explains. 'I mean, sure, I know he's healthy, and he's kind of sweet sometimes, but he's not exactly human, you know what I mean?'

'It's so damn frustrating not being able to communicate with him,' says Joe. 'Not to know all the things he must be thinking and experiencing. Our own kid. You can't help wondering, when he starts speaking, what is he going to say to us?'

'You could be disappointed,' Fred remarks. 'My father told me once that when I was a baby he used to look at me, having deep Wordsworthian thoughts about childhood, and wondering what message from the realms of glory I would bring down to him. Then finally I learnt to talk, and I said my first sentence, and it was, "Freddy want cookie."'

'How old were you when you said that?' asks Debby, failing to get the point.

'I haven't any idea.' Fred sighs.

'Most children don't start putting sentences together until they're about two,' Joe says. 'But they can usually produce single words a lot sooner. Ordinarily. Jakie babbles a lot, but nothing comes of it. I mean, what do you think?'

'He looks okay to me,' says Fred, who has no experience of babies. Maybe there is something wrong with Jakie; how the hell should he know? He has a hard time considering the subject, or any subject; he scarcely sees the picturesque scene through which he is walking: on the one hand a bank of long grass and wild flowering weeds, on the other the brightly painted barges and the tall horse chestnuts in the gardens on the opposite shore, which have begun to scatter their clusters of bloom onto the canal, transforming it into a floating carpet of cream and pink stars. London is visible to him now only in painful flashes of memory; most of the time he moves in a city of clouded gloomy shapes and noises.

Almost the only people Fred has seen anything of since Rosemary's party are the Vogelers, and he has seen more of them than he wants to, mostly because he hasn't the energy to invent excuses. Joe and Debby's opinion of London has improved with the good weather, but not much. Sure, the place looks better, Joe admits, but Jesus Christ, it ought to be warmer than this by June. Back home they'd have been swimming for months, Debby says. And you might as well forget about trying to get a decent tan.

The Vogeler's views are shared by several friends they have made here – two Canadian historians, met in the British Museum lunchroom, and another couple, relatives of the first, from Australia. All four of them agree with Joe and Debby about the inadequacy of British food, the lukewarmess of British beer, the chilliness of the natives, and the disappointing smallness of every national monument and tourist attraction.

They also have an explanation. Andy (the Australian) outlined it to Fred last week in a pub in Hampstead. The trouble with Britain today, he claimed, is that for three hundred years its boldest and most energetic, independent, and hardy citizens left the fucking place and went to the colonies – under which term he includes the U.S., right? The ones who stayed behind, by a process of natural selection, became progressively more timid, inert, slavish, and sickly. Hell, just look around you,

Andy said. The British are poor pale sad bastards now, the dregs of a once noble stock.

Sure, Andy admitted, Australia was settled by convicts – but wait a moment, mate, just ask yourself how they got to be convicts in the first place. What they really were was working-class blokes who wouldn't accept the class system shit, who weren't going to rot their fucking asses off slaving for pennies and live on charity porridge when they got too old to work. They had imagination and guts; they took risks, they made a grab for a fair share of what was going. Moll Flanders, not Oliver Twist.

Essentially the attitude of all these colonials – now including the Vogelers – toward Britain is that of successful people toward parents they have outgrown. They admire England's history and traditions; they feel a sentimental fondness for its landscape and architecture; but, Christ, they'd never want to come back and live here.

The experience of what Fred considers the real, inner London that Joe and Debby had at Rosemary's party hasn't affected their views. Most of the people they met there seemed to them 'kind of phony-baloney,' and they are still smarting from the reaction of certain guests to their baby's presence and behavior. Debby, in particular, seems to Fred to be nursing her grudge as if it were some ugly, fretful child – Jakie himself, maybe, on a bad afternoon. Fred's admission now that he and Rosemary have quarreled, and his account of his last meeting with her, only confirms their prejudice.

'That's how the English are, especially the middle-class types,' Joe informs Fred as they turn back down the towpath toward Camden Lock. 'You never really know where you are with them.'

'Perfidious Albion,' suggests Fred, who half agrees with Joe and half pities his ignorance.

'Yeh, okay.' Joe declines to register the irony. 'I don't deny that they can be damn pleasant if they want. I can understand how you felt about Rosemary Radley; I was kind of bowled over by her myself at first. But your mind-set and hers are light-years apart.'

'Mf.' Fred makes a noise of discomfort. Not for the first time, he wonders why it is that married couples feel perfectly free to analyze the affairs of their unmarried friends; whereas if he were to make some comment on Joe and Debby's relationship they would be righteously pissed-off.

'I absolutely agree,' his wife says. 'Oh, what is it now?' She squats to confront Jakie, who has begun fretting and squirming in the stroller; it is one of his bad afternoons.

'It looks like he wants to get out,' Fred suggests.

'He always want to get out. Well, all right, silly.' Debby disentangles the baby and sets him on uncertain feet – he has only been walking for a few months. 'Okay, wait a second. Jesus.' She straightens out the striped ticking overalls and cap that make Jakie look like a dwarf railway engineer, and takes a firm grip on his small puffy hand.

'You've got to reexamine your priorities,' Joe instructs Fred, as they continue, now at a toddler's pace, along the towpath, pushing the empty stroller.

Silently, Fred declines to do this.

'That's right,' Debby says. 'I mean, after all, there was never any future in it. Just for one thing, Rosemary Radley's much too old for you.'

'I don't see that,' Fred says with an edge in his voice. 'You're older than Joe, aren't you?'

'I'm fifteen months older; that hardly signifies,' Debby returns, not very pleasantly.

'All right. So Rosemary's thirty-seven. What the hell difference does that make, if we love each other?' says Fred, wishing he had never confided in the Vogelers or maybe even met them.

'Rosemary's not thirty-seven,' Debby says. 'No way. She's about forty-four, or maybe forty-five.'

'Oh, come on. She is not.' He laughs angrily.

'I read it in the *Sunday Times.*'

'So what; that doesn't make it true,' Fred says, recalling how often his love had complained of the disgusting lies printed about her and other actors. 'Screw them.'

'All right, don't believe it.' Debby's tone combines annoyance and condescension. 'No, no Jakie! You don't really want that.' She stoops and pries from the baby's fingers a half-squashed rubber ball with a cracked and faded Union Jack pattern. 'Nasty, dirty thing. Joe, would you hold onto him for a moment?' Debby transfers the struggling baby's hand to his father, then hurls the ball away up the weedy slope. Jakie stares after it, then lets out a surprised howl.

'Look, Jakie, look!' his father cries, trying to distract him. 'See the, uh, boat.' He points to a painted dinghy moored on the farther shore. 'Oh, hell.'

The squashed rubber ball has reemerged from the weeds; it bounces across the path ahead of them and into the sliding frog-green water of the canal, where it joins a flotilla of debris that includes a plastic bleach bottle, half an orange, and bits of water-logged wood and straw. 'No, Jakie!' He holds the straining, screaming child back. 'Bad germs. All gone now.'

'You don't want that dirty old ball,' Debby insists – an obvious lie, Fred thinks. 'Stop that right now!' The baby, in a paroxysm of frustrated desire, is kicking and screaming at the top of his lungs; his face is distorted into a red gargoyle mask.

'Oh, shit,' Joe sighs. 'Come on now, Jakie. Up you go.' He hoists the struggling, howling gnome to his shoulder. 'A-one, a-two.' Joe begins to bounce his son in what Fred supposes is meant to be a soothing manner, at the same time striding rapidly down the towpath, followed by Debby and the stroller. 'A-one, a-two. That's a baby.'

'Listen, I'm sorry if what I said annoyed you,' Debby remarks, as they outdistance the floating ball and Jakie's screams diminish to a fretful gurgle.

'That's all right,' says Fred, feeling magnanimously sorry for the Vogelers, parents of a retarded infant troll.

'It's just like, I don't like to see you so down over something like this.'

'Like okay,' Fred says. 'It'll pass,' he adds, thinking that with luck he and his love will be together again by this time tomorrow.

'Sure it will,' Joe tells him. 'Rosemary Radley's not what you really want anyhow.'

'Once you're back in America, I bet you'll read the whole experience a lot differently,' says his wife.

'Mh,' Fred mutters; it has just occurred to him that to the Vogelers his passion for Rosemary is more or less exactly equivalent to Jakie's passion for an old rubber ball.

'That's right,' Debby agrees. 'You need a woman with some real intellectual substance. That's what I've always thought,' she continues, mistaking Fred's silence for receptivity. 'Someone you can really communicate with on your own level. Share your ideas with.'

'Right,' Joe puts in. 'For instance, somebody like Carissa.'

'Carrissa wouldn't ever have behaved in such a flighty, irrational way. You always know exactly where you are with Carissa. She's really up front; I remember once when she –'

'Look Debby,' Fred interrupts, halting and turning to face her. 'Do me a favour: quit mentioning Carissa to me. Carissa is not the point.'

'But she is the point,' says Joe, 'Oh, all right,' he concedes, registering Fred's expression. 'If that's the way you feel.'

'That's the way I feel, God damn it,' Fred says. It occurs to him that he and the Vogelers are on the verge of a real quarrel – maybe of a break in their seven-year friendship. But in this present mood he doesn't give a shit.

All of them are stopped on the towpath now, facing one another. But the slippery greenish water still pours by, bearing its flotsam and jetsam. Jakie, gazing over his father's shoulder, sees his lost prize approaching and begins to babble excitedly. 'Oooh! Oo-ah-um! Ba – boo – ball!'

'Ball!' Joe cries. 'He said "ball", Debby!'

'I heard him!' Debby's cross, set face breaks into a delighted grin. 'Jakie, darling. Say it again. Say "ball".'

'Boo-uh-aw! Bah-aw. Ball!' The baby strains toward his object of desire as it floats by, surrounded by waterlogged crap.

'He said "ball",' his mother declares with triumph.

'His first word.' His father's voice trembles.

'Ball,' Debby breathes. 'Did you hear that Fred? He said "ball".' But she and Joe hardly wait for an answer; forgetting Fred, they gaze at their son with relief and awe, then clasp him in a double embrace and cover him with happy kisses.

Fred's confrontation with Rosemary the next day has been planned without her knowledge or consent. A listing in the Sunday papers had informed him that she was appearing on a radio program featuring the newly published memoirs of her friend Daphne Vane, and he had determined to be there. After a morning of trying (without success) to work on his book, he checks the time and the address again and sets out.

The studio, when he finds it, is discouraging – not the place anyone would choose for a lovers' meeting. Fred would have preferred the BBC building in Portland Place, where he once went with Rosemary: a comic temple of art deco design with a golden sunburst over the door and a bank of gilded elevators. Behind them was a warren of corridors down which eccentric looking persons hurried with White Rabbit expressions. The sound rooms were cosy burrows furnished with battered soft leather chairs and historical-looking microphones and switchboards; the Battle of Britain still seemed to reverberate in the smoky air.

The commercial station is cold and anonymous and ultra contemporary; its glass-fronted lobby is decorated in Madison Avenue minimalism. A dozen or so teenagers slump on plastic divans, chewing gum and jiggling their knees to the pounding beat of rock music.

'I'm here to meet Rosemary Radley,' Fred shouts through the din at a sexy young receptionist with magenta lips and greasy-green iridescent eyelids. 'She's going to be on the Lively Arts program at four.'

'What name, please?'

Fred pronounces it, thinking a second later that maybe he should have claimed to be somebody else.

'Just a sec, baby; see what I can do.' She gives him an openly admiring look and a glossy ripe plum smile, and lifts a red telephone. 'They're trying to locate her.' She smiles at Fred again.

'You from America?'

'That's right.'

'I thought so. That's my dream, to go to the States.' She listens to the phone again, her smile tightening from plum to prune; finally she shakes her head.

'Tell her it's important. Very important.'

The receptionist gives him a different sort of look, equally admiring but less respectful; Fred realizes that she has reclassified him from VIP to groupie. She speaks again into the shiny red phone.

'Sorry. Nothing doing,' she says finally. 'I'd let you go in, but they'd give me hell.'

'I'll wait till the program's over.' Fred makes for a cube covered in shiny black imitation leather. As he sits on its edge, waiting, other visitors approach the desk; after checking by phone the receptionist presses a buzzer, allowing them to pass through the quilted, metal-studded imitation-leather doors behind her. The rock music continues, then blares to a crescendo, inspiring some of the lounging teenagers to rise and dance with hysterical, jerky motions.

The music crashes to a halt and is followed by a string of deafening commercials. The teenagers swarm toward the rear of the lobby, some of them holding out what looked like autograph books.

'Don't miss this amazing opportunity! Call NOW! . . . Stay tuned now for the The Lively Arts.' There is a surge of mood-music.

'Welcome again to The Lively Arts.' A different voice, fluty and confiding. 'I am your host, Dennis Wither. This afternoon we have a real treat in store: we're going to be talking to Dame Daphne Vane, whose autobiography, *Vane Pursuits: A life in the Theatre,* has just been published by Heinemann. Dame Daphne is here in the studio, and with her is Lady Rosemary Radley, star of the prizewinning television series *Tallyho Castle. . .* '

The punk teenagers look grossed-out at this news; some groan, one pantomimes nausea. Fred gives him a hostile look. He knows that Rosemary's show, popular as it is, has detractors. Some high-brow liberals, for instance, consider its picture of village life sentimental and snobbish. But these idle, loud-mouth kids, pretending to vomit at Rosemary's name – He'd like to murder them.

'We'll be back in a moment.' While an idiotic musical plug for shampoo ('Dreamier – lovelier!') reverberates round the lobby, a skinny man in a nail-studded white leather coverall pushes his way out through the doors behind the reception desk, followed by two fatter men in cheap suits. The teenagers converge on him with shrill cries.

The celebrity, whoever he is, moves on across the lobby, smiling tensely. He stops to sign a few autographs, then breaks for the street doors and a waiting limousine, while the fat men run interference. I might as well be back in New York already, Fred thinks watching this scene with distaste.

Suddenly Rosemary's beautiful trilling laugh, electronically magnified to three times life size, fills the room. Fred's heart flops like a fish.

'Thank you, Dennis darling, and I think it's quite marvelous to be here.' Her sweet, clear, perfectly modulated upper-class voice echoes from one wall to another, as if an invisible Rosemary Radley sixteen feet tall were floating in the air above his head.

Fred sits listening, becoming more and more angry. Rosemary's praise of Daphne's autobiography is fervent but, he knows, false – she has already described it to him as 'a silly picture book' and made fun of Daphne for being too tight to hire a really good ghostwriter. Now she announces to anyone tuned to this station in Greater London – or, for all he knows, anywhere in Britain – that she 'was absolutely bowled over' by Daphne's 'wonderful charm and wit'. How can she tell such lies? How can she chatter on like that, laugh like that, exchange trivial theatrical reminiscenses with Daphne and those other fools? Obviously she isn't in the same kind of pain he is. She really doesn't give a fuck; she's forgotten he exists. Well, as soon as the show is over he'll remind her.

The closing theme begins; Fred approaches the padded doors. Five minutes pass, but Rosemary doesn't appear, nor do any of the other people who were on the program with her.

'Hey!' The receptionist calls to him through a renewed blast of popular music. 'Hey you.'

'Yeh?' Fred looks around.

'You still looking for Rosemary Radley?'

'Yes.'

'You're wasting your time. The talent doesn't use this way out, 'less they want to see their fans or something.'

'Thank you.' Fred approaches her desk, leans on it with both elbows, and projects as much sexual charm as he can manage in his present mood. 'What way out do they use?'

'Round the back, by the parking lot. But they're probably all gone by now.' She lowers her slime-green, thick-lashed eyelids, leans towards him. 'Anyhow, what does a hunk like you want with a bag that age?'

'I – ' Fred suppresses the impulse to defend his love; there's no time to lose. 'Excuse me.' He runs across the lobby, shoves open a thick glass door, and circles the block. Behind the studio building he finds another entrance, but the glass doors here refuse to open.

His heart thumping, he stands beside a stack of empty packing cases watching for Rosemary to come out – with Daphne and those other fools probably, he realizes. But he won't bother about them, he'll pull her away, he'll say . . . Slowly, as Fred rehearses his prepared speech, time leaks out of the air; slowly he realizes that Rosemary has left without waiting for him.

Furious with blocked impulse, Fred curses aloud. 'Goddamned bitch,' he cries to the empty parking lot, and much more. He says to himself that Rosemary is cold-hearted, cruel; that all her words and gestures – some rise to consciousness, but he shoves them down again – were false, theatrical. The Lively Arts, he thinks: so lively, so arty . . . Ah, fuck it. He kicks the side of a damp-stained packing case several times, stoving it in.

Maybe he should have used more lively art himself. He should have lied to Rosemary, told her that he'd resigned his summer-school job, enjoyed himself for the next few weeks, and then got on the plane – been the Yankee skip-jack Mrs Harris claimed he was.

But he couldn't have kept up the act; he's no thespian. Anyhow the whole idea made him sick. It wouldn't have been love any longer, it would have been calculation, exploitation. Rosemary could have managed that maybe, if she'd wanted . . .

And now a smog of suspicion and jealousy descends on Fred, as if the saturated smoky-purple clouds that hang over the parking lot had suddenly descended, blotting out London. Maybe Rosemary was faking all along. Maybe she staged that quarrel with him after her party deliberately; maybe she'd just met or renewed a connection with someone she likes better. Maybe even now she is in the arms of this man, whispering to him in her soft voice, giving her intimate trilling laugh. Again the idea that he has fallen into a Henry James novel occurs to Fred; but now he casts Rosemary in a different role, as one of James' beautiful, worldly, corrupt European villainesses.

What if it was false, everything she'd ever said to him, everything he'd believed about her? What if, even, Debby was right, and Rosemary is really years older than she'd said? She doesn't even look thirty-seven, but Nico had claimed that she'd had more than one face-lift, that all actresses did as a matter of course. Fred had assumed this was just fag spitefulness. But suppose it's true, what difference does it make? Whatever her age, isn't she still Rosemary, whom he loves? Who doesn't love him, probably, who may never have loved him, who won't even speak to him now; who lied to him, maybe, the whole fucking time.

What an asshole he is, standing here among the rubbish, like some lovelorn groupie waiting at the stage door for a star who isn't even there. Fred scowls at the smashed packing case, at the debris blown against the wall: scraps of soiled paper and foil, an empty beer can, a length of twisted red yarn of the sort Roo used to tie round her hair.

And suddenly, for the first time in weeks, he sees Roo clearly in his mind. She is sitting naked on the edge of their unmade bed in the apartment in Corinth, her round tanned arms raised to gather the heavy weight of her dark chestnut hair. Then she separates it into three parts and, with an unconscious half smile of concentration, begins to plait them in and out to form a single thick, shining cable like the hawser of some sea-going ship. As the glossy rope lengthens, she pulls it forward and braids on till only about six inches of loose hair remain. Then she stretches a rubber band three times round the end of the plait, and over that a twist of scarlet wool. Finally, with a toss of her head, she flips the finished braid and its soft tail of coppery filaments back over her bare brown shoulder.

Fred feels a rush of longing; he thinks that, whatever her faults, Roo is incapable of calculated theatrical falsity. The seas will all go dry and the rocks melt with the sun, to quote one of her favorite folksongs, before he will ever hear her voice announcing that it is quite marvelous to be in some fucking radio station.

Next he feels a rush of guilt, remembering Roo's letter, which is still lying desolate and unanswered on top of a pile of unread scholarly books in his flat in Notting Hill Gate. He'll write her now, Fred thinks as he turns his back on the studio and starts home. This afternoon.

But the mails are slow; it will take ten days for a letter to reach Roo. Maybe he should phone; the hell with the cost. But after such a long silence – over four weeks since she wrote, he remembers with a groan – Roo could be furious with him again;

she has a right to be. She could hang up on him, scream at him. Or there could be somebody with her when he calls, some other guy. She has a right to that too, damn it. No. He'll send a telegram.

9

I'll tell you the truth,
Don't think I'm lying:
I have to run backwards
To keep from flying

Old rhyme

At the London Zoo, Vinnie Miner sits on a slatted bench watching the polar bears. Several of them are visible: one splashing lazily in the artificial rock-pool; one asleep on its side at the entrance of a stone cave, looking like a heap of damp yellowish-white fur rugs; and a third padding back and forth nearby, occasionally turning its heavy muzzle, on which the coarse hair has separated into spiky clumps, to give her an inquiring glance from its small glittering dark eyes.

Though she lives only a few blocks from the Zoo, this is the first time Vinnie has visited it all year, and she's only here now because some American cousins insisted on coming. These cousins, who are frantically 'doing London' in three days, have already gone on to the National Gallery. Vinnie lingers here partly from the sense that, having paid several pounds to enter the Zoo, she might as well get her money's worth, and partly because it's a fine day and her project is ahead of schedule. All her London data has been collected; she has read most of the relevant background material, and she has traveled to Oxford, Kent, Hampshire, and Norfolk to talk with experts in children's literature and folklore.

It isn't in Vinnie's nature to be wildly euphoric, but today she is at the peak of her own emotional curve, even off the graph. She is happier than she has been in months – maybe even in years. Everyone and everything looks good to her: the animals, the other visitors, the graceful new-leafed trees and the damp, shining lawns of Regent's Park. Even her cousins, whom she usually thinks of as boring, today seem only forgivably naive.

She hasn't had a visit from Fido – or even thought of him for days. For all she knows, he has followed Chuck to Wiltshire.

As she sits alone on her bench, Vinnie not only feels happy but curiously free. She is far from Corinth University, and from the duties and constraints of the role of Spinster Professor. The demanding and defining voices of her colleagues and students and friends are stilled. Moreover, English literature, to which in early childhood she had given her deepest trust, and which for half a century has suggested what she might do, think, feel, desire, and become, has suddenly fallen silent. Now, at last all those books have no instructions for her, no demands – because she is just too old.

In the world of classic British fiction, the one Vinnie knows best, almost the entire population is under fifty, or even under forty – as was true of the real world when the novel was invented. The few older people – especially women – who are allowed into a story are usually cast as relatives; and Vinnie is no one's mother, daughter, or sister. People over fifty who aren't relatives are pushed into minor parts, character parts, and are usually portrayed as comic, pathetic, or disagreeable. Occasionally one will appear in the role of tutor or guide to some young protagonist, but more often than not their advice and example are bad; their histories a warning rather than a model.

In most novels it is taken for granted that people over fifty are as set in their ways as elderly apple trees, and as permanently shaped and scarred by the years they have weathered. The literary convention is that nothing major can happen to them except through subtraction. They may be struck by lightning or pruned by the hand of man; they may grow weak or hollow; their sparse fruit may become misshapen, spotted, or sourly crabbed. They may endure these changes nobly or meanly. But they cannot, even under the best of conditions, put out new growth or burst into lush and unexpected bloom.

Even today there are disproportionately few older characters in fiction. The conventions hold, and the contemporary novelist, like an up-to-date fruit-grower, reconstructs the natural landscape, removing most of the aging trees to leave room for young saplings that haven't yet been grafted or put down deep roots. Vinnie has accepted the convention; she has tried for years to accustom herself to the idea that the rest of her life will be a mere epilogue to what was never, it has to be admitted, a very exciting novel.

But the self, whatever its age, is subject to the usual laws of optics. However peripheral we may be in the lives of others, each of us is always a central point round which the entire world whirls in radiating perspective. And this world, Vinnie thinks now, is not English literature. It is full of people over fifty who will be around and in fairly good shape for the next quarter-century: plenty of time for adventure and change, even for heroism and transformation.

Why, after all, should Vinnie become a minor character in her own life? Why shouldn't she imagine herself as an explorer standing on the edge of some landscape as yet unmapped by literature: interested, even excited – ready to be surprised?

Today the Zoo, her immediate landscape, is at its best. An early-afternoon shower has sluiced the dust from the still-shiny leaves and the mica-flecked paths, and has lent the air a scented freshness. It has also given Vinnie a chance to wear her new raincoat: dramatic, full-cut, of shimmery silvery-blue water-proofed silk – the sort of coat she could never have afforded to buy, and in fact hasn't bought. In it she feels taller and better looking, almost proud of herself.

She is proud of London too today. She rejoices in its natural and architectural beauty, the safety and cleanliness of its streets, the charm and variety of its shops; in its cultural sophistication – the educated, ironic tone of its press, its appreciation of historical tradition, its deference toward maturity, its tolerance of, even delight in, eccentricity.

Today, events that at another time would have infuriated or depressed her seem mere annoyances. The arrival in this morning's post of the current issue of the *Atlantic*, containing a letter in praise of L. D. Zimmern's article, hardly rippled her mood. Poor stupid Zimmern, imprisoned in ugly, dirty New York and in his own sulky spitefulness. Vinnie imagines this spitefulness as a deep cold muddy rock-pool like the one in the polar bears' enclosure. She visualizes L. D. Zimmern as sunk in it up to his (in her imagination) pudgy chin, unable to climb out. Whenever he attempts to clamber up its slippery sides, the largest polar bear – who has now hauled himself out of the water and is lying dripping on the rocks beside the pool – places a heavy paw like a sopping-wet floor mop on his head and shoves him back down again.

Since she feels so good, and it is such a nice warm day, Vinnie refrains from actually drowning Professor Zimmern in her fantasy. It would be bad publicity for the London Zoo, such a death. Besides, it might be upsetting for the bear – and perhaps even dangerous, if the keeper discovered that his prize *Thalarctos maritimus* was a man-killer. She rather likes this particular bear. It is true that his movements are slow and rather clumsy and his coarse yellow-white fur coat none too clean; and he doesn't look awfully intellectual. But he is satisfyingly large, and he has a humorous, sly, agreeable expression. To tell the truth, he is a little like Chuck Mumpson. She saw exactly that look on Chuck's face when they were shopping in Harrods last week, just before he left for Wiltshire.

The expedition was the final move in Vinnie's campaign to improve Chuck's appearance, both for his sake and for her own. If she was to go about London with him – and evidently she was – she was determined that he shouldn't look like a cartoon American Packaged Tourist, Western Division, especially since he really wasn't one any longer. She didn't try to alter his cowboy costume. That, she realized, would be almost impossible; and besides it was if anything a social advantage here. But she did gradually manage to persuade Chuck not to carry around so many maps and guidebooks, and to leave his cameras and light meters at the hotel – suggesting that she could guide him, and that his constant picture taking interfered with conversation.

Getting rid of his deplorable plastic raincoat was harder. There was no point in telling Chuck how ugly it was, she finally realized. His aesthetic sense was poorly developed; he judged even art almost wholly by its meaning rather than its looks. (Probably this was just as well for her, Vinnie thought, since it meant that her appearance had little importance for him; his appreciation of her was tactile rather than visual.)

Vinnie therefore tried a moral and connotative approach: she spoke disparagingly of the raincoat, associating it with ignorant tourists, with traveling salesmen, and with the shower curtains of cheap motels. But even when – in a fit of exasperation – she compared the garment to a male prophylactic, Chuck remained unmoved.

'Aw, come on Vinnie,' he said, grinning. 'Nothing wrong with it that I can see. Sure, maybe it's not beautiful; but it keeps the water out real fine. Besides, it's just about brand-new.'

'Really,' she remarked, implying doubt.

'Yeh; I bought it specially for the trip. It comes in this little plastic case, made outa the same stuff as the coat, see? You can fold the whole thing up and put it in your pocket. Great for traveling. You oughta get yourself one.'

Observing his expression of satisfaction, Vinnie had despaired. Her only hope – a faint one, considering the English climate – was that when she and Chuck went anywhere together it wouldn't rain.

Two days later, however, Chuck came to lunch at her flat; and when he departed considerably later, with an even more satisfied expression, he left his raincoat behind. Vinnie found it lying on the carpet in a corner of the sitting room, looking like a large very dead fish. She picked it up with distaste, observing how the greenish-gray plastic managed to feel stiff and slimy at the same time. How could Chuck, who is really a quite attractive man, wear such a thing? And where could she put it until she saw him again? Certainly not in her hall closet – a mere doorless alcove – where it would be visible to anyone who came to the flat.

She lugged the dead fish into the bedroom, opened her too small wardrobe, and shoved her clothes aside. The pretty pale dresses and skirts and blouses, all of soft natural fibres, seemed to flinch away from the vulgar plastic companion she offered them. She put out her hand to pull them back. Then, on a sudden impulse, she dragged the coat off its hanger. She carried it back down the hall by the scruff of its neck, opened the door of her flat and then the front door, and descended the steps to the yard. There she lifted the metal lid of a trashcan and wadded the raincoat down inside beneath a green plastic bag of garbage and a stack of wet newspapers.

That's where you belong, she told the dead fish. And if Chuck asks, I'll say I never saw you, and he'll assume he left you somewhere else.

As it turned out, however, Chuck did not assume this. Nor was he convinced by Vinnie's protestations of ignorance.

'Naw. I know I left my raincoat at your place Thursday. I bet you hid it.'

'Of course I didn't,' she said easily, smiling. 'Why on earth would I do that?'

'On account of you can't stand the thing.' Chuck grinned.

'Oh, don't be ridiculous. It's probably somewhere back at your hotel.'

'Come on, Vinnie. I left it right here, day before yesterday.' His grin widened. 'You hid my raincoat; I can see it in your eyes. You can't fool an old con like me.'

'Really, I didn't.' Confronted with Chuck's steady, smiling gaze, Vinnie's voice faltered. 'Not that I wouldn't have liked to.'

'Uh-huh.' He glanced into the hall closet, then walked on into Vinnie's bedroom and yanked open the door of the wardrobe.

'Really, Chuck,' she exclaimed, following him. 'You can see it isn't here.'

'Maybe.' He looked behind her bedroom door; then he pulled out the drawers of her chest, glanced in, and banged them shut again. 'Okay, honey. A joke is a joke. Hand it over now, and I promise I won't wear it to the theatre tonight.'

'It's not here anymore. I mean, it never was.'

A loud guffaw burst from Chuck. 'You swiped my raincoat,' he said. 'That really beats all. A nice sweet lady professor like you. And where is it now?'

'Honestly, I didn't – ' But Vinnie was unable to sustain the pretense. 'The dustmen took it away yesterday,' she said weakly. 'And good riddance.'

'Great. And what am I supposed to do the next time it rains?'

'Well-uh.' Vinnie realized she was flushing. 'I'll buy you another one.'

'Okay; sure.' Chuck began laughing again. 'You can just do that.'

'But not the same kind,' she insisted.

'Any kind you like.' Chuck gave a final whoop of laughter, then folded Vinnie in a generous hug.

As she accepted and then, relaxing, returned Chuck's embrace, Vinnie said to herself that of course he wasn't serious. He would, she hoped, take her advice on the purchase of a new raincoat. But he would hardly expect her to pay for it – or at least, to be fair, he wouldn't expect her to pay more than the cost of the dead fish.

These were still her assumptions the following day in Harrods, when Chuck removed the very expensive trenchcoat she'd said she liked best and told the sales clerk that it would do fine.

'Shall I wrap it for you, sir?'

'No thanks, sir,' Chuck returned. 'I'll wear it. And the lady will pay,' he added. Then he stood there calmly, grinning, while Vinnie helplessly allowed nearly a hundred pounds to be charged to her Barclaycard, wondering meanwhile what on earth the man must think. That Chuck's some sort of kept man, perhaps, she decided, signing the receipt as if under a bad spell. Or perhaps that I'm his bossy, money-managing wife. She hardly knew which would be worse.

But she couldn't get up her nerve to protest; after all, she'd brought this on herself. Besides, if you added up all the lunches and dinners and theater tickets Chuck had bought her, she was probably still ahead. Nevertheless she felt tricked, cheated; she remembered that Chuck Mumpson was a former juvenile delinquent – an old con, as he put it.

'Wal, thanks a lot,' he said – to her or to the sales clerk? It was ambiguous – offering Vinnie his arm, which she pretended not to see. She was struggling to frame a graceful request for at least partial repayment, a tactful way of saying that it was all a good joke, of course, wasn't it, but now . . .But no words came to her.

'I'm real glad we came here,' said Chuck as they waited for the elevator. 'This is a damn good-looking coat, huh?'

'Yes,' Vinnie agreed helplessly.

'And you're a real good sport, too.' Chuck grinned; it was at this moment that, clad in his new pale-tan Burberry, that he most resembled the polar bear. 'The way you signed that receipt! Not a squeak out of you!'

'No,' Vinnie squeaked, smiling uncomfortably.

'Okay, we're quits. Now I'll buy you one.'

'Me? But I don't need a raincoat.'

'Sure you do.'

She protested, but Chuck was determined. 'You want to make me feel like a creep, a moocher, a travelling salesman, is that it?'

'No, of course not,' Vinnie said; and the result was the coat she's wearing now, with its romantic gathered hood and designer label – the most beautiful garment she's owned in years.

Vinnie's raincoat isn't the only surprising thing Chuck has given her. He has turned out to be wonderful in bed; so wonderful that Vinnie had broken her promise to herself and allowed – no, rather welcomed – him back once, twice, three times – almost every day until he left for Wiltshire again. And to think that if hadn't been for Posy Billings' watercress-and-avocado soup, she might never have known . . .

Sometimes Vinnie wonders why any woman ever gets into bed with any man. To take off all your clothes and lie down beside some unclothed larger person is a terribly risky business. The odds are stacked almost as heavily against you as in the New York state lottery. He could hurt you; he could laugh at you; he could take one look at your naked aging body and turn away in ill-concealed, embarrased distaste. He could turn out to be awkward , selfish, inept – even totally incompetent. He could have some peculiar sexual hangup: a fixation on your underclothes to the exclusion of you, for instance, or on one sexual variation to the exclusion of all else. The risks are so high that really no woman in her right mind would take such a chance – except that when you do take such a chance you're usually not in your right mind. And if you win, just as with the state lottery (which Vinnie also plays occasionally) the prize is so tremendous.

In over forty years Vinnie has held a lot of losing tickets. But when she's with Chuck she feels like one of those lottery winners who are occasionally pictured in the newspapers grinning dizzily, astounded at their own luck. She has had this experience before, but she never expected it again. Even though it has happened four times, she hardly believes it.

Her disbelief, Vinnie realizes, is the consequence not only of English literature but of contemporary culture. The media convention is that people like Chuck and Vinnie – especially Vinnie – don't enjoy sex very much or experience it very often. This convention may date from an earlier era, when most women were physically worn out, if not dead, at fifty. Or it may reflect the distaste many people seem to feel for the idea of their parents as lovers. Superego figures are supposed to be dignified and disembodied; above all that.

Of course, elderly couples can now and then be seen hugging or kissing in a friendly manner. The public regard this indulgently, as visitors to the Zoo do the two damp-stained polar bears across the way from Vinnie, who are now nuzzling each other with a playful, clumsy affection. Anything more serious on their part, however, and most spectators would sidle off embarrassed, dragging their children with them, though perhaps with a prurient backward glance. To imagine these bears – or Chuck and Vinnie – really going at it would cause mental discomfort. In books, plays, films, advertisements, only the young and beautiful are portrayed as making love. That the relatively old and plain do so too, often with passion, is a well-kept secret.

Now that Chuck has been gone nearly a week, Vinnie misses him acutely. She misses the way he strokes her back and behind, remembering all the right places; the slow, delicious way he licks her breasts, first one and then the other; the size, shape, and color of his most private parts, and its amazing mobility – it can, uniquely in Vinnie's experience, nod or shake its head in reply to a question. Remembering all this, and more, as she sits on the bench, she wants him back so much that it is acutely painful. On the other hand, his presence creates a difficult social dilemma.

For the sake of her London reputation, Vinnie believes, she would do best to remain, or at least seem, romantically uninvolved. In Edwin's set – among people like Rosemary Radley and Posy Billings – occasional love affairs are forgiven. But her social world overlaps Edwin's only slightly. Most of her English friends are rather old-fashioned in their views: even if they approved of Chuck, they would look askance at adultery. In their opinion, casual affairs are perhaps all very well for actors, students, secretaries, and people like that; but a woman of Vinnie's age and professional reputation, if not celibate, ought to be married – or at least permanently living with another respectable educated person.

Vinnie has no regrets about having taken Chuck into her bed – much the reverse – but she doesn't want anyone to find out that he's been there. Unfortunately, since they became lovers Chuck's public manner toward her has altered. He has developed a way of looking at her, a way of taking her arm, that – agreeable though they may be – are a dead giveaway, or would certainly have become so if he had stayed in London much longer. When he returns next weekend the public danger as well as the private pleasure will be renewed. Vinnie can hardly ask him to behave more formally toward her when other people are around: that would involve uncomfortable explanations of her motives, or even more uncomfortable lies. And to prevent him from meeting anyone she knows will be inconvenient – maybe impossible. At the same time, she can't go around explaining to all her acquaintances that in spite of appearances, she isn't sleeping with Chuck Mumpson, especially when it is no longer true.

Vinnie rises from her bench and walks on, as if her contemplation of the bear who looks so much like Chuck might in itself incriminate her, should some acquaintance appear. To be suspected of having a lover would be difficult enough, she thinks; to be suspected of sleeping with what, from the British point of view, is practically a polar bear, would be worse. It isn't that her British friends dislike Chuck. They like him: they find him amusingly original; they are vastly entertained by his American simplicity and vulgarity.

The problem is that if her friends find out that Vinnie is mixed up with Chuck, they will begin to mix her up with him, to redefine her. The mental process isn't typically British, of course, but universal. In certain cases the confusion of identities affects the lovers themselves: transported by passion, they believe that their souls have merged, or were always identical. As an American friend of hers once put it at a high point of their brief relationship, crossing the town park in Saratoga Springs: 'Sometimes I think we're the same peson.' 'Oh, I know,' Vinnie had replied, equally deluded. (She hasn't been affected by any such hallucination in this case – rather the reverse: when she is with Chuck she feels more than usually small, intellectual, and timid.)

Even more often, outsiders conflate the couple, and credit them with each other's characteristics. If a radical takes up with a conservative, both will be perceived as more moderate politically, regardless of whether their views have in fact altered. The man or woman who becomes involved with a much younger person seems younger, the latter more mature.

Vinnie doesn't want her London friends to confuse her with Chuck, to think of her as after all rather simple, vulgar, and amusing – a typical American. She wants them to accept her, to take her for granted. She wants to be, believes she has been considered up to now, one of them. Subject, not object;

observer, not observed, she thinks, stopping by the wildfowl enclosure, which resembles a gigantic wire-mesh mosquito net held up here and there by long aluminium poles. She is content, and more than content, to be one of the smaller, less noticeable brownish birds she can see swimming or wading among the rustling marsh grasses beyond the netting, looking busy, pleased with themselves, and totally at home. She has no ambition – rather a horror – of resembling one of the outsize, peculiarly colored and feathered exotic waterfowl at whom a knot of cockneys are now pointing and giggling.

The brilliant birds, and their audience, remind Vinnie of Daphne Vane, and of the publisher's party that is being given in less than an hour to launch her largely ghost-written memoirs. If Vinnie is to attend it in more appropriate dress and with clean hair, she must hurry. Luckily the party's in Mayfair, and easily accessible by the 74 or Zoo bus, which stops outside her front door.

Daphne's party in an elegant converted Georgian house, is well under way when Vinnie arrives. For the first half-hour she experiences it as lively and thronged; then it begins to seem noisy and crowded. Stand-up events are always hard on her because of her height: most conversations take place a foot above her head, and when she wants to move she feels like a child trying to make its way to a familiar face through a mob of unseeing adults, all heavy rumps and sharp elbows. And today many of the faces that at first seem familiar turn out not to be acquaintances, but only actors she has seen at some time on stage or television – and, like most actors, uninterested in meeting anyone not in their own profession.

'Having a good time?' inquires an actual acquaintance, William Just, looking down at her.

'Oh yes. Well, perhaps not especially. The publisher's party isn't quite my favorite social occasion.'

'It isn't a social occasion at all,' William says, reaching for a plate of hot hors d'oeuvres and offering some to Vinnie. 'Almost everyone here was invited for some ulterior purpose, as usual. They're connected with the firm, or with some paper, or they're in the theater – though I hear Nigel's very disappointed because so few of our leading dramatis personae have shown up. I'm meant to get Daphne's book discussed on the BBC, and you're supposed to tell everyone in America how thrilling it is.'

'Yes, I suppose you're right.' Vinnie cannot think of anything clever to say. Her head has begun to ache and her stomach to complain of the strong punch and the spicy canapés. She says goodbye to William and starts to move toward the door, stopping to greet the few people she knows. One of these, as might be expected, is Rosemary Radley.

'Lovely, isn't it all?' Though elegantly dressed and perfectly – if rather over-elaborately – made up, Rosemary seems somehow scatty and distracted, perhaps a bit tipsy.

'Oh yes.' Vinnie remembers that there's something she's supposed to tell Rosemary – what? Yes: she's promised to explain that Fred Turner really loves her and is going back to America against his true desire. The commission is uncomfortable, and this crowded room hardly the place to carry it out. Besides, what's the point? In Vinnie's opinion, the breakup of their affair isn't surprising; it was inappropriate from the start. Of course Rosemary is beautiful, and her life no doubt very glamorous, if you like that sort of thing. But she's much too complicated for someone like Fred, and probably bad for him as well: frivolous, egotistic, temperamental, and full of expensive false values. To reconcile them – even if anyone could, which seems very unlikely – hardly seems desirable.

But fate, perversely, provides Vinnie with the opportunity to carry out her promise. As she collects her coat, Rosemary reappears and asks if she needs a lift; she is going to a dinner party in Gloucester Crescent, and can easily drop Vinnie off. Feeling ashamed of her recent thoughts, Vinnie hesitates; but her increasing headache and the knowledge that the 74 bus becomes rare, almost extinct, as soon as the Zoo closes, change her mind.

Though it is always hard to find a cab in Mayfair at that hour, Rosemary spies one. Sprinting a little unsteadily down Upper Grosvenor Street in her high-heeled silver sandals, with her long pink cape billowing behind, she beats out two men in bowler hats who have already hailed the taxi. They begin to expostulate, but Rosemary, dazzling them with her smile, pulls open the door and waves Vinnie on. Once inside, however, she and her cape collapse into the corner with a sigh like a pricked balloon.

'Stupid party,' she announces in her sweet, well-modulated voice. 'Imbecile dons, think they know everything about the theater because they once read a play.'

Vinnie, who has recognized no dons beside herself at the party, and wonders if this comment is meant maliciously, makes no comment.

'Disgusting drink,' Rosemary continues. 'Nothing to eat, either.'

'Oh, no,' Vinnie corrects her. 'There was quite a lot of food.'

'Really? No one offered me any.' She laughs musically. 'Pigging it all for themselves, most likely.'

Unsure whether this is an accusation, Vinnie again says nothing. Rosemary too is silent, sulking within her silk cocoon.

Traffic is heavy; the taxi jerks forward and halts along South Audley Street; jerks and halts. At this rate it will take hours to reach Regent's Park Road; whereas if Vinnie were to get out now and walk to Bond Street Tube Station – But before she can solidify this intention Rosemary turns to her and begins to complain of what she calls 'your friend Fred' – thus simultaneously denying that she is Fred's friend and assigning responsibility for him to Vinnie.

'I'm not a complete simpleton,' she declares. 'I know your friend Fred doesn't really have to go back to that silly old college this summer.'

Annoyed, but bowing to fate, Vinnie assures Rosemary that he does; she begins to explain why. Rosemary listens with an ill grace, tapping her silver-sandaled toe on the floor of the cab and gazing away out the window.

'Oh, come on, Vinnie,' she interrupts. 'I don't need to hear all that drivel again. I know there's more to it; he's going back to that stupid wife of his, isn't he?'

Vinnie assures her that as far as she knows Fred isn't going back to his wife, all that is long over. 'It's you he cares for,' she adds, noticing that her headache is worse and wishing she could get out of the taxi. 'He thinks you're a wonderful woman.'

'Oh he does, does he.' Rosemary's voice has thickened and coarsened oddly; if they hadn't been alone Vinnie would have looked round to see who else was speaking.

'Yes, he told me so. And I believe him' she adds.

'I suppose you might,' Rosemary says, again in her

characteristic upper-class drawl. 'But you don't know much about men, Vinnie. They're liars, the lot of them.'

Vinnie glances nervously at the back of the taxi-driver's head; then she sits forward and tugs the glass panel shut.

'Listen, sweetie, when they're making up excuses to leave you, men always start telling everyone you're a wonderful woman.' Rosemary's accent continues to alternate disconcertingly between refined and vulgar, as if she were trying out for some inappropriate low-comedy role but was unable to sustain the illusion. 'That's what they always say, the bastards. It's a kind of omen.'

'It's not an excuse, really. You've got to understand . . .' With increasing weariness Vinnie begins to explain the tenure system in American universities.

'You're wastin' you breath, dearie,' Rosemary interrupts. 'I don't give a fart for all that. All I know is he's sneakin' out on me,' she says in her low-comedy voice – a voice Vinnie has heard before, but where?

'Fred isn't sneaking – ' she begins.

'I need him, Vinnie,' Rosemary wails, pathetically ladylike again, with a half sob. 'You tell him to forget his silly job. If he doesn't come back and stay with me, I'll be all alone again. You don't know what that's like for me.' She leans toward Vinnie as she speaks – breathes toward her; and Vinnie realizes what she should have realized sooner: that Rosemary isn't merely tipsy, but quite drunk.

Annoyed, she tries to calm her, speaking slowly and firmly as she would to an anxious class. 'Of course you're not alone. You have so many friends, so many beaux, I'm quite sure – '

'That's what you think, my dear. You think a lot of men want to sleep with me. I used to think that myself.' Her voice alters. 'Bloody little fool that I was. Men don't want to sleep with me, they want to have slept with me. They want to be able to tell their mates, "Oh, Lady Rosemary Radley, the television star? Yes, I do know her. In fact, I knew her *very well*, at one time."' Rosemary has slipped into a third voice: tenor, smarmily insinuating.

'That's how they all are, the bastards,' she continues, her accent shifting again. 'Except for Freddy. Freddy knew I was an actress, but it didn't mean fuck-all to him. He'd never even heard of *Tallyho Castle* before he met me. I thought all you Americans were mad about British TV, but he didn't even own a set, for Christ's sake. He never even saw the show, he loved me anyhow.' Rosemary is sobbing now, her face distorted in a way it never becomes when she weeps on camera. 'But he's a bastard like the rest of them.'

The taxi is in Oxford Street now, snarled in a skein of other vehicles. From either side their drivers and passengers, with the covert but avid interest of the British in personal disaster, regard the drunken and weeping woman from whom they are separated by only a sheet of glass.

'He keeps on phoning my service, but I don't dare see him or talk to him. I bloody couldn't take it, Vinnie, unless I knew he was coming back for good, I – ' Rosemary breaks off, perceiving that she has an audience.

'Yah!' she screams suddenly, turning with an ugly face and a coarse gesture to the nearest spectator, a portly well-dressed man in an adjoining taxi. He flinches visibly, then turns away with an unconvincing attempt at casualness.

Rosemary laughs wickedly, almost hysterically. Then she flings herself across the cab and repeats the performance at Vinnie's open window, horrifying a young woman at the wheel of a Mini. 'Yah, you nosy bitch! Why don't you mind your own business!' She flops back into her seat, grinning. The Pale silk cocoon of her cape has been sloughed off by all this activity, and lies crumpled on the seat beneath her; and what has emerged from it, Vinnie thinks, is not a butterfly.

The light changes, the taxi jolts ahead. Rosemary turns to her and says in a light sweet voice, 'Next time you happen to see Mr Frederick Turner – '

'Er-yes?'

'You might be kind enough to give him a message from me. Would you do that?' Her manner has become exaggeratedly gracious, almost caressing.

'Yes, of course,' Vinnie agrees, bewildered and even a little frightened by these rapid histrionic changes.

'I'd like for you to tell him, mm – Please tell him, would he be kind enough to stop telephoning me, and writing to me' – her voice alters again – 'and just bloody well go screw himself.'

'Now really, Rosemary. You don't mean – '

'Now really, Vinnie. That's exactly what I do mean,' Rosemary interrupts, caricaturing Vinnie's intonation and accent. 'I've had it with all you fuckin' Americans,' she goes on in the other voice, the coarse cockney Vinnie has heard somewhere. 'Why don't you stay home where you belong? Nobody wants you comin' over here, messin' up our country.' She waves at the souvenir shops and hamburger bars with which this portion of Oxford Street is disfigured. The loose, excessive gesture and grimace are those of a low-comedy stage character – of a music-hall charlady, say – of Mrs Harris. Yes. That's where Vinnie has heard this voice before: once or twice on the phone when she called Rosemary, and often at parties when Rosemary, telling some story, had imitated Mrs Harris.

'It wasn't me,' she starts to protest, with a strained laugh, trying to treat Rosemary's performance as a joke – which after all it must be. 'I certainly never wanted – '

'Of course not,' Rosemary interrupts smoothly. 'Tell me something, Vinnie. How old are you?'

'Uh, I'm fifty four,' replies Vinnie, who makes a point of answering this question accurately.

'Imagine that.' Rosemary smiles sweetly. 'I would never have guessed it.'

'Thank you.' She is pleased in spite of herself, and somewhat mollified, 'It's just because I'm small, really.'

'You know what's so wonderful about you, Vinnie?'

'Er – no.' Vinnie smiles expectantly.

'I'll tell you what's so wonderful about you.' It is Mrs Harris' voice again, speaking through the pink sweet-pea lips of Rosemary Radley. 'You're fifty-four years old, and you look sixty, and you don't know fuck-all about life.' .

The taxi has, with many stops and starts, negotiated the turn into Portman Square, and is halted next to a bed of yellow parrot tulips. Seizing the opportunity, Vinnie mumbles something about having to be home by seven-thirty, shoves the door open, and flees.

Not looking back, she makes her way hazardously through the traffic toward the 74 bus stop, walking too fast and breathing painfully hard, but congratulating herself on having had the nerve to get out of Rosemary's taxi and escape from her drunken insults. Messing up our country. Fifty-four, and you look sixty.

Standing on the curb, she shivers with rage and pain. She shouldn't have sat there and taken it, she should have said – But Vinnie can't think what she should have said. And after all, what's the point of arguing with a drunk?

Of course Vinnie has never liked Rosemary, and probably Rosemary doesn't like her. It's not as if they'd ever been friends. Vinnie's real friends don't like Rosemary very much either, except for Edwin, and even he admits that she is self-indulgent and erratic, though he excuses it because she's an artist, an actress – as if that were any excuse, Vinnie thinks, with another spasm of fury.

She's always thought there was something unpleasant about the art of acting, Vinnie remembers as she reaches the bus stop; something unnatural, really, in the ability of certain persons to assume at will a completely alien voice and manner. She has felt this often at the theater, where she is never really comfortable, however entertained or moved she may be. The mimicry of other living beings is a nasty business; the more successful the imitation, the more there is essentially something horrible and uncanny in it.

Uncanny; literally so, because it overturns our belief in the uniqueness of the individual, Vinnie decides as she stands waiting for the bus in a queue of half-a-dozen women of varied ages and walks of life, any one of whom Rosemary might presumably if she chose become, as she had a few minutes ago become Vinnie Miner. Again she hears what was supposed to be her own voice coming out of Rosemary's mouth: 'Now really, Vinnie – ' Does she always sound like that, so pert, nasal, and schoolmistressy? Of course no one likes their own voice; she remembers embarrassing moments with her tape recorder. Then she wonders whether Mrs Harris has ever heard Rosemary's impersonation of Mrs Harris. Somehow she doubts it – a woman of her sort wouldn't stand for that; she would fly into a rage, she would curse out Rosemary or maybe even smack her, the way Vinnie would have liked to.

Histrionic talent such as Rosemary's has other dangers besides the hostility of those who are mimicked, Vinnie thinks, breathing more normally now. It's possible to play a part once too often; actors can be typecast, so that they have to go on being silly ingenues or strong-silent detectives for years. Sometimes they become so identified with a role that it gradually usurps their own shallower and less defined personalities – in private as well as in the public eye.

Edwin was right, she tells herself as the tall red bus approaches. He saw what was happening before he left for Japan: he said that Mrs Harris was a bad influence. And now, from imitating her as a parlor trick, Rosemary has progressed to the point where, when her own rather weak ego is blurred by alcohol, the strong but disagreeable personality of the charlady takes over and says things Rosemary herself would never say, or probably even think. Because surely she doesn't think that Vinnie is personally messing up London and knows fuck-all about life.

Yes, that's an interesting theory, and a nice, reassuring one, Vinnie says to herself as the 74 bus grinds north toward Regent's Park. But isn't it more likely that Rosemary, however drunk, meant what she said? That her jealous rage at Fred spilled over onto Vinnie, and the real truth came out? But what she really thinks of Vinnie – what all her friends – maybe everyone in London – think of Vinnie couldn't be properly expressed by anyone as sweet and charming and refined as Lady Rosemary Radley. To say it she had to become, and because she is an actress could become, a coarse, ill-tempered, vindictive person like Mrs Harris.

When she reaches her flat, Vinnie's impulse is to go to bed and hide. But she resists it; she isn't really tired or ill, just angry and miserable and headachy. She doesn't feel up to going out again, even just up the road to Limonia to have supper with her cousins. She distrusts the world: people she has never done any harm to – or (as in the case of L. D. Zimmern) even met – are walking around in it wishing her ill. She decides to telephone her cousins and excuse herself. But before she can find the number of their hotel, her phone rings.

'Hi, honey, this is Chuck.'

'Oh, hello. How is everything in Wiltshire?'

'Great. I've got a heap to tell you. You remember that picture of the grotto with the Hermit of South Leigh that Colonel and Lady Jenkins showed me when I first came down here?'

'Yes of course.'

'Wal, I've been trying to get ahold of a copy, and this guy in

Bath just came up with one. Not the whole book, just that etching, but it's hand-colored and in great condition.'

'Oh, that's nice.'

'And yesterday we found a stone on the dig with real interesting carvings. Mike thinks – ' Chuck expounds; Vinnie, holding the phone with one hand and her headache with the other, listens, making appropriate noises. 'So it looks like – Hey, Vinnie. Are you feeling all right?'

'Oh yes, thanks,' she lies.

'You sound kinda low.'

'Well. Perhaps a little. A rather upsetting thing happened this afternoon.' Though she hasn't meant to, Vinnie finds herself relating her encounter with Rosemary, omitting only the characterization of her own appearance.

'Weird,' is Chuck's comment. 'Sounds to me like she's having some kinda crackup.'

'I don't know. It could easily have been deliberate. After all, Rosemary's an actress. Probably she just doesn't like Americans. And I expect she never did like me very much.' In spite of herself, Vinnie's voice wavers.

'Aw, baby. It's rough to be cursed out like that. I wish I was there; I'd make you feel better.'

'I'm all right, really. It's just that it upset me, the way she kept changing voices.'

'Yeh, I get what you mean. Myrna used to do something like that. She'd be screaming at me or the kids, or maybe the help, practically out of control. Then the phone would ring, and she'd answer it sweet and smooth as soft ice cream, talking to some client or one of her lady-friends. Just as easy as switching channels. It used to spook me.'

'I can understand that. You wonder which one is real.'

'Yeh. Wal, no, I never wondered that.' Chuck laughs harshly. 'Listen, honey. Maybe what you need is to get out of London for awhile. I mean, you don't hafta be back home till late August, right?'

'That's right.'

'Wal, I was thinking. There's a lotta folklore down here in Wiltshire. All these books and manuscripts and stuff in the historical society, I was looking at some of them the other day. And there's schools here of course, and kids. There oughta be lots of rhymes you could collect. I was thinking, maybe you could come down and stay with me for the summer. There's plenty of room for you to work here. I'd really like that.'

'Oh, Chuck,' Vinnie says. 'That's kind of you, but –'

'Don't decide now. Think about it awhile. Okay?'

'Okay,' Vinnie repeats.

Of course she can't spend the whole summer in Wiltshire, she tells herself after she has hung up; she doesn't want to leave the London Library and all her friends. But a short visit – several visits, even – that might be possible. And that way she could see Chuck every day, and every night, without anyone in London knowing about it. Yes, why not?

While she wasn't watching it, Vinnie's headache has dissolved. She feels able to go out to dinner after all.

10

'Why dost thou turn away from me? 'Tis thy Polly – '

John Gay, *The Beggar's Opera*

In Notting Hill Gate, Fred Turner is packing to return home. It is midsummer, and London is in full bloom. Tall horse chestnuts press their green hands and creamy candles of blossom against his windows, and through them a hazy vanilla light seeps into the room, transfiguring its scratched wooden furniture, turning its paint-clogged Victorian woodwork and flowery plaster ceiling decorations into confections of whipped cream. The air is warm and windy, the sky beyond the trees a deep, still blue.

Fred, however, sees little of this. His mood is gray, flat, icy, and bitter as a brackish winter pond. In less than two days he will be gone from London, without having finished his research, seen Rosemary again, or heard from Roo. More than two weeks have passed since he cabled an answer to his wife's letter: but though his message included the words LOVE and CALL COLLECT, there has been no answer. He had waited too damn long; or Roo never wanted him back in the first place.

As for his work, it is in a dead funk. He goes through the motions of scholarship, reading primary and secondary sources, copying down quotations from Gay's work and from eighteenth-century critical essays, contemporary records, and true-crime narratives, patching them together somehow into a kind of whole, but it is all false and forced. Everything Fred puts into his two battered canvas suitcases reminds him of failure, of waste. Stacks of notes – skimpy and disordered compared to what they should have been – half-empty notebooks, blank three-by-five-inch index cards. Unanswered letters, including one from his mother and two from students asking for recommendations which should have been dealt with weeks ago. A favorite snapshot of Roo at fourteen with a pet rabbit, taken by her with her first time-release camera; the innocent warmth of her smile, the openness, the trust, wrenches his heart: this Roo has never loved him or any man, never been hurt by him – A great lump rises in Fred's chest; he turns the photograph face down, sets his jaw, goes on with his packing.

Paper, envelopes, manila folders, all unused, mutely accusing. Programs for plays, operas, and concerts he'd attended with Rosemary – why the hell is he still saving these? Fred shoves them in the overloaded wastebasket. The long handwoven tan cashmere scarf that Rosemary gave him for his birthday, winding it round and round his neck with her own hands. A square of pocket mirror with the mauve-pink imprint of her mouth on it, commemorating their first kiss. They had just finished lunch at La Girondelle in the Fulham Road, and Rosemary was renewing her lipstick. Fred, suddenly realizing that they were about to part, leaned over the table toward her, saying something impulsive, passionate. She glanced up, smiling slowly and wonderfully, then blotted her open mouth on the glass to avoid smudging his. How charming, how thoughtful, he had marveled. Later he had put his hand on her wrist to stop her from returning the bit of mirror to her handbag, claiming it as a souvenir. Now it has another meaning: before she kissed him, Rosemary had kissed herself.

Stop thinking about it, Fred tells himself. It's over, for Christ's sake; he's leaving London the day after tomorrow and he will probably never see Rosemary Radley again. Also, as he realized this morning when he emptied his closet, he will never see again his Ragg sweater from L. L. Bean, his blue chambray workshirt, his *Oxford Book of Eighteenth-Century Verse*, and his spare toothbrush and razor, all of which he left at Rosemary's before the day of her party.

But he can't stop thinking about it. Angry as he is at Rosemary, he hasn't been able to forget her. Several times in the last two weeks, against his better judgment, and giving himself the lame excuse that he just wants to pick up his sweater, shirt, etc., he has dialed her number. Most of the time it rings on and on, unanswered, though once Mrs Harris picked it up, growled out, 'Nobody home,' and slammed down the receiver. He also tried the answering service, where a falsely refined female voice always informed him that Lady Rosemary was 'out of town'. A warble of amused condescension the last time he called suggested to Fred that the female voice knew all about him; that as soon as he hung up she would turn to other females and say: 'Guess who just phoned Lady R again, the moron; when will he smarten up?' Though he left his name, Rosemary never called back.

Suppose he were to leave the message that he wasn't going back to America, would Rosemary call him then? Yes, maybe, Fred thought. Maybe that's what she's waiting for. Or maybe not. It has occurred to him that in a way their love affair has reenacted Anglo-American history. Rosemary may have loved him, but she has the colonial mentality; she would do anything for him but grant him independence. When he demanded that, it was war.

Partly in order to stop himself from telephoning Rosemary again and leaving this self-destructive message, Fred has just had his phone cut off. His other, more rational motive was to save money. As it is, he's going home dead broke, and in debt on both sides of the Atlantic.

He shuffles through a pile of letters from relatives and friends, consigning most to the wastebasket. Among them is a postcard from Roberto Frank in Buffalo. The reverse of the card is a painting from the Albright-Knox Gallery by Sir Joshua Reynolds: *Cupid as Link Boy*, 1774 – selected because of Fred's interest in the period, he had assumed. Now he looks at the picture more closely.

Ostensibly, it is a half-length portrait of one of those urchins who for a small fee used to light travelers through the streets of eighteenth-century London at night. This Cupid is no plump, laughing, naked babe: He is slight, shabbily dressed in contemporary costume, and seems about nine or ten. He is good-looking – indeed, he rather resembles Fred himself at that age – but quite obviously a dark angel. He has small black bat wings, and holds his long smoldering dark torch in a phallic position, braced against his crotch; a spurt of flame and stained smoke rises from it into the sooty air. Cupid, however, looks away from the torch over his shoulder and down to the left, with a brooding, sorrowful expression – regret for what he has done to so many humans, maybe. Behind him, sketchily indicated, is a London street along which an ill-matched couple can be seen walking away: the man tall and stick-thin, the woman grossly fat, like Jack Sprat and his wife.

Yes, Fred thinks: this is the little dark god who has scorched him – he can feel the wound blistered and smoldering still – twice mismatched, to two beautiful angry impossible women he can't get out of his mind. To be unhappily in love with one woman is bad enough, but to be longing after two alternately is laughable. Roberto certainly would laugh.

Smarten up, he tells himself. Forget about them. Get on with your damn packing. He yanks out the jammed top drawer of the desk angrily, causing it to tilt downward and scatter its contents onto the floor; pencils, paper clips, old bus maps, pamphlets about tourist attractions. Among the avalanche of debris something falls with a heavier, more metallic sound. Fred bends to look and recognizes the keys to Rosemary's house in Chelsea, which he thought he'd lost weeks ago.

The house is empty now, probably. He could go there this afternoon and reclaim his possessions, which he doesn't want to lose – especially the book, which is annotated, and his Ragg sweater. Rosemary will never even know he's been there, or miss anything. Her books are many and disordered, and her closet, being outside Mrs Harris' theater of operations, is always in chaos. Okay, let's go. He jams the drawer back into the desk, and its former contents into the wastebasket, and sets out. At Notting Hill Gate, too impatient to walk, he descends into the tube station.

But as he sits on the Circle Line train being shaken toward South Kensington, its whining roar begins to sound a chorus of doubts. What if somebody is staying at Rosemary's? What if the lock has been changed? What if one of the neighbors sees him and calls the police? AMERICAN PROFESSOR HELD IN BURGLARY OF STAR'S CHELSEA HOME.

As he stands in South Kensington Underground Station, still hesitating, a sign pointing the way to MUSEUMS reminds Fred that he has been in London for five months without visiting the Victoria and Albert, so highly recommended by everyone as a repository of eighteenth-century furniture and artifacts. He decides to stop there first while he makes up his mind. If he doesn't go on to Rosemary's, at least he will have done something professionally useful.

Five minutes later he has passed from the warm sunny afternoon into the cool, cavernous galleries and halls of the V and A. They are almost deserted, maybe because of the weather outside. Thousands of decorative art objects lie unregarded in a shadowy gloom, through which here and there a dusty band of sunshine slants down from the tall Victorian Gothic windows to spotlight a carved medieval chest or a Georgian silver teapot. No such light strides into Fred's psyche: it remains uniformly clouded and chill. Everything before him is handsome, highly finished, the best of its kind; but he is unmoved. These great rooms full of national treasures don't seem to him rich and complex and historic, but overcrowded, overdecorated – collections of too many expensive old things. He has, as Rosemary and her friends would have put it, gone off England. London especially oppresses him; it seems so crowded with architecture and furniture and tradition that there is no room to move. The city is weighted down with ghosts, haunted by its long history just as he is haunted by his short one: by the history of his affair with Rosemary and by her own past history.

These last weeks in London Fred has felt as lonely and shut out of life as he did his first month here. He has hardly spoken to any of the natives, except as a tourist might; he hasn't seen a single one of the many people he met through Rosemary. Or, to be more accurate, he hasn't seen them in the flesh. In the media they are everywhere: explaining the human body and international law on television; appearing in plays and films; giving their opinions about cultural events on the radio; being interviewed by newspapers; answering difficult questions with charm and erudition on quiz shows and current affairs programs. Whenever Fred opens a magazine one of them is telling him what to think about Constable or how best to cook asparagus or support nuclear disarmament. And if they aren't quoted, they are referred to – most disagreeably, by an item in *Private Eye* noting that 'Lady Rosily Raddled', as it habitually calls her, has 'dissolved her Yankee connection', and making reference to a long list of other melted connections, some of them involving men Fred has met several times but never imagined that Rosemary had once slept with.

Of course he hadn't thought that she had no past, Fred tells himself as he wanders disconsolate down a long gallery of late

Renaissance furnishings toward a looming pillared structure described on a placard as The Great Bed of Ware and said to have housed up to a dozen sleepers a night. But to be referred to in print as just one of a series – Fred clenches his teeth and focuses again on the Great Bed, associating it in his mind with Rosemary and her lovers. There is room here between these twisted columns for all those mentioned or hinted at in *Private Eye,* and more. And no doubt there were more. He's only the most recent – by now, maybe not even that. Against his will he sees Rosemary, in her pale satin nightgown scattered with lace butterflies, sporting in the Great Bed with a dozen shadowy naked male figures. The legs, the arms, the cocks, the backsides – her tumbled pale-gold hair – the stained and tumbled bedclothes – the rebound of springs, the smell of sex . . .

To shake off this hallucination, Fred moves nearer and puts his hand on the unwrinkled brocade coverlet, receiving a shock: the Great Bed of Ware is as hard as stone.

But why should he be surprised? Functionally speaking this is no longer a bed. No one will ever sleep or fuck in it again. No one will sit in these high-backed oak chairs: their stringy crimson velvet seats, now faded to pink, are protected from contemporary rear ends by tarnished gilt cords. The engraved goblets in the glass cases will never again hold water or wine; the pewter plates will never be heaped with the roast beef of Old England.

Art museums are better. Paintings and sculptures continue to serve the purpose for which they were made: to be gazed at and admired, to interpret and shape the world. They live on, immortal, but all this stuff is functionally dead; no, worse, fixed in a kind of living death, like his passion for Rosemary Radley. There's something futile, something hideous, about this immense Victorian junkshop full of expensive household things: all these chairs and dishes and clothes and knives and clocks, so many of them, too many of them, preserved forever in frozen uselessness, just as his passion for Rosemary and his love for Roo are uselessly preserved.

A revulsion from the thousands of undead objects that surround him on all sides seizes Fred, and he starts to walk, then to run toward the staircase and the exit. Outside the vast cocoa-colored mausoleum he takes deep breaths of a living air that smells of auto exhaust and cut grass. Okay, what shall he do now? Is it safe to rescue his clothes from Rosemary's house, or should he abandon them to a V and A zombie existence?

If Rosemary were only in London – If only he'd found the damn key when she was still around – Yes, then he could have gone to the house whether she'd invited him or not, let himself in, and told her and showed her that he loved her, sworn he wasn't tired of her. How could he be tired of Rosemary, for Christ's sake?

If only he'd gone there sooner after their quarrel . . . Or, two weeks ago at the radio station, if only he'd been bolder, if he'd pushed his way into the studios behind some of those other people, found Rosemary, made her listen to him – Why has he become so slow, so cautious, so respectful of rules and conventions and public opinion; why has he become so – yes, that's it – so goddamn English?

Look at him now: nearly thirty years old, nearly six and a half feet tall, a professor at a major American university, standing dumbly in front of the V and A shifting from one foot to the other, too fucking chicken to go and get his own goddamn sweater back. For Christ's sake, stop acting like some British twit, he tells himself, and begins to stride toward Chelsea.

When Fred reaches Cheyne Square twenty minutes later, he understands his reluctance better. The house looks exactly, painfully the same; it is hard to believe that Rosemary – his real Rosemary, not the phony imitaton of the radio station – won't in a moment open the shiny lavender front door and hold up her heart-shaped face for his kiss. He feels deeply reluctant to enter the familiar rooms again, to pass through them as an intruder. If only it hadn't all gone wrong he might now, today – A tight choked feeling fills his chest, as if he'd swallowed a wet balloon.

Fighting down the sensation, fixing his mind on the image of a gray sweater, Fred climbs the steps and rings the bell; he hears the two familiar musical notes of the chime within, but nothing more.

'Rosemary!' he calls finally. 'Rosemary! Are you there?'

Silence. After ringing the bell again, and waiting a few more minutes, he puts his key in the lock.

The house, as he had expected, is darkened and silent. He

shuts the door behind him, and forestalls the shrill clamor of Rosemary's burglar alarm by clicking the switch under the gilt-legged hall table as he has so often done at her request.

The shutters are closed in the long drawing room, but even in this light its total disorder is evident. Newspapers and cushions are strewn on the floor, plates and glasses on the tables. Evidently Mrs Harris too is away on holiday. He searches round for his book, but can't see it anywhere; maybe it's upstairs.

As Fred starts for the hall he hears noises below: a thump and a scuffling of feet. He halts, holding his breath, listening. Has Rosemary lent the house to someone? Have burglars got in in spite of the alarm system? His first impulse is to turn and run, abandoning his possessions, but this strikes him as cowardly and twit-like. Instead he looks round for a weapon, then grabs a tight-rolled black umbrella from the Chinese urn by the hall table. The poker would be more effective; but if it's not burglars the umbrella will pass as part of his getup. That it's a sunny afternoon won't matter: in London many men carry such umbrellas in all weathers, as Gay and his contemporaries carried canes.

Clutching the bamboo handle so tightly that his knuckles whiten, Fred descends the dark, twisting backstairs. In the basement kitchen a greeny half-dusk seeps through the net of ivy that shrouds the barred window. A woman – Mrs Harris, he recognizes her by her headscarf, and the mop and bucket leaning against the sink – is sitting in a rocker at the far end of the long room. In front of her is a glass and a nearly empty bottle of what looks like Rosemary's gin.

'So it's you,' says Mrs Harris in a drunken, hostile cockney, hardly raising her head to look at him. Though Fred has seen her only once before, and then only briefly, he is aware of her appearance as greatly altered for the worse. Her shoes are off, and shreds of hair hang thickly over her face. 'I thought you were off to the States.'

'I'm leaving the day after tomorrow.'

'Y'are, are you?' Her voice is slurred, shaky. 'Then what the bloody 'ell are you doin' ere?'

'I've come to pick up some clothes I left,' Fred explains, repressing his irritation. 'I heard noises, so I came down to see what was going on,'

'Oh, yeh,' Mrs Harris sneers.

'Yeh.' He is not going to be intimidated by a drunken char woman.

'Creepin' into the 'ouse behind my back. I oughta call the p'lice.' She grins tipsily.

Fred doesn't believe for a moment that Mrs Harris will call the police, but it occurs to him that she will certainly report his visit to Rosemary, no doubt with disagreeable embellishments. 'And what are you doing here?' he asks, taking the offensive.

Mrs Harris stares at him through the gloom in a boozy, fixed way. 'You tell me, Professor Know-All,' she says finally.

Fred flinches. 'Professor Know-All' was one of Rosemary's private nicknames for him, used half-fondly, half-mockingly when he brought forth some item of general information. Where has Mrs Harris heard it? Either Rosemary told her, or Mrs Harris has listened in on their phone calls.

'Lady Rosemary's still away, isn't she?' Fred asks. A desperate hope has come to him that his love may have returned, or be about to return before he leaves London. Maybe Mrs Harris has been told to come in and prepare the house for her. Some preparation! But he tries to speak pleasantly, or at least neutrally. 'Is she coming back soon?'

For a long moment Mrs Harris does not answer. Finally she shrugs. 'Could be.' Either she doesn't know, or – more likely – she has been told, or chooses, not to say.

'I wondered if you were expecting her today.' No answer. 'Or tomorrow, maybe.' No answer. 'Well, I guess I'll go and get my things.'

'Right. Clear out all your bloody mess, and good riddance,' Mrs Harris growls, reaching for the gin bottle.

Fred climbs back up to the hall, thinking that when Rosemary does get home she is in for a shock, unless Mrs Harris manages to pull herself together first. Somebody, not him, should warn her – should tell her what her perfect charlady has been doing in her absence.

He returns the defensive umbrella to the urn and ascends the graceful white curve of the stairs to Rosemary's bedroom. It is much brighter here: one tall shutter of the bay window has been folded back, and a broad band of gold-dusted sunlight fans across what he has always thought the most beautiful room in this house: high-ceilinged, elegantly proportioned, lavishly mirrored. The walls are painted a subtle shade of rosy cream, the woodwork and the flowery plasterwork and fireplace are white; the furniture is white-and-gilt French provincial. Right now, however, the place is one hell of a mess. Drawers hang open, spilling their contents; a lamp lies fallen; the pillows and bedclothes of the four-poster have been dragged to the floor, and the dressing table is a confusion of overturned bottles and broken glass from which a stale sticky-sweet odor rises.

Fred feels a sinking of despair and guilt and longing at this mute testimony to Rosemary's state of mind when she left London; then fury at Mrs Harris. It is really disgusting of her not to have cleaned up, not to have spared Rosemary – and all right, himself – such a sight. This followed by a second spasm of guilt as it occurs to him that it was he who persuaded Rosemary to hire Mrs Harris. In a way he is responsible for the state the house is in, and for the drunken slut sitting in the darkened basement. Well, nothing can be done about that now. He glances into the mirrored, peach-tiled bathroom, but it is so littered and foul – the toilet, for instance, is full of turds – that he decides to forget his razor and toothbrush. Has Mrs Harris – disgusting idea – been treating the place like her own, pawing over Rosemary's things, using her bathroom, maybe even sleeping off a drunken stupor in her white-and-gold four-poster bed?

That would explain the disorder, and more logically. When he last saw Rosemary – when he heard her voice in the radio station, rather – she wasn't in an emotionally disturbed state, but very much in control. Perfectly happy, in fact. He hears her light melodious voice again: 'Thank you Dennis , and I think it's quite marvelous to be here.' She doesn't care about him anymore; maybe she never cared.

With a kind of shudder Fred picks his way across the debris-strewn pastel-flowered Chinese carpet and opens the walk-in closet. Yes; there is his sweater, sagging from a clothes hook at the back. He throws it over his arm and looks round for the shirt, but all he can see is Rosemary's clothes, hanging empty on all sides: her long pink cape, her forget-me-not-blue quilted robe, her gauzy blouses, and her rows of high-heeled sandals like the cages of delicate birds. Many of these garments flutter in his mind with some intimate memory. There is the trailing pale-gray evening dress printed with the blurred shadows of leaves; he remembers how he had caressed a cobwebby fold of it secretly between his fingers all through *Così fan tutte;* there is the apple-green silk voile she wore at her party, which whispered so caressingly as she moved.

Fred feels weak and exhausted, as if he had been running a marathon or playing squash for an hour. He leans against the frame of the closet door and tries to breathe normally. But it is no use; the balloon that has been in his chest ever since he got to Cheyne Square begins to deflate with a wet whinnying sound. Weeping, he knocks his head rhythmically against the door jamb to provide a counter-irritant. And as he does so, he becomes aware of another, less evenly rhythmical noise from below: the noise of Mrs Harris staggering up the stairs, banging into the wall as she comes. The way it sounds, she is so drunk she can hardly walk.

He retreats into the dimness of the closet, hoping she isn't headed this way or won't see him; but no such luck. She pauses in the hall, breathing audibly, then stumbles into the bedroom and leans for support on the chest of drawers.

'Missing your sweetie, are you?' she says. Fred realizes that even from the back his posture must be so eloquent of misery that a drunken charwoman can read it. Not trusting himself to look at her, let alone reply – and what would be the point anyhow? – he begins sliding Rosemary's clothes along the rod, searching for his blue workshirt and hoping that Mrs Harris will go away.

Instead she lurches across the room toward him, catching her foot on the bedspread and only saving herself by grabbing the bedpost with both hands; then she lurches on into the closet behind Fred.

'Don't do that now, lovey,' she says. 'Let's make hay.'

Fred stiffens. 'Making hay' was his and Rosemary's most private code phase. On bright days like this one the westering sun would shine into this room and onto the canopied bed. Rosemary loved to lie in it, to feel it warming and coloring her white skin.

'Come on, darling. Let's make hay while the sun shines,' she had said to him once, laughing softly. A few days later he had brought her a print of Breughel's *The Haymakers,* and she had tacked it on the pale-flowered wallpaper above the night stand; it is still there. He knows now for sure that Mrs Harris has been spying on them, sneaking round and listening at doors and/or on the kitchen extension. Sick, sickening. He turns away, giving up on his book and his shirt, wanting now only to get the hell out of here.

'Excuse me, please,' he says angrily.

But Mrs Harris doesn't move aside. Instead she stumbles even closer. Her dirty face, what little Fred can see of it under the peroxided hair, is smeared with what looks like a mixture of soot and lipstick; he can smell her unwashed odor and her foul breath. She puts out her hand, and the soiled flowered wrapper she is wearing falls open it; beneath it is incongruously white, voluptuous naked flesh.

'Oh darling!' she whispers in a drunken, wheezing imitation of Rosemary's voice. She grabs Fred's arm; she sags toward him and tries to rub her body against his.

'Quit that!' he cries. He tries to push Mrs Harris away gently, but she is unexpectedly strong. 'Let go of me, you dirty old cow!'

The charwoman's grip slackens. He shoves her aside with such force that she falls onto the closet floor among Rosemary's shoes, giving a kind of startled animal howl.

Fred doesn't stay to see whether Mrs Harris is hurt, or to help her up. Clutching his sweater, not looking back, he flees from the room and down the curving staircase two steps at a time, and slams out of the house.

Once in the street he keeps walking, at first not choosing any direction. But as he strides on, putting block after block between himself and Cheyne Square, his shock and disgust gradually moderate into embarrasment. He turns south toward the river, reaches the Embankment, and crosses the road. There he stops, leaning on the stone parapet, with the wide calm panorama of the Thames before him. The tide is almost full, and the houseboats moored upriver along the near bank rock rhythmically on its swell. To his left is the Meccano-set rococo of the Albert Bridge, with the high-summer green of Battersea Park beyond; to his right the solid Romanesque brickwork of Battersea Bridge. Slowly, the flow and pale shine of the water, the steady churning of a string of barges headed downstream, the passage of flocked clouds overhead in the glowing sky, begin to calm him.

He will never be able to dream sentimentally about Rosemary's bedroom again, Fred thinks; but hell, maybe that's for the best. Who wants to be haunted by some goddamn room? He admits to himself that he hadn't gone back only for his things, but in the stupid vain hope of seeing Rosemary again. In spite of everything he isn't over her. Maybe he only got what he deserved. His job now is to forget Rosemary, who has obviously forgotten him and is enjoying herself in some luxurious country place.

In a calmer state of mind, Fred leaves the river and heads home. He has more packing to do, and in a couple of hours he is having supper and going to a late film with two old friends who have just arrived in England for the summer.

By the time Fred meets Tom and Paula his equilibrium is nearly restored, though he remains depressed. Their pleasure at the reunion and their eagerness for information about London raise his spirits somewhat. He is reminded that all American academics are not like the Vogelers (whom he has seen too much of lately) or like Vinnie Miner. A keen homesickness comes over him, a longing for American scenes and American voices, for people like Paula and Tom who say what they think without irony, who won't ever pretend to like him and then drop him casually and graciously.

Over crêpes and Beaujolais at Obelix, around the corner from his flat, Fred recommends to his friends a number of London sights, restaurants, and cultural events, without revealing his disillusion with the place. (Why discourage them, after all? They're only here for a few weeks.) He also relates a censored version of the scene that afternoon with Mrs Harris. He doesn't say, for instance, that he had a key to the house; and Rosemary is transformed into 'some people I know who are out of town'. Stripped of these aspects, his own experience that afternoon begins to seem almost comic, in a rough way – a scene from Smollett, or maybe a cartoon by Rowlandson. It becomes a jocular tale, a kind of jest or fabliau, and is a riotous success with Tom and Paula.

'Great story,' Tom pronounces. 'It would only happen to you.'

*

As he lies in bed much later that evening Fred recalls this comment, which at the time made him uncomfortable. But of course Tom, who has never heard of Rosemary, meant it as a kind of compliment. Because of Fred's appearance, he was saying, it is comically appropriate that a drunken cockney charwoman should make obscene proposals to him.

It is true that over the years Fred has received other unwelcome – though less comically revolting – offers of this sort. Girls and women he has hardly looked at and never would look at have sometimes, there's no denying it, thrown themselves at him, or at least in his general directon, causing him acute embarrassment. His male friends have often been less sympathetic. Hell, they sometimes say, they wouldn't complain if girls were falling all over them – not realizing what it's really like to be heavily fallen upon by some woman you don't want, even if some other guy does.

Physical attraction is a mystery, Fred muses as he watches the lamplight playing on his wall through the leaves outside. It makes a pattern like that of the dress Rosemary wore to *Così fan tutte,* which folded itself closely round and floated loose below her apple-blossom breasts, that he will never see or touch or kiss again.

Why is it that something which makes a beautiful woman like Rosemary more beautiful – for instance, large soft white breasts – makes a slattern like Mrs Harris even more disgusting? Mrs Harris's breasts aren't really any heavier than Rosemary's, he thinks, allowing himself to visualize the scene in the closet for the first time; they are about the same size. They have the same kind of big strawberry-pink nipples, and there was even the same sort of pale-brown mark on her left one, like an ostrich feather –

No. Lying between the sheets, Fred shudders from head to toe. No, he must have imagined it.

But the memory is photographically clear. Mrs Harris has Rosemary's breasts. She is about the same size as Rosemary; she has almost the same color hair. She seems to be living in Rosemary's house, drinking Rosemary's gin, sleeping in Rosemary's bed.

Of course her voice and accent were completely different. But Rosemary's an actress; she's often imitated Mrs Harris. Oh,

Jesus Christ. Fred sits up in the darkened room with his mouth hanging open as if he were seeing some foul ghost.

But hold on a minute. He's met Mrs Harris before, he would've noticed – Yeh, but he only met her for a moment, one evening when he'd got to the house too early. Mrs Harris had opened the door a crack, and hardly looking at him, grumbled that Lady Rosemary wasn't home yet. She wouldn't even let him in to wait; he had to go to the pub round the corner.

She wouldn't let him in – she wouldn't let anyone in when she was working there – not because she couldn't stand people underfoot, like Rosemary said, but because they might recognize her – because she was – Because the drunken harridan whom he called a filthy old cow and knocked onto the bedroom floor this afternoon was his false true love, the star of stage and screen, Lady Rosemary Radley.

Oh Jesus. Oh Jesus Christ. Though he is unconscious of having got out of bed, Fred now finds himself standing naked in a patch of blurred moonlight, pounding his fists against the wall. He stops only because he hears steps overhead; the repeated reverberating thud has woken another tenant – or worse, his landlord.

Maybe there was a Mrs Harris once. And then she left, only Rosemary didn't tell anybody, and she kept on answering the phone in Mrs Harris' voice. Or maybe there never was any Mrs Harris; maybe Rosemary was cleaning the house herself the whole goddamn time.

How could he have been so dumb and deaf and blind this afternoon? Why hadn't he known?

Because Rosemary had fixed in his head the idea of herself as beautiful and graceful and refined and aristocratically English, and anyone who wasn't that, even if they were living in her house and sleeping in her bed and speaking with her voice, wasn't Rosemary. So when she decided she didn't want to see him or talk to him all she had to do was put on Mrs Harris's clothes and Mrs Harris's accent. That was what she'd done today. And she'd deliberately mocked him by using their private lovers' language; she'd destroyed everything they'd ever had together.

And maybe that's how it had been the whole goddamn time, Fred thinks, staring out the open window into the windy half darkness. Because if Rosemary had ever really loved him, she wouldn't have pulled a trick like that. All these months he's loved somebody who was as much a theatrical construct as Lady Emma Tally. She'd been putting him on the whole goddamn time, pretending to be Lady Rosemary when she wanted him and pretending to be Mrs Harris when she didn't – and God knows who she really was.

Well, now he's got the message. She doesn't want to see him again. And he doesn't want to see her either. Even if she were to welcome him back passionately, to be again the Rosemary he'd loved, he wouldn't believe it. He'd always be looking and listening for clues that she was only acting a part.

Fred flings himself onto his bed, where he lies for a long time staring at the play of nervous shadows on the paint-clogged Victorian plaster garlands of the ceiling. At last, despairing of sleep, he gets up. He pulls on some clothes, turns on the light, and starts cleaning the fridge and the kitchen cupboards, throwing out most of the food and saving the rest for the Vogelers, with whom he will be having a final supper this coming evening. A bottle with an inch or two of Scotch remaining in it doesn't seem worth lugging to Hampstead Heath, so Fred pours it into a glass, adds lukewarm tap water, and drinks as he works.

As he clears the cupboards over the sink, he stops dead with a package of McVitie's Cream Crackers in his hand, suddenly remembering Rosemary's party, and Edwin Francis standing on the stairs eating one of these crackers overloaded with pâté, and confiding in his nervous nice-old-lady manner that he was worried about Mrs Harris's effect on Rosemary. He hears Edwin saying: 'She can get a bit frantic . . . She can get into rather a state sometimes.'

Suppose Rosemary hadn't been playing Mrs Harris as a joke, out of rage and spite when she saw Fred, whom she thought she'd got rid of, walk into her kitchen. Because she couldn't have expected him. Whether he'd been there or not she would have been sitting drinking in the basement in Mrs Harris's clothes.

Suppose she wasn't just acting; suppose she was 'in a state', whatever that meant. What if Fred isn't the only one who doesn't know who Rosemary is? What if she doesn't know either? What if she is a disturbed person, and there's something really wrong with her?

Maybe Rosemary has started to drink at other times before

this; maybe she's become 'frantic' – had some kind of breakdown – in the past, maybe more than once. Is that what Edwin was hinting? Was he trying to warn Fred?

No. More likely Edwin was asking for his help, just as he'd claimed, twittering that he wouldn't feel comfortable unless Fred promised to 'look out for our Rosemary'. Fred hadn't paid any attention; he hadn't looked out for their Rosemary. He hadn't been able to, because an hour or two later she'd thrown him out of her house. Anyhow, he hadn't thought she needed to be looked after.

But maybe she needs it now, he tells himself as he stands in the kitchen holding the box of crackers. If she's on a binge or having a nervous breakdown or both, somebody ought to be taking care of her. The trouble is, who?

By three a.m. he has finished the Scotch, two leftover beers, and most of a bottle of souring white wine. He is drunk in Notting Hill Gate, and Rosemary is drunk or mad in Chelsea. It's all too goddamn much for him. He wants to go home to America; he wants to see Roo again. Only by now she probably doesn't want to see him, he thinks, falling back onto the bed without bothering to take off his clothes, and dizzily spiraling into unconsciousness.

When Fred comes to, with a headache like an ax blow, the sun is high in the sky and hot on his disordered bed. Too ill to think of eating anything, he stands in the shower for a long time soaking his headache, with little effect. The one clear thought in his mind is that he's got to tell somebody to look out for Rosemary before he leaves. He bundles his dirty clothes together with the dirty sheets and towels and drags them through the streets to the laundromat. While they slosh about in the machine in a queasy way that makes his headache worse, he goes to the pay phone and tries to call Edwin Francis, who ought to be back from Japan by now. Then he tries to get Posy's or Nadia's number from William Just at the BBC. Finally, because he can't think of anyone else, he calls Vinnie Miner. None of these people are in, and for the rest of the day and the evening they continue not to be in. But he keeps on trying.

11

Don't care was made to care,
Don't care was hung,
Don't care was put in a pot
And boiled till she/he was done.

Old rhyme

At the London University School of Education, Vinnie Miner is attending a symposium on 'Literature and the Child' and becoming steadily bored. The subject is promising, and the first panelist was a friend of hers and an amusing speaker; but the other two have begun to annoy her greatly. One is a fat educational psychologist named Dr O. C. Smithers; the other a tense young pedant called Maria Jones who is devoting her life to a study of early etiquette books.

In Britain, Vinnie has observed, most lecturers feel an obligation to entertain their listeners and to avoid jargon; it is therefore usually sage to attend any public talk if the topic seems interesting. Maria Jones, however, is too nervous to think of her audience, and is made almost inaudible by shyness; and Dr Smithers is too self-satisfied. He has, as he puts it, 'studied extensively in the United States,' and delivers his platitudes with a bland transatlantic pompousness. Like some American educators, he insists upon speaking of The Child as a sort of abstract metaphorical figure – one of those Virtues or Graces represented in stone on public monuments. Smithers' abstract Child is full of Needs that are in danger of being 'unmet' and of Creative Potential that must be 'developed' if 'he-or-she' is to become a 'full human being'. Vinnie has always especially detested the latter phrase; this evening it has an ironic ring – seeming inevitably to refer to Smithers' own physique, which is of a rotundity rare in Britain. In Vinnie's own country, according to statistics (borne out by her own observation) one out of three men over thirty is overweight. Here most remain trim; but those few who do become fat, as if by some law of averages, often becomes excessively so. In the same way, those British minds that allow themselves to be filled with jargon swell to sideshow proportions.

Warming to his subject, exceeding his allotted twelve minutes, Smithers declares that The Child's 'moral awareness' must be awakened by 'responsible literature'. The frictions and stresses of Our Contemporary World press hard upon The Child; he-or-she (Smithers, no doubt aware that the majority of his audience is female, has used this awkward pronoun throughout his talk) must be able to look to literature for guidance.

Vinnie yawns angrily. There is no Child, she wants to shout at Smithers, there are only children, each one different, unique, as we here in this room are unique – perhaps more so, for we are all in the same profession and have been sanded down over time by the frictions of your nasty Contemporary World.

How much nicer and less boring it would be if we were all still children, Vinnie thinks. Then, as she often does on boring public occasions, she relieves her restlessness by imagining the weight of years lifted suddenly from everyone in the room. The older members of the audience, like herself, become children of ten or twelve; the undergraduates mere babies. Whatever their new age, all those present, upon finding themselves transformed, share a single thought: Why am I sitting here on this chair listening to this nonsense? At their table, the speakers and the moderator look at each other with surprise. Smithers, who is now a fat, earnest boy of six, drops his notes to the floor. Vinnie's friend Margaret – already at nine a sensible, kind, observant little girl – leans over to comfort Maria Jones, who is now only about three years old, but already painfully anxious in public. Margaret wipes Maria's brimming tears and helps her to climb down from the platform. In the audience the baby students toddle about, playing house under overturned chairs, scribbling on the walls with pencil and chalk, building and demolishing textbook towers with shrieks of mirth.

It would be only just if some minor, humorous god, perhaps The Child Him-Herself, were to work such a metamorphosis, Vinnie thinks. The very idea of making children's literature into a scholarly discipline, of forcing all that's most imaginative and free in what Smithers calls Our Cultural Heritage into a grid of solemn pedantry, pompous platitude, and dubious textual analysis – psychological, sociological, moral, linguistic, structural – such a process invites divine retribution.

Though it has given her a livelihood and a reputation, not to mention these happy months in London, Vinnie has a bad conscience about her profession The success of children's literature as a field study – her own success – has an unpleasant side to it. At times she feels as if she were employed in enclosing what was once open heath or common. First she helped to build a barbed-wire fence about the field; then she helped to pull apart the wildflowers that grow there in order to examine them scientifically. Ordinarily she comforts herself with the thought that her own touch is so light and respectful as to do little harm, but when she has to sit by and watch people like Maria Jones and Dr Smithers dissecting the Queen Anne's lace and wrenching the pink campion up by its roots, she feels contaminated by association.

Smithers now figuratively spreads out his collection of dead flowers, pours a final slow molasses-jug full of clichés over them, and sits down looking self-satisfied. The discussion period begins; earnest persons rise and in assorted accents direct self-promoting speeches disguised as questions to the panel members. Vinnie yawns behind her hand; then she unobstrusively opens the latest *New York Review of Books*, bought at Dillon's on her way to the symposium. She smiles at one of the caricatures; then she receives an unpleasant shock. On the facing page, in a prominent position, is the announcement of a collection of essays entitled *Unpopular Opinions*, by L. D. Zimmern, whom she hasn't thought of for weeks.

She is startled too by the accompanying photograph, which doesn't at all resemble the figure in her imagination, the victim of polar bears and the Great Plague. Zimmern is older than she has pictured him, thin and angular rather than heavy, and not bald – indeed, he has more hair than necessary, including a short dark pointed beard. His semi-smile is ironic, verging on scornful or pained.

But it doesn't matter what Zimmern actually looks like. What matters is that he is about to publish, probably already has published, a book that is almost certain to contain his awful *Atlantic* article. This disgusting book, available both in hard cover and in paperback, is at this very moment in bookshops all over the United States, lying in wait for anyone who might come in. It will be – or has already been – widely reviewed; it will be – or has been – purchased by every large public and university library in the country. Presently it will be catalogued, and shelved, and borrowed, and read. It will shove its sneering way even into Elledge Library at Corinth. Later, probably, there will be an English edition, and possibly – especially if he is one of those awful post-structuralists – a French edition, a German edition . . . The hideous possibilities are endless.

Vinnie feels a sour, burning pain beneath her ribs, the gift of L. D. Zimmern. To relieve it she tries to picture him as a child among the instant children here: an unpopular child, scorned and persecuted by the others. But the scene won't come clear. She can transport Zimmern to London Unviersity mentally, but she is unable to make him young. Persistently fixed in sour middle age, he stands by the deserted speakers' table glancing round condescendingly at the roomful of riotous children, including or especially Vinnie.

And even if she could imagine another suitably sticky end for Zimmern, she thinks what's the point? This violent fantasizing is unhealthy; also useless. There is no way Vinnie can actually revenge herself; no forum for her except magazines like *Children's Literature* that Zimmern and his colleagues will never see. She can't even complain to her friends any longer, not after so many months – it would make her seem neurotic, obsessed.

Besides, Vinnie is reluctant to relate her troubles at any time. She believes that talking about what's gone wrong in one's life is dangerous; that it sets up a magnetic force field which repels good luck and attracts bad. If she persists in her complaints, all the slings and arrows and screws and nails and needles of outrageous fortune that are lurking about will home in on her. Most of her friends will be driven away, repelled by her negative charge. But Vinnie won't be alone. Like most people, she has some acquaintances who are naturally magnetized by the unhappiness of others. These will be attacted by her misfortunes, and will cluster round, covering her with a prickly black fuzz of condescending pity like iron filings.

The one person Vinnie could safely complain to is Chuck Mumpson. He is outside the operations of the magnetic system, and nothing printed in any book can alter his view of her, for it does not depend on her professional reputation or the opinions of others. To Chuck, L. D. Zimmern is a non-account sorehead that nobody in their right mind would pay any attention to. 'Who gives a hoot in hell what some creep says in a magazine?' as he once put it. Vinnie finds this ignorance of the ways of the academic world both wonderfully restful and very frustrating, just as she does many things about Chuck. It is this ambivalance, no doubt, that keeps her from fixing a date for her visit to Wiltshire.

Chuck has, for instance, an intellectual resilience she hadn't suspected earlier. By now, for instance, he has not only managed to reconcile himself to the fact that the Hermit of South Leigh was an illiterate farm labourer, but to take as much pride in him as if he had been a learned earl. When she remarked on this, he generously attributed his change of heart to her. 'The way you love me – it makes everything that happens okay,' he said. Vinnie opened her mouth to protest, and then shut it again. 'I don't think I love you,' she had been about to say. But she's never said she did, and probably Chuck only meant 'the way you make love to me'.

That she can accept; can affirm. Physical pleasure of the sort she's known with Chuck does improve the entire world; it becomes a humming, spinning top in which all the discordant colors are blurred and whirled into a harmony that spirals out from that center. When she is away from him the spin slackens; the top totters, lurches, falls, showing its ugly pattern. Lying alone in bed under only a flowered sheet, these warm short nights of late June when darkness seems merely to blow over the city and the sky begins to flush with light at three-thirty a.m., she longs physically for Chuck. But then morning comes; the telephone gives its characteristic excited double ring, higher-pitched and more rapid than in America. June is a highly social season in London, and Vinnie's appointment book keeps filling itself up with interesting parties, leaving no room for a trip to Wiltshire.

Besides, if/when she does go, what will it be like staying with Chuck, in his house? It's ages since Vinnie shared a place with a man – or with anyone. And after all, it is partly by choice that she hasn't done so. In the score of years since her marriage ended she probably could have found a housemate if she'd wanted one – if not a lover, then some good friend.

'Don't you ever feel frightened living alone? Don't you ever get lonely?' say Vinnie's friends – or rather, her acquaintances, for any friend who asks these questions is instantly, though sometimes only temporarily, demoted to an acquaintance. 'Oh no,' Vinnie always replies, concealing her irritation. Of course she feels frightened, of course she gets lonely – how stupid can they be? Obviously she only put up with it because for her the alternative is worse.

Sometimes, in spite of her disclaimers, her acquaintances go on to suggest that it really isn't safe for a small aging single woman to live alone, that she ought to get herself a large unfriendly dog. But Vinnie, who dislikes dogs and is unwilling to conform to the stereotype of the lonely old maid, has always refused to do so. Fido has remained her only companion. It has occurred to her that she treats him much as the traditional spinster does her pets: until two months ago he went almost everywhere with her, and was alternately indulged and scolded.

The truth is that Vinnie isn't temperamentally suited to a shared life. The last time Chuck was in London, nice as that was (she recalls a particular moment when they were lying moving together on her sitting-room carpet, looking up through the bay window at a sky full of green moving leaves), even then she sometimes felt – how to put it? – crowded, invaded. Chuck is too large, too noisy; he takes up too much room in her flat, in her bed, in her life.

And it isn't only Chuck who makes her feel this way. Whenever she stays with friends, however fond she is of them, she is uncomfortable. So many things about sharing a house bother her: for instance, the unending necessity for politeness, both positive and negative. The Please and Thank You and Excuse Me and Would You Mind If; the daylong restraint of the natural impulse to yawn, to sigh, to scratch her head or pass wind or take off her shoes. Then, there is the sense of being constantly, even if benevolently, observed, making it impossible to do anything odd or impulsive – go for a walk in the rain before breakfast, for instance, or get up at two a.m. to make herself a cup of cocoa and read Trollope – without provoking anxious inquiry. 'Vinnie? What are you doing down there? Are you all right?'

And then there is the noise and clutter that's involved in having someone else always around, walking from room to room, opening and shutting doors, turning on the radio, the television, the record player, the stove, and the shower. Having to negotiate with this someone before you did the simplest thing: having to agree with them about when and where and what to eat, when to sleep, when to bathe, what film to see, where to go on holiday, whom to invite to dinner. Having to ask permission, as it were, to see her friends or hang a picture or buy a plant; having to inform someone every single damn time she felt like taking any action whatsoever.

It had been that way with her husband almost from the start. And even with Chuck, who is wonderfully easygoing, sharing a flat was like playing a permanent game of Grandmother's Steps. 'I think I'm going to have a bath now and go to bed.' 'Okay, honey.' 'I'm going up to the shops now.' 'Okay, honey.' And if you didn't remember to ask permission before you did anything: 'Hey, honey where were you? You just disappeared – I was kinda worried.' (Go back: you forgot to say 'May I?') And of course the whole thing was reciprocal, so that when whoever you were living with wanted to go to the store, take a bath, move a piece of furniture, or any of a hundred other things, you had to listen to them asking you for your permission.

And then finally, after you had begun to tolerate living like this, because you'd begun loving the other person – after you'd learned even to like it, maybe, and depend on it – they walked out on you. No thanks, Vinnie thinks.

The trouble is, it's too late to say No thanks. She will go to Wiltshire soon because she wants to go there; she won't be able to stop herself, because somehow by accident Chuck Mumpson, an unemployed sanitary engineer from Tulsa, Oklahoma, has got into her life in such a way that she cares about him and depends on him to a degree she would be embarrassed to admit to her London friends, and even more to her American ones.

And when she goes down to Wiltshire it will be worse. There is a terrible danger that she will become wholly entangled, caught. Vinnie imagines the English countryside in June – in itself a seduction. Then she imagines walking with Chuck between flowering hedgerows, lying beside him in some grassy flower-strewn glade in the woods . . . All her caution and reservations will give way; she will be lost. She will feel more and more for him, and the more she feels the worse it will be when he comes to his senses later.

Vinnie knows, she has taught herself to know in over thirty years of loss and disappointment, that no man will ever really care for her. It is her belief, almost in an odd way her pride, that she has never been loved in the serious sense of the word. Her husband had once said he loved her, of course, but events soon proved this a delusion. The few other man who claimed to do so had made the assertion when carried away by desire, telling her then, and only then, what soon enough turned out to be a lie. Chuck, she admits, has said it on other occasions – out of politeness, she had told herself, or out of some antiquated code of Wild Western honor that made it necessary for him to believe he loved in order to justify what was, after all, adultery. He has even praised her looks ('Everything about you, it's so kinda little and neat; you made most of the women back in Tulsa look like plow horses.')

Perhaps at the moment Chuck does think he loves her, because she was nice to him when he was in a state of despair; because she took him in and scolded him and cheered him up – just as she had done with her former husband years ago. But once his confidence has been fully restored, he – like her husband – will look at Vinnie again and see her for what she is, a small, selfish, unattractive, aging woman. He will turn away to someone younger and prettier and nicer, and nothing will remain of his love for Vinnie except a kind of tired guilty gratitude.

Vinnie knows all this – and yet she also knows that she cannot prevent herself from going to Wiltshire. All she can do, and that not for very long, is put it off. She can accept invitations in London. She can remind herself of Chuck's faults; she can cast a cold eye on her own passion, telling herself that he isn't even her type physically: he's too large-boned, beefy, and freckled; his hair is too thin, his features too blunt. True, all true – but no use: she wants him still.

After the symposium, and the reception that follows it, which is well supplied with wine and with literary conversation, Vinnie returns to her flat in a superficially improved but essentially down mood, brooding about *Unpopular Opinions* and her helplessness in the face of L. D. Zimmern's persecution. She has a strong impulse to telephone Chuck in the country; but it's almost eleven, and he will surely be asleep, for the archaeologists keep early hours. As she looks indecisevely at the telephone, it rings. It isn't Chuck on the line, however, but a young strong female American voice, with a tremor of urgency.

'This is Ruth March,' it announces, as if Vinnie ought to recognize the name, which she doesn't. 'I'm calling from New York. I'm trying to get in touch with Fred Turner; I have his number in London, but it's been disconnected. I'm sorry to bother you so late, but I have to reach him, it's really important.'

'Really,' Vinnie repeats flatly, annoyed at the voice for not being Chuck's. 'Are you one of his students?'

'No, uh,' Ruth March stutters, then declares, 'I'm his wife. I met you at an English Department party in Corinth.'

'Oh yes.' A vague image appears in Vinnie's mind, the image of a tall, dark, annoyingly handsome young woman in a black jersey. Not for the first time, she thinks that the feminist practice of keeping one's unmarried name, though politically admirable, has social disadvantages. 'Well, I wish I could help you, but I think he's about to leave for New York anyhow – tomorrow, I believe.'

'I know he's coming back tomorrow. But the thing is, I won't be in Corinth then, I have to fly to New Mexico about a job there. I was away before, on a photo assignment, so I didn't get the telegram he sent me, so I couldn't call him, otherwise I would have.' Fred's estranged wife is beginning to sound almost out of breath. 'I want to get hold of him now, so we can meet in New York, because I'll be there tomorrow night.'

'Yes,' Vinnie says neutrally.

'I thought maybe you might know where he is.'

'Well.' As a matter of fact Vinnie does know where Fred is now. When she saw him the day before yesterday at the British Museum he told her that he was going to have dinner with Joe and Debby Vogeler on his last night in London, and then go with them to watch the Druids perform their midsummer solstice rites on Parliament Hill. 'Yes; I think he's with some friends, people named Vogeler.'

'Oh yeh. I know who you mean. Do you have their number?'

'I think I have it somewhere. Hang on just a moment.' Vinnie runs into the sitting room, thinking again how stupid it was of her landlord to have the telephone installed in the bedroom. 'Here . . . no, sorry. Wait a sec.' Embarrassing moments pass as she shuffles through scraps of memo paper and cards from mini-cab companies, increasing Ruth March's transatlantic telephone bill. 'Well, I'm sure I can find it if I have time to look,' she says eventually. 'I tell you what; when I locate the number I'll phone and give Fred your message.'

'Oh, would you? That's wonderful.' Ruth releases a grateful sigh. 'If you could just ask him to call me in New York, as soon as he gets into Kennedy.'

'Yes, all right.'

'I'll be at my father's place. I think he has the number, but anyhow it's in the book: L. D. Zimmern, on West Twelfth Street.'

'L. D. Zimmern?' Vinnie repeats slowly.

'Uh, huh. Maybe you know him? He's a professor.'

'I think I've heard of him, yes,' Vinnie says.

'And hey. When you speak to Fred, you could tell him, if you wouldn't mind – '

Stunned by what she has just learnt, Vinnie is silent. Ruth March takes this for assent.

'Tell him I love him. Okay?'

'Okay,' Vinnie replies mechanically.

'Thanks. Thanks a lot. You're a real sport.'

As soon as she hangs up, Vinnie begins searching for the Vogelers' phone number. At the same time, rather distractedly, she wonders why Fred's wife is not named Ruth Zimmern or Ruth Turner. Maybe she's been married before. The idea in the forefront of her mind, however, is that her wish has been granted. Her generic and specific enemy has been, in a manner of speaking, delivered into her hands; the sins of the father can be visited upon the daughter, a young, beautiful, and loved woman. Without the slightest effort Vinnie can prevent Ruth and Fred from having a reconciliation – for surely that is what it would be – in New York. And her subconscious seems eager to cooperate, for the Vogelers' phone number refuses to surface. Vinnie is positive that she has it somewhere, written on the back of a British Museum call slip; but this slip, in league with her worser nature, has concealed itself completely. Yet her better nature, which doesn't believe in the law of genealogical justice – what harm has Ruth March ever done her? – continues to search.

Of course it doesn't really make any difference, she thinks, giving up at last. If Fred doesn't meet his wife in New York tomorrow they'll get back together eventually. She will phone him from New York tomorrow, or from New Mexico, or wherever she is going.

Or maybe she won't phone him, because she'll believe that he got her message and deliberately ignored it. She'll take the job she mentioned and move to the opposite corner of the United States and that will be the end of their marriage.

Well, too bad – or maybe not so bad after all. Since she is L. D. Zimmern's daughter, Ruth may very well take after him. She may be spiteful, inconsiderate, destructive; the sort of wife Fred or any man is well rid of – just as her first husband, if he exists, was well rid of her. Probably it's her fault that her marriage broke up in the first place; nobody could say that Fred was hard to get on with. Anyhow, Vinnie can't do anything for her. She hasn't got the Vogelers' phone number, and she doesn't know anyone who might.

The trouble is, she does know where Fred is, or at least where he soon will be: on the highest part of Hampstead Heath with the Druids. But she certainly can't go out at this time of night and look for him there. Nobody would expect her to do that. Let events take their course. Vinnie turns off the sitting-room lights and begins to prepare for bed.

No, most people Vinnie knows certainly wouldn't expect her to go to Hampstead Heath. But one person would, she thinks as she sits on the side of her bed with one shoe off and one on. Chuck Mumpson would take it for granted that she'd go, without even stopping to consider the great inconvenience and even possible peril of such an excursion. And when he hears that she hadn't delivered Ruth March's message, he will stare at her in a surprised unhappy way, as he did once when she said she'd never met a dog she liked. She can see exactly how his face will look, and hear his voice. 'You mean you didn't even try?' it says. 'Aw hell, Vinnie.'

Vinnie returns to the sitting room and turns on the lights. She unfolds her bus and Underground maps and opens her *A to Z*. Getting to Parliament Hill, as she suspected, would be a real chore. The London Transport Authority has made it easy for her to shop at Selfridges, consult a doctor in Harley Street, or see friends in Kensington; but it hadn't conceived that she or any well-bred resident of Regent's Park would ever wish to visit Gospel Oak, and little provision has been made for such a journey. She'll have to walk all the way to Camden Town Station, take a bus or the Underground to Hampstead, and then tramp another mile or more across the Heath. And after she finds Fred – if she finds him, which is unlikely – it will be too late to return by the same route; she'll have to pay for a taxi home.

She refolds her maps, thinking how expensive and tiring and difficult, if not dangerous and impossible, it would be to find Fred Turner on Parliament Hill at midnight; how easy and satisfying it will be to stay home and cause lasting pain and grief to a close relative of L. D. Zimmern. As for Chuck, he needn't ever know. But at the same time she finds herself putting her shoes back on; taking her passport, bank card, and all but five pounds and some change out of her wallet as a precaution against pickpockets and muggers; and getting her raincoat out of the closet – for though it is a warm summer night it may be cool and windy up on the Heath.

Even at past eleven Regent's Park Road is familiar and reassuring, with only a few respectable-looking people walking dogs, or on their respectable way home. But as Vinnie crosses the intersection and starts down the Parkway toward the center of Camden Town her breath becomes tighter. It is the worst time of night now, just after the pubs close; and numbers of the homeless unemployed men who hang about Camden Town have been released onto the street in a drunken and confused and possibly violent condition. She sets her mouth and walks faster, turning her head away as she passes each moldy figure or group of figures, ignoring remarks that may or may not be directed to her; once crossing the street to avoid two especially dubious-looking individuals lounging in a dark doorway, thinking that each step she hammers onto the pavement with her size 5 heels is another step further away from comfort and safety.

When Vinnie reaches the town center, rather out of breath, there are no buses at the stop, and no one waiting for them. She scurries into the station, though it hardly seems much of a refuge. It is a disagreeable place at any time of day, with a cold blast of air rising from below and the loud, loose, continuous death rattle of the antique wooden escalator. Three scruffy young men shove their way onto the moving stairs ahead of Vinnie, glancing at her in an unfriendly, possibly threatening way. Utterly against her better judgment, she steps on behind them. At the bottom, however, without a backward glance, they disappear down a corridor.

Vinnie takes the opposite tunnel, descends the stairs, and waits for the train to Hampstead. How horrid the dark holes at each end of the platform are: they suggest that something huge and nasty is about to come rushing out of them, heading for her. A stupid thing to think, almost mad. Is it perhaps some vestigial folk-memory trace, some lingering Jungian subconscious dread of caverns and giant slimy serpents?

What does finally come out of the cavern, of course, is a train: ordinarily no danger but a kind of sanctuary. The London Underground is usually in all respect the opposite of the New York subway: well lit, warm, relatively clean, and full of harmless passengers. The car Vinnie enters, however, is less reassuring. It is almost empty, littered with old newspapers, and dimmed by some fault in its electrical system. Well, she has only three stops to go; fifteen minutes at the most.

But after Belsize Park, as sometimes happens on the Northern Line, the train slows, shudders convulsively, and grinds to a halt. The engine dies; the lights blink and dim further. There are only two other passengers in the car, both male, sitting alone at the other end across from each other. One, younger, stares angrily at the floor; the other, older, seems half drunk or half asleep or both.

In the sudden silence another Jungian monster can be heard far off, roaring through distant tunnels. Vinnie stares at her own smudged reflection in the opposite window, and then at the notice above it, which recommends a poison for blackbeetles. As the minutes pass, she begins to feel time has stopped; that she will never reach Hampstead or anywhere else, that she will sit on this seat forever.

If it hadn't been for L. D. Zimmern, she wouldn't be here. If he had never existed, he wouldn't have had a quarreling inconsiderate daughter for Fred Turner to marry. Fred would have married some other much nicer girl, who would not have quarreled with him, who would have come with him to London. He would never have had an affair with Rosemary Radley, and Rosemary would never have insulted Vinnie in a taxi.

It is Zimmern who should be here now, imprisoned in time on an almost empty half-lit train. Vinnie imagines him sitting across from her under the advertisement for blackbeetles, looking rather like a blackbeetle himself. She imagines how as the minutes lengthen toward hours the insects so graphically depicted above Zimmern's head will begin to crawl out of the poster and down the window frame toward him, how they will crawl in procession onto his shoulders and arms and neck and head; how he will try to brush them off, but it will do no good, for more of them will come out of the picture, and more and more. Zimmern cries out for help, but Vinnie only sits looking steadily at him, watching what happens to him, willing it to happen . . .

The lights blink brighter; the image of L. D. Zimmern fades and vanishes. The engine gives a drunken hiccup and begins to hum. Finally, with a jolt, the train starts off.

Hampstead, when Vinnie reaches it, is at first unthreatening. A blurred haze of interlocking street lights hangs over the High Street, which is well populated with harmless-looking pedestrians, and here and there an illuminated shop window. But the side streets are empty and silent. Now and then she hears the echo on the pavement of some other late walker's tread, and occasionally a car rushes past her. At East Heath Road she halts, gazing at the path opposite, which disappears between overhanging heavy trees into acres of windy darkness. Really, to venture onto the Heath at this hour would be plain stupidity, just asking for it. The only sensible thing is to turn around and go home now, while the Underground is still running.

Impelled by this idea, Vinnie starts back down Well Walk. 'I tried,' she says in her mind to Chuck Mumpson, 'but the Heath was pitch-black, and I really didn't want to get myself mugged.'

'Aw, come on, Vinnie,' his voice replies. 'You got this far, you can do it. You just gotta have a little gumption.'

All right, damn it, she says to him, turning round again. But as she crosses the road and starts onto the Heath her heart begins to pound warningly. A hazy, pale, nearly full moon is just clearing the trees, and the sky is a strange fluorescent smoke-red. In the fitful night breeze every stooping bush, every overhanging tree is a moving presence; and there are other, worse presences: voices and figures. Vinnie keeps stupidly walking on, feeling more and more frightened and angry at herself for having come, swerving away from every blowing leaf or strolling couple, thinking how insane it is for her to be wandering across Hampstead Heath in the middle of the night on this wild-goose chase. Who knows if she can find the goose Fred Turner on Parliament Hill, among the drifters and tramps and thieves that maybe – probably certainly are – prowling about in the dark? Who knows if she can even find Parliament Hill?

And whether or not she is robbed and injured on this foolish excursion, Vinnie realizes, there is a more certain, though more intellectual danger: the danger that her vision of London will be injured, even destroyed. So often she has boasted to her American friends that this is a benign and nonviolent city, in which her flat may be burgled when she is away, perhaps (not that this has ever happened), but she herself will never be attacked or threatened; a city where even a small woman in her fifties can go out alone at night in perfect safety. If she really believes this, why is her pulse so fast, her breathing so tight? What if it isn't true, never has been true? How long is it since she was last alone in an unfamiliar part of London at midnight?

It is not only L. D. Zimmern's fault that she is here, but Chuck Mumpson's. If it weren't for Chuck, she would be safe at home now, probably already asleep. And if she is attacked or murdered tonight on Hampstead Heath, he won't even know what she was doing there; no one will. Vinnie almost wishes she hadn't ever met Chuck Mumpson, or even heard of him. But it is too late for that now. So she walks on, as fast as possible, across the shadowy grassy common, under the watery moon.

At the summit of Parliament Hill, near a thicket of bushes and trees, a small and rather scattered crowd has gathered to watch for the Druids. Among them are Joe and Debby Vogeler and Fred Turner. None of them feels the least anxiety about being out on the Heath at midnight, but their minds are not at ease. The Vogelers are a bit worried about Jakie, whom they have left with a sleepy-looking teenage babysitter. Fred, though he is actively trying not to think of it any more, is silently haunted by the overlapping images of Rosemary Radley and Mrs Harris. What has happened to her/them since yesterday afternoon? Where/how is/ are she/ them now?

Awful scenarios flicker before him of Rosemary/Mrs Harris staggering round her house in a drunken, schizophrenic state, or dead of a broken neck at the foot of her graceful curving (but slippery) staircase. Also of her quite happy and well, laughing with friends at a dinner party, relating what a clever trick she'd played on boring old Fred: pretending to be her own charlady, pretending to be drunk. It had been so easy to fool him, she says: he was like that silly rude clerk who wouldn't charge her groceries, and then complained about not being able to recognize Lady Emma Tally in jeans and a sweater. Maybe he'll never know which scenario is right, or what really happened to him yesterday. He still hasn't been able to reach Rosemary or any of her friends, and in twelve hours he'll be on a plane to New York.

Fred is also brooding about his uncompleted book on John Gay. The directness and brilliant energy of Gay's work, to which he had been so strongly attracted, now seem to him a façade. The more he studies the texts, the more ambiguity and darkness they reveal. It strikes him now with greater force than before that everyone in *The Beggar's Opera* is dishonest; even Lucy, its heroine. Its hero, the highwayman Macheath, named after the common on which Fred now stands, is nothing more than an urban mugger on horseback, and cheerfully false to all his women. London in Gay's time was filthy, violent, corrupt – and it hasn't changed all that much. The streets are still dirty, the newspapers are full of crime and deception – in low-rent districts, mostly, but is it basically any better elsewhere? Who in this town gives a shit about anything except using one another and getting ahead?

Fred also compares himself, unfavorably, with Captain Macheath. The women in his life hate rather than love him; and if he is presently to perish it will not be like Macheath for what he has done, but for what he has failed to do: specifically, for his failure to write and publish a scholarly work.

Apart from their anxiety about Jakie, the Vogelers' mood is

cheerful. In the last few weeks – ever since the weather became really warm – their view of England has altered. They still don't care much for London; but a trip to East Anglia, where their Canadian friends have been lent a cottage, has given them a passion for the English countryside. 'It's like being back in the nineteenth century, really,' Debby enthuses. 'Everybody in the village is so friendly, not like here in London, and they're all such perfect *characters.*'

Next month, Joe tells Fred, they and the Canadians are planning to rent a boat and cruise on the canals. 'It's too damn bad you have to leave tomorrow, otherwise you could come along. It's going to be great.'

'Yeh, it sounds like fun,' Fred says, thinking to himself that being confined for a week on a canal boat with the Vogelers and their friends, not to mention Jakie, isn't his idea of great. While their opinion of contemporary England has improved, his has worsened. Everywhere about him now he sees all that they used to complain of: the meaningless imitation and preservation of the past, the smug hypocrisy, the petty regulations, the self-conscious pretense of refinement and virtue. London especially – like Rosemary – seems to him alternately false and mad. He wishes it were already tomorrow evening and he were back home where he belongs, though Christ knows nothing awaits him there. Roo never answered his telegram; she's probably off him for good.

Because of his height Fred is one of the first to see the Druids approaching up the path from the east: a procession of maybe two dozen persons hooded and robed in white, many of them carrying lanterns of antique design. At a distance, climbing the dark hill in the hazy moonlight, they are mysterious, even moving: numinous ghostly figures from the prehistoric past come back to life.

Joe and Debby suck in their breath, and Fred awed in spite of himself, thinks a kind of prayer at the Druids and whatever supernatural powers they may be in touch with – in much the same spirit in which, as a child, he used to wish on a white horse and a load of hay. Make everything come out right, he whispers silently.

But as the Druids draw nearer, the illusion, like so many of

Fred's illusions about England, wavers and is shattered. At close hand these figures are undeniably modern, middle-class, and middle-aged or worse. Under their loose monkish hoods are long smooth pink-and-white English faces of the kind Fred used to see everyday at the British Museum; they wear solemn self-conscious expressions and, in many cases, glintingly anachronistic spectacles. And beneath their long robes is an assortment of leather and plastic sandals, only a few pairs of which could pass even on stage as Early British.

The Vogelers don't seem to be disturbed by these incongruities, or even to notice them. 'Hey, this is great,' Joe says as the procession continues past them and forms into a straggly circle before the clump of trees that crowns Parliament Hill.

'Really pretty impressive,' Debbie agrees; and in an almost reverent whisper she points out that many – in fact more than half – of the celebrants are female. Druidism is a gender-neutral faith; she read that in the *Guardian*.

Joe isn't so sure. Maybe that's the way it is now, he whispers back, but weren't all the original Druids men?

Whatever the truth of the matter, Fred thinks as the Vogelers continue to debate the point sotto voce, these modern London Druids are patently phony and amateurish. The elbowy gestures with which their leader flourishes his ceremonial sword are awkward and unconvincing, and so are those of the two bespectacled women waving leafy branches toward the four points of the compass. The fragments of liturgy blown toward Fred on the night wind suggest an Edwardian rather than an Anglo-Saxon religious service; the manner of delivery reminds him of college productions of Greek drama. There's something almost mad about them too, he thinks, as the Druids raise their lanterns aloft in semi-unison, chanting a hymn to what sounds like The Great Circle of Being in thin well-educated voices, and incidentally revealing a large number of anachronistic wrist-watches and trouser legs.

Fred turns away, disgusted with this mummery, and with all the phoniness that surrounds him as far as his eye can see, from Bloomsbury to Notting Hill, from the lights of Highgate in the north to Chelsea in the south, and further.

As he stares toward Hampstead Village he sees another, even

stupider-looking Druid climbing the path, coming from the wrong direction and obviously late for the show. At the crest of the hill she halts, peering anxiously about at the crowd of spectators; then she trudges on, wavering this way and that as if uncertain whether or not to approach her fellow-worshippers. Her welcome seems doubtful to Fred, for she is not only late but ill-equipped. She has forgotten her lantern; and small as she is her hooded robe is far too short; it doesn't reach the ground by almost a foot, and exposes a pair of modern pumps.

Yes, Fred thinks as the foolish figure drifts nearer, this is what England, with her great history and traditions – political, social, cultural – has become; this is what Britannia, that vigorous, ancient, and noble goddess, has shrunk to: a nervous elderly little imitation Druid –

No. Wait a second. That isn't a Druid, or even an Englishwoman. It is Vinnie Miner.

Eight hours later Fred is sitting on the front steps of Rosemary's house in Chelsea, surrounded by all his luggage. Or maybe not all; when he jammed stuff into his canvas backpack early this morning he was still groggy from a second night of interrupted sleep. But if he's forgotten anything, it's too late now; his plane leaves from Heathrow at noon.

Though tired, Fred is in a far better frame of mind than he was last night. He knows now that Roo is waiting for him in New York; and he has managed to pass on his anxiety about Rosemary first to Vinnie Miner and then, with her help, to Edwin Francis, who is back from Japan and staying in Sussex with his mother.

'Oh dear,' Edwin said when Fred called early this morning and related his story. 'I thought she must be away; she didn't answer the phone. I was afraid of something like this. Well, I've nearly finished breakfast; I'll take the first train in and go straight to Rosemary's from Victoria.'

'All right. I'll meet you there.'

'I don't see the point of that. Besides, I thought you just told me you were leaving for the States this morning.'

'I can make it. My plane isn't until noon.'

'Well – '

'I want to.'

'If you insist,' Edwin says with a sigh. 'But promise me you won't try to get into the house until I come.'

Restless now with waiting, Fred rises, crosses the street to the park in the center of the square, and scans the front of the house, both hoping and fearing that Rosemary will come out of it before Edwin arrives. The place looks deserted; all the shutters are closed and the stoop is littered with throwaway papers and advertising brochures. It's hard to believe there's anyone inside – let alone the woman he saw the day before yesterday. Or he thought he saw. Was that really Rosemary, or was it only Mrs Harris after all? What if his identification of the two was a delusion, a mental aberration caused by frustrated desire?

'Oh, there you are,' Edwin Francis says, getting out of a taxi; he looks white and anxious. 'Did you try the bell? No? Good. Well, oh dear, let's see now. I think perhaps you should go down the street a bit; it might upset her, seeing you suddenly.'

'I – All right,' Fred agrees.

He retreats, and from a middle distance watches Edwin ring and wait, then beckon him back.

'It's rather worrying,' he says.

'Yeh.' Fred realizes that for Edwin, as for many Englishmen, the word 'rather' is an intensifier.

'I think I'd better see if I can find the spare key.' He turns to one of the stone urns by the steps and begins to poke about in the earth under the ivy and white geraniums with a broken twig. 'Yes, here we are.' Edwin takes out a large linen handkerchief of the sort Fred's grandfather used to carry, and wipes the key and his small neat hands.

'I think you'd better wait,' he says, holding the door only slightly open. 'Let me see what the situation is first.'

'No, I want –'

'Back in a moment.' Before Fred can protest Edwin slips into the hall and shuts the door behind him.

Fred sits down again on the steps beside his luggage. There is no sound from the house; all he can hear are the ordinary noises of a London summer morning: the wind shuffling the leaves in the square, the high voices of children playing, the lazy chirp of birds, and traffic on the King's Road. The well-kept Victorian terrace houses, enameled in eggshell colors, glow in the warm sunlight; it is hard to believe that there is anything unpleasant behind their façades.

The door opens; he clambers quickly to his feet. 'What –? How – ?'

'Well, she's there,' says Edwin. In the few minutes he has been inside something has happened to his face; he looks less worried and more angry. 'She's all right – physically that is. But she's rather confused. She's not quite awake yet, of course. And the house is in a dreadful state. Dreadful.' He gives a little shudder.

'Let me – ' Fred tried to push past in the hall, but Edwin holds onto the door.

'I really don't think you'd better come in. It will only upset Rosemary.'

'I want to see her.'

'What for?'

'For Christ's sake. To know that she's all right – To tell her I'm sorry about the other day – ' Fred is younger, stronger, and much larger than Edwin Francis; if he chose, he thinks, he could easily get past him.

'I don't see the point of that. She's in no condition to have visitors, believe me.'

'But I want to do something. I don't have to leave for' – Fred checks his watch – 'twenty minutes.'

'I think you've done quite enough already,' Edwin says with a spiteful emphasis; then, registering Fred's expression, he adds: 'I expect it's going to be all right, you know. I'm going to phone now and ask the doctor to come round, just to be sure.'

'I want to see her, damn it.' Fred puts a hand on Edwin's shoulder and starts to shove him aside.

'Really, you make me rather cross,' Edwin says, not budging. 'I'll tell you what though. If you're prepared to stay in London and make Rosemary's life work, very well; I won't stop you. Otherwise, anything you do is simply going to make it harder for her.'

'Just for a few minutes – ' Fred realizes that in order to get past Edwin he will have to use force, perhaps even violence.

'You want to remind her that you're leaving and make her feel worse, is that it?'

'No, I . . . ' Feeling accused, Fred drops his arm and steps back. 'I only want to see her, that's all. I love her, you know.'

'Don't be selfish.' Edwin begins to close the door. 'It won't do either of you the least good. Anyhow, the person you think you love isn't Rosemary.'

Fred hesitates, wrenched between the desire to see her again and the fear that Edwin might be right; that he may do harm. He looks round for help or advice, but the street is empty.

'You go home now, Freddy,' Edwin says. 'And really, I think the best thing you can do is forget Rosemary as fast as you can. Well, have a nice trip. And please don't write,' he adds, shutting the door in Fred's face.

Though he's allowed himself what seemed enough time to get to the airport, Fred has reckoned without the scarcity of taxis in Chelsea and the heaviness of daytime traffic. For the next hour he is mainly preoccupied with the idea of catching his plane; if he had seen Rosemary, he realizes, he would certainly have missed it. Once he is safe in the departure lounge at Heathrow, however, all the confusion and anxiety of the past two days floods back over him.

Along with his boarding pass Fred has received a brochure listing what travelers are allowed to import into the United States. He crushes and discards it. He is too broke to buy any duty-free goods; besides, he is already weighted down with all he has acquired in England over the past six months. Physically this isn't much: a few books, the cashmere scarf Rosemary gave him, a stack of notes on John Gay and his times. His mental baggage is bulkier: he is carrying home a heavy weariness and disillusion with London, with Gay, and with life in general and himself in particular.

In the past Fred has thought of himself as a decent, intelligent person. Now it occurs to him that maybe he's not so unlike Captain Macheath after all. His work, like all scholarship emptied of will and inspiration, has over the past months degenerated into a kind of petty highway robbery: a patching together of ideas and facts stolen from other people's books.

And his love life is no better. Like Macheath's, it follows one of the classic literary patterns of the eighteenth century, in which a man meets and seduces an innocent woman, then abandons her. Sometimes he merely 'trifles with her affections'; at other times he rapes her. There are many possible endings to the story. The woman may fall into a decline and die, give birth to a live or dead baby, go on the streets, become a nun, etc. The man may go on to other victims, be exposed in time by a well-wisher, meet a violent and well-deserved end, or repent and return – either too late, or in time to marry his former sweetheart and be forgiven.

In these terms, Fred thinks, you could say that he had seduced both Roo and Rosemary and then deserted them when they needed him most – just as Macheath deserted Polly and Lucy. He hadn't ever thought of it this way, of course. Because Roo was, in her own phrase, 'a liberated woman', because Rosemary was rich and famous, he had assumed he could do them no damage. Well, if he's learned one thing this year, it's that everyone is vulnerable, no matter how strong and independent they look.

Roo had wanted very badly to come to England, but he had made it impossible by quarreling with her. When she wrote in May she must have hoped that he'd ask her to join him here at once; instead he let her letter lie on his desk unanswered for weeks. He had encouraged Rosemary to love him unconditionally, while intending to love her only as long as it was convenient for him . . . Well, he had been caught there. Some part of him will probably always love her – even if, as Edwin put it, the Rosemary he loves doesn't exist.

A notice flops on overhead announcing the boarding of Fred's flight. Gathering his things, he follows the other passengers out into the corridor to the moving walkway that will carry them to the gate. As he stands on it, watching the same colored posters of scenic Britain that he saw six months ago – or ones much like them – move slowly backward past him, Fred feels worse about himself than he has ever felt in his adult life.

But he is, after all, a young, well-educated, good-looking American, an assistant professor in a major university; and he is on his way home to a beautiful woman who loves him. Slowly his natural optimism begins to reassert itself. He thinks that after all *The Beggar's Opera* doesn't dispense strict poetic justice. Gay steps into his play in the third act, like a god intervening in human affairs, to give it a happy ending. He interrupts the hanging of Macheath and reunites him with Polly, as Fred will soon be reunited with Roo.

Did Gay do this only to please the audience, as he claims? Or did it satisfy his own natural affection for his characters? Did he know, from experience or the intuition of genius, that there is after all hope – not for everyone, maybe, but for the most fortunate and energetic among us?

Fred's spirits improve. He ceases to stand like a lump on the moving rubber sidewalk, and begins to walk forward along it. The colored views of Britain stream backward twice as fast as before, and he has the sensation of striding toward the future with a supernatural speed and confidence.

12

Sticks and stones may break my bones,
But names will never hurt me.
When I die, then you'll cry
For the names you called me.

Old rhyme

It is a sopping wet summer afternoon in London. Rain pours from a gray sky, drenching everything outside Vinnie's study window: houses, gardens, trees, cars; people huddled into raincoats or defending themselves with umbrellas – unsuccessfully, for the sheets of water deflected from above splatter up again from the pavement and blow at them sideways. Vinnie gazes irritably through the downpour in the direction of Primrose Hill and the West Country, wondering again why she hasn't heard from Chuck in nearly a week.

Or not exactly wondering: rather guessing, almost knowing that his silence must be deliberate. It has turned out just as she feared, just as it always does for her. Chuck's affections have cooled; he has realized as many others have before him – notably her former husband – that he had mistaken gratitude for love. Possibly he has also met someone else, someone younger, prettier . . . Why should he think any more of Vinnie, who isn't even around, who when they last spoke on the phone declined to set a date for her visit to him?

Until that moment their conversation had been easy and intimate as ever. Chuck was interested to hear about Roo's telephone call and Vinnie's midnight excursion to Hampstead Heath.

'You're a good woman,' he said during her story, and again at its end; and for the first time Vinnie almost believed him. She isn't a good woman; but perhaps she has done one good thing.

As for Chuck himself, he seemed to be in high (too high?) spirits. Work on the dig was going great, he told her, and so was his genealogical research. 'I've found a lotta Mumpsons now. All of them related some way, I guess, if you go back far enough. One of Mike's students, he was saying maybe that's why I feel so good down here. Said it could be a genetic memory, didja ever hear of that?'

'I know the theory, yes.'

'Sure, it sounds kinda crazy. But y'know, Vinnie, I really like this place. I could stay here forever, that's how I feel sometimes. I even got the idea of buying myself a house. Nothing fancy, no castles. But there's a lotta nice property for sale round here. Going for practically nothing, too, compared to what it'd be in Tulsa.'

The people in the local historical society had been a big help, Chuck said. One of them had even suggested that Chuck's family might have been descendants of an aristocratic follower of William the Conqueror called De Mompesson – of which the name 'Mumpson' may by a plebeian contraction. Most of Chuck's recorded forebears, however, from what Vinnie can gather, were like Old Mumpson: illiterate or near-illiterate farm laborers. One such family, he recently learned, may have lived in the cottage where he is now staying.

'That really got to me,' Chuck said. 'Last night I was looking at the furniture in my room – it's real old, like most of the stuff here – and I was lying there wondering if maybe one of my ancestors slept in that same room. Maybe even in that same bed. And then this morning when I was out on the site – Mike was rushed because of the rain coming on, so I was lending a hand – it came to me, maybe Old Mumpson or one of his relatives dug in that same field. Maybe he even turned over that same shovelful of earth. It makes you think.'

'Yes.'

'Y'know I've been planning to go over to the next county to track down those De Mompessons. But what's kinda weird, I almost hope I don't find them. I don't know if I want some Frenchy lord for an ancestor. All the same, I figure I'll drive over there tomorrow if it's raining like it is now. They say it's going to keep up. Unless you might be coming down, of course.'

'No,' Vinnie said. 'I don't think so, not this weekend.'

'Okay.' Chuck gave a sigh – of disappointment, she had

thought then. Now she wonders if it wasn't also of exasperation, even of rejection. 'Wal then. Maybe I'll give you a call day after tomorrow, let you know what I find.'

Or maybe I won't, he should have said, Vinnie thinks now; for Chuck did not call on Friday, or on Saturday, Sunday, or Monday. He's sulking, she thought. Or he's met someone else, just as she had predicted. These ideas upset Vinnie far more than she would have expected; indeed, they preoccupied her the entire weekend. On Monday morning she telephoned Paddington to inquire about trains to Wiltshire; and late that night, after a considerable struggle with her dignity, she picked up the phone and dialed Chuck's number in Wiltshire, planning to say that she would be coming down to stay with him this week. Against her better judgement, yes; expecting it all to turn out badly in the end, yes; but still unable to stop herself. But there was no answer, neither then nor any time the next day.

Presumably Chuck is still away in Somerset, which must mean that he's found more relatives, possibly even some aristocratic ones. But in that case, why hasn't he called to tell her all about it? Because he's angry at her, or tired of her, and/or because he's met somebody he likes better. Well, she might have foreseen it. As the old rhyme puts it,

> She that will not when she may,
> When she would she shall have nay.

Vinnie feels an irritability rising to anger at Chuck and at herself. Until she took up with him, she had been content in London, almost happy, rcally. Like the Miller of Dee, as long as she didn't really care for anyone, the fact that nobody cared for her could not trouble her. She's just as well off now as she was before Chuck got into her life, but she feels miserable, hurt, rejected, and sorry for herself.

Vinnie imagines the long sitting room of a large expensive country house, far away in the southwest of England in a town she has never seen. There, at this very moment, Chuck Mumpson is having tea with newly discovered English cousins named De Mompesson, who have a rose garden and hunters. Charmed by his American naïveté and bluntness of speech, they are plying him with watercress sandwiches, walnut cake, raspberries, and heavy cream.

Beside the chintz-covered armchair in which Chuck sits, an invisible dirty-white dog yawns and lifts his head. He directs a discouraged look at Chuck; then, slowly, he rises to his feet, gives himself a shake, and pads across the peach-colored Aubusson carpet toward the door. Fido is abandoning Chuck, who no longer has any need of him; he is on his way home to Vinnie.

Well, there's no point in brooding about it. When the rates go down at six she'll phone again. Meanwhile she might as well get back to her own less fancy tea and to the piece she promised to the *Sunday Times* a month ago.

Vinnie is deep into this task, with the four collections of folktales she is reviewing spread open round her typewriter, when the telephone rings.

'Professor Miner?' The voice isn't Chuck's, but female, American, nervous, very young. Vinnie classifies it generically as that of a B-minus student, perhaps one of her own B-minus students.

'This is she.'

'You're Professor Miner?'

'Yes,' Vinnie says impatiently, wondering if perhaps this call, like the one last week, relates to Fred Turner. But the flat, anxious tone of voice suggests not so much a lovelorn condition as some serious touristic crisis: stolen luggage, acute illness, or the like.

'My name is Barbie Mumpson. I'm in England, in a place called Frome.'

'Oh, yes?' Vinnie recognizes the names of Chuck's daughter and of a large town far from South Leigh.

'I'm calling you because of this picture – I mean because of my father' – Barbie's voice wavers.

'Yes,' Vinnie prompts. An awful unfocused uneasiness has come over her. 'You're visiting your father in South Leigh?'

'Yeh – No – Oh gee, excuse me. I guess maybe – Oh, I'm so stupid – ' To Vinnie, everything seems to be falling apart: Barbie Mumpson's grasp of the English language has failed, and the room is full of darkness. 'I thought maybe Professor Gilson told you. Dad, uh – Dad passed on last Friday.'

'Oh, my God.'

'See, that's why I'm here.' Barbie goes on talking, but only a phrase here and there gets through to Vinnie. 'So the next day . . . couldn't get a seat on the plane till . . . Mom decided.'

'I'm so sorry,' she finally manages to say.

'Thanks. I'm sorry to have to tell you.' Barbie's voice has become even more wavery; Vinnie can hear her clearing her throat at the other end of the line. 'Anyhow, why I was calling,' she says finally. 'There's this old antique picture Dad had, and Professor Gilson says he wanted you to have it if anything happened to him – I mean Dad did. He was planning to give it to you anyhow, because you helped him so much with the research on his family, Professor Gilson says. So the thing is, I'll be in London day after tomorrow, on my way home. I thought maybe I could bring you the picture then. If it was convenient.'

'Yes. Of course,' Vinnie hears herself reply.

'When should I come?'

'I don't know.' She feels incapable of making any plans, almost of speech. 'When would you like to come?'

'I d'know. Anytime. I'm free all day.'

'All right.' With what feels like a major effort Vinnie gathers her wits. 'Why don't you come about four. Come to tea.' From a distance, she hears her own voice, sounding horribly normal, giving Barbie Mumpson her address and directions.

Vinnie hangs up, but she is unable to let go of the phone. As she stands in the bedroom holding it and staring out through the gray gauze curtains into a blurred street full of rain, a frightful image comes to her: the image of a smashed rented car on a muddy country road, of the death that Chuck had also imagined for himself, and even courted.

He'd said he wanted her to have some picture if anything happened to him. Because he knew something was going to happen? Because he was planning it? Or was it some awful premonition? But his daughter hadn't said it was an accident. She'd said nothing about what happened, only that he'd 'passed on'. Would she have said that if it were an accident? Because if it was an accident, or rather, not a real accident – Vinnie's head had begun to ache horribly – it would mean Chuck didn't want to live, that he wanted to pass on. Stupid euphemism, what you'd say of someone who'd stopped for a moment on the street to speak to you, and then –

A choking, sinking feeling comes over Vinnie, as if the rain outside were pouring into her flat and rising up the walls of her bedroom. But all the euphemisms are stupid. Passed on, passed away, kicked the bucket, gone over to the Other Side – as if Chuck had committed a foul or switched teams in some awful children's game.

What he has done is died; he's dead. He's been dead – what did Barbie say – since last Friday. All these days she's been calling him, all the days he hasn't been calling her . . .

That's why he didn't call, Vinnie thinks. It wasn't that he was tired of me. Joy and relief flash across her mind, followed by a greater pain than before, like the beam of a lighthouse that on a dark night first pierces the gloom, and then illuminates a frightful shipwreck. Chuck wasn't tired of her; he was dead, is dead. There is nothing left of him but his awful family, one member of which is coming to tea the day after tomorrow. And until she gets here, Vinnie will know nothing.

When Barbie Mumpson arrives it is raining again, though less heavily. She stands dripping in Vinnie's hall, struggling with a wet raincoat, a vulgarly flowered umbrella, and a damp cardboard portfolio tied with tapes.

'Oh gee, thanks,' she says as Vinnie relieves her of these burdens. 'I'm so dumb about these things.'

'Let me.' Vinnie half closes the umbrella and sets it to dry in a corner.

'I never had an umbrella before, really. I just bought this one last week, and for days I couldn't get it open. Now I mostly can't get it shut. I'll figure it out some day, hopefully.'

Barbie is large and fair and healthy looking; she has a deep tan and wears an ill-fitting wrinkled pink polo shirt with a crocodile crawling across the left breast above the heart. She is also somewhat overweight, and older than her high, childish voice had suggested on the phone – perhaps in her mid-twenties.

'Please,' Vinnie says. 'Come in and sit down.'

Out of some private sense of congruity, she has provided for Barbie the lavish country-house tea she had only the day before yesterday – weeks ago, it seems now – imagined the mythical De Mompessons serving to Chuck. His daughter's appetite, like his, is good; her manners less so. She shovels in the raspberries and cream almost greedily, pronouncing them 'really yummy.'

'And what do you think of England?' asks Vinnie, who feels it would be both awkward and impolitic to move at once to her real concern.

'Aw, I don't know.' Barbie wipes cream from a square, slightly cleft chin – a disturbing feminine version of Chuck's. 'It's not much of a country, is it?'

Repressing her reaction, Vinnie merely shrugs.

'Kinda poky and backward, you know?'

'Some people think that.' Vinnie realizes that Barbie not only has Chuck's large, blunt, regular features and squared-off jaw (more attractive on a man than on a young woman), but his habit of blinking slowly at the end of a question.

'I mean, everything's so small and kinda worn-out looking.'

'I suppose it might seem so, compared to Tulsa.' Vinnie allows Barbie to run on, to run down her beloved adopted country in the usual stupid tourist way. You are rightly named, she thinks, silently christening her guest The Barbarian.

'And it's so awful wet.'

'Mm.' Vinnie doesn't want to start an argument; she is pacing herself, waiting for the moment when she can politely ask the question that has been repeating itself in her mind and interfering with her sleep for forty-eight hours.

'How did it happen?' she bursts out finally.

'Pardon?' The Barbarian lowers a fistful of cake, shedding crumbs. 'Oh, Dad. It was his heart. He was in this town hall, see, over in the next county. He went there to look at some old records, you know.'

'Yes, he mentioned he might do that.'

'Well, it was a real hot day, and the office was on the top floor. There wasn't any elevator; you had to walk up three long flights to get to it. Anyhow, even before the librarian could bring Dad the book he wanted, while he was just standing there by the desk waiting, he just kinda collapsed.' Barbie chews and swallows audibly, rubs one fist into her left eye, then reaches for another watercress sandwich. Crocodile tears, Vinnie thinks. 'Anyhow, by the time the ambulance came and they got him to the hospital he had passed.'

'I see.' Vinnie lets out a long sigh. 'It was a heart attack.'

'Yeh. That's what the doctor said.'

What they call natural causes, Vinnie thinks. Not a deliberate or half-deliberate act, not his fault – not her fault. Maybe. But if it weren't for her, Chuck wouldn't have died in a provincial English records office; he wouldn't have been there in the first place. ('If it hadn't been for you' – she hears his voice again – 'I never woulda thought of looking for my ancestor.') But what does it matter whether he died because of her, or in spite of her? Either way he is dead. He will never enter this room again, never sit where his stupid daughter is sitting now, smiling stupidly at her.

With great difficulty, Vinnie remembers her manners and focuses again on Barbie. 'That's awful,' she says. 'An awful shock for you.' She frowns, recognizing that her remark is as much of a cliché as The Barbarian's.

'Uh, well.' Barbie chews and swallows. 'I mean, naturally it was, but in a way we were sorta prepared for it. Dad had been alerted, after all.'

'Alerted?'

'Oh, yeh. He'd had a couple of what d'you call them, episodes, already. The doctor in Tulsa told him he oughta take it real easy: he was s'posed to give up alcohol and cigarettes and avoid exertion as much as possible. Even then there was always some risk. I mean, he could've gone anytime. Maybe he didn't mention that to you, I guess.' She blinks slowly.

'No, he didn't mention it,' Vinnie says. Images of Chuck drinking and smoking appear in her mind, followed by one of him engaged in a particular kind of exertion.

'He shouldn't have climbed all those stairs in that dumb old town hall,' Barbie says. 'But that was how Dad was, y'know. When he got some project in his head, he had to finish it.

'Like I remember once when we were kids, I said I wished we had a treehouse,' she goes on. 'And Dad got interested, and started drawing plans, and the next Saturday he was up in our big catalpa tree all day building it. Gary and me were helping him, and he made Consuelo – she was our cook then – bring out sandwiches for all of us so we wouldn't have to stop working for lunch. By the time we got done it was nearly dark, and we had a pinic up there, we had . . . pink . . . lemonade . . . Excuse me.' She snuffles back tears.

'That's all right.' Vinnie passes Barbie another napkin, since she seems to have lost her own.

'Thanks . . . It's just . . .' She blows her nose loudly on the hand-hemmed linen. 'I'm okay now. I haven't been crying much. Just at first when Mom got the cable, and on the plane. And then with the cremains.'

'Cremains?' Vinnie repeats, baffled.

'Yeh. Ashes, I guess you could call them. See, Mom decided to have Dad cremated over here. Well, like she said, there wasn't anything else to do, really. Professor Gilson arranged it: he was wonderful. He didn't know Dad had passed till Mom phoned him, but then he got in touch with the hospital, and him and his students took care of everything. They found me a place to stay and met me at the train; they were just great, honestly. They really thought a lot of Dad. I'm so stupid, I didn't know what to do about anything, but they helped me, like, finalize everything: pay the bills, and sort out dad's stuff, decide what to send home, and what to give away.'

'That's good,' Vinnie says, trying to prevent herself from imagining the process.

'They took care of everything, really. Except for the cremains. That was kinda weird and awful, y'know. Professor Gilson had them saved for me. I thought they'd be in a big heavy silver urn or something, but it wasn't anything like that.' Barbie snuffles, stops.

'Nothing like that,' Vinnie prompts.

'Naw. They were in a, I don't know, a kinda waxed cardboard carton like you get with store-packed ice cream, about that size. Inside it was a plastic bag full of this kinda pale gritty gray stuff. I couldn't believe that was all that was left of Dad, just a coupla pounds of what looked like health-food soy mix.' Barbie snuffles again, swallows.

'Then I didn't know what to do with it,' she continues. 'I didn't know if it was legal to take cremains on a plane. I mean, suppose there was a customs inspection? I couldn't see putting that carton in the suitcase with my clothes anyhow, y'know?' She begins to tear up again. 'Sorry. I'm so stupid.'

Barbie's continual assertion of her lack of intelligence has begun to annoy Vinnie. Stop telling me how stupid you are, she wants to say. You graduated from the University of Oklahoma, you can't be all that stupid.

'That's all right,' she says instead. 'I think you've done very well, considering everything.' Almost against her will, she reclassifies The Barbarian as an innocent peasant – the victim rather than the accomplice of that Visigoth realtor her mother, who is no doubt responsible for Barbie's low opinion of her own intelligence.

'Anyhow, when I phoned home next, Mom said not to bother,' Barbie resumes presently. 'She said what I should do was scatter the cremains somewhere. So Professor Gilson drove me out in the country to a place he said Dad had liked. It was nothing special. Just this little field, on the side of a hill, that one of Dad's ancestors owned once. It wasn't a bad place really: kinda quiet. And Professor Gilson said hopefully it'll never be built over; it's too out-of-the way, and the land is too steep.

'So I climbed over the fence by these wooden steps they have here, what did he call them?'

'A stile?' Vinnie suggests.

'Yeh. That's right. Anyhow, I got over it. And I walked up the field a ways, and sorta dumped the cremains out into the long grass and flowers. I guess I shoulda scattered them around more, but I was crying too much, and I couldn't put my hand into the bag. It seemed kinda rude, y'know?'

'Yes, I see what you mean.'

'Poor old Dad.' His daughter sighs and reaches for the last watercress sandwich. 'Mom was right. It was pathetic really, his chasing around the country looking for ancestors.'

'I don't see that,' Vinnie says a little snappishly. 'Why shouldn't your father have been interested in his genealogy? A great many people are.'

'Sure, I know. But they've mostly got someone worthwhile in their family tree. Like Mom: her side of the family is real distinguished. She's a D.A.R., and she's descended from a whole lot of judges and generals. Hiram Fudd, the senator, y'know, he was her great-uncle.'

'Really,' Vinnie remarks. In her mind a catalpa tree appears, with monkeys dressed as judges and generals and senators sitting in the treehouse and on the nearby branches.

'I guess Dad thought if he went back far enough he might find somebody he could be proud of too. Professor Gilson told me he was looking for months, all over the country; but all he ever came up with was a lot of farm workers and a blacksmith and this old hermit . . . At least I guess that's what he was doing down there, besides helping Professor Gilson out sometimes. Mom wondered if maybe he'd got involved with . . . uh, you know, a woman.' Barbie blinks at Vinnie, but inquiringly rather than suspiciously. It is clear that in her mind Professor Miner is not 'a woman' and probably never has been one. 'I mean, do you think there coulda been anything like that?'

'I have no idea,' Vinnie says frostily, thanking heaven for the existence of British Telecom. Because of it, there will be no incriminating and distressing letters from her for Barbie or her mother to find later among Chuck's effects. And she too has nothing of Chuck's, not even a note – only a few of his winter clothes.

'I sorta don't believe it. Dad wasn't like that. He was a very loyal person, y'know.' Barbie blinks.

'Mm.' Vinnie glances involuntarily in the direction of the hall closet, where she seems to see Chuck's sheepskin-lined winter coat glowing with a guilty fluorescence. 'More tea?' She holds up the pot, aware that tea is all she can offer now: Barbie, in spite or perhaps because of her grief, has eaten all the watercress sandwiches and walnut cake.

Chuck's daughter shakes her head, causing her long sun-bleached hair to flop about. 'No, thanks very much. I guess I oughta be going.' She gets up clumsily.

'Well, thanks for everything, Professor Miner,' she says, moving into the hall. 'It was real nice to meet you. Oh, hey. I almost forgot to give you Dad's picture. Boy, am I stupid. Here.'

'Thank you.' Vinnie places the portfolio on the hall table and unties the worn black cotton tapes.

'Oh,' she gasps, drawing her breath in as she lifts a creased sheet of tissue to reveal a large hand-colored eighteenth-century engraving of a forest scene with a grotto and a waterfall. A figure dressed in rags and bits of fur and leather stands before the grotto, leaning on a staff. 'Your father told me about this picture. It's his ancestor, The Hermit of South Leigh; "Old Mumpson" they called him.'

'Yeh; that's what Professor Gilson said.'

'You don't want it yourself,' Vinnie says rather than asks, hoping for the answer No.

'I d'know.' Barbie looks larger and more helpless than before. 'I guess not.'

'Or perhaps your brother might like it,' says Vinnie, realizing at the same time that Old Mumpson, in spite of his honorary title, looks no older than Chuck and a good deal like him (if Chuck had grown an untidy beard), and also that she wants the picture so badly it frightens her.

'Aw, no.' Barbie almost recoils. 'Greg? You gotta be kidding. That guy looks like some kinda hippie weirdo; Greg wouldn't have him in the house. Anyways, Dad said if anything happened to him, Professor Gilson was s'posed to give the picture to you.' She smiles awkwardly. 'You could throw it out, I guess, if you want to.'

'Of course not,' Vinnie says, taking hold of the portfolio as if it might be snatched from her. 'I like it very much.' She looks from the engaving to Barbie, who is standing there dumbly.

'You must have had rather a hard time of it these last few days,' Vinnie says, suddenly realizing this. 'It's too bad your mother or your brother wasn't able to come to England with you.' Or instead of you, she adds silently to herself. Because surely either one of them would have been able to manage things better, and not had to lay it all on Professor Gilson. But perhaps that was the point: Barbie had been sent because she was helpless.

'Uh, well. Mom woulda come, only she was closing an important sale, a big condo deal she's been putting together for months. And Greg's always busy. Besides, his wife's expecting a baby next month.'

'So they sent you.' Vinnie manages to keep most of her disapproval out of her voice.

'Yeh, well. Somebody had to come, y'know.' Barbie blinks. 'I don't have a family, or much of a job, so I was kinda disposable.'

'I see.' Vinnie has an image of those shelves in her Camden Town supermarket that hold 'disposables' – paper plates and napkins, plastic cups and spoons, aluminum-foil pie tins and the like: made to be used on unimportant occasions and then discarded. A strong dislike for Barbie's living relatives comes over her. 'Well, you'll be able to go home now.'

'Yeh. Well, un, no. I've got to stay another couple days in London. Mom decided we'd better plan on ten days. Anyhow it costs a lot less that way, on the charter. I have a free hotel and everything.'

'Not a very nice hotel, I should imagine,' says Vinnie.

'Uh, no. It's not specially nice. It's called the Majestic, but it's kinda yucky really. How did you know?'

'Because they always are. And what are you planning to do while you're here?'

'I d'know. I haven't thought, really. Look at some tourist attractions, I guess. I've never been to England before.'

'I see.' The thought come to Vinnie that she ought to do something about Barbie; that it's what Chuck would have wanted. She tries to remember some of the things he'd told her about his daughter, but all she can recall is that Barbie's keen on animals. There's the Zoo, of course – But the idea of another visit to the Zoo – where only a few weeks ago she was so happy watching the polar bear that looked like Chuck – upsets and depresses Vinnie so much that she can't bring herself even to mention it.

'Well, so long, then,' Barbie says awkwardly. 'Oh, thanks.' She accepts the ugly umbrella, which Vinnie has closed for her since it is no longer raining. 'Thanks for everything, Professor Miner. Have a nice day.'

No, Vinnie thinks, shutting the door behind Barbie. It's too bad what Chuck would have wanted. There's nothing she can do for someone who, on an occasion like this, would say 'Have a nice day.' And hasn't doing things for other people caused most of the trouble and disruption and pain in her life? Yes, but it has also caused most of the surprise and interest and even in the end joy. Does she, for instance, really wish that she'd never lent Chuck Mumpson that book on the plane?

She begins mechanically to clear away the tea things, thinking of Chuck – that all the time she knew him he had been ill, and had known he was ill. That's why he'd told Professor Gilson he wanted her to have the picture of Old Mumpson 'if anything happened to him'. He knew something might happen to him; all these months he had been living under a kind of death sentence, but failing to take any of the precautions that might have commuted it. He didn't put much faith in doctors; he had said that to her more than once, the stupid, unlucky . . . Vinnie has to put down the plate she is rinsing and catch her breath. She is shaken by pity for Chuck, living on the edge of a cliff all this time, and knowing it – and shaken by fury at him for deliberately walking so near the edge, for not taking decent care of himself.

And of her too, she thinks suddenly. Because he could very well have died right here in this flat, with a glass of whisky dropping from one big freckled hand and a smoldering cigarette falling from the other as he pitched heavily, fatally, onto her carpet.

Or worse. Vinnie stares out the window, letting water splash unheeded over the rim of the sink. He could have died in her bed, on top of her. She recalls vividly how red Chuck's face got – with passion, she had thought; how he gasped at the climax – she had thought, with pleasure. Why did he keep taking that chance? How could he do that to her? Is that why he never told her he was ill, fearing, and perhaps rightly, that if she'd known she might never have let him . . . All those times . . .

Miserable, furious, even frightened – though the danger, of course, is past – without knowing exactly what she is doing. Vinnie turns off the faucet and, holding the colander she has been washing, walks back through the flat into her bedroom. She stands staring at the double bed, now smoothly covered by its brown-and-white flowered comforter, so often before stirred into a whirlpool of sheets. The last time Chuck was here, she suddenly recalls, he hardly smoked at all. He was trying to give it up, he had told her. And he hadn't drunk anything to speak of either: only one glass of soda with a little white wine. He must have decided to live, he must have wanted to live –

But if Chuck really wanted to live, why did he go on making such passionate love to her? Wasn't that just plain stupid?

No, Vinnie thinks. Not stupid on his terms, because that was one of the things he had wanted to live for. He loved me, she thinks. It was true all the time. What a horrible bad joke, that after fifty-four years she should have been loved by someone like Chuck, who on top of everything else that's wrong with him is dead and scattered on the side of a hill somewhere in Wiltshire.

If she'd believed him; if she'd known; if she'd said –

A wave of confused memory and feeling churns up inside her; still clutching the wet colander in one hand, she falls onto the bed, weeping.

'Rosemary? Oh, she's fine now, really.' Edwin Francis says, helping Vinnie to more shrimp salad. It is a warm afternoon a week later, and they are having lunch in his tiny, beautifully tended Kensington courtyard.

'Really?' Vinnie echoes.

'I saw her two days ago, just before she left for Ireland, and she was in top form. But I don't mind telling you, it was a near thing.'

'Really,' she says, with quite another intonation.

'Now this mustn't go any further.' He pours them both more Blanc de Blanc, then looks hard at Vinnie. 'I wouldn't say anything even to you, but I want you to understand the situation, so you'll see how important it is for us to be very very discreet.'

'Yes, of course,' Vinnie says, becoming a little impatient.

'You see, there have been, mm, other episodes in the past . . . Well, nothing quite like this, but Rosemary often gets . . . well, a bit odd when she isn't working steadily.'

'Oh?'

'It's no joke, really, you know, always having to be a lady. Or a gentleman, if it comes to that. The best of us – and I do believe, in a way, that Rosemary is one of the best – might find it a strain.'

'Yes,' Vinnie agrees. 'It must have been rather difficult for you,' she prompts, since Edwin remains silent.

'Well. Initially. Then . . . Well, as it happens, there's this extremely gifted doctor – Rosemary's seen him before, actually. He was tremendously helpful. Luckily, she has a complete amnesia for most of the worst period.'

'Really.'

'Yes. You know, drink does that sometimes. She doesn't remember Fred's coming round to the house at all, for instance.'

'I suppose that's just as well.'

'Oh, I think so. A mercy, the doctor said. But you mustn't say anything about any of that to anyone. Seriously. Promise.'

'Of course, I promise,' Vinnie says. The British hush-hush attitude towards psychotherapy is something that, in spite of her

Anglophilia, she has never quite understood. Eccentricity, even eccentricity of a sort that would be designated 'sick' in America, is admired over here. Men who dress up like Indian chieftains and hold pow-wows, women who keep fifty Siamese cats in royal splendor, are written up admiringly in the newspapers. But ordinary neurosis is denied and concealed. If you consult a psychologist, it is something to be hidden from everyone while it is going on and forgotten as soon as possible afterward.

If Rosemary were an American actress, Vinnie thinks, she would already be in therapy, and would refer with easy familiarity to 'my analyst' on every possible occasion. She might very well give interviews about her problems with drinking. And her split personality – if in fact it was really split, and not just an act – would be discussed on talk shows and celebrated in *People* magazine.

'And you mustn't say anything to Fred, either. Let him think it was all theatrics. Have you heard from Fred, by the way?'

'Yes, I had a letter – well, a note. He wanted to tell me that he and his wife have reconstructed their marriage, as he put it.'

'Really.' Edwin rises and begins to clear the garden table. 'And is that a good thing?'

'Who knows? Fred seems to think it is.' Vinnie sighs; she has a deep distrust of marriage, which in her observation has an almost irresistible tendency to turn friends and lovers into relatives, if not into foes.

'It's just as well really that he couldn't get in touch with Posy,' Edwin says a little later, returning from the basement kitchen with a plate of fruit and another of macaroons. 'She would have coped magnificently, of course, but she's not as discreet as she might be . . . Please, help yourself. I especially recommend the apricots.

'I had my suspicions about Mrs Harris all along, you know,' he continues. 'She simply sounded to good to be true.'

'Yes, I thought Rosemary was improving the story sometimes,' Vinnie says. 'Or do you mean – do you think there never was any Mrs Harris?'

'I do rather. It's hard to imagine Rosemary doing her own housework, though. I expect she just went on hiring those part-time people – only rather more of them, perhaps, so that Fred would stop complaining of how the place looked.'

'But Fred saw Mrs Harris at least once. He told me so.'

'Yes, well . . . You know, Rosemary's always been annoyed that she's so narrowly typecast. She's convinced she could play working-class characters, for instance, only no one will ever let her.'

'But she was scrubbing the hall floor, Fred said. I can't believe –'

'You have to remember her training. She always gets tremendously into her parts. Almost carried away, sometimes. When she's taping *Tallyho Castle*, for instance, she starts to have this frightfully gracious lady-of-the-manor manner. I can easily imagine her washing a floor just to get the feel of it.'

'Ye-es.' Vinnie is aware that Edwin is skillfully rationalizing and diminishing what would otherwise seem highly neurotic or even psychotic behavior. 'But I think there must have been someone like Mrs Harris for a while,' she insists. 'Even if that wasn't her real name. I spoke to what I thought was Mrs Harris on the telephone twice at least. She'd have to be an awfully gifted actress.'

'Oh, she's gifted,' Edwin agrees, carefully skinning a ripe peach with one of his ivory-handled Victorian fruit knives. 'She can imitate just about anyone. You should hear her do your cowboy friend, Chuck what's-his-name. How is what's-his-name, by the way?' he adds, changing the subject with his customary deftness. 'Is he still digging for ancestors down in Wiltshire?'

'Yes – no,' Vinnie replies uncomfortably. Though she has been at Edwin's for nearly two hours, and spoken to him earlier on the phone, she hasn't dared to mention Chuck. She knows it will be nearly impossible for her to tell the story without falling apart as she has been falling apart at intervals for the past ten days. But she plunges in, beginning with Barbie's telephone call.

'So the wife and son couldn't make it to England,' Edwin remarks presently.

'No. Of course, it's just a convention that when someone dies you have to hurry to the fatal spot. It doesn't actually do them any good.'

'I suppose not. Still, it does give one a certain opinion of Chuck's relatives.'

'It does.' Vinnie continues with her story. Several times she hears a tell-tale wobble in her voice, but Edwin seems to notice nothing.

'So there's some corner of an English field that is forever Tulsa,' he says finally, smiling.

'Yes.' Vinnie strangles the cry that rises in her.

'Poor old Chuck. Rather awful to go out like that, so unprepared and sudden and far from home.'

'I don't know,' Vinnie says, lowering her head and pretending to be spitting out a grape-seed to conceal her face. 'Some people might prefer it. No fuss, you know. I think I'd rather have it that way myself.' She imagines herself dead, and her ashes scattered like Chuck's over a hillside field that's she's never seen and never will see. A longing comes over her to look upon that place; to visit the grotto where Old Mumpson lived, the cottage in which Chuck and his ancestors slept; to talk to Professor Gilson and his students about Chuck. And she could do all this . . . Nothing prevents her from doing it except a sense of the hopeless ridiculousness of such an excursion.

'Not me.' Edwin helps himself to the last of the macaroons, of which he has already had more than his fair share. 'When I die, I want it to be in my own bed, with flattering interviews in the papers and tearful farewell visits from all my friends and admirers. I want to be prepared for it, not just hit over the head.'

'Well, Chuck should have been prepared,' Vinnie says. 'The doctor told him not to drink or smoke; he told him to be careful, his daughter said, but he wouldn't listen. Climbing three flights of stairs on such a hot day! It really makes me furious. And he probably had a cigarette and a drink in some pub before that. So stupid of him.' Realizing that she has spoken with more feeling than is appropriate, Vinnie gives a false laugh.

'Poor old Chuck,' Edwin says again. 'He was quite a character, wasn't he? Do you remember . . .'

Yes, Vinnie thinks as Edwin relates his anecdote; for her London friends Chuck Mumpson was a character, a comic type – not a real person. And she, who had known him better and should have known better, had put off going to him in Wiltshire not only because she was afraid to trust herself to any man, but because she didn't want to be associated with him in their minds or even in her own. It was as if, in her blind Anglophilia, she had even taken on what are said to be the characteristic English weaknesses of timidity and snobbishness – neither of them, in fact, particularly characteristic of those English she knows best.

'Still,' Edwin concludes, 'I did rather like him, didn't you?'

'No,' Vinnie is extremely surprised to hear herself say. 'I didn't "rather like Chuck", if you want to know. I loved him.'

'Really.' Edwin moves his chair back from the table, and incidently away from the force of Vinnie's statement and perhaps its content.

It's true, Vinnie thinks. Chuck had loved her, and – she says this to herself with surprise and difficulty – she had loved him. 'Yes.' She meets his stare, his insulting slight smile.

'Well, we did all rather wonder sometimes,' he says at last. 'But I never really thought you – ' He recollects his manners and breaks off. 'I do understand,' he says in another tone, consoling and sympathetic. 'These things happen. As I know all too well, you can love someone you don't admire – love them passionately, even. Of course that's not very nice for either of you.' A cloudy, fixed look comes over his small neat features; he stares past Vinnie and the orderly little courtyard with its clean white gravel and clipped roses, into the part of his life that she has always preferred to know nothing of.

'But I did admire Chuck,' Vinnie says, realizing the truth of this as she speaks.

'Really. Well, no doubt he was admirable, in his own way. One of nature's noblemen.'

'I – ' Vinnie begins, and chokes herself off. The patronizing phrase enrages her, but she doesn't trust herself to speak without screaming or crying. And after all, what right has she to scream at Edwin for thinking as she had thought for months?

'Well,' he says, splashing the last of the wine into their balloon glasses. 'We mustn't judge everyone by our own silly standards. I suppose we ought to learn that at our mother's knee.'

'I suppose so,' says Vinnie, thinking that she did not learn it then, and that if she had, her whole life might have been different. 'How is your mother, by the way?' she adds, hoping to divert Edwin.

'Oh, very well, thank you. Her arthritis is much better – one good effect of this frightful heat.'

'That's nice.' To Vinnie the day is only pleasantly warm, but she is used to the British intolerance of temperatures over seventy-five degrees.

'If she stays well, I'm thinking of giving a little luncheon for her next week; I hope you'll be able to come.'

'I'm not sure,' Vinnie says. 'I may be going down to the country this weekend, and if I do I won't be back until next month.'

'Oh dear. Really?'

'I'm afraid so,' says Vinnie, who is as surprised by her declaration as Edwin is.

'And when are you leaving for the States?'

'On the twentieth, I think it is.'

'Oh, Vinnie. You can't possibly. That's very naughty of you.'

'I know. But you see I've got to get ready for my fall term.'

'Come on, now. That's ages away.'

'Not in America it isn't.' Vinnie sighs, thinking of her university's academic calendar, revised recently to save on fuel bills. Classes now start before Labor Day, and by August 24 known and unknown advisees will be fidgeting in her office.

'Besides, you've only just come.'

'Silly.' She smiles. 'I've been here since February.'

'Well, good. Anyhow, I think of you as living here always. Why don't you?'

'I certainly would if I could.' Vinnie sighs again, well aware that she cannot possibly afford to quit her job and move to London.

'Never mind. I'll make the most of you now. Let's have some coffee. And I've got a rather shameless strawberry mousse; I hope you have room for it.'

An hour later Vinnie is on her way back to Regent's Park Road in a taxi, feeling somewhat overfed. Ordinarily she would have taken first one and then another tube train, but an extravagant impulse came over her. If she does go down to Wiltshire – and she realizes that she's probably going to, ridiculous as that is – she'll be in London so little longer; why should she waste any of her remaining time here underground? Especially on an afternoon like this one, when everything seems to shimmer with light and warmth: the trees, the shop windows, the people on the pavement. Why does London looks so marvelously well today? And why does she feel for the first time that she's not only seeing it, but is part of it? Something has changed, she thinks. She isn't the same person she was: she has loved and been loved.

The taxi turns into the Park, and Vinnie gazes out the open window at the smooth green lawns, the nannies with their carriages, the gamboling children and dogs, the strollers, the joggers, the couples sitting together on the grass: all these fortunate people who live in London, who will still be here when she is alone and exiled in Corinth. Even Chuck, in his own way, will be here forever. The cold nauseous ache of past and coming loss squeezes her heart, and she shivers in the heat.

As they swing east into the Bayswater Road she leans back against the seat, feeling tipsy, tired, and low. She thinks again how inconsiderate and wrong it was of Death to come for Chuck just when he had begun to want to live. Then she thinks how inconsiderate and wrong it was of her not to have agreed to visit him in Wiltshire that last weekend. Chuck wouldn't have gone to look for the De Mompessons then, or climbed those stairs in the Town Hall.

And even if he had gone there some time later, it mightn't have been so hot that day; or she might have been with him and made him ascend more slowly (she could have saved his dignity by pretending that it was she who needed to stop awhile on each floor to catch her breath). Then he would be alive now.

If only he had told her that he was ill . . . If only she had gone to stay with him, made sure he didn't drink too much, encouraged him not to smoke, to see a doctor regularly . . . He might have lived many years; and she might have lived with him, here in England. She might have resigned her job and given all her time to research and writing ('Money is no problem'). She would have kept the flat, so that they'd have a place in town as well as the old house in the country Chuck had talked about buying, with a flower garden, raspberry and currant bushes, an asparagus bed . . .

Why does she keep having this stupid fantasy? It's not what she wants at all, not what would ever have worked, even if Chuck were alive. It's not her nature, not her fate to be loved, to live with anyone, her fate is to be always single, unloved, alone –

Well, not completely alone. From the corner of the taxi comes a snuffle and whine inaudible to anyone in the world but Vinnie Miner. She recognizes it at once: Fido has returned from

Wiltshire. Slowly he becomes visible to her inner eye: considerably smaller than ever before, only about the size of a Welsh terrier now; dusty, travel-worn, and not quite sure of his welcome.

'Go away,' Vinnie says silently. 'I'm perfectly fine. I'm not a bit sorry for myself. I'm a well-known scholar; I have lots of friends on both sides of the Atlantic; I've just spent five very interesting months in London and finished an important book on playground rhymes.' But even to her the list seems painfully incomplete.

The taxi pulls up in front of Vinnie's house; she gets out, followed at some distance by a small invisible dog, and pays the driver. As she turns to enter her gate, she sees Fido standing by the wall, pale and shadowy in the summer sunlight, looking up at her with anxious devotion and wagging his feathery white tail.

'Well, all right,' she says to him. 'Come along, then.'

Elizabeth Berridge's crisp and distinctly English style of writing established her as one of the most significant novelists of the post-war years. Now that her best work is at last available in Abacus Paperback, a new generation of readers will be able to discover the quiet brilliance of her writing . . .

Elizabeth Berridge

ROSE UNDER GLASS

'An eye for the beauty of humble and familiar things, and a gift for expressing it in a language sharp yet delicate. She has a quiet, wicked sense of humour.'
New Statesman.

ABACUS FICTION 0 349 10303 8 £2.95

Elizabeth Berridge

ACROSS THE COMMON

'Entirely good and most beautifully written. I love her subtlety and observation and impeccable characterisation.' Noel Coward.

ABACUS FICTION 0 349 10304 6 £2.75

Elizabeth Berridge

SING ME WHO YOU ARE

'One of the best English novelists presents something of a tour-de-force.'
Martin Seymour Smith.

ABACUS FICTION 0 349 10305 4 £2.95

BILGEWATER

Jane Gardam

Shortlisted for the Booker Prize
Winner of the Whitbread Award and David Higham and Winifred Holtby Prizes

'Superbly told . . . adolescent anguish has no better friend than this poignant ode to its hopes and fears.' *Times Educational Supplement*.

'The best of all her novels. It is funny, beautifully constructed, deeply moving, and I cannot get it out of my mind.' *Daily Telegraph*.

'Jane Gardam has a deep, intuitive sympathy for victims of this age group . . . not without an equally sharp comic appreciation of their plight. Lively . . . excellent.' *The Times*.

'A very good book indeed, witty, enriching, and a pleasure to read.' *The Listener*.

'One of the funniest, most entertaining, most unusual stories about young love.' *Standard*.

GENERAL FICTION 0 349 11402 1 £2.50

Also by JANE GARDAM in ABACUS paperback:
THE PANGS OF LOVE AND OTHER STORIES
A LONG WAY FROM VERONA
GOD ON THE ROCKS
BLACK FACES, WHITE FACES
THE SIDMOUTH LETTERS